The Waters of Hercules

The Legend of Gaura Dracului

"Books you may hold readily in your hand are the most useful, after all."

— Dr. Johnson

Emily and Dorothea Girard

The Waters of Hercules

The Legend of Gaura Dracului

Introduction by A.K. Brackob

Addison & Highsmith

Addison & Highsmith Publishers

Las Vegas ◊ Oxford ◊ Palm Beach

Published in the United States of America by
Histria Books, a division of Histria LLC
7181 N. Hualapai Way, Ste. 130-86
Las Vegas, NV 89166 USA
HistriaBooks.com

Addison & Highsmith is an imprint of Histria Books. Titles published under the imprints of Histria Books are distributed worldwide.

Library of Congress Control Number: 2021940692

ISBN 978-1-59211-132-9 (hardcover)

Contents

Introduction 7

The Legend... 13

The Prologue 18

Chapter I Katzenjammer 21

Chapter II A Legal Advisor 34

Chapter III The Ash Wednesday Visitor.............................. 43

Chapter IV A Victim of Science 53

Chapter V A Glimmer of Fortune 64

Chapter VI When Doctors Disagree..................................... 75

Chapter VII On the Wing 84

Chapter VIII The Valley-God... 95

Chapter IX The Sleeping Beauty 103

Chapter X A Love Letter.. 115

Chapter XI The Valley-King... 124

Chapter XII The World Above 130

Chapter XIII "Sir Hovart" 146

Chapter XIV The Bohemian... 157

Chapter XV Devotions and Emotions 171

Chapter XVI Pater Dionysius... 184

Chapter XVII Broken Glass 194

Chapter XVIII Tristezza 212

Chapter XIX More Tristezza.. 224

Chapter XX The Home of Her Ancestors...................................... 230

Chapter XXI Josika's Grave 243

Chapter XXII Princess Tryphosa.. 252

Chapter XXIII Fishing.. 266

Chapter XXIV Public and Private Amusements............................. 280

Chapter XXV The Story of the Broken Heart 295

Chapter XXVI A Sultana 308

Chapter XXVII The Oath of Hercules.. 320

Chapter XXVIII A Modern Martyr 334

Chapter XXIX By Torchlight... 343

Chapter XXX A Granted Prayer 355

Chapter XXXI Dulcétia and Daggers.. 372

Chapter XXXII István's Stirrup-Cup 390

Chapter XXXIII The Fallen Signpost 403

Chapter XXXIV Gaura Dracului.. 415

Chapter XXXV A Riddle 432

Chapter XXXVI The Day of Reckoning 444

Chapter XXXVII Wisdom and Ignorance...................................... 455

Chapter XXXVIII The Story of a Toadstool 462

Chapter XXXIX The Political Spy... 464

Chapter XL Gretchen's Fortune... 486

Chapter XLI The Hour and the Man 495

Chapter XLII The Missing King 502

Chapter XLIII What People Said 505

Introduction

Written by two Scottish sisters, Emily and Dorothea Girard, *The Waters of Hercules* is a long-forgotten Gothic novel of the Victorian era, with ties to Bram Stoker's *Dracula*. In the only newspaper interview that Bram Stoker gave about his famous novel, *Dracula*, the author of the interview, Jane Stoddard, draws a connection between the two novels:

> *One of the most interesting and exciting of recent novels is Mr. Bram Stoker's "Dracula." It deals with the ancient mediaeval vampire legend, and in no English work of fiction has this legend been so brilliantly treated. The scene is laid partly in Transylvania and partly in England. The first fifty-four pages, which give the journal of Jonathan Harker after leaving Vienna until he makes up his mind to escape from Castle Dracula, are in their weird power altogether unrivaled in recent fiction. The only book which to my knowledge at all compares with them is "The Waters of Hercules," by E.D. Gerard, which also treats of a wild and little-known portion of Eastern Europe.*[*]

While Stoker never mentions reading the novel during the course of the interview, he does acknowledge his use of Emily Girard's other works on Transylvanian

---

[*]Jane Stoddard, "Mr. Bram Stoker: A Chat with the Author of "Dracula" in *The British Weekly*, 1 July 1897, p. 185.

folklore, "Transylvanian Superstitions"* and *The Land Beyond the Forest*† in crafting *Dracula*: "No one book that I know of will give you all the facts. I learned a good deal from E. Gerard's 'Essays on Roumanian Superstitions,' [sic] which first appeared in the *Nineteenth Century*, and were afterwards published in a couple of volumes."‡

Emily and Dorothea Girard were both born in Scotland, Emily on May 7, 1849, and Dorothea on August 9, 1855. The sisters' connection to Eastern Europe began when the family moved to Vienna in 1863. The girls, who had been home-schooled up to that time, continued their formal education at the convent of Sacré Coeur in Austria. They both demonstrated a remarkable talent for languages and writing. On October 14, 1869, Emily married a Polish cavalry officer named Ritter Miecislaus von Laszowski, who served in the Austro-Hungarian army. This marriage ultimately led Emily to Transylvania, where she lived from 1883 to 1885 while her husband was stationed in Brasov (Kronstadt) and Sibiu (Hermannstadt). It is likely that Dorothea joined her sister here for at least some of this time as they penned *The Waters of Hercules*.

While each sister wrote independently, *The Waters of Hercules,* published in 1885, is one of a series of novels they collaborated on, using the pen name E.D. Girard, between 1880 and 1891. Their other works include *Reata or What's in a Name* (1880), *Beggar My Neighbour* (1882) and *A Sensitive Plant (1891)*. Their literary collaboration ended following Dorothea's marriage to an Austrian-Hungarian military officer, Captain Julius Longard. Longard later rose to the rank of Major General and received the title Longard de Longgarde. Although the sisters did not pursue any more collaborative literary efforts, each continued to write on their own.

---

*Emily Girard, "Transylvanian Superstitions" in *The Nineteenth* Century 8 (1885), pp. 128-144, published the same year that *The Waters of Hercules* first appeared in print.

†Emily Girard, *The Land Beyond the Forest: Facts, Figures, and Fancies from Transylvania*, New York: Harper, 1888.

‡‡Jane Stoddard, "Mr. Bram Stoker: A Chat with the Author of 'Dracula'" in *The British Weekly*, 1 July 1897, p. 185.

Dorothea embarked on a prolific literary career, authoring 40 books between 1890 and her death on September 29, 1915. Emily, although less prolific than her younger sister, also continued to write. She even befriending the famous American writer Mark Twain in 1897, to whom she dedicated her 1901 novel *The Extermination of Love*. Emily died in Vienna on January 11, 1905. Although during her lifetime, Dorothea was certainly the more famous writer of the two, today Emily is somewhat better-known due to the connection of her non-fiction work with Bram Stoker and *Dracula*.

Much of the story is set in Transylvania in the resort town of Băile Herculane (meaning Hercules' Baths) in the latter half of the nineteenth century, from which the novel takes its name. The city is a real town in Transylvania, in modern Romania, which was then under the domination of the Austro-Hungarian Empire. It is an idyllic setting for a Gothic novel. Set in a narrow valley along the Cerna River (called the Djernis in the book), the town has been inhabited since ancient times. Legend has it that Hercules once passed through the valley and stopped to rest and bathe at the site, hence the name of the town. Băile Herculane is famous for its hot springs, with their healing properties, which is the reason the protagonists of the novel come to visit the town. One popular tourist destination is the *Peștera Hoților* (Cave of the Thieves), not far from the town center. It may have inspired the Girard sisters in their creation of the fictional *Gaura Dracului*, (the Devil's Pit). The bronze statue of Hercules that adorns the Town Center and is mentioned in the story was erected in 1874 and can still be seen by visitors today.

On the surface, *The Waters of Hercules* is a Victorian romance. Gretchen, the heroine of the story, is an intelligent young German woman, who distinguished herself in school by winning the *prix de logique*. A very practical-minded girl, Gretchen, influenced by her Italian friend, Belita, considers marriage an economic proposition and is determined to marry a man of wealth. When the decent, respectable family lawyer Vincenz Komers, an older man of modest means, but who truly loves her, seeks her hand in marriage, she rejects him, not once, but twice. As different suitors appear during the course of the novel, Gretchen must grapple with her ideas of love and financial security. One is tempted to speculate as to whether the story of the romance between Gretchen and her much older suiter Vincenz somehow parallels Emily Girard's own love story as she married a man twenty years her senior.

Amidst the romantic conundrums of the story's heroine, Gretchen's father is seriously injured in an accident. This leads the family to set off for Transylvania, to the Baths of Hercules, in hopes that the waters of Hercules, known for their curative powers, will rehabilitate her ailing father. As they set out, Gretchen's father, Adalbert, tells his daughter of a mysterious place in the surrounding forest, called *Gaura Dracului* (the Devil's Pit) that he had discovered during a visit to the valley years earlier, but whose precise location is now a mystery. Hercules, considered the god of the Valley, is said to have sworn that the pit would receive a sacrifice of human blood once every century. The legends of a mysterious treasure associated with *Gaura Dracului* serve to inspire Gretchen to consider an alternative means to make her fortune, something that would allow her to marry any man of her choosing. Her efforts are redoubled when a long-expected inheritance of a family estate proves illusory.

As Gretchen relentlessly pursues the secrets of *Gaura Dracului* and the hidden treasure it is said to hold, she is courted by the handsome, wealthy, and debonair Baron István Tolnay, called the King of the Valley, who could provide the financial security that both she and her family seek. Aided by the Baron, Vincenz, her brother Kurt, and others, she sets out to find the mysterious bottomless pit in the nearby forested mountain. Will Gretchen discover the elusive *Gaura Dracului*? Will its secrets finally be revealed? Will Gretchen find the lost treasure? Or will she achieve financial security for herself and her family by marrying the wealthy Baron? These are questions that the reader will answer within the pages of this intriguing novel.

There is a great deal of symbolism in the novel and one could spend a great deal of time discussing its meaning, but we are reminded of Stoddard's interview with Bram Stoker in which she writes, "In a recent leader on "Dracula," published in a provincial newspaper, it is suggested that high moral lessons might be gathered from the book. I asked Mr. Stoker whether he had written with a purpose, but on this point, he would give no definite answer, 'I suppose that every book of the kind must contain some lesson,' he remarked; 'but I prefer that readers should find it out for themselves.'" Readers of *The Waters of Hercules* will also have a great deal to ponder as they sort through the underlying meanings of the novel and its portrayal of the values of Victorian society.

This long-forgotten, but remarkable piece of nineteenth-century literature will be of interest to anyone who enjoys Victorian romance, Gothic literature, and particularly Bram Stoker's *Dracula*.

A.K. Brackob

The Legend

h E obeyed the war-trumpet which echoed throughout the Roman Empire. He went forth to fight under the Eagle of the mighty Trajan. His young wife, who had been his for scarcely three moons, hung once more on his arm. He kissed the mute lips which did not trust themselves to speak. Trajan called, and he must follow, but she should be safe. He would send her to the far-distant province by the Danube, where the wild Dacians had long since bowed before Trajan's victorious sword. A trusty escort should guide her to that peaceful valley; the sweet society of her friends, the noble ladies Flavia and Lavinia, should help to cheer her; the sacred waters of Hercules should give back the roses which had faded from her cheek.

He kissed her lips, and taking from his neck a sacred chain of gold, he whispered, "Keep it, and never forget that thou art my wife."

Once more the Roman Eagle triumphed. Flushed with victory and crowned with laurels, the young general hastened to that distant province by the Danube. Had she guarded the mystic chain as he had bid her? The "aquae Herculi sacrae" — had they rekindled the beams of her eyes? Did the roses bloom again on her cheek? Yes, the roses bloomed again; he saw that from afar. He saw her smiling, radiant, her friends beside her, and — someone else. Was not that fair-haired stripling the puny Aurelius Ciispinus, whose arm had been too weak to fight for Rome? Was that smile, so heavenly sweet, for yonder boy?

A devil clutched the warrior's heart; his fingers felt for his sword-hilt. Venomous tongues spoke to him; they whispered that she had been false.

He watched from afar; he saw her leave the spot; he saw the stripling bend over something in his hand; and still watching, he followed step by step. A gold line glittered on the youth's neck; the warrior's eagle eye caught the shine; it was the sacred chain, the chain which was to have been the token of her fidelity; and now that white-faced boy was mumbling over the dishonored pledge.

They must both die; but the blood should never stain his sword. He knew the man who would do any deed for the love of heavy gold; that man should do this deed. A wild cavern in the rocks was the ruffian's abode. The warrior sought it and spoke:

He. Dost thou know a grave so deep that it will tell no tales?

Brigand. Master, I do.

He. A place whence the dead cannot return to trouble me?

Brig. Even so, I know the place.

He. A woman must sleep in that grave tonight; but neither word nor step must I hear. Here, take this purse.

Brig. Name me the woman.

He. My wife.

The valley slept. The young wife softly slumbered on her couch; but a dark rude hand has touched her arm.

What is this massive muffled figure that confronts her? Her eyes, as death, flash for one moment.

"Follow me, lady; I have come for thee."

"Follow thee? By whose order?"

"Thy lord's."

"Dost thou take me to him? Then will I follow thee gladly."

The way was long and steep; rough with rocks and sharp with brambles. Trees on all sides threatening her with their arms; thorns which caught her silken hair; stones which cut her tender feet.

"Kind man, let me rest a while; see, my sandals are rent."

"Nay, thou shalt rest presently, and deeply too. The end of thy journey is at hand."

"Good man, is it here I will find my lord?"

She stood still with a shriek. What was this black abyss, blacker than the night around her, which yawned at her feet? Whence came this hideous gaping void?

"What is it?" the woman asked, trembling.

"It is thy grave."

They were alone, the woman and the man, and the vast forest was around them. No human ear could hear her shriek, no human eye could see her death. Shame on the trees which nodded to each other over the murderer's head; shame on the breeze which whispered the black secret through the forest; shame on the golden stars, oh, shame on them, not to hide their twinkling eyes from the sight of so foul a deed! The eagle started from its nest at the sound of that shriek, and circled flapping through the darkness; the lynx-eyed cat, listening, dropped her prey, then rose and fled swift-footed to the inmost fastnesses of her rocky den.

The guiltless wife had not yet ceased to breathe when the husband had learned his error. Before his mighty sword the stripling sank to the ground, but with his last breath he whispered the truth. Aurelius had loved her, but she was innocent; that chain was no love-token from her; he had stolen it from her as she dropped it going to the bath.

" Cruel man, she loved no one but thee."

Wildly did the warrior press up the hillside to find that deep grave which could tell no tales. That grave should be his grave, if he were too late.

The valley awoke, and the portals of the baths stood open. The sacred Hercules Waters bubble boiling from the rock, and are caught in marble basins to be the health of thousands. The priests are offering their morning sacrifice to the god *Hercules sanctus augustus invictus salutifer*. Fair ladies enter the baths, or stroll along the tessellated pavement.

The noble ladies Flavia and Lavinia walk with linked arms.

Lavinia. How has the sweet Flavia rested?

Flavia. But poorly. The fate of my beloved friend robbed my couch of all its softness. It is the common talk of the valley. I shall never be consoled. Wilt thou?

Lav. Never. Ah, she was beautiful! How red were her lips!

Fla. And how shapely were her arms! But didst thou never think that her hair was too black?

Lav. Now that I reflect, I think it was too black.

Fla. And her eyes too large?

Lav. How justly thou speakest! And, sweet Flavia, what say'st thou of her skin? ·

Fla. Any suckling could see that it was over-white. She had not thy roses, Lavinia.

Lav. Nor had she thy noble stature, sweet Flavia; her figure bad not the pleasing roundness of thine. ·

Fla. Nor seems it to me that her lips were so — very red.

Lav. Nor her arms so very shapely.

Fla. Now that I call back her face to mind, I cannot say that she was beautiful.

Lav. We shall be friends forever, my Flavia!

[*They embrace; then stand looking down at the rolling Djernis river.*]

Lav. They say she was innocent.

Fla. They say so.

Lav. Even now the high-priest waits to implore the gods with sacrifice that they should pardon her cruel bloodshed.

Fla. The high-priest has a tender heart. He is ever compassionate to the erring.

Lav. Didst thou say-erring?

Fla. I was but speaking my thought.

Lav. Tell me thy thought, sweet Flavia.

Fla. It came to my mind that we unhappily hold no proof of her innocence. Aurelius had a fair face.

Lav. Methinks her lord was of nobler gait.

Fla. The man who is nearest is always the comeliest to a pleasure-loving woman; we will not say more than a pleasure-loving woman, Lavinia.

Lav. Oh, wise Flavia! oh, far-seeing Flavia! Yes, she deserved to die. But hush! let us speak softly.

Fla. and *Lav.* [*in one breath*]. No word of ours shall taint her memory.

Lav. What if I whispered the truth to young Sabina? She is a discreet matron.

Fla. And I have no secrets from Lucrezia; we are as sisters to each other.

[*The noble ladies have readied the entrance of the sacred temple. They pause on the steps to adjust the folds of their trailing gar-ments. To the left of the temple the wooded bank slopes upward, dark green against the clear blue sky/ from below on the right comes the sound of rushing water, for there the Djernis tosses moaning over its stony bed.*]

Lav. When last we stood here, she was by our side. Canst thou tell me if my *palla* falls smoothly?

Fla. As smooth as moonbeams on a lake. And mine?

Lav. Thou art draped like a goddess in the clouds. Say, is it not pitiful that she had to die so cruel a death?

Fla. Truly; but the pity is greater that he should have thrown himself after her. He was a well-favored man.

Lav. [*looking into the steel mirror which hangs by her side*]. He might have known that there are many more comely women in the world. But hark! the voice of the flutes invites us to the temple.

Fla. Come, let us sacrifice to the immortal gods! [*Exit.*

The Prologue

WHEN Alexius Damianovics de Draskócs, sometimes known as Count Damianovics de Draskócs, died, he left his widow and two children under the care of his brother Jósika. Jósika had long waited for this opportunity. Some fifteen years previously Alexius had taken possession of the paternal estate, merely on the ground of being the nearest to the spot, for no will was forthcoming; and indeed, in the lower Danubian provinces of Austria, where these cir-cumstances occurred, wills were rarely heard of, and everything was settled by the right of might. Jósika, who in his father's lifetime had already spent considerable sums of money, made no objection when Alexius took possession of the estate; he merely said to him- self, " I have a long life before me; I can wait."

Scarcely twelve months were passed since Alexius's death when Jósika's waiting was crowned, and he had virtually become master of Draskócs. He had begun by proposing to the widow, who refused him; and had ended by boldly declaring that he had as good a right to the estate as Alexius had ever had. This resulted in much indignation and tears on the part of Eleonore, the widow; and finally, in her abrupt flight to Pesth, whence she threatened Jósika with the terrible word "Justice!"

Twenty-two years passed, and the lawsuit begun by the furious Eleonore still trailed its slow length along. "I have a long life before me," was Jósika's set formula: "I can wait. I hope to survive the end of the lawsuit.

Meanwhile, the widowed countess experienced another heavy blow.

Her son Alexius, who betrayed a weakness for alcohol had been placed in the hands of a young German tutor, named Adalbert Mohr. The widow's daughter, As-celinde, being then an impulsive creature of twenty-nine, lost her heart to the tutor, and told him so or "betrayed her feelings" in an unguarded moment. Adalbert really admired her; and what between that and surprise, he took the bait. The engagement was kept secret, but Eleonore had suspicions, and lost no time in sending off tutor and pupil on a holiday tour. The choice of locality had been left to Adalbert, and he gladly seized this opportunity of visiting a spot which he had long wished to see. This was a romantic valley on the southern confines of Hungary, which, though possessing strong sulfur springs, was little known and rarely visited. Historical research happened to be Adalbert Mohr's pet form of study, and this wild spot was known to harbor fragments of great antiquity. Eagerly he set to work, forgetful of his pupil. His enthusiasm grew daily.

"I have at last," he wrote to Ascelinde in the second week of his stay, "come upon the track of that curious place called *Gaura Dracului*, which the peasants of the valley speak of with dread. I shall devote my last fortnight to the search, for I have a theory that some interesting discoveries might be made on the spot; but not one of the peasants will act as a guide."

A few days after the date of this letter, Adalbert was standing beside a giant beech tree high up among the hills. He had found the spot he sought, but darkness was close at hand, and he must hurry home. "Tomorrow I shall return," he said to himself, while with his penknife he cut three crosses in the beech-stem, which was to serve as a sign-post, "and I shall bring torches and ropes."

But his plan for the morrow remained unrealized. That same evening a letter from Ascelinde recalled him in frantic haste. There had been discovery and family scenes, after which Ascelinde had left her mother's house, or, more properly speaking, had been turned out of it.

A few words sum up the rest. Adalbert and Ascelinde were married and soon began to find thorns among their roses. Two years later Ascelinde was summoned to her mother's deathbed and went to receive her parent's last blessing — or curse, she hardly knew which to expect. It turned out to be a blessing but in a conditional shape. She was to be forgiven if henceforward she would devote herself to fighting the Draskócs' battle for her brother Alexius, who was. too apathetic to fight for himself. Through her tears Ascelinde assented; her heart had clung secretly to "the family cause" all along.

"You have made a fatal mistake in life," murmured the countess, "and you must redeem it."

"Yes, a fatal mistake; I confess it," sobbed the daughter, "and I will redeem it!"

A fatal mistake! And this after barely two years of married life.

Alas, that love should be woven of so ephemeral a tissue!

Chapter 1

Katzenjammer

"C'est une etrange affaire qu'une demoiselle"

— Moulière

I F you look in the German-and-English dictionary for the translation of the word *Katzenjammer*, you will be startled to find it defined as " an indisposition in consequence of intoxication."

The definition is correct, and yet many victims of this complaint do not as much as know the taste of wine. Ask the fine ladies who shudder at the mere approach of Bacchus, what complaint it is which stretches them on their soft sofas and opens their lips to innumerable yawns, and, if they are Germans, they will answer you *Katzenjammer*. The truth is, that not wine alone intoxicates. Pleasure can intoxicate, passion can inebriate, success can make you quite as drunk as champagne. The waking from these several stages of delights will bring the same result — *Katzenjammer*. In English you would call it reaction; but whole pages of English cannot express the sick, empty, weary, vacant feeling which is so concisely contained within these four German syllables. This disease is, at certain seasons, apt to become epidemic; but Ash Wednesday in Catholic countries is the day on which it reaches its climax. On that dreary day — whose first stroke is the knell of dissipation and pleasure, warning us to stop amusing ourselves and to begin undoing all the mischief which the Carnival has done

— that sickly specter *Katzenjammer* creeps into many a gilded drawing-room, and slinks into many a fair lady's bower.

On the Ash Wednesday of which I write, the sickly specter was making his round of the town in search of victims. He stole in by every door, and slipped in by every window, exactly as it pleased him; and he came, among others, to an apartment which seemed to please him unusually well, and to a victim whose torment afforded him a special enjoyment.

The specter waved his wand, and the comfortable room looked dreary, the well-filled bookshelves became oppressive, the solid chairs appeared clumsy, the dark-green window curtains gloomy. Never had raindrops run so dismally down the pane, never had the clock ticked so monotonously, never had the mirror thrown back so pale a reflection of the victim's face as it did on this Ash Wednesday afternoon.

It was at the writing-table that the sufferer had at last taken refuge from her tormentor; and as she sat there in the shadow of the green curtain, with her eyes fixed on the paper before her, and with a somewhat weary droop of her fair head, she looked so like a piece of exquisite fragility that it was a wonder the tormenting specter took no pity on his victim.

This very fragility made her beauty peculiar, though by no means faultless. She was too slight in figure to be called handsome, too irregular in feature to be called classical, too faint in coloring to be called brilliant; yet this graceful girl, with the faintest bloom on her cheek, with the fairest of hair lying on her forehead like a cloud of feathery gold, had never been denied the supreme right of beauty. The complexion was of a flawless transparency; the eyelashes so long and thick that they threw a distinct shade on the cheek, and fringed her eyes so heavily as to leave them in a sort of mysterious darkness. It wanted but the uplifting of those downcast eyes — blue, dreamy eyes, they surely must be — to complete the whole of the picture consistently. She looked like a figure stepped straight out of an old-fashioned poem.

As yet the fringe remained obstinately lowered, and the eyes fixed steadily on the open page before her. That page belonged to a leather-bound, gilt-edged book —

She looked like a figure stepped straight out of an old-fashioned poem.

just such a volume as young ladies love to cherish as the confidant of their secret inspirations. The broken lines upon the paper looked most curiously, most suspiciously, like verses; and the way in which her white fingers counted out little raps upon the table, might have made one think of a measure that would not fit or a stanza that would not scan; and when she now and then paused frowning, and bit the tip of her penholder with her pearly teeth, any spectator would have been irresistibly reminded of a poetess brought up for want of a rhyme.

At length she threw down the pen and rose.

"Impossible!" she said, aloud.

What was impossible? Would *Thräne* not rhyme satisfactorily with *gräme*? Or was *Schmerzen* too commonplace to be coupled with *Herzen*?

"Impossible," she repeated. "Impossible to be quite happy under twenty thousand florins a year," and she raised her eyes at last. There was no one in the room to meet her gaze, no one to be surprised at the revelation it afforded. For, after all, they were not blue, those eyes, they were not dreamy; there was no touch of the muse in them. They were of a brilliant gray; keen, quick eyes, very wide-awake and very direct in their gaze. It seemed almost as if nature had here been guilty of an anachronism; for this girl's eyes were distinctly and characteristically nineteenth-century eyes, while the fragrance of old-world poesy which seemed to linger about her features, and the floating grace of her movements, belonged rather to the ideal of an age long passed. "I have calculated it every way," she remarked, still aloud, closing her leather-bound book with care," and twenty thousand is the very lowest figure possible in order to —" She broke off, for the door opened just then, and two letters were placed in her hand.

Her face fell as she opened the first; it was the bill for the wreath of apple blossoms which she had worn last night, at the last ball of the Carnival. Eight florins, which had seemed so cheap for the fresh, crisp flowers in the shop, looked quite out of proportion now that the petals hung limp and lifeless, and the pleasure was behind her. Rather despondently, she crushed up the envelope and opened the second letter. "From Belita," she pronounced, as she took the sheet to the window to read it.

Belita was this girl's one solitary great friend. If she was not quite the *Herzens-freundin*, almost indispensable to German girlhood, and who has the right to share all thoughts and feelings, she was at least the nearest approach to such a confidante that the other had ever known. They had been for some years together in a private school, whither the Italian girl had been sent to acquire the northern tongue, and where circumstances, as well as a certain sympathy in some of their ideas, had thrown them very much upon each other's society.

"CARISSIMA MARGHERITA, I will risk the possibility of crushing my lace ruffles; I will even risk making ink spots upon my pale green silk before the *corso*, and all this in order that you may be the first to hear my news. Margherita, it is all settled: I am going to be married. You are surprised? *Eh certo*, I am as much surprised myself. Two days ago the matter was decided *for* me, of course, and not *by* me. How much more satisfactory is our custom than yours! You Germans would take several months to decide what is settled by our good parents in a few hours; and after all, the result is the same. I was sent for and told my fate; and before my mother had done speaking, I had, with my usual presence of mind, realized my position, and resolved to present the two new muslins I had just ordered to my younger sister. The eyes of a married woman must be directed towards higher things than muslins. I want your advice on a weighty point — my toilet for the 30th, the day the *contratto* is to be signed. Blue or lilac? is the question which pursues me day and night. Yellow is too lively, not enough *recueilli* for the occasion; and pink I have been obliged to discard, for I have not got your adorable complexion. It must be elegant, and yet not too *voyant*; it must be rich, but not heavy; it must soar above the simplicity of a girl's dress, and yet not attain the elaboration of a *toilette de jeune femme*. A judicious compromise between all these qualities, and a happy mixture of the maiden and the matron, are what is requisite. Added to all this, it must not cost much money. For a little time more I shall require to continue my economy; but the mystic words at the altar-foot once spoken, I shall be trans- formed into a rich contessa — and such a rich one, Margherita! No more dresses to be turned, no more trimmings to be scrimped, every fashion-paper *rêve*. I must stop, the carriage is at the door. No, I have a moment's respite. Mamma is gone to change her velvet mantle; she is afraid of the pelting of the *confetti*. I tremble for my green silk; but, *basta*! I am wasting my time. Margherita, do you remember our words of parting? How we two poor penniless girls swore to each other that we would make our fortune in the world? That we would fall into no such mistake as that which your parents have made? It was in August we spoke thus; it is March now, and my fortune is made. And yours? It may take you a lit-tle longer, for you have the disadvantage of having to choose for yourself; but answer me truly: what has your first Carnival brought you? I am curious, but I am not uneasy; for, thank Heaven, you are not one of those silly, sentimental, romantic girls, so frequent among your countrywomen, and who never fail to fall in love with the wrong people. That same clear little head which enabled you to carry off the *prix de logique* at school will help you to take a prize in the world as well, and a very big prize it will be. I hear my mother coming — goodbye; but now, on glancing through my letter, I perceive an omission — I have not mentioned my future husband's name. It is Conte Luigi Francopazzi, distantly related to me on my mother's side. He is young, good-looking, and I have no objection to make to him, except — except — Margherita, I can have no secrets from you; there is no use blinding myself to the fact — he is not tall enough for me. Not that he is a very small man, either, but you know my unfortunate height. This is all the harder, as throughout life I have noticed that a tall husband makes a better background; but I console myself with the reflection that low *coiffures* are coming into fashion, and I have secretly vowed that nothing but tall hats shall find their way on to his head.

Now I am off. Do not expect another letter just now; for tomorrow I enter on the delights and agonies of the *trousseau*.

Your devoted friend.

BELITA PEGRELLI."

The perusal of this letter was scarcely completed when the door opened once more, and a middle-aged gentleman appeared on the scene. This middle-aged gentleman was Adalbert Mohr.

The last twenty years had slowly changed Adalbert from a slim, clear-eyed student to a mature man, whose glance had gained in shrewdness and lost nothing in vivacity. His active habits had saved him from that heaviness of appearance and manner with which almost every German on the verge of fifty is beset. His light hair was only sparsely sprinkled with gray; and his bearing was as straight and easy now as it had been at thirty.

"Papa," began his daughter, without the smallest preliminary, "Belita has made her fortune."

"Her fortune!" repeated Herr Mohr, somewhat staggered at this abruptness. "Has she struck a gold mine? or invented a new steam engine?"

"No, she is going to marry a rich man."

"Ah!" said Adalbert, "I comprehend;" and he sat down on the chair beside him. He was holding his hat in one hand and his um-brella in the other; he twirled the umbrella between his fingers, and looked at his daughter with a glance that was both curious and a little uneasy. He appeared altogether like a man who is in a hurry to be gone, and yet has something to say which he hesitates how to put forward.

"And so, Gretchen, Belita has made her fortune, has she?"

"Yes; and now I mean to make mine."

"And in the same way?" asked Adalbert, again rather staggered.

"In exactly the same way."

Gretchen left the window and calmly took a chair straight opposite her parent. She had announced her intention of making her fortune in a tone as matter-of-fact as if she had been announcing her intention of making a pudding.

Adalbert began to laugh. "Many a young lady has started with that same idea, Gretchen, and has ended by eating bread and cheese in a garret, and darning her husband's stockings by the light of a tallow-candle."

Gretchen gave a sniff of her fine-cut nostrils.

"Stockings and tallow-candles, indeed! Of course, I know that there are lots of foolish and romantic girls in the world; but what are they there for, unless those sensible girls should profit by their experience?"

"No man has ever grown wise through another man's experience, and no woman either."

"Then why should I not be the first woman who does?"

"How young you are, child; and how much more foolish than you think!"

"Young!" repeated Gretchen, with an accent of the most supreme, the most delicate scorn in her clear voice. "Why, I am eighteen and nine months; in a year and a quarter I shall be out of my teens. When a woman is out of her teens, her first youth is passed; therefore it stands to reason that in fifteen months my first youth will be passed."

Adalbert laughed out loud.

"What are you laughing at, papa?"

"At my dogmatical daughter, whose confidence in life I am trying in vain to shake."

"I wish you would stop; I have said nothing ridiculous. What has age got to do with it, after all, when you look at it from a logical point of view? Some people are born sensible, and others die foolish.

It cannot make any difference whether one is nineteen or twenty-nine or thirty-nine; and it is only a stupid old prejudice to say that because a woman happens to be young and — "

"Pretty," completed Adalbert, with a mischievous smile.

"Pretty," repeated Gretchen, steadily, "that because a woman happens to be young and pretty, she must necessarily also be foolish. If you insist on the number of years, I am only eighteen, but much, much older in experience."

"Of the world and its wicked ways," finished Adalbert.

"Laugh if you like, papa; I know what I am talking about. I have been out a whole season, without counting the two dancing parties last year; and I have been to fourteen balls — five public and nine private."

"Accurate, Gretchen — always accurate," put in her father. "You were born a master of the exact sciences."

"I have watched other girls," continued the daughter, unheeding, "and the way they go on; and I have danced and talked and listened, and made acquaintance with dozens — just simply dozens, of men — "

"And broken dozens, simply dozens, of hearts — "

"Nonsense, papa! Hearts do not break."

"Well, I am bound to say that they make everything unbreakable nowadays, even china; that comes from living in the nineteenth century. And yet — and yet — " Adalbert twirled his umbrella rather nervously, and looked with anxiety at his daughter — " and yet, even in this century I think there are a few hearts still left which might break in an old-fashioned manner. What should you say, Gretchen, if you were to have an opportunity of testing the solidity of a nineteenth-century heart — an early opportunity, Gretchen?"

"Papa, I do not understand you," said Gretchen, with a stare and a sudden flush. "What — what do you mean? And where are you going to?"

For Adalbert had risen now, and was buttoning his great coat in a hurry. Gretchen rose likewise, and stood gazing at her father, while a sort of vague excitement began taking possession of her mind.

"Where am I going to? Did I not tell you? To the *Frauenkirche*, to examine that old vault they have come upon. They want my opinion about some of the half-obliterated inscriptions on the tombs." Gretchen was accustomed to these expeditions of her father's; for Herr Mohr had long since become an authority in matters of historical research. His name was honorably known far beyond the limits of Schleppenheim, the provincial German town in which he had settled. He had worked hard, but he had not worked in vain; and though, since his marriage and the births of the son and daughter with whom Providence had blessed him, he had not been able to indulge his passion for travel and active exploration, yet he had succeeded in realizing that comfortable independence for himself and his family which once had seemed to lie so far out of reach.

"Yes, papa, the vault, I understand," said Gretchen, with a rather palpitating heart; "but — and — You were going to say something else?"

"Only that I think it not improbable that during my absence you should have a visitor."

"A visitor, on Ash Wednesday?" repeated Gretchen, somewhat mockingly. "That is not likely, papa."

"But if I happen to know that this unlikely thing is a fact?"

"Happen to know!" she echoed, scornfully.

"Well, I was told so."

"By — "

"By the person himself."

"*Himself!*" repeated Gretchen, significantly. She stood close to her father — her eyes were devouring his face. "Papa," she said, suddenly, clutching at his arm, "who is it?"

"Nonsense, Gretchen," laughed Adalbert. "I know nothing. Let me go. I am in a hurry: they are all waiting for me in that vault. Where are my gloves? Let me go."

But the gray eyes were still fixed on his face, and the fragile white hand was still on his sleeve; and fragile though it appeared, its grasp was surprisingly firm. It might look like a snowflake, but it was not to be shaken off like one.

"Who is it?" was all she said.

"Gretchen, you will be the ruin of that vault; let me go. Don't pretend that you cannot guess his name." And with an unexpected movement, Herr Mohr freed himself and escaped through the door, remarking, as he reached it, "I shall be back again in two hours."

"Who is it?" called out the disconcerted Gretchen; but she only heard her father laughing to himself halfway down the staircase.

Once more left solitary, Gretchen looked slowly round her, and to her astonishment she perceived that everything was changed. The bookshelves were not oppressive, the green curtains were not gloomy, there was a quite surprising variety in the tick of the clock; the tormenting specter was laid at last.

Gretchen's form of *Katzenjammer* had been severe, but it had been a different species of the malady from that which usually attacks young ladies of eighteen. She did not regret the Carnival for the Carnival's sake, nor sigh over the dancing and gaslight because she liked dancing and gaslight; she never looked at them otherwise than as means which might help her to reach an end. The Carnival was a campaign on whose battlefields she had hoped to win a victory. If she had felt dull and dispirited it was because this campaign was over, the next so far in the future, and the victory not gained — or so it had appeared. But now — her father's words — his smile — the visitor who was to come — oh, there could be no doubt that the victory was won and her happiness secured.

With regard to this vast word happiness, Gretchen's ideas might have been worth analyzing. In her opinion it was a question of arithmetic. Since there existed laws for measuring the distance of sun, moon, and stars — since there were rules for weighing the earth and determining the compounds of chemicals — she saw. no reason why, by judicious calculation and a logical blending of elements, happiness should not be attained. Her recipe would have been something as follows:

Take of silver florins as much as will buy a house in town and keep a villa in the country; mix to flavor with golden ducats; consolidate the whole by a handsome balance at some well-established bank; throw in a coronet, and add to it a husband who will let you have your own way.

Result: (Who could doubt it?) Happiness. Some tastes might prefer more town and less country, or vice versa, but those were details.

Gretchen stooped to pick up a paper — the bill for the apple-blossoms; eight florins was really not much, considering the result. Belita's letter was still in her hand; she slowly folded it up. Perhaps — perhaps her answer to that letter might contain as important a piece of news as the one here announced. Her fortune might be made as well as Belita's, perhaps as brilliantly as Belita's; for surely he would be as rich as the Conte Luigi Francopazzi — possibly richer? And having reached this point, Gretchen repeated her question aloud," Who can it be?" The father, as he walked down the street, had laughed to himself at the idea of a girl of eighteen pretending not to guess such a riddle; but in very truth Gretchen was in the dark. During her first Carnival many looks and words had flattered her vanity, but none had succeeded so far as to touch her heart. She had met with much admiration, but she had not been prepared for so rapid and immediate a triumph. She began to go through the names of all her most constant partners.

Gretchen was nothing if she was not methodical. She had formed a cut and dry opinion of every single one of her acquaintances. Her eyes were accustomed to take stock of every object and every person they saw, and by a quick contraction of the delicate mouth a sharp observer might guess at the nature of the judgment instantly passed. Her acquaintances were all catalogued and ranged in order within a secret storehouse of her brain. She had seldom been puzzled as yet as to the judgments to be passed, or the exact place to be assigned in her liking. She found no difficulty whatever about the matter: she had as yet found very little difficulty about anything of any kind. Mentally, she wrote out the designations as follows:

"*Lieutenant Stumpfenspor* — Good-natured and slow; the sort of man to be trusted with untold gold; but as he has none of his own, and I none to trust him with, must not let him go too far in his attentions."

"*Herr von Sattleben* — A shriveled worldling; thinks I am a toy to be played with; but he shall soon find out that some toys have sharp edges, and can cut people's fingers."

Such an intangible catalogue is useful for occasional reference, and Gretchen referred to it now; taking the list to hand, she looked up a special column which was marked "*Epouseurs,*" and here she alighted, among others, upon the following names:

"*Herr von Barten* — Not so stupid as he looks, but quite as heavy as the cloth he manufactures. *N.B.* — The cloth trade is improving daily."

"*Baron Federbusch* — Gentlemanlike; rather amusing, and very conceited; but I think I could cure him of that."

This last name was, so to say, mentally underscored; and there was a note added, which had all the emphasis of italics, "*The best parti of the season.*"

It was upon these last two names that Gretchen's attention remained fixed; the balance of her surmises was pretty equally divided between them, although a few others were not quite out of the question.

"If it is either of these," she decided," I shall not say 'Yes' quite at once; but I shall certainly not say 'No.' If it is any of the lancer lieutenants, then I must be stern, for I know that they are all penniless. But, really, I wonder who he is, and I wish he would not keep me waiting so long; I am quite prepared now — not in the least flurried."

A ring at the bell cut the words short. There was a step in the passage, and Gretchen, though she was not in the least flurried, turned rather pale, and began to wish that after all the apple blossoms had not taken such immediate effect, and that nobody was coming to propose to her.

Chapter 11

A Legal Advisor

"I too a sister had, an only sister; She loved me dearly."

— Coleridge

HILE Gretchen had been settling the amount of her future income, at the opposite end of the town a tall man was walking leisurely through the streets.

The rain splashed in heavy drops on his hat, each drop squirting up again like a tiny fountain, then joining into little torrents, which ran merrily down his forehead and his nose, blurring the glass of his massive spectacles, then losing themselves a little in his beard, and ending by drawing long wet lines all down his winter coat. He had an umbrella with him, but it was tightly rolled up in his hand, instead of fulfilling an umbrella's vocation. He walked on with a long but unhurried step, as unconcerned about the weather as if there had been a dry pavement beneath his feet and a blue sky overhead, and evidently plunged in some deep and absorbing thought. Still, with that abstracted look on his face, and with a mere mechanical sense of locality, which spoke of constant habit, he turned into a narrow lonely street, and entered a door.

A steep staircase took him up to the second story, and there, on a brass plate, stood engraved the name —

"DR. VINCENZ KOMERS."

That was his door, and the name on the brass plate was his name. He was Vincenz Komers, lawyer, or *Doctor der Rechte*, coming home rather late from his office to his dinner.

Before he had had time to touch the bell handle, the door was opened quickly from the inside, and a thin, sallow-faced lady confronted him.

"I knew it was you; I heard your step," she greeted him in a tone of shrill reproach. "Too stingy, of course, to give himself a cab home in the rain; never minds whether he frightens his sister into fits by coming home late; overworks himself, catches a cold, and I have to nurse him when I need nursing myself."

She had drawn him into the room by this time, and was looking at him critically.

" Preserve us! he has not opened his umbrella; he has ruined his best hat and soaked his collar. Nothing like a lawyer for nice practical commonsense!"

Certainly, Dr. Komers presented a rather striking sight, as he stood there with his neatly rolled-up umbrella in his hand, and the raindrops dripping from his clothes. His sister contemplated him with a sort of affectionate contempt, then curtly prescribed dry clothes as the prelude to eating his "cold dinner."

Vincenz meekly complied, and presently reappeared, metamorphosed from an amphibious into a terrestrial being.

His sister looked at him again critically.

"Did you not see your slippers standing ready for you? Why have you not put them on?"

"Because I must go out again this afternoon," answered Vincenz, his pale face flushing ever so slightly.

"Indeed! to your office?" "No, not to my office."

"Might I venture to inquire where to?" "To the *Krautgasse*."

"Oh, there again!"

Vincenz laid down his spoon to let his "cold" soup cool, but he did not answer.

Having waited for a minute, Anna found herself obliged to add, "Anything new about their precious lawsuit? Is it going to come to an end at last?"

"Not that I know of; matters remain perfectly unchanged."

"Then what is it you are going to do in the *Krautgasse?*"

Vincenz looked up with marked impatience.

"Does it not strike you, Anna, that a man need not always go there as a legal adviser? Why should I not call in the *Krautgasse* as a friend?"

There was a sort of pride in the way he said the last word.

"As a friend — ah!" repeated Anna. Then she looked from her brother to the girl who was waiting upon them; and then she sat silent for some time, eating her dinner and throwing stolen and piercing glances at Vincenz opposite.

Although she had, with cheerless emphasis, invited him to come to his *cold* dinner, the dinner was in fact scalding hot. Anna was too good a *Hausfrau*, and far too devoted a sister, to let anything but a steaming repast be set upon the table. She dearly loved to receive her brother, when he came late from his office, with promises of discomfort and over-cooked meat — but she would rather have cut off her right hand than have fulfilled these prophecies. Had she not stood in the kitchen herself today, roasting her face over the fire, and earning for herself one of her chronic headaches, merely in order that Vincenz should get his fried carps crisp and hot, as he liked them on fast days?

Anna was four years older than her brother, and long before she had passed the barrier of her fortieth year she had given up all claim to feminine charms. But feminine she remained in mind and manner; womanish and womanly in the highest degree, in spite of the commanding mien and cutting tone with which she armed herself, and in defiance to the dash of strong-mindedness she carried on the surface. It was a mere coat of varnish, and under the thin glaze her true nature lay.

She was tall, meagre, and already wrinkled — her features cut so sharply as to be almost a caricature; ill health it was, more than years, which had so quickly withered her cheek.

She never could have been beautiful; but there had been a time when that exaggerated profile had not been without its charm; and even now there were moments when, entering the half-lighted room, or looking at her without his spectacles, Vincenz was vividly reminded of what she had been in the days when they were both young and prosperous, and before Anna had had that mortal illness which had ended her youth with one blow.

The maid-servant had scarcely closed the door behind her when Anna looked at her brother and said, "Well?"

"Well, what?"

"How about that visit? Explain yourself."

For a moment Vincenz hesitated. Should he confess or evade? "Evade" was the first instinctive answer which rose in his mind; but in the next second he had felt that he ought to confess. The remembrance of a past obligation, the consciousness of a heavy debt, for which his whole life could not repay Anna, rose before his eyes. She had a right to his confidence. What a minute before had irritated him as womanish curiosity, now appeared to him in the light of sisterly solicitude. He threw down his napkin, and taking off his spectacles, began to rub them with much unnecessary zeal, looking straight at his sister, while, with a touch of defiance in his voice, he said,

"I am going to try my chance with her."

Anna returned her brother's look without the slightest surprise, for she had known perfectly well what was coming. She had seen it coming all these long months, although never had he breathed one word to her. She had seen it coming before even he had seen it coming himself. Therefore, when, after a moment's pause, he began explaining who "she" was, and what "taking his chance" meant, Anna interrupted him —

"You need not tell me — I know it all."

Here was a shock for Vincenz, who all this time had been priding himself on his masculine impenetrability. He had never written a single love-verse which might have fallen into her hands; he had never hung up the sacred photograph in his room;

he had never pronounced the name, whose very sound stirred his heart, except in what he considered to be a studiously indifferent tone. He had never, he was quite sure — he had never been caught in the act of kissing that battered old pocketbook which she with her own fingers had so amiably and deftly stitched up for him. No, he was quite confident that he had not comported himself like a heartsick lover, and yet Anna had guessed!

Her voice broke in upon his thoughts. "Why must you do it today?"

"I should have done it long before today, only that during the Carnival weeks there was no possibility of approaching her. I dare not now delay."

"Nobody but you would think of choosing Ash Wednesday as the day of your betrothal."

"It remains to be seen whether it is the day of my betrothal," said Vincenz, with an anxious smile.

"Vincenz, this is nonsense! What can you fear?"

"Rivals, Anna; she is so young and beautiful."

"So sweet and tender and helpless, why do you not add?" retorted Anna, sharply. "Oh for the blindness of men! Do you not see that that girl, who looks as delicate as an angel going into consumption, is in reality as wiry as a man, as tough as a sailor, as hard-headed as a lawyer — ay, and as hard-hearted too? I believe, more hard-hearted than some lawyers" — she added, with a severe glance at her brother. "No, Vincenz; angels may have golden hair, but golden hair does not make angels."

"Anna," said Vincenz, unheeding, "what do you think of my chance?"

"Your what?"

"My chance of winning her."

"It may amuse you to call it a chance, but you must know perfectly well that you cannot seriously contemplate the possibility of a refusal."

"It is not a grand marriage for her," said Vincenz, musing; "but, after all, I do not ask her to share a crust of bread with me; she need not go without the comforts which she has in her father's house."

"I will tell you what I think," burst out Anna. "You are throwing yourself away. Not a grand marriage for her? Pooh! You are ten times too good, and too handsome, and too clever for her. She ought to thank you on her knees for your condescension."

Vincenz smiled absently; he was used to such speeches. If he could have seen himself with Anna's eyes, he would have beheld a sort of impossible demi-god, as far above his fellow creatures in loftiness of character and majesty of countenance as the sky is removed from the earth. Even as it was, he had been sufficiently influenced to think himself both clever and good-looking beyond the average of men, until a certain day, when he had for the first time looked at himself in the light of a suitor for that flower-faced girl in her teens; then only his mirror had told him that his youth was past, and then only he discovered all the qualities which he wanted, and wished, with all the strength of his strong mind, that he could be twenty times better looking, and greater and more brilliant, for her sake.

"I wonder you never thought of marrying Barbara Bitterfreund," said Anna, "instead of that chit of a girl. Barbara would have suited you much better. She has just written a pamphlet upon the prospects of lady dentists."

Vincenz shuddered a little.

"Why, Barbara is seventeen years older than —"

"And two years younger than yourself," interrupted Anna; "and you don't call yourself old."

This was a new view of the case for Vincenz. Hitherto Barbara Bitterfreund had always appeared to him in the light of an old scarecrow; and yet it was quite true that she was two years younger than himself. Was it not barely possible that he might appear in the light of an old scarecrow when looked at by eyes of eighteen? He lost himself in the train of thought suggested by this idea.

Brother and sister were in their sitting room now; there was a long pause. On one side, the raindrops fell against the pane; on the other, there was the clatter of plates as the maid-servant was clearing away the remains of the fried carp.

Anna lay back with closed eyes, for her head was beginning to ache. Vincenz stood and looked round the room, as he had never looked at it before. The wallpaper seemed to him dingy today; he had not till now noticed how shabby was the piece of carpet in the middle of the room; how unshapely looked the pile of law papers which loaded his writing-table; and really it was time that Anna should replace that starved-looking pot of ivy by some brighter plant.

"I wish the stairs were not so steep," he said aloud. Anna understood the thought underlying that wish.

"If they are good enough for you they will be good enough for her."

He scarcely heard the words.

There was another pause, longer this time, and then Vincenz, looking at his watch, walked to the table and took up his hat.

Anna opened her eyes and followed his movements. "Are you really going now?"

"Yes, it is time," said Vincenz, brushing his hat, and speaking with forced composure.

Anna's lips tightened as if in pain. She thoroughly disapproved of the step he was about to take; but she knew perfectly well that it would be taken. She could bully Vincenz about his coats, and his boots, and the pattern of his neckties; but she never could move him an inch in such a resolution as this. Fortunately, she was wise enough to spare the unnecessary annoyance of attempted persuasion both to herself and to him. '

It was a moment of trepidation as Vincenz took up his hat, and in spite of herself, the trepidation touched Anna also. The sound of the hat-brush even had something solemn in it, and the fact that Vincenz was not much given to the polishing of his hats gave all the more weight to the circumstance. He would not have thought of doing it if it had not been for her: henceforward everything would be done for her.

Anna watched him, and it seemed to her that a great deal more than mere dust was being brushed away in this minute.

When the hat had been operated upon with a perseverance which threatened to be destructive, Vincenz turned, and said slowly, "I am going; if it is 'Yes,' you need not expect me home till late." Then, with a change of tone, "If it is 'No,' I shall be back at once, in half an hour."

"If," echoed Anna, firing a last shot. "I wish — I wish with all my heart that it could be no, but that is impossible. Of course, I shall have to sit up late. There is no hope of a refusal."

"Goodbye," said Vincenz from the door; "will you not wish me luck, Anna?"

But Anna leaned back again with closed eyes, and gave no an-swer. He shut the door softly, and went out.

She let him get as far as the top of the staircase, and then, springing from her chair, overtook him, breathless.

She did not speak to wish him good luck, but she first seized his hand, and then threw her thin arms around him.

For one minute, brother and sister held each other thus clasped. Anna was some-what less profuse in her caresses than the generali-ty of German sisters, and Vincenz understood her now, though she said no word. She was meagre and withered and unbeautiful, but she was his sister, and they had been all in all to each other during so many long years; for these two stood alone in the world. The same thing was in both their minds. I do not know what strange train of ideas it was which made them both think now of another day, long past, as decisive as this one — the day on which Anna's youth had been ended.

When his steps had died away on the steep staircase, the old maid went back to her room and to her knitting. Her head ached acutely, but the click of the needles would at least break the silence of the lonely room.

She sat till the rain ceased and the early dusk fell; then she knit-ted on by the light of the lamp, pausing every now and then to listen for his step.

The clock from the nearest church spire struck ten, and Anna rose. "It is no use sitting up later," she said aloud, as she rolled up her knitting. "There is no sense in waiting; I shall hear it soon enough."

But though there was no sense in waiting, the stroke of the next hour still fell upon wakeful ears; and the young moon, looking in doubtfully at the window, saw the figure of a thin woman with idle knitting needles in her lap.

Eleven o'clock, and Anna still sat up — for Vincenz had not yet returned.

Chapter III

The Ash Wednesday Visitor

"Alas! syr knight, how may this bee, For my degree's soe highe?"

— Sir Cauline.

G RETCHEN, though somewhat pale, stood resolutely facing the door when she heard the sound of a man's step in the passage. It was not quite jaunty enough for Baron Federbusch, nor ponderous enough for Herr von Barten; and there was no clank of spurs to betray a lancer lieutenant. Who could it be?

"Dr. Komers," announced the servant, opening the door and closing it again behind the lawyer.

Gretchen's pulses calmed down instantly, and the color came back to her face; relief, disappointment, and amusement all took possession of her at once. On the whole, amusement had the upper hand. Here she had been listening for the approach of a suitor; and after all, that step had belonged to Dr. Komers, the family lawyer, whom she had known for years, and who had probably brought some scanty shred of information about the Damianovics' case. It was provoking that he should have been shown in here, and just at this critical juncture when any minute might bring the expected wooer.

Her first impulse was to vent her displeasure on Dr. Komers; but looking at the matter from a logical point of view, it struck her that Dr. Komers was not to blame.

It should have been made clear to the servant that the visitor she expected was a young gentleman, and not middle-aged like this one. No doubt, her mother would appear soon to take him off her hands, and in the meantime she must entertain him. It was a respite; and perhaps a little calm conversation with the family lawyer might help her to prepare for the coming crisis.

"Does mamma know that you are here?" she graciously inquired. "I am sure that she will appear directly," and Gretchen motioned Dr. Komers to a seat.

"There is no hurry," said Dr. Komers, first peering at the chair in his short-sighted manner, and then sitting down upon it.

"I hope your sister is quite well?" inquired Gretchen, noticing the extra shade of gravity on the lawyer's face.

"Thank you, as well as she ever is."

"You have not brought mamma any bad news "I have not brought any news at all."

"Then why have you come?" was rising to Gretchen's lips; but she checked herself in time, remembering that it would not be logical to show her vexation.

The conversation seemed likely to drop here, for Vincenz was wondering whether, after all, her father could have prepared her; and according to his invariable habit, when he became involved in a train of thought, had lost for the moment all sense of his surroundings.

Vincenz Komers had two distinct and quite opposite manners. In the law court or at his desk he was the clear-minded, keen-sighted lawyer, who never for a moment permitted his vagrant thoughts to carry him from the point in hand; but no sooner was his office door closed behind him than the whole man underwent a transformation. He became absent, dreamy, awkward sometimes, although never shy. His nature was unsociable; and a loss of fortune and position in early youth had fed this disposition, until he had become a systematic shunner of his fellow creatures; he was what is termed *sauvage*. He struck attention everywhere as a conspicuous figure — an absurd figure, perhaps, with his tall, stooping frame his short-sighted gaze, and gold-rimmed spectacles; but not all the absurdity in the world could make him look otherwise than a gentleman. The Mohrs were the only family with whom circumstances had thrown him intimately in contact. For several years, he had been in the habit of visiting there — merely as a legal adviser, he persuaded himself; but though, since the death of old Zanderer (who had been his principal, and from whose hands he had received the legacy of the Damianovics case), it is true that there had been many business conversations between Ascelinde and Dr. Komers. It is equally true that business had often been followed by a warm invitation from Adalbert, and a friendly supper in the family circle.

A very tall man, with spectacles and a beard, was the first general impression which Vincenz produced; but the nearer he was looked at, and the longer he was known, the more there was to be discovered in his face. The thick, rich brown beard, which almost reached the middle of his chest, did its best to conceal the fine molding of the jaw and the classical cut of the mouth; but the curve of the nostrils and the bold sweep of the high white forehead were enough to show that it was both a handsome and a proud face. It was a calm face as well, and grave, and would have exactly accorded with the manner, only that the short-sighted eyes had a habit of lighting up suddenly in a way which betrayed that that calmness owed some of its existence to training and not all to nature. In stature he was not only tall but massive and large-limbed, although utterly lacking that straightness of carriage which a large frame requires.

A painful want of drill betrayed itself in both his sitting and his standing attitudes. Placed in tender youth under a drill sergeant, he might have learned how to manage his long legs with more ease and grace, and a certain degree of rigidity would have replaced the general looseness of his appearance. A connoisseur of human physique would have sighed to see such breadth of shoulder stooping over a desk, instead of breasting the beating waves; a recruiting sergeant would have measured his general build with an approving eye; a worshipper of virile muscle would have cast an envious glance at the shape of those long legs which always were in the way in a small room, but which in the wrestling arena would have been pronounced "adorable."

The ruddy color of health should have been on those features instead of that pale, bureaucrat complexion; those long-jointed hands should have grown brown with the sun, and not have whitened within closed rooms. To look at Vincenz Komers was to think of some great fund of power lying waste and useless: of some strongly wrought piece of machinery, for instance, iron-sinewed and giant-limbed, built up with care and wit, and now standing silent — the huge joints rusting in their sockets, the wheels growing helpless with inaction; or else, to change metaphors, you might have compared him to a wide tract of land on which only the puny bluebell trembles and the foolish convolvulus twines, but which on its broad and generous breast might have borne corn to nourish thousands; or else you might have thought of him as of a mighty cataract, with the power of thunder in its voice and the strength of legions in its rush, and which yet falls useless upon mossy stones, and wastes its spray upon untrodden banks.

Fate is very provoking sometimes. If everyone's business were measured out by his strength, we should at least be spared· the absurdity of seeing a man with the strength of a gladiator and the arms of a Hercules passing his day in tying up little parcels neatly with red tape; while that puny youth with thin legs and peaked features is sent out to defend his country from her enemies.

Having waited in vain until Dr. Komers's train of thought should have come to a natural conclusion, Gretchen at length considered herself justified in yielding to her first impulse, and asking, "What have you come for?"

"I wanted first to inquire whether you were quite well?" began Vincenz, starting out of his thoughts.

"But you are always asking me that, Dr. Komers, and you know that I am always quite well. You cannot have called here to ask that? Are you quite sure you have no news for mamma?"

"Quite sure. It is not your mother I wish to speak to, but yourself."

He paused for a moment, and then added, "I am glad of this opportunity of finding you alone."

"I shall not be alone long," said Gretchen; and she rose from her chair, and walking to the window, threw a searching glance up and down the long street, wondering from which side the suitor would come.

"Are you ·waiting for anybody?" asked Vincenz.

"Ye— es," said Gretchen, hesitating. "Yes, I am expecting a visitor," she added, more collectedly, thinking by this threat to drive away Dr. Komers.

Dr. Komers showed no signs of flight. "Your father told me that you would be alone this evening," he remarked, in a tone of disappointment.

"My father!" said Gretchen, turning slowly from the window. "Why it was he himself who told me of the visitor; he never mentioned you at all."

"He told you that you would have another visitor this evening?" asked Dr. Komers, rising, and, according to his habit at critical moments, taking off his spectacles to rub them.

"Yes," she answered, staring at him with parted lips; but already the light of understanding was dawning in her eyes. One moment more and it flashed out.

"You are the visitor!" she cried, and sank down trembling in her chair.

"Yes, I am the visitor," said Dr. Komers, with his spectacles still in his hand. "And surely you know why I have come?"

"I know nothing," retorted Gretchen, setting her teeth and shutting her eyes as if to blind herself to the truth.

"You must know why I have come," Vincenz was saying, and there was a tremor in his deep bass voice. "You must know that I love you, and have loved you for long. It was years ago that I first set eyes upon you, and my heart went out at once to the lovely child, but it was only months ago that I found out my own feelings, and since that moment I have known that there is but one woman on earth for me, and that you are that woman."

He paused, though the words were crowding to his lips; he paused in dismay at the expression of her face. She had listened to his words in a mood that hovered between laughter and tears; her lips parted, her hands clasped, her eyes fixed into a stare of utter bewilderment. All her air-castles were tumbling to the ground, and on their ruins was springing up again the old weary feeling of *Katzenjammer*, which had made the day seem so long.

"I have frightened you," cried Vincenz, with a pang of remorse and a vague apprehension that she was going to faint before his eyes. He never could rid himself of the feeling that this girl was a sort of perishable flower, which could not be touched or scarcely looked at without the bloom coming off. If he did not approach her absolutely on tiptoe, yet there was always a certain instinctive caution in his movements: unconsciously, he would lower his voice in addressing her. A constant dread haunted him lest a breath should blow her off her feet, or a rash gesture knock her down; or lest her hand, if shaken too roughly, might break, like a piece of alabaster. It was always when beside Gretchen that Vincenz felt most conscious of his height, his breadth, and his awkwardness.

"I have frightened you," he repeated, as she still sat silent. "This has been too sudden — too abrupt. I have no right to be as hot-headed as a man of twenty-five. But, believe me, I have tried so hard to be calm, and I have waited so patiently till now; do not ask me to wait longer, Gretchen — let me speak today. Whatever the truth may be, let me hear it; it is better than this devouring suspense."

His eyes were upon hers, forcing her to look at him, but his eloquence had not the power of reaching her just now. She was still plunged too deeply in her disappointment — still too much stunned by his audacity to be touched as yet by his passion.

"You must have known that I loved you," said Vincenz again. "Will you not give me an answer?"

Gretchen raised her head at last.

"Yes," she stammered; "I do not quite understand. You are asking me to — to —"

"To become my wife."

There could be no doubt that she heard aright. The stupor of consternation was dispersed at last.

"Dr. Komers" — and her cheek began to burn — "this surprises me so much that I — I find it difficult to believe that you are serious."

"Surprises you! Oh, Gretchen, have you never guessed it? Have you never known it?"

"I never knew anything — I never thought of you at all — in that way."

"But it is not too late," he said, watching her eagerly. "I cannot ask you to love me in a day, but I know I should win your love in time; and rest assured that there is no man on earth who will love you as I do. Will you not think of me now?"

"No," said Gretchen, with an involuntary shudder, "I can never think of it."

"And why not, Gretchen?"

"Because you are only a poor lawyer," Gretchen would have answered had she spoken her inmost thought; "because you have to scribble for your bread; because you have not got twenty thousand florins a year; because you are not a *parti*."

Poor Vincenz! Had he but known his designation in the mental catalogue, he might have passed his afternoon peaceably at home with his sister and his slippers; for surely no man who is described as "long-legged and short-sighted," and who is, moreover, referred to as "papa's best friend, and a nice, fatherly sort of man, though with a tiresome habit of paying long visits," would ever be foolhardy enough to present himself before the author of these remarks in the character of a lover.

"And why not, Gretchen?" urged Vincenz once more.

But by this time Gretchen's sole feeling was one of indignation. What! She, the ambitious Gretchen, who half an hour ago had been planning how she was going to make herself precious to the rich Baron Federbusch — she who had never been allowed to forget that she carried Damianovics blood in her veins — here she was, the ballroom queen, the courted beauty, receiving an offer of marriage from the family lawyer! What would Belita have said to this? And, to crown his audacity, Dr. Komers was not even comporting himself as a humble and diffident lover should. He was not on his knees, begging for her love in deprecating accents. He was standing there looking at her — with impassioned eyes, it is true, but with nothing in his face to show that he thought she would be lowering herself by loving him — with nothing to say that he considered himself a bit worse than she was. He was not entreating for her love as a favor; his tone said that he almost asked for it as a right.

"Why not?" she repeated, coldly, but her voice shook a little with the tumult of feelings within her. "I cannot give you one reason, for there would be thousands to give; because it is impossible, incongruous — not to be thought of for a moment — because —"

"Because what?" asked Vincenz, coming a step nearer in his excitement, while his burning gaze plunged deep into hers.

"Because I shall never be a poor man's wife," flashed out the girl, scarcely knowing what she said. She threw back her head against the cushion, and dropped her gaze to the floor. Vincenz could no longer see the expression of her eyes, but she could watch him very well through her long lashes. They were a silken curtain that hid her thoughts from the world when she chose, but they never hid the world from her.

Was the family lawyer's audacity crushed at last? No; he did not look crushed, or in the slightest degree humbled. On the contrary, he was holding his head higher than before. He did not look humbled; he only looked sorrowful, and he was gazing at her with a sort of pitying wonder. The tall man looked very gentle as he stood there, no longer attempting to speak; but it was not the gentleness of the lamb — not that gentleness which springs from meekness of disposition, but rather that which comes from an excess of strength. With Vincenz it sprang from a passion which he dared not show, a power which he dared not use, when dealing with so frail a creature. If Dr. Komers had looked angry, or drawn himself up sternly, Gretchen might never have bestowed a second thought on the words that had escaped her; but when he gave her only one sorrowful look, and then walked slowly and silently to the window, a revulsion of feeling was the natural consequence.

What had she said? She hurriedly questioned herself, and blushed with shame as the ungracious phrase came back to her memory. She had seen by that look how deeply she had wounded the man, and she understood now, all at once, how cruel she had been. And not only cruel, reasoned Gretchen, but also illogical, and consequently unjust; and justice was the very virtue on whose possession Gretchen especially piqued herself. The combination of circumstances had been unfortunate; but Dr. Komers need not have been ill-treated on that account: *he* had not combined the circumstances. Clearly, an apology was due to him.

Gretchen looked towards Dr. Komers; he was standing at the window now, and had put on his spectacles again, preparatory to departure. She was not usually diffident of speech, but that man at the window seemed so utterly and so suddenly to have forgotten her presence that she hesitated for a moment as to how she should remind him of it.

There was a carriage rolling down the street, and the clatter which it made on the pavement would have drowned her voice. Gretchen thought she would wait till the carriage was past before she began her apology. Dr. Komers was looking out of the window very intently.

The carriage did not pass, but the clatter came suddenly to an end — almost under the window, it seemed. Gretchen, though not forgetful of her apology, yet felt her curiosity aroused; she wanted to see why the carriage had stopped here, and at what Dr. Komers was peering down so earnestly through his spectacles. With a double purpose in her mind, therefore, she rose from her chair and advanced towards the window.

The rain had stopped some time ago; and now at the eleventh hour the setting sun burst forth, and, with one shower of light, made the dripping streets glorious. Every chimney and window pane all along the street took fire as if by common consent; the small knot of foot passengers who had gathered at the house door were framed in a golden halo; the wet pavement at their feet had turned into a path of yellow light.

"Dr. Komers," said Gretchen, advancing to the window; but before she had reached it Dr. Komers turned round. His expression was quite changed; his face looked pale in the sunset. He put out his hand and stopped her in the act of advancing.

"You must not come here," he said, in a quick, peremptory tone; "you must not look out of the window."

His look was so strange and his words so hurried that Gretchen began to tremble with a nameless dread.

"Sit down," said Dr. Komers, and he pointed to a chair; and Gretchen, wondering at her own obedience, sat down as she was told. Her trembling lips could form no question, only her eyes followed Dr. Komers with a beseeching gaze as he rapidly walked to the door. She was conscious of a great reluctance to being left alone.

He seemed to have read her thought, unspoken though it was, for he turned at the door.

"Do not be frightened, and do not move from here till I return. I think there has been an accident in the street."

He had closed the door almost before he had done speaking; his hurried steps went down the passage; but Gretchen sat as he had left her, and stared only at the door, too much frightened to ask herself what it was that she feared.

Chapter IV

A Victim of Science

"Wherefore let him that thinketh he standeth take heed lest he fall."

— 1 Cor. x.12.

ACCIDENTS, together with concerts, balls, births, marriages, adventures, and discoveries, are to the world at large neither more nor less than a newspaper item — a food for daily gossip which stands rather higher in interest than natural death, and rather lower than willful murder. The column of accidents will scarcely be scanned with as much attention as the column of exchange; and though the habitual newspaper reader may feel somewhat ill-used if nothing more exciting has occurred than the drowning of a couple of village boys out bathing, his interest in the accident column is not likely to take any shape but this.

How wonderfully, how selfishly callous we are towards the misfortunes of all except that handful of fellow creatures with whose features and voices and manners, neckties and coats, we happen to be familiar! How little we are touched by the destruction of unknown men! Oh, strange want of imagination! Amazing poverty of fancy!

Who loses a night's sleep because some peasant lad has been killed by lightning? Whose appetite suffers because of the list of charred corpses that were dragged from the ruins of a theatre? Whose spirit is dejected because a workman has fallen from his scaffolding and been picked up dead? Workmen falling from scaffoldings is a thing which happens every day, and, according to the average number of houses being built, must continue to happen. If we take the trouble to say, "Poor man!" this certainly is the greatest length to which our good nature goes. We never stop to follow up the thought, nor picture to ourselves the dead man brought home, his orphans' faces, and his widow's tears. "How fortunate that I did not pass down that street this afternoon!" we perhaps remark; for we think more of the shock that has been spared our nerves than of that unknown individual's death. Next paper most likely brings the account of a more sensational accident — perhaps a gigantic explosion, or a mysterious murder, which feeds our appetite for romance with higher seasoned food — and the workman is forgotten while he still lies unburied.

But the selfishness of youth is a more refined and more perfect form of the general selfishness of humanity; and Gretchen possessed this first bloom of selfishness in a not inconsiderable degree. Moreover, she had a spirit which inclined to the sanguine order. Never once had she contemplated the possibility of misfortune coming her way. She had always felt blindly confident that the train in which *she* traveled would not run against any other train; that the house in which *she* lived would not fall to pieces and bury her. All the more utterly overwhelming was the agony of the moment which had now come.

Never in after-days was she able to recall exactly the details of this terrible evening. There had been a period of suspense — how long she did not know: it might have been hours, or perhaps only minutes, that she had sat rigid in her chair; then there was the darkened bedroom, which to her bewildered eyes seemed to be unaccountably full of people — the servants in a flutter — her mother in hysterics; hurried whisperings and hushed footsteps; two unknown men with grave faces, whom she guessed to be doctors; a thin fussy gentleman whom she vaguely recognized as Herr Steinwurm, one of her father's scientific friends, and who in a quick staccato voice, and with much agitation of manner, was talking incessantly and excitedly.

On the bed lay a motionless figure bleeding from a wound in the forehead. The hair had been pushed back and drenched with water; the white face was painfully distorted.

This was the father from whom Gretchen had parted so carelessly only two short hours ago.

She was conscious of a strange feeling of unreality as she lay on her knees and held the cold white hand in hers. What she said, or whether she wept, she could not afterwards remember; but she knew that Dr. Komers had spoken to her, that the physicians had tried to drag her away, and that even Herr Steinwurm had put in his word of exhortation.

"Dear Fraulein Mohr," he implored, while moving about restlessly on his thin legs, which, together with his face and general frame, bore an appearance of mustiness and mildew, as if he himself had been recently dug out of some dark and gloomy catacomb —" dear Fraulein Mohr, avoid agitation, and try and resign yourself to Providence. No one can be more distressed than I am. These are the sacrifices that Science demands. I was within an ace of being smashed myself. I can still see it hovering — all over in a minute — man and stone disappearing together; but," he added, with a touch of pride," I insisted on the man being attended to before the stone. Science may suffer; but humanity first, I say. Dear Fraulein Mohr, these sacrifices are unavoidable. You must have heard of the destruction of twenty-seven workmen last year — just in the same way, only on a larger scale, that is all; but the same, radically the same. Science — yes, Science is cruel. Think of Providence, think of Science, Fraulein Mohr." Thus Herr Steinwurm prattled on, unheeded and unchecked.

There was much whispering and consultation around the bed; the two doctors contradicted each other in a polite undertone, and refuted each other's opinions with due regard to professional etiquette.

"Is there any hope?" Gretchen managed at last to inquire, with apparent calmness.

The whispering began again; the doctors cleared their throats, hesitated, glanced irresolutely around them; finally, the least evasive of the two admitted grudgingly that there existed a certain conditional possibility of hope — "for his life," he added, after a second's pause.

Gretchen drew a long breath. "The wound has almost stopped bleeding," she remarked, in a more hopeful whisper.

The doctor who had spoken looked at his learned friend, and his learned friend looked back at him, and then bent over the patient. The first doctor cleared his throat again and stared at Gretchen.

"The wound in the head? Ah yes, it has stopped bleeding," he said, doubtfully. "So it is that which frightened you?"

"Yes," she said, with a shudder.

"That is not the mischief, though."

"Is there anything else the matter?"

The doctor coughed again, and looked down at his knees, then towards the bed; and, following his glance, Gretchen for the first time perceived the unnatural twisted attitude in which her father lay: the line of the coverlet showed that the legs were half drawn up, in a way which suggested some horrible mutilation.

Now Gretchen understood why the doctor had said that he hoped — for his life. Her heart sickened at the thought of the future.

"But broken legs can be set again," she resolutely suggested.

The doctor, who was bending over the bed, observed, without looking up, "Knee-cap splintered, compound fracture of the hip-bone, both ankles severely injured."

It was all the more appalling for being incomprehensible. Hitherto Gretchen had always believed that a thing was either broken or it was not; and, once broken, you had only got to mend it again and it would be all right. These nice definitions, these ghastly nuances, were strange to her.

"Can I be of any use?" inquired Herr Steinwurm, tripping about the room, addressing himself to the company collectively. "Shall I be required to stay? Somebody ought to take charge — ah, I perceive — Dr. Komers; I am forestalled." And the thin antiquarian breathed a sigh of undisguised relief. His very breath seemed to bring with it a whiff of underground air. "Do you intend to stay, Dr. Komers?"

Vincenz bowed.

"Ah — exactly; a man without family ties can always dispose of his time. Now I am a family man; my wife must have waited supper for me during the last hour. I scarcely feel justified in staying longer. Domestic duties, you know. If it had been cold supper, I might possibly" ("we have cold supper twice a week," he explained, parenthetically) — "but this is not the day; I am *so* distressed! Goodnight, Dr. Komers. Try and keep up your spirits, Fraulein Mohr; I am *so* distressed!" and Herr Steinwurm sidled out of the sick-room, home — and supper-wards — feeling very clear in his conscience. What could a man be expected to do for his mutilated friend, beyond bringing him home in a cab and sending for a doctor?

It was not long after Herr Steinwurm's departure that one of the doctors took his leave; and then, when another half hour of unbroken silence had trailed away, the second physician drew on his gloves.

"Are you going also?" asked Gretchen, wistfully.

"I must; a more pressing case awaits me. I may be back towards morning, and I shall bring a nurse. Can you sit up till then?" He looked towards Vincenz.

"I will sit up," answered Gretchen.

"There is no need," said Vincenz from across the bed; "I know how these bandages are put on." He had one in his hand as he spoke, and bent forward to lay it right, but Gretchen snatched it away.

"Leave that to me," she said, hotly. "It is I who must sit up."

Vincenz made no answer, but walked to the farther end of the room, out of the feeble circle of light.

"Yes, yes; a woman's hand is lighter," agreed the doctor, as he took his departure.

Every ten minutes the bandages were to be changed, and with the scrupulous over-exactitude of a novice Gretchen counted the seconds of each interval. She thought she knew the watch that lay beside her, but she did not recognize it as Dr. Komers's.

The faint ticking of the watch was the only sound in the room; it throbbed like the heart of some living thing; only now and then the trickle of water broke the silence, as, with her white fingers, Gretchen wrung out a bandage.

The shutters were closed and the curtains were drawn, she noticed and vaguely wondered who had done it, for no servant had been in the room.

After a time, she felt her knees aching, and sat down on a chair. Dr. Komers was still at the far end of the room; he had not again offered to help her.

Could it really be possible that within these same twenty-four hours Gretchen had been dancing in a lighted ballroom, wreathed in garlands of apple blossoms? It seemed like yesterday, it seemed like a week ago.

She closed her eyes for an instant, and then opened them again at a sound. Dr. Komers was standing beside her.

"I think you had better drink this," he was saying, holding a glass of wine towards her.

She took it mechanically; and the first taste of wine on her lips made her feel how weak and hungry she had been till then. She held out the empty glass towards Vincenz without looking at him, and he went and sat down again on his distant chair.

The wine had made her feel quite strong again, thought Gretchen, and strangely wide awake. She sat with her eyes on the watch, counting the seconds. Still three minutes, still two minutes, before the bandage must be changed; and then her head sank back, her eyelids closed, and she was fast asleep, with the wet linen in her hand.

The scene of her dream was the vault of the Frauenkirche; and pictures conjured up by Herr Steinwurm's broken phrases passed busily through her brain; but, like most dreams, these pictures were false and fantastical, for Gretchen still ignored the facts of the case, which in reality were as follows:

In the, vault of the Frauenkirche, an old and somewhat dilapidated edifice, some repairs, recently begun, had been the source of an interesting discovery. An inner opening had been found leading to a small and hitherto unknown crypt, which, judging by the inscriptions and the half-effaced ciphers on some of the stones, appeared to be of an older date than the body of the church. A few lines in a local paper calling attention to this fact had been enough to bring a swarm of historians and antiquarians buzzing round the Frauenkirche. Correspondences were started, in which learned men said sarcastic things to each other, and commissions were organized to ascertain the truth and settle knotty points. Adalbert Mohr, as a well-known authority, was among the first who were asked for their support; and he lent his help with all the energy and eager love of discovery, which had not grown weaker but stronger with years.

There were eight men who descended together to the vault — a queer assembly of withered faces and gray heads, keen eyes and parchment complexions — men who had spent their lives in digging in dark corners, and grubbing the secrets of the past out of deep holes. Adalbert Mohr, with the slight sprinkling of silver on his hair, was the youngest, and at the same time the keenest, among them. A question arose about the date of a large flat tombstone, which had sunk rather lower than its neighbors into the irregular floor. The Roman ciphers, carved deep into the soft stone, had been partially eaten away by damp.

"I should advise caution," Professor Nagelrost, the eldest and coolest of the antiquarians, had said warningly, as six of his colleagues crowded excitedly round the tombstone, crouching painfully in the low space, and all but setting fire to each other's hair with the candles they held. "You know the state of the foundations;" and he pointed with an experienced finger to the low and threatening ceiling against which the head of even the smallest man among them was perforce pressed.

"Ah, but Science — remember the interests of Science," exhorted Herr Steinwurm, who, with his candle held so that it could drop wax only on other people's clothes and not on his own, was hopping about on the outskirts of the company, keeping well out of reach of the treacherous spot in the ceiling.

It will not do Science much good even if you do succeed in ruining my coat with grease-spots," said Assessor Feuchtkeller, with a little temper. "I wish you would not stand behind me; there is room enough in the front.'

"Grease-spots! Is it possible? I am so distressed! Much obliged, very much obliged," as the assessor stood aside to make room for him; "but I really do not feel justified. I have no right to forget that I am a family man. Infinitely obliged;" and the two men stood opposite each other, each with a dripping candle held at a slanting angle, and each gracefully waving the other into the honorable but perilous place, quite willing to forego the prestige of standing exactly below the critical spot in the ceiling.

"Give me another candle," said Adalbert Mohr, kneeling down on the edge of the stone whose date stood in dispute. He was a family man too, but in moments like this he was somewhat apt to forget it. More than one candle was held forward, and he took the nearest and bent down, passing it slowly along the worn inscription, and striving to connect the surviving fragments.

He was still bending, and the others still crowded round him, when in the silence a slowly grating sound jarred on their ears.

The ceiling! They thought instinctively of the ceiling; all their eyes turned towards it in terror. And while they stared up stupidly the catastrophe was accomplished, for danger never comes from the point we anticipate. It is an enemy which clutches us in the rear while we are guarding our front.

To seven of the antiquarians the ground seemed to heave for a moment, and the flickering light of their candle flames to blind them. The slow grating swelled gradually, until there burst forth a crash, and then followed a sweep as of slipping sand, and then there was silence again.

The central light, on which all their eyes had been fixed, had vanished, and the eighth antiquarian, Adalbert Mohr, who had been kneeling on the disputed stone, had vanished too. There was a black hole, irregularly square, in their midst; for more than one stone had been dragged down by the center one.

A universal destruction and a common grave threatening, was the first thought of the seven terror-stricken men. Herr Steinwurm, being the nearest to the entrance, reached it with two quick little strides, and then turned to see what more was going to follow. But nothing followed, except a little more ominous rattling of what sounded like tiny stones and an invisible avalanche of dry mortar.

"Where is the stone gone to?" gasped an opened-mouthed historian.

Then it was that Herr Steinwurm, standing well out of the vault, displayed his lofty fellow-feeling by exhorting his companions to rescue the vanished man.

"Humanity first, I say. Drag him out of that hole; it is a tomb — a larger tomb than we guessed at. A sacrifice to Science — but humanity first!"

In what precise condition Adalbert Mohr was dragged out of that hole has already, in the attending doctor's words, been told.

The hole itself was, as the sharp-witted Steinwurm surmised, an unusually deep and ancient tomb, the resting place of some long-dead man; but of whom exactly would now never be known. Perhaps it was the grave of some peace-loving mortal who in his lifetime would have shrunk from injuring a fly, but whose tombstone now, against his own will, was destined to cost the life of a fellow-creature; or perhaps some blood-thirsty warrior slept there, whose span of breath had been too short for all the destruction he brooded, and who must needs carry on his murderous practices, and strike another blow with his fleshless arm centuries after his weapons had rusted away and crumbled into dust.

But of all this as yet Gretchen knew nothing. In her dream, the vault was a ballroom, where the venerable Professor Nagelrost sat astride on a tombstone and drummed dance music on a skull, while Herr Steinwurm offered her bouquets of petrified flowers, which, flying from her hand, came showering back upon her head; and at last, as they rattled past her ears, she awoke with a start.

Everything was unchanged, the bandage in its place; only Dr. Komers had left his distant chair, and was sitting at the other side of the bed. She looked down, and saw that there was a rug thrown over her knees, and felt that there was a pillow behind her head. Dr. Komers was sitting quite motionless in his chair, and did not look towards her. His spectacles and beard were as expressionless as ever.

"Have I been asleep long?" she asked, in alarm. "Not very long."

"How long? Ten minutes?"

"Rather more than that — an hour and a half."

"How could you not wake me? You knew that the bandages must be changed."

"I changed them," said Vincenz. She leaned back again, relieved.

"What o'clock is it?" she asked, after a pause. The watch was no longer beside her.

"A few minutes past one."

"So late! Why are you staying so late, Dr. Komers? Why do you not go home?"

"I am not wanted at home," said Vincenz, rather coldly.

"But I really can do without you," said Gretchen, sincerely.

"I dare say," was the short answer.

"Will your sister not be waiting for you — for supper?" she asked, with a mechanical remembrance of the warm supper to which Herr Steinwurm had been forced to hurry back.

"I don't know — I dare say," said Vincenz, indifferently, and again a long silence fell over the room.

Gretchen was beginning to collect her bewildered thoughts. Af-ter all, it was rather good-natured of Dr. Komers to make himself so useful as a sick-nurse. Of course, he was the family lawyer; but a family lawyer's duties do not include dipping bandages in water, and losing his supper, whether warm or cold. Now that she thought of it, it was he who had charged himself with the solving of all difficulties: he had calmed her mother's tragical agitation, and had insisted on the hysterical woman's removal from the sick-room; he had restored some degree of self-possession to the terrified servants; it was he who had procured the second doctor and written the directions for the apothecary. The family lawyer had done every- thing, and nobody had thanked him for it. And now, like a thing forgotten and far away, the scene of the afternoon rose again before Gretchen's mind. She had wounded this man most sorely, and had said no word to heal the wound. Could she not say it now? She glanced furtively towards him; but at once she felt conscious that the apology would not be such a simple thing now as it would have been at first. Neither his expression nor his manner afforded her any point of attack. He was no longer the lover, he was again the sober family friend. He spoke only what was strictly necessary, he never looked towards her; the business of the moment seemed to be his only thought, as, peering through his spectacles, he bent over the bandages. Was it indeed possible that that look of wounded pride had ever been in his eyes? Was it really this same man who a little while ago had been wooing her with such passionate eloquence?

The night was beginning to wane when Vincenz quitted his post at last, and, leaving the patient in the hands of the hired nurse, turned his face homeward. The clock of the Frauenkirche had struck three before he reached his own door.

He started as it flew open in his face; and his sister, with weary eyes and her rolled-up knitting in her hand, stood before him. He had scarcely thought of his sister all these hours.

"Anna, why are you not in bed?"

"I knew I should have to sit up late," she cried, between alarm and a sort of breathless inquiry; "but I did not think it would be as late as this. Well, Vincenz, am I to get no news for my pains?" and the lean old maid hung on his arm, and gazed up with mingled pride and burning curiosity into his face.

"No news of that sort," said Vincenz, looking straight before him; "she will not have me." But in the next minute he stooped and kissed the withered cheek.

"Anna, we must go on being satisfied with each other. I was a fool to think that I could ever win her."

Chapter V

A Glimmer of Fortune

"Uneasy lies the head that wears a crown."

— King Henry IV.

A FTER the events last recorded, the Frauenkirche was more talked about but rather less visited than usual. The principal Schleppenheim paper had a feuilleton article upon the subject, with a double title: "The Sacrifices of Science; or, A Noble Life Nobly Lost." The article was published anonymously, but certain peculiarities of style and expression pointed towards Herr Steinwurm as the probable author. It was much read and commented on, and Herr Mohr's personal qualities were discussed with a freedom and frankness hitherto unknown. When, however, a few days had passed, the literary production suddenly dwindled in interest, and the charm of the style was robbed of its principal point; for it became generally understood that the sacrifice to Science was not quite as absolute as bad been supposed, and that the life, although it might be noble, was not yet on the point of being lost.

Adalbert Mohr was pronounced out of immediate danger: one of the doctors attending him was reported to give fair hopes of his recovery; the other would not do more than admit the possibility of his living. There was also understood to be something wrong beyond the question of life and death; but the reports which circulated were uncertain, and would probably remain so until the consultation of doctors which had been called should have pronounced their verdict.

It was in the forenoon of the day destined for the medical consultation that Dr. Komers received an agitated note from Madame Mohr, summoning him to a business interview. "Business," as Vincenz well knew, was synonymous with "Draskócs;" and so, with a business-like but unenthusiastic punctuality, the family law-yer obeyed the summons.

It must be explained that, during the last ten years, the Damianovics cause had been lingering through one of its most sleepy periods — consisting, in fact, of little else than conversations and unanswered letters. Dr. Komers had received it in this state of coma from the hands of his dying principal, old Zanderer, and had been satisfied to use it as a pretext for visiting the Mohr house, without feeling specially inspired to accomplish the work which had trailed on for over forty years. Dr. Komers was received by Madame Mohr and her daughter in a retired sitting-room, and the lawyer immediately became aware that there was a certain excitement pervading the manner of both ladies. The daughter, though outward-ly calm, betrayed an unwonted exultation in the luster of her gray eyes; and as for Ascelinde, she made no attempt whatever to mask the joyful agitation which glowed within her.

During the painful week that had passed, Madame Mohr had played a passive though lachrymose part. Hysterics and tears were more congenial to her dramatically inclined nature than the commonplace duties of a sick-nurse. If Adalbert's hurt had been the wound of a poisoned arrow, instead of the more prosaic blow of a stone, Ascelinde would not have hesitated to suck the venom from his arm. She would have wept and torn her hair at his funeral, and sprinkled the holy water on his grave, with all the gestures of a despairing widow; but it was not in her nature to sit in a darkened chamber for hours, with nothing more heroic to do than to put his pillows straight or drop out his medicine in a glass. Her ideas were too large to be satisfied with such puny services.

Therefore, after a week of inaction, she hailed the revival of a more sympathetic subject.

"I have heard from Alexius," were the words with which she opened the interview.

"Hearing from Alexius" usually meant the petition for the loan of a few hundred florins; and Vincenz, with some impatience, inquired, "Is your brother in debt again?"

"The count is in difficulties," corrected Ascelinde.

"And he wants more money?"

"He applies for pecuniary assistance; but — "

"But," broke in Gretchen, "he makes a proposal in return. There, Dr. Komers, read that!" And she placed a letter in his hand.

In this letter, Alexius Damianovics, in plain if somewhat ungrammatical terms, offered to resign all claim upon the estate of Draskócs in favor of his sister, in return for the payment of ten thousand florins immediately and in hard cash. The count likewise hinted that the modest sum he had named would enable him to live in a manner more suitable to his august constitution, and to enjoy some of the small comforts which his precarious state of health required. The precarious state of health meant, as Vincenz was aware, an inclination to *delirium tremens*; and the small comforts implied an unlimited quantity of Magyar wine, diversified by spirits.

This letter and the proposal it contained were the source of Ascelinde's exultation. For twenty years, she had held faithfully to the vow required of her by her dying mother; she had fought the battle for her brother, feeling glorified enough by the reflected light which fell upon her. But the task had been hard. She had grown subdued in speech and action, and somewhat melancholy in expression as it became one on whose hands rested so heavy a work. Like a dethroned queen, she sat on the ruins of her grandeur, mourning over the splendor that had departed. Today there was new life in her veins: she was offered the possibility of gaining for herself that which she had been striving to win for Alexius; and the light thus suddenly presented to her blinded her with delight.

Two pairs of eyes were fixed on Vincenz while he read; and when he laid the letter down, the mother said, "Well?" and then the daughter said," Well?" and then they both paused for his answer.

"Well," said Vincenz, with unaccountable calmness, "do you think of accepting the proposal?"

"Can you imagine me blind enough to my own interests to hesitate for a moment?" asked Ascelinde, in amazement.

"But there is a question as to which way your interests lie."

She smiled a broad smile of pity. "You talk like a blind man, Dr. Komers, for you have never seen the home of my ancestors. I almost feel as if I were taking an unfair advantage of my brother in accepting his thoughtless offer; for ten thousand florins cannot be the half — what am I saying? — not the quarter of the value of Draskócs. But poor Alexius will never marry; his unfortunate health forbids him to contract family ties. It is upon me alone that the weight falls." And Ascelinde bowed her head as though the crown which pressed it were too heavy to bear.

"How long is it since you last saw the place?" inquired Vincenz, coolly.

"I was seven years old when we left it."

"That is scarcely the age at which we form correct ideas as to the value of land."

But Ascelinde was losing herself in visions of the past. The scene of departure was rising before her eyes. A great house, many-windowed and many-chimneyed; a flight of lofty steps, on which her uncle's tall figure stood bowing them farewell; the family coach; the avenue down which they had rolled — all these things rose up again before the eye of her inner soul.

"Ah, Dr. Komers!" she cried, "it grows more distinct in my mind every year."

"Really!" said Dr. Komers, dryly.

"How well I remember the entrance hall — I think there were pillars that supported it — and the open colonnade that ran round the house on three sides!"

"With a dark red pavement," supplemented Gretchen. "Was it not red, mamma? It must have been marble, I think."

"And my father's books, my mother's jewels," flowed on Ascelinde; "her wardrobe — it was all left there; even my toys remained behind, in our big nursery upstairs. Ah, what a panorama we viewed from our nursery window!"

"It must have been a fine house," remarked Vincenz, "but the value of the land is a separate question."

"Oh, I remember the land as well as the house, of course. There was the courtyard and the fountain, and there were stablings for ten horses, and a high park wall all round. I remember the fields too, and the lake."

"Yes," said Dr. Komers, stifling a yawn, "so you have told me."

"The fields and the lake," repeated Gretchen, impatiently. "Are you listening, Dr. Komers?"

"Ah, yes, the fields and the lake," he re-echoed; and, strangely enough, though the words had conveyed no special meaning to him before, the Draskócs fields now suddenly became invested with a wonderful fruitfulness, and the Draskócs lake assumed an abnormal charm of aspect in his fancy.

"And then there was the garden," pursued Ascelinde. "Ah, if you had seen the garden! The trees bent under the weight of the fruit. And the roses!" Ascelinde paused here, apparently overcome by the impossibility of describing the Draskócs roses. "Even the Emperor has not got such roses here; they had to be carried away in cart loads."

"In cart lords!" emphasized Gretchen, forcibly.

"In cart loads — yes," said Dr. Komers, beginning to think, as he watched her, that Draskócs must be a fine place after all. "But," he added, "the finest places are sometimes the most encumbered. If your uncle has not been a careful manager, you might find the value of the estate much diminished — in the event of its coming into your hands."

"My guardian," corrected Ascelinde, who always scrupulously clung to this designation of her unscrupulous relative. Anybody could have an uncle, but a guardian implied a certain degree of social importance, even though it happened that this particular guardian had appropriated to himself the worldly goods of his wards. Ascelinde had felt the first shadow of this social importance when, a few weeks after her father's death, Jósika had kindly but firmly removed from her small fingers the golden watch which she had found on a shelf of her deceased parent's room. "I will take care of it for you, my dear; I am your guardian," Jósika had said, patting her on the head; and the deprivation of the watch, bitter in itself, had been sweetened by the accompanying circumstances. It had seemed a greater thing to have had a gold watch taken away by a guardian than to have received the present of one from an uncle. From that day to this, Ascelinde had never again set eyes on the watch; but the feeling of importance had survived. She knew him to be a scoundrel, and she had devoted her life to unmasking him as a traitor, yet for all that he remained her "guardian;" for Ascelinde, at fifty, had retained many childish characteristics beyond the mere incompleteness of geographical and historical knowledge. She had never for a moment felt disgraced at the thought of being related to this man. In her secret heart of hearts, she even cherished a lurking and unspoken admiration for this bold usurper, whose audacious robbery had deprived her brother of his birthright. It would have been shame unbearable to be related to a thief who had stolen a purse or a ring, but no one need disown an uncle whose crime was accomplished on so large and royal a scale.

"Your guardian," repeated Dr. Komers, " but that reminds me that my last letter down there has remained unanswered. We really have no reason to suppose that your guardian is still alive. There seems to be a sort of death-like stillness settling over Draskócs; I cannot awaken a single answer. Let me see, what would his age be now?"

"He was ninety-eight when we heard from him last," said Gretchen.

"And that was three years ago, when the decision of the Landesgericht was reversed in his favor."

"Why that would make him a hundred and one," exclaimed Ascelinde whose arithmetic fortunately reached as far. "My guardian always said that he had a long life before him, and the Damianovics are a long-lived race."

"There was a shoemaker who died near here the other day at the age of a hundred and five," remarked Vincenz; "so there is, after all, no reason why your uncle — your guardian — should not still be alive."

"Oh, indeed!" said Ascelinde, coldly, and she immediately dropped the subject of the Damianovics being a long-lived race, not caring to divide the privilege of high age with anything so low as a shoemaker. She began to think that her guardian must be dead after all.

"And even if he is dead," said Gretchen, "it does not really alter the case. It is evident, then, that he has long ago carried out his threat of marrying his housekeeper — probably he has left heirs, and we shall have several enemies instead of one."

"Very likely," agreed Vincenz; "and this uncertainty makes it all the more advisable to decline the count's proposition."

"Decline — the — pro — proposition!" stammered Ascelinde, staring at Vincenz as if he had suddenly become transformed into a monster before her eyes. "Decline the possibility of possessing Draskócs, the home of my ancestors, Dr. Komers!"

"The question is," said Vincenz, "what is Draskócs worth?"

"No, the question is not that," broke in Gretchen all at once. "The question is quite different. Neither you, mamma, nor you, Dr. Komers, are looking at the case from a logical point of view. Mamma is much too quick, as you are much too slow, in the matter. It stands to reason that a house such as mamma has described, with fields, lakes, stabling, avenues, and — and roses, must be worth much more than ten thousand florins; therefore the question of the worth of Draskócs is settled — the real question is, can it ever be ours? Shall we survive the end of the lawsuit?"

"I hope so," said Vincenz, somewhat absently.

The fair orator bit her lip, and a rather threatening glance shot towards the lawyer.

"You hope so," she repeated. "Tell me the truth, Dr. Komers, do you see any chance of a conclusion?" '

"No very immediate chance, I fear."

Gretchen could contain herself no longer. "You fear," she burst out, in a voice which vibrated with anger — "you fear, and you hope, and you reflect, and write letters, and hold conversations, but when do you act? When has anybody acted in this long-trailed-out, this unfortunate cause? How much paper and ink and words have been wasted on the Draskócs, case, and how little energy! Oh that during forty years and among fifteen legal advisers there should not have been found one man who would put his heart into the work instead of only his pen! We are just as near the recovery of our fortune now as at the moment when my grandmother left Jósika in possession; and, at this rate, my brother's grandchildren and my own may use the same words half a century hence. What is the use of being a lawyer if you can do no more than hope and fear, and express doubtful opinions? Neither your hopes nor your fears, Dr. Komers, will end the cause which has dragged on for forty years. Oh, that I were only a man!"

Gretchen had risen in her excitement, and, in the warmth of her harangue, her fair cheek began to glow. Like Portia addressing the senate, she stood before the two admiring auditors, dropping her logical arguments from lips that seemed made only to speak the softest poetry or to breathe the most tender love; alluding to her grandchildren in a voice that carried the spirit of the enraptured lawyer to dreams of nightingales and musical fountains, although it certainly did not move him to second the wish which formed the climax of her speech. And with her last words she unveiled her eyes before him.

She did not mean it, nor had she calculated any effect in this sudden uplifting of those eyes, of whose full power she was not even aware. All memory of what had passed between her and Dr. Komers, scarcely ten days ago, was blotted out for the

moment; she forgot that he had ever been anything but the family lawyer and coun-
selor. That uplifting of the eyes was an impulse of the moment, done in the heat of
her earnestness; but the most refined coquetry, the most subtle management, could
not have worked a more telling effect. From the reproach, the fire, the brilliancy of
that gaze, Vincenz drank an inspiration that made his pulses flutter. With a sudden
subtle flash, he felt all his ambition fired. Why should he not do what so many others
had failed to do? Why should he not end the cause which had dragged on for forty
years? — If only to earn her gratitude, if only to belie her reproach?

There was silence in the room. Gretchen had sat down again, trembling still a
little from the vehemence of her speech. Ascelinde, with clasped hands, was gazing
at her daughter in speechless admiration. Dr. Komers had risen and had taken a turn
down the room. Suddenly, he stopped before Madame Mohr's chair.

"I have a new idea," he said, abruptly. "I do not ask you absolutely to decline the
count's proposition, but only to defer your decision."

"To defer it? And till when?"

"Until we have got out of the dark."

"I do not understand. What do you propose?"

"I propose that I should go down to Draskócs myself, and look at the land with
my own eyes — ascertain whether your guardian is alive — judge of the value of the
estate."

"Go down to Draskócs!" broke in Ascelinde, clasping her large hands in small
feminine bewilderment, and staring at Dr. Komers as if he had just announced his
intention of going straight to heaven. "Do you mean really? Are you sure? When will
you start?"

"Not quite yet — I have work on hand; in May, perhaps, or June. It is no use
starting until all necessary information has been collected. I shall need some references and directions."

References and directions! Ascelinde could supply him with any amount, as she
eagerly explained; for she was all fire in a moment, sanguine and voluble, as she gazed

There was silence in the room.

with wistful eyes at the enviable mortal who was so soon to behold the home of her ancestors. "There are some addresses written down in that old desk of my mother's," she explained; "perhaps they may help you to find people. I shall look them out. There is one of Pater Dionysius, the priest, who baptized us all; but he must be dead long ago. If he had lived, he might have convinced my guardian of the sinfulness of his conduct — for he was very pious, and attended my grandfather on his deathbed; and my mother said that he preached remarkably well."

All this time, Gretchen had not spoken, for surprise had locked her lips. She felt more startled than triumphant at the unexpected result of her words. Her mother could not guess the motive of this newborn energy; but Gretchen could guess it only too easily, and something like remorse smote her heart. Had Fate decreed that she should always and ever be in the debt of this man? Was he to sacrifice himself to every wish of hers, and she in return do nothing but wound his feelings and mortify his pride? This was not justice, this was not logic. She rose, and going up to him put out her hand.

"Thank you, Dr. Komers," was all she said; but Vincenz felt rewarded above his deserts. If the resolution had brought him this, what would the accomplishment bring him?

It was from that moment forward that his resolve was sealed.

Chapter VI

When Doctors Disagree

*"I am no such pil'd cynique to believe
That beggary is the onely happinesse,
Or, with a number of these patient fooles,
To sing, 'My miude to me a kingdom is!'"*

— Ben Jonson.

ON the afternoon of that same day, three doctors sat in conclave to pronounce the verdict on Adalbert Mohr. After two hours passed in examination, and consultation, and wordy discourses, much adorned with Latin, they all heartily agreed that a watering-place and a course of powerful baths was the patient's best chance of furthering the cure of those local injuries which still remained un- healed, as well as of reestablishing his shattered constitution; and all as heartily disagreed as to which watering-place was to be selected, and what species of powerful baths were to be taken. Each of the medical authorities had a pet scheme of his own. Doctor No. 1 spoke for Baden-Baden; No. 2 defended Teplitz, in Bohemia; No. 3 advised Aix-la-Chapelle. '

"Aix-la-Chapelle!" laughed the first doctor, who was of a sarcastic turn of mind. "Is my learned friend serious in advising our patient to traverse some hundred and odd miles in search of sulfur baths, which he can have almost at his door?"

"And which, according to my humble opinion," put in the second doctor, "would be as effectual as ditch water. It is not a case of sulfur at all; it is clearly a case of iron."

"If traveling be an object," remarked the first speaker, still sarcastically, "why not send him to Iceland at once? There are sulfur springs at the extremity of Northern Europe, and so there are on the confines of Southern Hungary. If traveling be an object, send him there, by all means."

Up to this moment, the patient himself had taken no part in the discussion around him.

"Let me die where I am," he had said once or twice with a fretful impatience; but now he turned his head sharply on the pillow. "The south of Hungary?" he repeated. "What baths do you mean?"

"Sulphur baths," said the second doctor, "but as I said before, sulfur is, in my humble opinion — "

"What is the name of those baths?" asked Adalbert, fixing his eyes on the doctor.

"The baths of Hercules."

"The baths of Hercules!" echoed the sick man, speaking as if in a dream. "The baths of Hercules! Yes, I remember them; I have been there."

But the war between sulfur and iron, between Baden-Baden and Aix-la-Chapelle, was raging so hotly round the patient's bed that no one had time to attend to his words.

"I remember — yes, I remember," the sick man repeated, with eyes that were shining and fixed, as though he were looking at the memories, so far off, which were crowding back on his mind. "Let me go there. I think that there I should get well."

That night in his sleep Adalbert Mohr moved restlessly, and in his dreams a black hole yawned, and ivy crept around it.

From that day forward, the house and the sick room became alive with discussion, and the family entered on a period of restless indecision. The center of discussion, and the cause of indecision, was the choice of the watering-place which was to restore to Adalbert the use of his crippled limbs. Opinions were as numerous as the friends consulted. Personal experiences poured in on all sides, unfortunately of a perplexingly conflicting nature. One old gentleman asserted with a savage persistence that he had known another old gentleman who, in the April of the last year, had been carried to Pystian, forty miles, in a litter, speechless with pain, and crippled in all his joints, and who, in the June of the same year, had without the slightest inconvenience walked up a mountain five thousand feet above the level of the sea; and on the same day that he came down again, put all men over twenty to the blush in the ballroom.

"Think of what I was last year, and look at me now!" said a bachelor acquaintance of the family, sounding the trumpet for Rohitsch, in Styria. As none of the family had happened to see him last year, and as there was nothing very striking to notice about him now except a decided limp in the left leg, this argument some- what missed its effect.

Gräfenberg was, by several enthusiastic ladies, declared to have cured hundreds, and, by one skeptical gentleman, hinted to have killed as many thousands. Whenever Doctor No. 1 mentioned Baden, Doctor No. 2 laughed; when No. 2 talked of Teplitz, No. 1 smiled; both, however, agreed that Aix-la-Chapelle, as suggested by No. 3, was not to be thought of for a moment; and he, in return, raised his eminent shoulders at both Teplitz and Baden. The only point on which 1, 2, and 3 were unanimous and unshaken, was the absurdity, not to say the insanity, of the patient's whim concerning the far-off Hercules Waters.

For throughout all these contradictory opinions, counsels, testimonials, and anecdotes Adalbert Mohr persistently held to his first inspiration. No one recounted anecdotes about the Hercules Baths, for no one had ever been there. The few acquaintances who were aware of the existence of the place, believed in a general way that it was beautiful, but were of opinion that nobody in their senses would go to the confines of civilization to see a beautiful place. Better informed people declared that

it was a nest of robbers, and exposed to every possible bodily peril, and more particularly so in the present disorganized state of the Romanian and Servian armies. " If
you escape the robbers you will be eaten by bears," somebody said by way of dissua-
sion. But Adalbert reflected that if he could only be well enough to get within reach
of a bear, he would be satisfied to run the risk of the eating. "I will either go to the
Hercules Waters or I will die where I am," he repeated with morbid persistence.

It was a sick man's fancy, everybody said; and they soothed and humored him,
as one would humor a child with the measles who cried for his playthings. But no
child had ever cried for his playthings with this perseverance. Adalbert, usually so
practical and so sober-minded, could not be made to understand the difficulties and
the risk of this long and troublesome journey. After a time, the family began reluctantly to consider that sick men's fancies sometimes work their cure. Men on their
deathbeds have been known to ask for a bottle of champagne, and to come back to
life as soon as they have swallowed it. Might not the Hercules Waters, considered as
a bottle of champagne, accomplish this same miracle? While matters were still in this
undecided state, there occurred one day a short and stormy scene, a sort of verbal
duel, between Gretchen and Anna Komers, the subject of which was one destined
apparently to imbitter the peace of Gretchen's days — to wit, the family lawyer.

Anna possessed a fair amount of average intellect, and yet her mind was incapable
of grasping the simple fact that her brother Vincenz was a man with failings and
virtues crossing each other — in all respects a man like his fellow-creatures. She loved
to scold him, adoring him all the time; but if anyone had ventured to hold up to him
a reproving finger, the old maid would have turned into a catamountain and flown
at the enemy's throat. As to the contingency of a woman who had the chance of
marrying him refusing to avail herself of that chance, the idea was pure madness to
her. She had assured her brother to his face that a refusal was her most devout hope;
but when this hope was fulfilled, a sort of stupefied disbelief took the place of the
expected satisfaction, while upon the disbelief there followed a fever of burning indignation. The severest self-restraint was necessary to keep her silent, even during the
first weeks of the Mohrs' affliction; and it was with all the bitterness of a long pent-

up grievance that, finding herself alone with Gretchen one day, she burst out at last, without preface or preamble.

"Ah, Fraulein Mohr, have you no remorse for what you have done? Have you no feeling at all for my noble brother?"

"What have I done?" asked Gretchen, coldly, but turning rather pale.

"What have you done? Why, you have ruined his existence — is that nothing to have done? And such a life to have ruined! Such a man to have lost!"

But Gretchen was already recovering from the sudden attack.

"Fraulein Komers," she said, straightening her slight figure, and knitting her finely penciled eyebrows in displeasure, "I really do not see what right you have to call me to account?"

"And I dare say you did not see either what right he had to propose to you? I told him he was a fool to do it. It was the narrowest escape he ever had in his life, and I thank Heaven for it!"

"Then," said Gretchen, seizing her advantage, "you should thank me too; for it stands to reason that — "

"Thankful? Did I ever say I was thankful?" cried Anna Komers, beginning dimly to see that her arguments were not convertible, and that she could not both run with the hare and hunt with the hounds. "It is you who should be thankful for the love of such a man! Oh, you may shrug your shoulders now, but you will find out his value someday when it is too late perhaps. I dare say you have heard me talk of Barbara Bitterfreund. *She* would not make such a mistake as you have made."

Gretchen had heard of Barbara Bitterfreund as of an unprepossessing old maid, and she smiled a little at an unconscious comparison between herself and that middle-aged female.

"She has written a very superior pamphlet upon the prospects of lady dentists," Anna was saying triumphantly, "and has translated some works from the Greek — *several* works; just the sort of woman to be an intelligent companion to my brother."

"Then if your brother thinks so, what prevents his marrying her?"

"What prevents him?" broke out Anna anew. "Why, it is you who prevent him. Have you ever come across a man who knows what is good for him? Ah, Fraulein Mohr, what have you done? and how could you do it? What possible reasons could move you to such — such folly?"

"Enough that I had my reasons."

"And not difficult to guess either. But what, after all, is the difference of a few years, when such a man is in the question? He is not old at all, though he may be double your age; I defy you to find a single gray hair in his beard."

"I see that you misunderstand both me and my motives entirely," said Gretchen, with rising temper. "It is not because your brother happens to be double my age that I refused him. A man might be three times my age, and have all the hairs in his beard gray, if only he had also — "

"Also what?" asked Anna, breathlessly.

"The — necessary qualifications for a husband."

"And what may those be?" was the sneering question.

"You would not like to hear them."

"Oh, pray, do not spare me!"

"Position and fortune," said Gretchen, shortly.

Anna gave a rather hysterical laugh. "Worldly advantages, you mean!" she cried, raising her thin hands in consternation.

"Yes, worldly advantages," repeated Gretchen, with the most exasperating calmness. "Do you not see the case, Fraulein Komers? It is simply that I am poor and ambitious."

"Mercenary, that is to say."

Gretchen smiled an enraging smile. "Well," she said, with a great distinctness of utterance, and a wicked pleasure in the horror she was provoking, "call it mercenary if you like; I call it practical. But we need not quarrel about names; the fact remains the same. I am poor, and I mean to make my fortune."

"That is, sell yourself to Mammon!" nearly shrieked Anna Komers. "You have the — the unblushingness to say it?"

"I have the courage to say it — yes," and Gretchen gracefully inclined her fair head in acquiescence. The almost terror-stricken expression of Anna's features was only an additional inducement to paint herself far blacker than she really was. There was no shrinking in the fearless glance of the clear gray eyes, no wavering in the steadiness of the smile which parted the rose-tinted lips.

"So young and so untender!" thought poor Anna, staring at the lovely face before her with feelings that baffled all description.

"Ah," she broke out, after a minute of stupefied silence, "if those are your sentiments, if those are your thoughts, I do not wonder any longer at the cruelty which broke my brother's heart; for his heart is broken — he will never recover it, never! Oh, poor Vincenz, my poor Vincenz!"

"Fraulein Komers," said Gretchen, calmly, "we are neither of us children, and so we can neither of us seriously believe in broken hearts. Such romantic fancies can surely only belong to the very earliest and most foolish period of youth."

"In which you now stand," retorted Anna, with sudden excitement, "or you would not talk of things about which you know nothing as yet."

"And never wish to know anything either. Tell me the truth, Fraulein Komers; have you ever seen a broken heart, except set in verses, and bound in morocco leather?"

"I have," said Anna, becoming all at once very quiet, and her shrill voice dropping into a lower key.

"What! do you mean to say that you believe in broken hearts?"

"And you mean to say you do not?"

A disdainful gesture was the only answer.

"Not even," faltered Anna — "not even when I tell you that I — that my own heart has been broken?" She was trembling, and her eyes had grown dim.

The smile on Gretchen's lips faded; and for more than a minute these two women sat and faced each other in silence. So this, thought Gretchen, was a woman with a broken heart; here was a living specimen of that which poets talked of in verses, and which she had never thought to come across in real life. She did not choose to display this newborn curiosity in an open gaze, but from under the shelter of her eyelashes Gretchen was contemplating Anna Komers with a quite new attention. She examined the woman with the broken heart as she might have examined some fabulous creation — a unicorn or a sea serpent, for instance — which had suddenly taken shape before her eyes. It struck her that, after all, a woman with a broken heart does not look so very different from a woman with a whole heart; but nevertheless there was a question rising to her lips — " How did it happen? What broke your heart?" Fortunately, she checked herself in time. As she did not believe in broken hearts, it stood to reason that she could take no interest in the recording of so preposterous a history. Her own curiosity provoked her; and for fear of another such impulse, she hastened to end this painful pause.

"I know very well," she began, in a voice much more subdued than her former tone — "I know very well that there is a great deal of such talk in the world, and that people often make themselves unhappy about — about these sort of things; but I am not afraid for myself — I am not the sort of girl who will ever fall in love and break her heart."

"Because you have no heart to break," flared up Anna, with a double return of bitterness after that soft moment. She had not read anything of what had passed in Gretchen's mind. She knew only that she had been on the verge of a confidence, and that her confidence had been tacitly rejected. "Oh, I never understood you before, but I understand you now. I thank Heaven again that poor Vincenz is free. He is a thousand times too good for you."

"Then he is better without me."

"Of course he is better without you, and he will come to see it soon enough. I dare say he will have quite got over it by this day next year; and then Barbara Bitter — "

Anna's phrase never got beyond this; a timely interruption bad intervened, and the baffled sister had beaten her retreat. Neither did the weeks that followed bring her a second such opportunity, for it was a time of disturbance and business. Everyone's thoughts were occupied, and everyone's hands were full; and it was only on a late day in April that Gretchen could snatch a spare hour wherein to answer at last that long-unanswered letter of Belita's. There were two pages devoted to Adalbert's illness, and one to the new aspect of the Draskócs affair. "My turn of fortune may be coming too," she wrote exultantly, "even if in a different way from yours. Just think of Draskócs becoming ours! For the lawsuit must end someday. How rich we shall be! What splendid fortunes we shall have, my brother Kurt and I!" On a farther page she wrote,

"So you have no objection to your *futur* except his height? I don't like short men much; a man can never be too tall. May I ask a question? Is he very fond of you, Belita? Does he tell you so often? Does he say that there is only one woman in the world for him, and that you are that woman?

"Where are you going for your honeymoon — I mean wedding-tour? Honeymoon is a ridiculous expression. Could you not come to — ah! For now I must give you my news. Belita, I am so happy that I can scarcely steady my pen. A tremendous resolution has been arrived at today. At last — at last poor papa has borne down all opposition, has wearied out all objections. No dusty streets for us this summer, no dustier public gardens; no barrel-organs, no rattling carriages, no baking pavement. I shall not have to watch the airing of those carpets opposite, of whose very pattern I am sick. What shall I see instead? I hardly know. I have no idea what to expect; for this day week we start for the Hercules Waters!"

Chapter VII

On the Wing

"So be it mine (thine equal now)
With thee to see what eagles see,
With thee to know what eagles know,
What eagles feel to feel with thee!"

— Lord Lytton

NOT since autumn leaves fell had the air been so pure or the sky so blue as in this May midday hour; and the eagle on the cliff drank in the air, and gazed at the sun in the blue May sky, and his eagle heart swelled with the pride of eagle glory. When last May's sun had shone the eagle had been a downy fledgling, sharing the nest on the rocky ledge with two brother fledglings. Where were those brothers now? The soft eaglets who had huddled together to keep each other warm, who had craned their necks side by side to peep over the rocky ledge at the wonderful world below? Where was the earnest, anxious father eagle who had watched for them, and the mother who had crammed such delicate morsels of murdered hare or fresh-killed squirrel down their throats, and who had gorged them lovingly with the legs and wings of tenderer and downier fledglings torn from the nests of weaker birds?

Alas! alas! Even an eagle's family history can have its tragic passage. One brother eaglet had peeped too far over the rocky ledge: the strongest, boldest eaglet, the pride of the parent birds, he had been; but they could not save him, though they swooped down round him with their sharp despairing cry, as he tumbled from rock to rock, flapping his useless wings; and before he reached the bottom — while the two surviving fledglings were spreading themselves more comfortably in the now roomy nest above — the useless wings had ceased to flap. The other brother eaglet had flown out into the world long since — soft down had stiffened into strong feathered pinions; and this young king now loosens his hold on the cliff he grasps, and spreading his giant wings, with a whir, and a flap, and a rush of the air, sails forth into the May sunshine. What recks he of his brothers, alive or dead, or of the parents who hatched him out of a dull gray shell? The parents are hatching other dull gray eggs now, and have forgotten the very memory of the luckless fledgling who broke his neck through his own rashness.

The eagle, slowly sailing with wide majestic flaps, has shaken off all care. Is he not a king of birds in the first dawn of his beautiful strength? He wants no support but his firm pinions. An eagle's family ties are not of a lasting nature; he would not know his mother if he met her, nor would he hesitate to measure his strength against that of his father should they chance to fall out over the carcass of a new-born lamb, or if there arose a question of possession regarding a fat carp, fresh and dripping from the river. What delight more glorious than to gaze into the sun undazzled, to live on peaks where no human foot can ever tread, to circle in wide curves, with the keen air ruffling his feathers; while far, far below the great river crawls, and a black speck, with a trail of smoke floating from it, creeps slowly along? The eagle knows that speck well. Specks like that creep daily down the river, or come up the river, creeping more slowly still. The eagle never sees that speck without feeling thankful that he has been born an eagle and not a man. Pain and toil are the only means by which those poor wingless creatures can work their way from place to place, while he has but to raise his pinions and cleave the air at will.

To the fisherman who lives alone in the hut at the cliff's foot that speck with the trail of smoke is familiar too — the only link which makes him feel as if he belonged to the outer world; only that to him it is not a speck, but a large black monster, puffing gray smoke from its grimy chimney, and lashing the water to foam with its flanks. In the dusk, when he steps from his hut into his boat to throw out his nets for the night, that monster has rushed past him with fiery eyes; and in the cold dawn, when he goes out with numbed fingers to draw them in, the spirit of that same monster has seemed to flit past him like a ghost. He has stood watching the half-defined phantom through the gray mists of morning, while he pulled at the net on which his livelihood depends. He knows by the first tug what his luck for the day is going to be. He can tell by the mere weight on his fingers what number of shining Danube trout or sleek carps will presently be drawn in a wriggling silver mass into the boat — so experienced, so unconsciously sensitive have those poor, rugged, work-worn fingers become. Ten fish more or less is a question with the fisherman. It may mean luxury in the shape of an extra pull of *rachiu* (brandy), or a fuller pipe of tobacco; or else it may mean deprivation of his usual allowance of black bread, no breakfast, and a meager supper. The fisherman at the bottom of the cliff has lived so long in his hut built of branches and mud, and has thrown out and drawn in his nets for so many consecutive evenings and mornings, that there is no other interest conceivable for him except the interest of counting his fish. He could have understood no other form of excitement; that, for instance, of gamblers and speculators, whose fingers tremble as they number out the coins they have won. He has never seen gold, except in the heart of a mountain flower, or in the west of the sky when the sun was setting. A pile of ducats would have raised no wish in his breast, for they would have conveyed no impression to his mind; he would much rather have had a pile of fish. Fishing is the one form of gambling which exists for him; fish are his nourishment and his trade. It is a wonder he is not grown into a fish himself. If he was not half a fish, he might love the lonely hut which stood with its back to the straight, precipitous rock, and with its face looking out across the water, its threshold to be reached only from the boat. Had he not built it with his own hands — carrying the fresh branches in his boat, and standing in his boat as he built, since the spot was not to be reached in any other way? It must have been long ago that the branches were green, for now they are bare, dry wood; but strong enough still to keep out the rain and the wind. The fisherman at the bottom of the cliff may be as happy as any of the people in the steamer; and yet the people in the steamer, getting a fugitive glimpse of him, think him the most lonely of mankind.

Everything depends on the point of view from which we look at it. Now the fisherman never looked at the eagle at all, though they lived in the same wilderness; and the eagle only looked at the fisherman as a usurper who was robbing him of his rightful prey. The fish, if they had any point of view, probably thought it made no difference whether they were caught by the man or by the bird.

To the eagle and to the fisherman the steamer is a familiar thing — a different thing according to their separate points of view, but still familiar. To the people on the steamer — to many of them at least — both the eagles and the fisherman are new.

There are many people on the steamer today, and much variety in the contrasts they present — the usual medley to be found on every lower Danube steamer. The most conspicuous, because the most unusual, figure here today is a tall, stiff, middle-aged man, who has not spoken to any of his fellow passengers, but who as everybody knows, or instinctively feels, is an Englishman. '

Nobody but an Englishman could travel with so many different sorts of portmanteaus, and with such an unlimited choice of railway-rugs; nobody but an Englishman would guard that long thin bundle (which must be a fishing-rod) with such stern yet tender care; and nobody but an Englishman could consult his red guidebook regarding the beauties of the lower Danube, when he might be looking at the beauties themselves. No wonder he is conspicuous when compared with the figures around him, just as any one of those figures would be conspicuous anywhere else — hook-nosed Jewish merchants, fiery-eyed Hungarians, straight-featured Greeks, white-cloaked Circassians, with their long guns slung on their shoulders, a ragged but inexpressibly serene Turk smoking his *chibouk* under an *improvisé* tent of carpets, and keeping an eye upon the harem with which he is traveling. The modest allowance of wives he has found good to take with him are, for the greater safety of the passengers' morals, dressed, or rather smothered, in coarse linen sacks, in which a few slits are cut in order to supply the necessary amount of oxygen, and leaving a passage for the small and fragrantly steaming coffee cup which repeatedly finds its way to their invisible lips. There is the sound of a plaintive fiddle coming from a corner of the deck, where a gypsy player is plying his bow. Here on the ground lies a bundle, the personal luggage of that fat Greek merchant, who calls it his traveling-rug, and probably considers it a rather shabby rug, but which, in virtue of its fleecy texture and blue-green shades, would create a furor in any English drawing-room. All over the deck there are touches of color, and slight but unmistakable revelations of habits, which make you wonder whether you are still in Europe. There are amber mouthpieces to long pipes, strings of coral on a woman's neck, sheepskin fur on a peasant's back, as many turbans and fezzes as hats and bonnets. At one end of the deck a perfect hillock of brilliant pillows is stocked, the property of some provident family changing quarters. Behind this brilliant mountain sits ensconced the middle-aged Englishman aforenamed.

The captain of the steamer, walking hurriedly to the front for the purpose of superintending the steering at a dangerous turn of the river, has to pass between the pillows and the Englishman. The Englishman looks up from his guidebook, and asks, in very bad German, "Where is the rock they call Babakei?"

The captain, besides being in a hurry, is rather short-tempered, and explains impatiently that Babakei has been passed some time ago — a tall bare stone standing by itself in the water — a very nasty point to pass at night. There is a legend about it, too.

Yes, the Englishman knows all about the legend of the pretty Turkish woman, carried off by an audacious Hungarian, and being recaptured, left exposed on the rock in the river, while her captors, sailing off, called back mockingly, "*Babakei!*" — that is, "Repent." The Englishman knows all this, but he has unfortunately missed seeing the stone while he was occupied in reading about it.

The captain passes on, and the Englishman resumes his reading, being so much engrossed in a description of the Danube cataracts and the perils attendant on their passage, that he scarcely notices a slight swaying in the movement of the steamer.

Having completely mastered the subject, he looks up again, and sees the captain returning the same way he came, only in a more leisurely manner, with his hands in his pockets.

The Englishman asks politely whether the captain will kindly point out the cataracts.

"Just got out of them, thank Heaven!" says the captain, with less temper this time; "and very nasty they were today; have not seen them so rapid for long. It will be all plain sailing after this."

The Englishman is much distressed at having missed the cataracts, and expresses his regret in worse German than he used before.

"We were just getting into the thick of them," says the captain, "at the time you asked me about Babakei."

"And Trajan's Road, which they tell me is about here?"

It appears that the beginning of Trajan's Road has just been missed while the Englishman has been inquiring about the cataracts. After this, he comes to the conclusion that it would be better to read the descriptions in the guidebook later, and to look about him in the meantime.

And now it requires all his British calmness to suppress a long-drawn "Ah!" of wonder, so sudden and so vivid is the revelation of the scene around him.

Here is Servia on one side and Hungary on the other; straight cliffs with craggy ledges high up, their points and hollows almost out of eyesight, their sharp cut eyes streaked with broad veins of red stone. Then, in ever-recurring succession, wooded slopes, which slant down to the water's edge, opening now and then to reveal the glimpse of a narrow creek winding off into a valley, steep-sided, and all clothed with young beech and clustering hazelnut bushes.

On the Hungarian side, there is but little life: now and then, at long intervals, a mass of white with a steeple, which means a village; now and then something alive moving along the road, which means a cart; here and there a speck at the water's edge, which means a human being. On the Servian side there is less life still. No villages here, not even single houses; nothing in the way of a human habitation, except lonely watch towers planted on the hills, with wide intervals between; and more rarely still, a fisherman's hut where the sun catches the light on the wet nets hung out to dry' and where large pieces of roughly cured fish are stuck about upon wooden stakes, bearing at this distance a ghastly resemblance to the heads of murdered men.

With one hand on his fishing-rod and the other on the brim of his flapping wide awake, the Englishman stood and gazed at the shifting scene; at the woods where the lowest trees dipped their branches in the water, and where the highest rocks seemed to run their heads against the very door of heaven; at the bold outline of some protruding cliff, and at the lonely peaks, so far above, which the wild birds of prey have all to themselves. A few days ago, he had believed that there could not be anything more beautiful than the Rhine; but now, as he recalls the trim vineyards; the well-perched ruins (whether real or artificial) smiling down with such perfect self-satisfaction at their own images in the water; at the life and the brightness of picturesque peasants at work, tying up graceful vine tendrils, it all seems prettily weak, amiably conventional, beside this rugged and wild loneliness of the Danube. The endless change which feeds the eye there, the constant succession of neatly framed pictures, falls flat beside the grand monotony here, where each towering rock is like the other, yet each beautiful, and where you only see, perchance, some dark-faced Oriental frowning at you with sullen brow from under his faded turban.

Not one of these things had escaped the eyes of Gretchen Mohr; she had studied the cataracts, passed judgment on Trajan's Road, catalogued the fishermen, and registered the eagles. But now she was weary of them all, and it was with a heartfelt "At last !" that she greeted the sight of the pier. At last, the end of their week-long wanderings was approaching. Tortuous are the paths, and questionable the conveyances, by which alone the Hercules Baths can be reached. The Mohrs had spent quite as much time in waiting-rooms as in railway carriages; had shivered on piers quite as often as they had been suffocated in cabins; they had slept in dirty inns, and had lived on strange and unknown food, had been cheated by railway officials and misguided by railway guides, until Gretchen had begun to think that the Hercules Baths were a myth.

The pier was as crowded and as lively as the steamer itself. A great number of men and boys, scantily dressed in dirty linen, wearing leather belts which almost reached their armpits, their feet curiously swaddled in checked flannel rags, stood grouped at the edge: their savage appearance and ferocious glances were not calculated to reassure an ignorant passenger, who might well be excused if he thought himself in presence of one of the wild robber-bands of this mountain country.

The moment of landing was one of inextricable confusion. The Englishman appeared disturbed in his mind. He asked the person next him whether the "Iron Gates" have been passed or not, and was told that they lay farther down.

"You will see them in your book," said a young Hungarian, jocosely.

The Englishman was not in a humor for jests. He had quickly given up the idea of the Iron Gates, and in very good English was requesting everybody not to press against his fishing rod, exclaiming at the same time that it was a rod of Farlow's make.

The savage half-naked men and boys suddenly disclosed themselves as porters, by seizing upon every available article of luggage and rushing off headlong in various directions, regardless of proprietorship, the great object apparently being to disperse the portmanteaus and boxes with the least possible delay. The mountain of pillows on deck was levelled with magical rapidity; the Englishman's fishing rod was wrenched out of his hand, and carried away in triumph through the crowd. There was an interval of uproarious confusion, of jostling and bustling, of hand-to-hand fighting with the porters, and unsuccessful bargaining with the drivers, and then at last the Mohrs found themselves on their way up the valley, while the confusion of tongues behind them grew fainter every moment.

Here there was peaceful green on all sides, and giant vegetation bordering the very edge of the road. The Djernis river rushed along with much splashing and frothing and musical murmur. Now the road hung over it, and the travelers could plunge their eyes straight into its pools and eddies; now the river was far off, apparently just winding out of sight — but it was always there, a running accompaniment to the drive. Gretchen stared and stared about her — at the steep hillsides, at the scraps of sprouting corn planted on such tiny ledges, at the spring flowers which thickly carpeted every green spot, at the bushes heavy with twining blossoms, at the lights and shadows of the fresh May evening.

The valley was quite silent, except for the bells on the harness of their small team, and the everlasting rushing of the Djernis. At every turn, they seemed to be leaving all signs of human life farther and farther behind them; only at long intervals a solitary peasant woman would trudge past them, with coins glittering on her neck, her red-fringe apron giving her the appearance of some wandering flower of tropical size and brilliancy.

They had been driving for three hours, but the sun was not yet set; for the mountain-tops still bore a yellow flush, though down in the deep valley the air was chill with the breath of evening.

Was it in this wilderness that they were seeking the Hercules Baths? Would not the ever-deepening and ever-narrowing valley close at last before them and block their passage?

Some such question was rising to Gretchen's lips when the carriage rattled over a bridge, and in another minute she saw houses on both sides, as with a jerk they drew up in the center of the Hercules Baths.

Three or four gigantic white buildings loomed chill and monstrous through the dusk. Any European capital might have been proud of possessing them. How, then, had these giants of civilization been dropped into this wild valley? The rampart of the hills rose straight behind them, and below a fountain splashed, and the stone Hercules leaned motionless on his club.

*...she saw houses on both sides, as with a jerk
they drew up in the center of the Hercules Baths.*

"The Hercules Baths at last!" said Adalbert, with a sigh of mingled bitterness and hope. The bitterness was for the past, the hope was for the future. When last he had looked upon these mountains, he had had both youth and strength.

The Waters of Hercules, which have cured so many crippled men, why should they not give back to him some of his lost strength? But his lost youth nothing can evermore restore.

Chapter VIII

The Valley-God

"...denn sehr geliebt von den Göttern
Wohnen wir weit abwärts."

— Voss's Odyssey

WHEN the Romans — so says Romanian tradition — wearied with the conquest of the world, began to sigh after rest and refreshment, it was to the valley of Hercules they came to seek it. Here, to heal their wounds and strengthen their enfeebled limbs, they passed three days and three nights sitting up to their necks in the hot sulfur springs — a proceeding, let it be parenthetically observed, which would have meant certain death to anything short of an ancient Roman. But an antique constitution could defy anything, it seems; for on the third day of this memorable bath, the heroes, emerging from the sulfur waves, found that they had not only regained their former strength, but had doubled and quadrupled it. Their muscles were iron, their blood was fire; and in the drunkenness of their new-born life they cried aloud, "What enemy is strong enough to be worthy of our sword? Behold, all countries of the earth are trampled, let us measure our strength with Heaven!"

In spite, however, of the sulfur-springs, the war between Rome and Heaven proved unequal; and the conquerors of the world, repeating the angels' fall, lost not only the battle with Heaven but their possessions upon earth as well. And thus, according to the Romanian peasant's theory, the Hercules Waters caused the fall of Rome.

Notwithstanding this magnificent failure, the sulfur springs to this day retain power enough to do almost anything, except raising man to the level of a god — so, at least, say the people of the country; and it must be confessed that in the lonely depth of that valley, penetrated with its wildness, intoxicated by its beauty, even a stranger feels inclined to share the half-superstitious and almost adoring awe with which the Romanian peasant regards the "sacred" springs of Hercules.

Some lingering trace of heathendom seems indeed still to hang about the valley. In this remote corner of the earth the ancient gods are not quite forgotten. It is scarcely an exaggeration to say that, though he has his blest medals and his relics, though he beats his breast and tells his beads, yet every peasant of the valley is at heart a little bit of an innocent pagan. He will never fail to sprinkle himself with holy water on leaving the church; yet, if the truth were known, the *Ava Hercului* (Hercules Water), whose almost miraculous effects he daily sees, is to him the holier water of the two. He will never forget to bend his head low when he passes by a wayside cross; but — with unconscious idol-worship — he bends it still lower when he passes by the stone Hercules, that stands like the guardian spirit of the place, and has stood here since the time of the Romans. Mythology and Christianity are inextricably jumbled up in the rustic mind; and though, practically, the valley inhabitants may be as good Christians as any peasants of any country, their idea of the Creator of the world is yet slightly mixed up with their idea of the hero of the twelve great labors of antiquity. It is by his name that the men of the valley swear; it is with the fear of his club that the women of the valley silence their crying children. He is at once their patron and their bogy.

"The god of the valley" is a phrase so current in the popular mouth, that even strangers adopt it; and though they be enlightened enough to laugh at superstition, and learned enough to understand the chemical analysis of the Hercules Waters, yet unconsciously they slip into the habit of talking of the "Sacred Springs."

Perhaps the deep shade, so seldom lifted from the valley, serves to feed this mysterious awe; for the hours of sunlight are short and rare. When Gretchen opened her eyes on the morning following their arrival, the forenoon was well advanced, and yet no sunbeam had reached the depth of the valley. The morning mist still lingered, weaving a soft chill bloom over everything. The sun will burn that bloom away when it has risen high enough to look over the mountains. The mountains! How wonderful they were! Gretchen's eyes rose towards them and hung there entranced. The picture had a strange power of fascination: the cold shadowy valley, the mountains yellow with the morning sun, and towering so near as to shut out the sky. It might have been awful if it had not been so beautiful.

I do not suppose that there is in Europe any watering place of importance which compresses itself into such a limited space as the Baths of Hercules. The Baths of Hercules have had no choice in the matter; compression was unavoidable, for the simple reason that there was no more room in which to expand. Two rows of houses, forming a short street, is all that the width of the valley will allow of — the river Djernis filling up what remains in breadth. Most of these houses are old and shabby, but three of the buildings belong to a more modern date. The *Cursalon*, graceful and majestic, seems to press its Byzantine walls and elaborate roof straight against the rock behind, which falls in a sheer precipice from the mountain. On each side a sweep of covered arcades connects the *Cursalon* with a monster hotel. A tiny church stands as the last building of the miniature town; and when that is passed, there is nothing but solitude. The very road dies away, and the footpath grows rougher, and the Djernis's voice louder, the higher the explorer strays up the valley.

This spot of earth seems to be connected with nothing else on earth: the beautiful wilderness is a kingdom by itself, and to the kingdom there is not wanting a king. A Hungarian of high family and large fortune was the present lord of the valley — or, to put it more plainly, Baron István Tolnay was the tenant who held the place in lease direct from the hands of Government, and under whose sway every visitor and doctor, every hotel-keeper and *restaurateur*, found himself perforce placed. The "valley-king" enjoyed a regard next only to that paid to the "valley-god;" and could the rustic conception of power and authority have been summed up in three words, the result would have been — *Dumnedeū* (the Lord God), Hercules, and the Baron.

"I shall certainly fall asleep if I sit still much longer," said Gretchen, on that first afternoon as they sat at the hotel window. One night's rest had not been enough to make up for the many that had been lost, and the sound of the rushing river hummed in her ears like a lullaby.

Ascelinde was not to be moved from her sofa; so contenting herself with the escort of her brother Kurt, Gretchen started on her first journey of discovery.

Kurt Mohr, be it here observed, was a rather strange specimen of humanity. Neither exactly a boy nor exactly a man, he had never really been the one nor was he yet the other, and yet he was both. His sixteenth birthday had been passed some months ago; but though by his stature he might have been taken for less, in expression and manner he generally was taken for more. In frame, he was short and somewhat thickset, in face sallow and square-featured: there was no particle of his sister's beauty about him; the difference between the two was the difference between a goblin and a fairy. But Kurt was not a goblin of the repulsive sort: a look of careless contentment sat forever on his face; he had never been known to lose his temper, never been seen flurried, never was in a hurry, never was excited. Throughout the whole of the worries of traveling his contentment had remained unflawed: no noise seemed to disturb him; no dust could succeed in clinging to him; no midday sun could heat him; no sight betray him into an exclamation of wonder. With his hands in his pockets, he had stared at each prospect in turn, and taken it all for granted.

As he now walked down the valley beside Gretchen, he looked as cool and careless as if he had walked down precisely this same path every day for years past, and had contemplated this same prospect ever since he possessed eyesight. He took everything for granted — from the peasant women who carried their babies in wooden boxes on their backs to the mountain ranges which obscured the sky.

Brother and sister strayed into the small *Curgarten*, and from there into the covered arcades, where in the height of the season all shopping is done. Everything as yet bore the stamp of the opening season: most of the shops were still closed; some were entering on preparations; glass panes were being polished, and packing-cases opened. They looked into the *Cursalon* and saw a lofty space handsomely decorated in the Oriental style, and with piles of velvet chairs stowed into a corner. At the far end, one puny youth in shirtsleeves was languidly rubbing the floor with a cloth; the sound of his steps echoed round and round the large apartment. The hotels seemed all to be breathing in a supply of fresh air for the summer; every window was wide open; within the bathhouses thermometer and shower baths were being tested and put to rights.

Farther on, the air was charged with sulphur-fumes; but when the last building was passed, and the loneliness of the valley gained, there were only the wildflowers to scent the breeze. The footpath ran on the top of the riverbank; and the noise and gurgling of the water was so great, that it seemed to fill the whole valley with its sound. The overhanging rocks re-echoed it, and the trees nodded in the wind as they bent to listen to it. They came to a bridge, and caught sight of a path winding up into the wood at the other side. Its tempting invitation was not to be resisted.

"Kurt," said Gretchen, "if I thought there were no bears and wolves in that forest, I should go up at once; it looks so beautiful there!"

Kurt having expressed the greatest contempt for the bears and wolves suggested, the ascent was accordingly risked.

It was indeed beautiful in the wood. From between the stones of the rugged pathway the maiden-hair and spleenwort were beginning to peep in tiny, tender, green points; young brackens were uncoiling their crisp, brown rings; the lilac-bushes, growing wild, flung their fresh scent on the air, and clustered in colored masses against the young green of beech trees, just bursting into perfect leaf. The branches of hawthorn and bramble, white with blossom, broke through the midst of green tangles and floated on each breath of air. A few late violets still lingered and hung their bleached heads, drooping in the shade of rising cowslips, and fading beside the brightness of blue lobelia, which spread itself up and down the banks in gaudy patches. The wild vine was only now beginning to spin fine threads round the branches on which it hung; soft green tendrils clung timidly where still rustled the dry brown stalks, and here and there dangled a withered leaf of last year's growth. Only the sober fir trees, solitary among the beeches, had not thought of putting on summer garments; tall they stood and dark, well-nigh black, amid all the freshness of young flowers and bursting buds.

It was beautiful, but it was silent; for silence is the peculiarity of these secluded forests. There was not a bird's note in the whole height and depth of the woods, nor coming from the mountains around. There was no chirrup and flutter to tell you of a thrush family learning to fly, nor any cry of an anxious parent-bird; there was no blackbird flying up startled from its nest in the hawthorn bush. It was all a death-like silence; only the rush of the Djernis down there, turned to a far-off murmur here, and the rattle which a squirrel made high above Gretchen's head, as slowly she climbed the steep path.

In this country, the people explain everything by legends; and the peasant of the Hercules valley has a legend to account for the silence of his woods. Once the valley not only had songsters, but such wonderful songsters that their voices attracted the attention of the gods and awakened their jealousy. "We have nothing like that in Olympus," they said; and having apparently a taste for good music, they robbed the feathered musicians for their own service and delight. But the gods had reckoned without their host; soon there arose in the valley music of another sort. The cries of the deprived people were so piercing that they quite prevailed over the birds in Olympus; and in order to pacify the screamers and enjoy their orchestra in peace, the gods caused the Djernis river to flow, and gave it a voice of musical sweetness.

More learned but less poetical people account for the want of singing birds by the injurious effects of the sulphur steams. To this latter theory, as being the more logical of the two, Gretchen would probably have agreed. But the want of birds did not strike her; for she had never been in a wood before, and even a wood without birds was enchantment enough. She did not stay long on the path; the first clump of cowslips on which her eyes fell was inducement enough to leave it. She returned with her hands half full; she went off again for a branch of pink and white hawthorn; she broke her way through the bushes back to the path; but just then the sunlight, which fell slanting into the wood, had touched a drooping head of lilac, melting it into liquid color, and Gretchen felt that she must have that lilac. She reached it and tore it down; but there were more slanting sunbeams, and they fell through the branches upon other lilacs, and upon yellow cowslips, which under their touch glowed into living gold; and they bronzed the uncurling brackens, and speckled the moss, until Gretchen, wandering on from bush to bush, and always meaning to turn back and never doing so, stood still at last with both her hands full, and looked around her in perplexity, wondering where the path could be.

"Kurt!" she called out; "Kurt, where are you?" and then she stood still and listened.

The bushes rustled, and Kurt appeared with his hands in his pockets. "Kurt, have you a notion where the path is?"

"Not the faintest."

"We cannot have lost our way," said Gretchen; "it stands to reason that the path is close at hand, but I am not going to look for it till I have rested."

Gretchen, as she spoke, threw down her armful of flowers and sat down beside them on the sloping bank. Her hair had got loosened as she broke through the bushes; it floated over her shoulders like a veil of gold; a head of white hawthorn had been caught in the silken net, and hung there a willing prisoner.

Gretchen drew a long breath of the evening air, and half unconsciously, she sank back upon the bank. It made such a luxurious couch, and the loose sheaf of flowers she had gathered was such a soft pillow for her head. She put up her hands and clasped them behind her neck, and lay staring up into the branches and the quivering leaves overhead.

"You look like a large babe in a wood," remarked Kurt, crouching on the ground and pulling up an ivy trail with his fingers.

"Leave me in peace," was the drowsy remonstrance.

"So I shall, presently," said Kurt, throwing the ivy trail across his sister, and looking up at the nearest beech tree with the eye of a connoisseur, as if marking its most favorable points of attack. There was a long silence before he spoke again.

"You are not going to sleep, are you?" he asked, showering a handful of anemone heads over Gretchen.

"Oh no," she murmured, in luxurious drowsiness. "What are you throwing at me? What have you put round my arms? Cannot you leave me alone?" She stirred her arm and heard some leaves rustling. Kurt was laughing in his impish way; but her eyelids were too heavy to raise themselves.

It was so pleasant to lie here — the moss so soft — the trees rustling — or was it the Djernis?

It did not matter which, for Gretchen was asleep.

Chapter IX

The Sleeping Beauty

*"There she lay, and was so beautiful that he could not turn away his eyes;
and he could not help himself, but bent down and gave her a kiss. And
scarcely had he kissed her than she opened her eyes."*

— GRIMM's Fairy Tales

THE coffeehouse and restaurant in the old street of the Hercules Baths
had not slept through the winter, like the *Cursalon* and the big modern hotels. It lived through the cold months in a state of half torpor,
blinking its open eyes at the many shut eyes around it. When the whole valley is
bound in ice, and when each tree up the mountainside hangs heavy with snow, the
shabby room in the interior of the old coffeehouse is a sort of bear's den, where the
small handful of men, whose duties chain them here in season and out of season, sit
drawn together in a narrow circle — their wants attended to by a couple of inferior
waiters on half-wages — while the snowflakes fall on the window, and the smoke of
their cigars curls up to the low ceiling and slowly stains the dingy walls. In the height
of summer, the guests spread themselves on the veranda outside, and eat their food
in the shade of alternate pomegranates and oleander trees, and to the music of the
Hercules fountain; for it is here that the stone figure stands, leaning on its club,
guarding the waters which flow at its feet.

But now the pomegranates and oleanders are still stowed away at the back; the
veranda outside is bare and chairless, and everything still concentrates itself in the

low-roofed, dingy dining room; for the beginning of May is scarcely the beginning of the season here.

The inferior waiters are attending to the wants of the solitary occupant of the room — a Romanian doctor, who practices in winter at Bucharest and in summer at the Hercules Baths. This Romanian is enormous, black-haired and unkempt, and his wants are strong coffee and spirits. The enormous doctor is a good deal bored with his own society, and glances up and down the short piece of street in hopes of an acquaintance, but there is nobody in sight.

"Bring me a paper, will you?" he calls to a man in a shabby black coat who is passing through the room.

The man in the shabby black coat looks at him over his shoulder, and does not bring the paper. A fussy waiter rushes in, waving a paper four days old, and whispers in an awestruck tone that the man in the shabby coat is the landlord, and you could hardly expect a landlord — etc.

"Why?" remonstrates the Romanian; "he always used to be a waiter; I remember him changing my plate every day last year."

"Oh, last year! yes," whispered the frightened waiter; "but you know — in winter — married the landlady ;" — in a deeper whisper — "first husband shot himself — winter before that again;" — in a whisper so profound as to be scarcely audible — "nothing else to do."

"Ah, I understand," says the Romanian, grasping the situation.

The surroundings of the Djernis valley in winter were indeed such as to reduce a man to marrying his grandmother, or murdering her, for the sake of a variety. The Romanian doctor had had glimpses of the landlady, and from what he remembered of her charms, it appeared not improbable that the second husband should shoot himself next winter, as the first had done the last; leaving thus an alternate wedding and suicide, relieving each other in an endless vista for many more winters to come. Dreary winters! The marriage as dismal as the suicide; the suicide as gay as the marriage.

"Bah! bring me another paper — the *Pester Lloyd*."

"Don't keep it yet; begin most of our papers on the 15th. Only keep two in winter. The new landlord" — lowering his voice again" — has cut down things."

"Me Hercule!" ejaculated the Romanian, pushing his unwashed hand through his uncombed hair, which, unchecked by any scissors, had been allowed to reach his shoulders, and hung there in a heavy black fringe.

This Romanian was of what he himself called a soft and impressionable nature. In private, he was much given to scribbling verses in the Romanian tongue; and by a strange coincidence, or a strange string of coincidences, these sonnets happened never to be addressed to his wife. In public, he was equally given to arranging fire-works, musical entertainments, and other means of public amusement. Public amusement, indeed, appeared to lie nearer his heart than the public health. He always declared himself to be passionately attached to each of his eight children; but the anxieties which he occasioned to the practical-minded mother were obstacles in the way of their bringing-up, scarcely to be made up for by effusive caresses and showers of kisses.

The picture of winter desolation sketched out by the whispering waiter was enough to depress his sensitive mind, though he had often before heard the like pictures described; and he sat with his fingers among his hair, plunged in melancholy reflections, until the opening of the coffee-room door aroused him from meditation.

The German *Bade* doctor, Funk by name, a timid startled man, slipped into the room, and answering to a vociferous invitation, joined his Romanian colleague at the table. Some minutes were passed in discussing the landlady's marriage, the prospects for the season, the few interesting cases which had as yet appeared.

"I don't believe there are more than twenty names on the *Curliste* yet," said the Romanian, with a groan. "I never saw such a late season. I wonder if there are any more guests expected this week. The baron ought to know. Where can he be hiding himself all this time?"

"I saw Baron Tolnay with his gun a little time ago," ventured Dr. Funk. "I think he mentioned something about a bear, or several bears;" not daring to be too positive on the point.

"Bah! I wish I had stayed at Bucharest till the 15th," said the Romanian, shaking the shaggy hair from his forehead. "There is nothing to be done here. Are you treating that English lady they speak of? The first English patient who has ever strayed so far!"

Dr. Funk confessed that he was treating the English lady.

"And her husband came last night," pursued the Romanian. "He is an English lord, they say. How on earth will he pass his time here — unless, to be sure, he takes to writing sonnets? *Uitisce! uitisce!* (see! see!) what is that? Softly, my friend!" as the door flew open under the scratch of a heavy paw and a large gray dog stalked majestically into the room.

"Where is your master, Pasha?" asked the Romanian, stretching out a big hand; "he cannot be far off if you are here. I thought you were after the bears, eh?"

"He is coming," whispered the *Bade* doctor to his companion. "Ha! by the club of Hercules, here is the baron himself. Perhaps he can tell us more."

The coffee-room door again creaked on its hinges, and a young man, wearing a fancy sporting attire of gray and green, and having a feathered hat on his head, and a gun slung over his shoulder, entered the room whistling.

"A glass of cognac, quick!" he called out, standing just within the door.

The nervous waiter fluttered his napkin, and executed a series of agitated bows; while the landlord himself, returning for the moment to his servile habits, ran nimbly for the cognac, and brought the glass deftly balanced on a plate, in the manner which had been acquired in the days of his past obscurity.

Both doctors had risen, and had inclined themselves, each after his fashion — the German doctor profoundly, the Romanian theatrically — and then remained standing as though in the presence of royalty, until a careless gesture of the sportsman told them to resume their seats.

"Baron Tolnay," began the Romanian, whose nature was not prone to be over-awed for long even in presence of the omnipotent valley-king, "can you not tell us what the new English lord is going to do with himself here?"

"Hang himself, probably," said the young man, having tossed off the cognac with the gesture of an *habitue*, and holding out the empty glass towards the cringing landlord.

"But cannot we devise a plan for saving him from suicide?" and the doctor pushed a chair suggestively towards the baron.

"You must devise it without me then, Kokovics; for my men are waiting up there," shrugging his left shoulder in a general way towards the mountains. "I settled the place and the hour, and I shall hardly reach it in time as it is."

Tolnay made a step forward into the room, and stood with one hand on the back of the chair which the Romanian had pushed towards him. He was a man not over twenty-eight, looking younger from the vivacity of his manner. Thanks to his expressive eyes — black eyes full of the fire of youth — and thanks to his slight, well-knit figure, he was handsome, though his features were not regular, nor his stature tall above the average.

"I will tell you what," said Dr. Kokovics, after a reflective pause, during which he had been searching his memory for some traditional scraps which lingered there; "we must give the English lord plenty of water — water in all shapes — water to drink, water to fish in, water to wash in — particularly to wash in" — he repeated with a sort of wondering emphasis — "that is what they do all day long — wash, wash, without resting. They are very mad, those English;" and the Romanian shook his head as he contemplated the complexion of his own hands, and thought how well they got on without soap and water.

"More charitable to drown him at once, my dear Kokovics," interpolated young Tolnay, with a yawn expressive of *ennui*.

"No, baron; depend upon it, water will create the happiness of Lord — what is he called?"

"Ouare," completed Dr. Funk.

"Hovart," corrected the baron.

Dr. Funk yielded the point at once.

"As for the other guests that came last night," chattered on Kokovics, "they will present no difficulty, for they are Germans, and Germans are proverbially content with their knitting and the delights of their family circle. Have you heard their name yet, Baron Tolnay?"

"*Mohr*, I fancy, it stands. Madame Ascelinde Mohr, *née* Contesse Damianovics de Draskócs, or some wonderful nonsense of the sort; and a daughter, if I remember right, and a son. Has anyone seen the daughter, by-the-bye?"

No one had seen the daughter.

"Patience," said Tolnay, taking his foot off the bar of the chair and jerking up the gun on his shoulder. "No daughter can remain hidden here for long. Pasha, come away with you!"

"So you are really going, baron," said Doctor Kokovics in a tone of dissatisfaction, as the Hungarian turned and whistled for his dog. "What is your game? Bears?"

"Yes, bears; or anything else either. Probably bears."

"Probably — anything," repeated the Romanian, squeezing one of his eyes shut, and heaving a sentimental sigh. "Oh, baron, you look like a very keen sportsman indeed. I suppose bears will do as well as anything else to pass the time with until Princess Tryphosa makes the valley glorious again with her presence."

The Hungarian pushed up his feathered hat and settled it more firmly on his forehead. "Nonsense, Kokovics! Mind your own business; you have enough on hand to need your attention, I fancy." He made an attempt at a frown, as he pressed down his hat with his hand; but his black eyes sparkled, and an expressive smile made his face more handsome, as a row of even white teeth shone for a moment in sharp contrast to the blackness of his hair.

"Good luck, baron," cried Kokovics as Tolnay reached the door, which Pasha, with a blood-thirsty eagerness, was impatiently scratching open, as though he already smelled a flavor of bears.

"My luck never fails me," said Tolnay as he slammed the door, and walked out whistling into the spring evening; while Pasha, having given one bound, and barked one permissible bark of excitement, settled down into a stately stalk at his master's heels.

Up the valley, Tolnay's road led him, past the Catholic chapel, into the solitude beyond. His men were waiting for him up there on the mountainside, and as he struck up the path he cast a glance at his watch.

"Half an hour late — that is Kokovics with his chatter. I must take the shortcut;" and leaving the path, he breaks his way through the bushes and tramps over mosses and ferns upward, and always upward.

István Tolnay never throws a glance on the hawthorn branches which he pushes aside and leaves hanging broken behind him, nor at the cowslips which lie with crushed stalks after he has passed, and do not rise again. He has seen these spring flowers here so often, growing in just the same way, that they can make no impression on his mind. He does not notice them, nor think of them. What is he thinking of, as he walks up whistling through the thickly grown flowers? Is he thinking of Princess Tryphosa? Or is he in imagination face to face with a bear-like Pasha, whose paws sink heavily into the emerald moss, and whose lowered head and fixed eye denote a stern concentration of mind?

It is not late yet. Outside in the wide flat world the sun will not sink for another hour; but in the Djernis valley the day is shorter by several hours than elsewhere. The last blaze of sunshine is falling on the hillside to the left, and will presently die away behind the lofty rampart, and leave the rocks and trees cold, and the valley in black shadow till late tomorrow morning.

István treads down a clump of sprouting fern, and puts out his hand to bend aside a branch.

Ha! What is this? A low sound at his heels coming from the depth of Pasha's capacious chest, as with glaring eye he presses forward.

The Hungarian's gun is unslung already, and his fingers on the trigger.

A bear so low in the valley at this season! How could this be?

Cautiously he makes a step forward, holding the hawthorn twig for fear of its snapping, and then stands motionless, with extended neck and searching eyes which glance over the space beyond.

He has not long to search, for it is here that the vanishing sun is throwing its rays in a shower, and right in the middle of the yellow light a girl lies asleep on the bank.

But how is this? Can this figure be mortal indeed? Is this a creature of flesh and blood? Or not rather some fairy of the woods, some princess who has slept here for a hundred years; who has slept for so long bewitched that the ivy has grown over her, trailing round her feet and in her hair, and on her arms clasped high behind her head? Some sleeping princess, surely — and is he the lucky man who is to waken her? Her very dress seems to be grown from the bank; garments woven of the leaves and the dark-green moss on which she lies. So softly they fall around her, so gently they shape themselves to the curves of her graceful figure! Her head is thrown back upon her clasped hands, showing the line of a milk-white throat, and pillowed on a great sheaf of flowers, yellow and purple and pink; and on the crowded flower heads, turning them into transparent gems, and on the waves of her loosened hair, drawing through it trembling threads of red fire, the last of the sunlight falls.

István Tolnay was twenty-eight, and he was a Hungarian; his imagination was inflammable and his nature impetuous. This sudden vision of beauty bursting upon his eye, under all the flattering, magical influence of the checkered sunlight, made his thoughts grow wild for a moment, and his heart beat fast; while his fancy, ever ready at a touch, set to weaving the realities of the surroundings into the fit frame-work of a fairy tale.

He let the hawthorn branches fall together behind him, with a gentle hand this time, and in wondering bewilderment he made a step forward, his gun sunk by his side, while with the other hand he held back the eager dog who dragged at his collar, flaring and straining; too much in awe of rightful authority to bark, or even to growl, but not quite able to suppress a mournful whine, expressive of mental agitation. István made a step forward, wondering, and then made another step, and wondered still more, always standing still again, for fear of breaking the spell of that sleep. There was a white flower hanging in her hair, half on it and half on the moss — a head of white hawthorn, drooping and fading already, but the magical light had touched it too, and it shone like a fairy star.

Now he stood close to her, looking down at the lovely face, where the curling lashes, gold-tipped like the hair, swept the fair, flushed cheek. His heartbeats quickened; a desire almost irresistible rose in him, a powerful curiosity to see of what color these closed eyes might be — a wish to stoop and wake the sleeping beauty in the way that the prince always wakes her in the fairy tale. He was not used to denial of the things he wished; he stooped, and his hand was on the hawthorn, while on his other side the forgotten Pasha, half-choked by the unconscious hold on his collar, turned up his eyes with a humble inquiry as to whether he was to lick the sleeping beauty's hands or tear her to pieces.

István held the flower, then he gazed at it, then he kissed it, for his fancy was on fire. That girl on the ground seemed to lie drowned in a flood of gold. One wave of hair, straying forward over her shoulder, rose and fell with her breath. He must act the fairy prince, though it were madness to repent of ever after. The kiss upon the white flower had been sweet, but the kiss upon that living red flower would be sweeter still. He stooped again, lower this time.

Something rattled through the branches overhead, and hit him sharply on the neck, on the shoulders, and dropped into the moss. Has the fairy princess got fairy guards to watch her, or have all the squirrels of the forest risen in an army to defend her? He started back, upright in a moment, coloring and conscience-stricken; and he scanned the beech beside him. The leaves were thick, and the branches close, but his eyes were piercing. Up there, grinning at him over the shining bark, a goblin crouched, with eyes that glittered in mischievous delight, and skinny fingers that clutched the tree. The face vanished like a face in a nightmare, and there was a sharp rustle in the branches. Down came another and more vigorously aimed handful of dry beechnuts; they landed on his hat, in his pockets, and they showered upon Pasha's lowered head. There are limits even to a dutiful dog's subordination; and finding himself pelted with beechnuts, Pasha considered that those limits were reached. He tore himself free from his master's relaxing hold, threw himself against the haunted tree, and, reared up to his fullest height, pawed the slippery trunk with his unavailing claws, while the forest resounded with his deep-toned bay.

The first of those barks was the breaking of the spell. The fairy tale faded and was gone, before even the fast-dying sunlight had vanished. István Tolnay with a start found himself transported back into the prose of real life. He was not a prince, he was only István Tolnay, with his gun by his side; the trees around were not whispering to each other with magic tongues, they were only shaking in the evening breeze: that goblin up there was nothing but a sallow-faced youth perched upon a branch. The princess herself was no more than flesh and blood — very fair flesh and blood indeed, as she started up, rubbing her eyes — and her moss-woven garments but a tumbled green dress.

The awakening was rude for a sleeping princess; and starting up at the harsh sound of the bark, Gretchen stared around in fright. She saw a man with a gun gazing at her with intense fixity· her eyes, still clouded with sleep, shone dim and deep for a moment; and with the movement her hair lost its last hold, and shook itself down in waves and rings and wonderful networks of silk.

István, becoming conscious of his own prosaic identity, recovered his presence of mind with what haste he could, and with a rather uneasy bow retreated a few steps towards the bushes, for his inbred *savoir-vivre* told him that it was scarcely correct to stand rooted and staring open-mouthed at an unknown young lady, whatever might be the habit of princes in fairy tales.

"I am afraid my dog has frightened you," he began, in his rich, well-modulated voice, and with eager eyes still fixed on the girl.

She looked at him critically.

"It stands to reason that he has frightened me."

István made a gesture expressive of unmitigated despair.

"How can I prove my distress for the wretched beast's misdemeanor?"

"By removing him," said the beauty, promptly — "and yourself too," her tone almost seemed to add.

She was rising as she spoke, but the ivy trails were an obstacle, and she stumbled and caught at the bank. István stepped forward, but the *ci-devant* goblin brushed past him disdainfully, and the *ci-devant* princess told him with a glance that he was not wanted. In the next moment, she bit her lip, and her cheek flushed crimson. Was it the unwavering look in his bold black eyes that made her blush? Or had she seen the hawthorn in his hand, and guessed at the theft committed? She walked two steps away, and with her back towards him began twisting up her long loose hair; while István, standing by the hawthorn bush, felt almost perplexed, almost foolish — he who had never been perplexed in his life before, and certainly not in the presence of a woman. The decision of the beauty's manner, her matter-of-fact tone, the critical, almost severe glance of her gray eyes, had taken him aback.

He was not wanted here; and calling to Pasha, he slowly turned and walked through the bushes, but his steps lagged strangely, and he looked over his shoulder oftener than was wise, considering the roots and stones in his way. She had done with her hair, she had put on her hat, and now the two were turning to go. Now István stood still, for whatever other doubt there might be, there could be no question that it was his duty to save two strangers from being inevitably lost in the forest and possibly eaten by bears, as might well chance to be their fate, seeing that they had struck into a direction exactly opposite to the Hercules Baths.

Gretchen and Kurt, starting, as they believed, homeward, heard a crackling of twigs, and quick steps behind them, and found themselves overtaken by the hunter with his dog.

"Excuse me," he said, eagerly, "you are going quite wrong; you will be lost in the mountains if you follow that direction," Ile spoke with a marked respect, but the intense expressiveness of his eyes never faded for a moment.

"Thank you," said Gretchen, with her head rather high. "Which is the right way?"

"Down there; the path is not far off; you will allow me to escort you that far."

She made no sign of acquiescence — indeed it had been more an assertion than a question — but she turned the way he pointed, and followed him as he forced the passage in advance.

It was not more than fifty paces; and having reached the path, the hunter turned round, and raising his hat, left them without another word.

The dusk was falling fast by this time, and Gretchen and her brother hurried home in unbroken silence.

Meanwhile, the hunter, with the dog beside him, pursued his way upward towards the place where his men were waiting for him at the rendezvous. They must have given him up for lost; but he dragged along lazily, in no hurry, it seemed, to relieve their minds.

Is he thinking of the Princess Tryphosa now, as he loiters along whistling, or is he thinking of some other princess? What is he thinking of as the shadows darken the wood around him?

A little while ago he had played the knight in a fairy tale; now he is only a man in real life, called István Tolnay.

But István Tolnay holds in his hand a faded hawthorn flower.

Chapter X

A Love Letter

"Oh waly, waly, but love be bonny
A little time when it is new;
But when 'tis auld it waxeth cauld,
And fades away like morning dew."

— Anon.

NEXT day, Gretchen took no walk in the wood. True, she had met neither bears nor wolves there yesterday; but she had discovered that there were other dangers to be feared in the shade of the lonely forest. It was quite as warm an afternoon, and quite as clear: the bank of green forest opposite glistened in the sunshine and quivered in the breeze. Through the open window every sound floated in with perfect distinctness; sometimes a step, a voice, more seldom the rattle of a carriage. In the room, there was silence, except for the rustling of paper under Gretchen's fingers. Her father, who reclined half dozing in his chair, was the only other occupant of the large apartment.

Gretchen sat with her back to the window; before her there stood open an old leather desk, whose contents she was submitting to a rather listless examination.

Madame Mohr had directed her daughter to search for a paper she required, and which she believed was contained in this old desk, inherited from her mother, Countess Eleonore Damianovics.

The paper in question was the address of the dead Pater Dionysius, who had preached so remarkably well and baptized all the young Damianovicses, with which address Ascelinde was desirous of furnishing Dr. Komers, as an undefined and unexplained means of assisting him on his impending Draskócs journey. Not very sure of recognizing the paper, she had wisely delegated the office to the quicker eyes and sharper wit of her daughter.

Gretchen was dissatisfied with the office — she could see no logical reason why a dead priest's address should in any way favor the Draskócs cause; and so, with indolent fingers and half-hearted interest, she turned over the musty bundles before her, thinking perhaps more of her forest walk yesterday, and of the adventure which had there befallen her, than of the papers she was handling.

There were a great many papers in the desk, the accumulations of years. There were bills and addresses and letters; many in unknown handwritings; some from her uncle Alexius, easily distinguishable by the round cramped hand, and shining a cold white among more faded epistles. In the place of honor lay a bundle religiously fastened with silk ribbon, and labeled, "From my guardian, Count Jósika Damianovics."

All these Gretchen tossed aside, but under the last bundle, crushed and perhaps forgotten, there lay another solitary letter, and this attracted her attention. Even though the ink was so faint with years as to be in places scarcely brown, and though the yellow paper was falling asunder at the creases, Gretchen at once knew the letter to be one of her father's. It was dated "The Hercules Baths," and with aroused curiosity she unfolded the limp and ragged sheet. She did not know it, of course; but this was the very letter which, by falling into the hands of her grandmother more than twenty years ago, had been the direct cause of her mother's elopement and marriage. It looked so worn and haggard, this· old letter, so marked with lines that might have been the crow's feet of care, so furrowed with age, and so stained with unsightly spots, as if it had gone through a world of trouble, instead of having only lain here for years forgotten and uncared for.

"My beloved Ascelinde," it began. A love letter — really and truly a love letter. Gretchen contemplated it with something of the same wonder with which she had contemplated the woman with the broken heart; and as her eyes traveled along the faded lines, her wonder grew apace. There was so much tenderness written there in bleached ink — so many loving words about the sadness of the separation, and the sweetness in the hope of meeting again — so many assurances about her living continually in his thoughts — that Gretchen, letting her hands sink slowly into her lap, began to ask herself where all that love and tenderness was gone?

If it had ever been, how could it have turned so chill in twenty years? Was it indeed gone? Gone, without leaving a spark behind it? Merged into that half-impatient indifference which was the spectacle that Gretchen daily saw? crumbled away like this poor faded paper, which, even as she held it in her hands, dropped asunder, while one worn-out fragment floated quivering down to the floor? True, Gretchen had never heard a hot and angry, but neither had she ever heard a warm and tender, word exchanged between her parents. What was the use of all that dead affection since it had borne no better fruits? Ah! but it was to bear fruits of another sort, reflected Gretchen; for was not her experience gathered for her be- forehand? And once more she vowed that it should not have been gathered in vain.

She stooped as she reflected thus, and picked up the fallen scrap of paper. It was as soft as a linen rag, too weak even to rustle; but the ink was better preserved here than on the rest of the letter, and one word, written somewhat larger than its neighbors, caught her eye at once.

To judge from her bent head and parted lips, some interest within her was aroused, and presently the silence of the room was broken. "Papa, what is *Gaura Dracului?*"

"*Gaura Dracului?*" repeated Adalbert, slowly. "Who has been telling you that name?"

"I have found it written here," said Gretchen, crossing the room and holding the torn paper towards him.

Adalbert took the old letter and read it in silence. A shade crossed his face while he read, then a bitter smile, then a gleam of interest; but it was with a sigh at last that he laid down the paper.

"Another of my dreams which will never be realized. I was young and foolish then, and presumptuous enough to fancy that I had got on the trace of some discoveries valuable to history."

"And did you never find the spot of which this letter speaks?"

"Yes, I found it after weeks of search; but I only saw it once; for next day — next day I had to leave," he finished with a frown. "It was a strange spot — a very strange spot indeed; weird, startling, fascinating. I hardly know whether to call it more terrible than beautiful."

"They tell me it is a deep, deep chasm" — read Gretchen, again taking up the letter — "a horrid yawning black hole in the wildest part of the hills, in the thickest shade of the forest. Bottomless, the peasants say; and, according to all accounts, of measureless depth."

"Yes, of an enormous depth," said Adalbert, in whose mind a long-dead interest was beginning to stir again. "I remember throwing a handful of stones down the monstrous hole, and for seconds I could hear them falling and falling, and they never seemed to stop."

"And the historical discoveries?" asked Gretchen.

"The historical discoveries were broken off, as I tell you, by my abrupt departure. Possibly there were none to make; but I was a little *monté* by the scenery, and listened only too greedily to the wild legends of the country; and certainly," went on Adalbert, warming as he proceeded, "I had more than one rational ground to believe that the spot had been known to the Roman conquerors of this valley. There is a tradition still alive among the people here, that a tribe of Dacians, driven to bay among the mountains, preferred to throw themselves headlong down this abyss than submit to the Roman eagle. It was that story that first attracted my attention. I was bent on investigation. I fancied then that I should make my name known through the book with which these mountains inspired me."

"A book about this place, papa? About the Hercules Waters? I did not know that you had written one?"

"Attempted to write one," modified Adalbert, "and under different circumstances might perhaps have succeeded, for these forests breathed an inspiration which I never found elsewhere. I felt almost as though they would tell me their secrets if I asked them. But the work was broken off very soon; the old manuscript has lain locked away for these last twenty years. I have scarcely looked at it since I put it aside. A mere fragment it was, and a fragment it will remain."

Adalbert sighed again, and was silent; he considered the subject disposed of, but Gretchen did not.

"Papa," she said after a minute, "why should it remain a fragment?"

Her father opened his eyes again languidly.

"And my discoveries?" he said, with a faint smile, "my investigations? How is the book to be finished without them? And how are they to be made? *Gaura Dracului* lies at three hours' distance from here. Do I look as if I could reach it?"

"When your course of baths is over, of course you will be able to reach it, papa; and in the meantime — "

"Well?"

"In the meantime, I can reach it."

Adalbert looked at his daughter, and smiled incredulously.

"Where is the difficulty?" demanded Gretchen, somewhat baffled by his glance.

"The difficulty is everywhere."

"No generalities, please, papa; particularize the obstacles."

"Begin rather by particularizing your intentions. To start with — how do you mean to find the way?"

"I shall get a peasant to guide me."

"Exactly the answer I expected. You cannot get a peasant to guide you."

"Why not?"

"Because, as you have yet to learn, the Romanian peasant is the most perfect personification of religious superstition that walks the face of the earth; and because round *Gaura Dracului* there hangs a cloud of superstition not easy to pierce. The name alone is enough to show in what horror the place is held; literally translated, it is 'Devil's Hole.' Of all spots among these hills, it is shunned and detested, by the few who know it, as a place accursed; though to nine men out of ten it is no more than a name, hardly as much, perhaps, for even twenty years ago the stories about it were sinking into forgetfulness."

"Then I shall try bribery," said Gretchen, still undaunted. "A Romanian peasant must have his price like any other man."

"His honor has, but his superstition never; of that I have assured myself."

Gretchen held her tongue for a little while, but her courage was not yet quelled.

"Tell me, papa, would you find the way there again yourself?"

"I almost fancy so, were I once on the track; every circumstance of that walk is vividly printed on my mind. I marked a beech tree not far from the spot. I cut three crosses into the bark with my penknife — the finest beech I have seen in my life — the stem like a pillar, the leaves a canopy of green. When that tree is once found, *Gaura Dracului* lies not a hundred yards off; but one might be nearer still without suspecting it, it lies so strangely hidden."

"Then, papa, surely your directions will be enough to guide us to the place?"

The sick man fairly burst out laughing.

"Oh, innocent ignorance! And how about the long, pathless, bewildering, indescribable forest that stretches between us and that beech tree — one among a million of beech trees, its very images and copies? No, Gretchen, your plan will not work."

"And yet, Gaura Dracului must be found!" exclaimed Gretchen, and brought down her small hand clinched on the table. "I have made up my mind that it is to be found!"

Adalbert stopped laughing, and eyed his daughter in some surprise.

"How now, my cool-headed damsel, what means this sudden fire? What betokens this wonderful interest in a perfectly illogical black hole in a forest? You talk like a maiden in a romance this evening. Have the mountains bewitched you too?"

"Oh, papa," said Gretchen, coloring, "what nonsense!"

Of course, it could not have been the mere sound of the description which had tempted her; of course, it was not the black chasm yawn-ing in the wildest part of the hills, in the thickest shade of the forest, which had aroused her curiosity; nor the place that was as terrible as beautiful, nor the superstition that guarded it, which had caught her fancy. All these grounds might have had weight with a girl of the romantic class; but how could they boast of any influence over the young lady who had carried off the *prix de logique* at school, and who ever since had shown herself worthy of the reputation there gained? No; with her some other motive must have been at work, and she hastened to explain what this motive was.

It appeared that neither the yawning abyss, nor the wild forest, nor the dark superstition, had anything to do with her interest; *Gaura Dracului* was not to be sought for its sake alone, but only as a means towards an end. And that end? What was it to be? Oh, she had her arguments all ready. The end was nothing less than the pursuance of the investigations, and the completion of the long-abandoned manuscript, which, written on the spot, would possess a peculiar interest, and therefore, as she further argued, command a large sale. "And it stands to reason," completed Gretchen, "that in such a case you will realize a great deal of money. Oh, papa, *Gaura Dracului* will make your fortune yet, if you would only believe me!"

"So your love for *Gaura Dracului* is, in reality, a love for florins," remarked Adalbert, with a cynical smile, having listened in silence to his daughter's speech.

"Exactly, papa; and you accused me of romance! Confess now that you were wrong!"

"Absolutely wrong. How strange, to be sure, is my paternal *role!* While other fathers are forced to bridle the romantic follies of their children, I, on the contrary, have to restrain my daughter's sense."

"You acknowledge, then, that I am sensible?"

"So terribly sensible, Gretchen, that you sometimes frighten me." Adalbert was gazing at her, as he spoke, with a look of keen inquiry. His daughter was to him, and always had been, a beautiful riddle which he had tried in vain to read. She baffled him at every point. Was he to believe the account which she gave of herself? Or might he still hope that underneath that brilliant and seemingly hard surface there lived a genuine tenderness? Sometimes he thought the one, and sometimes the other. The first doubt had arisen years ago, when the four-year-old Gretchen had sat on her father's knee, listening to the story of a baby brother and sister, who, cast adrift from out of a sinking ship, had gone down into the deep blue sea, holding each other's hands to the last. It was an affecting story, and towards the close a big tear shone in each gray eye. The anxious father feared that a burst of sobs would follow, and was half reproaching himself for the choice of so harrowing a tale, when his little daughter took him by surprise. The gray eyes had suddenly cleared, though there was still a bright stain on the cheek; and having sat silent for a moment, she inquired, "Was everybody in the ship drowned?" "Everybody," said the father, imprudently. "Then who told the story?" "A little bird, perhaps," said Adalbert, laughing; but in the next moment he almost quailed before the look of supreme scorn which shot towards him. "Little birds do not speak."

Since that evening he had often asked himself in perplexity whether his beautiful daughter had sense alone, or whether she had a heart as well — whether the outspoken thirst for wealth, which year by year she came to display, was in itself more perilous or less so than the secret longings of many a worldly maiden. She was not like other girls, and therefore she frightened him. Other girls, even when they worshipped the golden calf, had at least the grace to worship it in private. The world has no chance of guessing at the nature of that veiled and shrouded idol before which the votary kneels in enraptured prayer. Oh, if hearts could be sacked like churches, what a booty of golden calves could be torn from the sacred shrines, where they have throned unsuspected in many a spotless virginal bosom!

Gretchen built her altar in public, and strewed her incense in the face of the world. The world was scandalized — her own father was alarmed. What was to come of it? If she had married Vincenz Komers (as Adalbert had been shortsighted enough to hope she would), then, knowing her in the hands of an honorable man, her father would have felt his mind at rest; but now, what was to come of it? These questions were in Adalbert's mind today, while his eyes followed his daughter's movements.

She had returned to the desk; but though she was stowing back the papers, the words with which she broke the pause betrayed that her thoughts were still clinging tenaciously to their former object.

"But at any rate," she remarked aloud," if we do succeed in finding the place — for we may come across it by chance, you know — you must promise me, papa, to finish that book."

"I think we had better count our chickens after they are hatched, Gretchen. My energy is not what it used to be, nor my enthusiasm either, I fear; twenty years have ground it out of me."

An indignant protestation was rising to Gretchen's lips, but she was interrupted by a disturbance in the passage. There were quick steps, then voices, a question and answer; and in the same minute, the door was flung wide open, and an awestruck servant announced — "The baron."

Chapter XI

The Valley-King

"*Jul.* What think'st thou of the rich Mercatio?"

"*Luc.* Well of his wealth; but of himself, so so."

— Two Gentlemen of Verona

BEFORE more than a rapid questioning look had time to pass between Herr Mohr and Gretchen, the baron was in the room.

"A thousand apologies for intruding myself in this way," he began, advancing hat in hand," but there was a little matter connected with the *Curliste* which seemed to require explanation; infinitely distressed to have to trouble you on so trifling a point." While he spoke, his eyes were sweeping eagerly round the room; he broke off as they fell on Gretchen. "Ah!" he exclaimed, with a start of surprise, almost too natural to be quite natural, "I perceive that I have more than one apology to make; what can I say in defense of my dog's conduct in the forest yesterday?"

Gretchen had half turned on her chair; a beautiful blush dyed her cheek. She had seen both the eager glance and over-perfect start that followed it, and quick as lightning she had read his motive. Her heart began to beat tumultuously. Even within these first two days, she had had opportunity to observe the respect and almost veneration with which the name of "the baron" was pronounced by every inhabitant of the mountain valley, and the semi-royal prestige which environed his person. What wonder, then, that her heart beat now, and her cheek flushed crimson, when in the valley-king she recognized the sportsman of yesterday?

The little matter connected with the *Curliste* proved to be a very little matter indeed. Baron Tolnay, having got through the preliminaries of apology and introduction, launched into a voluble explanation as to an uncertainty which had arisen respecting the spelling of a word in one of the names, expressing himself with as much apparent concern as if the matter had not been invented on the spur of the moment. Was Herr Mohr quite certain that the names had been given correctly? Was Madame Mohr's name undoubtedly Damianovics de Draskócs, and not perhaps Draskócs de Damianovics, or not possibly some other variation of the sort? Mistakes so often occurred, printers were so negligent, handwritings were so difficult to decipher. Something to the effect of all this, Baron Tolnay explained, while he took the seat which was offered him; and then in a tone of well-bred anxiety, though with a confident smile, he again expressed a hope that he was not intruding.

The hope was so evidently considered a mere matter of form by the visitor himself, and the pretext was such a flimsy disguise, that it required all Gretchen's self-possession to put on even an appearance of belief in the slender fiction.

To one person at least there was nothing flimsy in the pretext; anything relating to the great cause was too sacred a matter to be trifled with. Ascelinde, whom the rumor of the baron's appearance had conjured to the spot, was in raptures. She thanked him with effusion; she explained to him with minute detail that the name had been correctly spelled; she gave him a *résumé* of the family cause; she favored him with an outline sketch of the home of her ancestors; she dwelt at length upon her guardian's unscrupulous conduct; she was just stopped on the verge of her brother Alexius's biography by Adalbert's interposition.

"An unfortunate family cause, as you see," he said with a smile, which sufficiently betrayed his sentiments on the subject; "but it is scarcely fair to inflict it upon you."

Baron Tolnay bowed easily and gracefully, as much as to say that he was only too happy to be made the recipient of these troubles, and would be more delighted than he could express if Madame Mohr should be ready to impart to him her brother's biography at this or any future opportunity. Something was murmured, too, about regretting that he could not serve the family cause in any other way, and a wish that they should command his services in whatever need should arise during their stay in the Hercules valley.

Ascelinde's heart was won from that moment. "We have to thank you for one service already, baron," she rapturously exclaimed. "Without your kind guidance my children would never have found their way home yesterday."

This gave Baron Tolnay the opportunity of turning from the mother to the daughter.

"Ah, you have not learned the lessons of our valley yet, or you would not have the imprudence to move from the beaten track; our forest is a perfect maze, even by daylight; in the dusk sometimes a dangerous maze."

"Every maze has a key," said Gretchen, "therefore it stands to reason that this maze has one too."

"To be sure," said Tolnay, rather wondering at her decisive tone. "And I flatter myself — "

"That you possess the key?" she interrupted. "Is that really true, Baron Tolnay? Do you know the forests well? All the forests?"

"I should think I do; and I am about as tired of them as they must be of me."

"And you know all the hills here? Every path, every track?"

"Every stick. every stone," said Tolnay, not thinking so much of his words as of their effect upon her, which he was still at a loss to explain.

"Then," cried Gretchen, with a ring of triumph in her voice, "you can tell me where to find a spot that I am seeking for — "

"Any spot that you wish."

"Called *Gaura Dracului*," she finished, rising in her eagerness. "Do you know it, Baron Tolnay? You must know it if you know the hills."

"Ah, *Gaura Dracului*," repeated Tolnay after her, though for a second he looked blank — " of course I must know it. There are so many of these caves here; the whole mountains are riddled with them."

"No — not a cave," said Gretchen; "it is a hole. Papa, what was your description?"

"I cannot call it anything but a sudden break in the forest floor," answered Adalbert; "there is no reason why it should be there, except that it is there."

"Yes, a sudden break in the forest floor," echoed Tolnay, slowly. Gretchen's eyes were severely scrutinizing him.

"Well, Baron Tolnay," she said, laughing," what makes you hesitate? Are you also one of those perfect personifications of religious superstition about which papa has been telling me? Are you afraid of the devil's vengeance if you betray to me the devil's hole?"

Religious superstition! At the mere notion, Baron Tolnay broke into an irresistible laugh — a very light and airy laugh — but which jarred on the expectant Gretchen.

"Or perhaps you do not know the place?" she asked, stiffly. "You must either know it, or you must not."

Tolnay's laugh broke off, and he hesitated for a moment before he spoke. He was very quick of thought, and perhaps in that moment of hesitation he had recognized the advantages of the position, or perhaps his memory had grown alive all at once.

"Of course, I know it — why should I not? Are you interested in it?"

"Not in the least; but papa is, for historical reasons," she promptly added.

"And you want to visit it?"

"To investigate it, that is to say, or to have it investigated, sounded, examined, measured," said Gretchen, in her most business-like tone of voice. "Don't you understand?"

"Perfectly," said Tolnay, who understood nothing; "but" — he cast a rather doubtful glance over the fragile figure before him — "you will never be able to get up one of these hills; you must have a horse, and — "

"Ah," broke in Ascelinde, who all this time had been an uninterested listener, "if we only had one of my guardian's horses here! There are stablings for twenty horses at Draskócs, Baron Tolnay!" It was a noticeable fact that the Draskócs horses possessed a rabbit-like propensity for multiplication; at every enumeration their number showed a steady increase.

Tolnay bowed and bit his black mustache; and Gretchen laughed at the idea of the required horse almost as much as Tolnay had laughed at the idea of his religious superstition. "I want neither horse, mule, nor donkey," she assured him; "the only thing we need is a guide. Can you tell me of a guide, Baron Tolnay?"

"I can," said Tolnay, readily.

"And who is he?"

"He is here," said the baron, laughing; "behold me at your service."

"Oh," said Gretchen, somewhat staggered, "I did not mean that; but — "

"But you will not reject me, since you can find no other?"

"Nor surely could have no better," said Adalbert, politely. "You are really very kind, baron, to trouble yourself about this fancy of my daughter's."

"Of your own, papa, you mean," corrected Gretchen. "Think of your manuscript!"

"Well, of my own," said Adalbert, in a tone almost of concession, though his face betrayed more interest reawakened than he chose to confess. "There is no reason, certainly, why the investigations should not be pursued."

"And pursued at once," broke in Tolnay. "When shall we start? I feel an historical fever on me already."

"Next week, perhaps," suggested Adalbert.

But next week was much too indefinite a term to suit Baron Tolnay. He was burning to investigate the traces of defunct Dacians; he could not possibly rest quietly for many days longer without having satisfied his mind as to the existence of Roman relics in the hills. Why be devoured with curiosity for a whole week longer? Why not take advantage of the still comparative coolness of the weather? Why not say this week? Why not tomorrow? Or was Fraulein Mohr alarmed at so short a notice?

Fraulein Mohr was not in the least alarmed; deeds were always more congenial to her than words. And so, between Baron Tolnay's historical fever, and Gretchen's business-like energy, and Adalbert's revived interest in what had once been the pet scheme of his life, it was settled before they parted that the start should be made at daybreak next morning. "And by this hour tomorrow," said Gretchen, exultantly, "we shall have made the first step towards the historical discoveries. "Oh, papa, where are now all the obstacles that you would build round *Gaura Dracului?* You promise really to take me there, Baron Tolnay, do you not?"

"If she asked me in that voice," said Baron Tolnay to himself, "I would promise really to take her to the moon."

Chapter XII

The World Above

*"And after all, what is a lie? 'Tis but
The Truth in masquerade."*

— BYRON, *Don Juan*

HERE were two worlds here: the world of the valley below and the world of the mountains above; the one all the more beautiful because of its life, the other because of its desolation.

To this latter world, the ascent is precipitous — at places well-nigh perilous — feasible, indeed, only at one or two rare points of attack. Therefore, that world above is as well-defended against invasion as though it were fortified according to strategical laws; and as far away, though it is so near, as a country floating in the clouds.

The inhabitants of the world above can watch the movements of their lower neighbors — as the bears sometimes do when they creep to the edge of the rock and listen in comfort to the band below, whose strains float up distinctly through the pure mountain air — but to the world below the world above is a sealed book. Of a hundred people who visit the Hercules valley, ninety-nine will be content to admire these rocky heights from below, as they would look at the stars or the sunset, without the ambition to approach them. But the hundredth man, perchance, may stand and gaze so long and so deeply that the Spirit of the mountain throws his spell upon him, and bids him ascend; which he does with pain and toil, fighting for each step, and battling for breath till he reaches the confines of this enchanted country. Once here, he has gained the battle; and for hours he can walk at ease, in such a forest as he will have scarcely fancied in his dreams. He may have seen black pine forests, shaking their fragrant fringes to the ground; he may have walked in the shade of time-honored oaks, or have seen the sunshine making filigree work of silver birch tree branches — but none of these sights will have impressed him as do these forests of the Hercules valley.

For here, all is vast, all is wide, solemn, majestic — awful without gloom, calm without monotony. Here the intruder, threading his way through the pillared corridors, starts as the sound of his own step breaks the breathless stillness of the aisles around him. The forest is one vast cathedral of tremulous green; a temple which Nature has built so manifestly for herself alone, that the mere presence of man seems rude profanation. Surely this mossy mosaic was not laid to be trodden by human feet? These garlands which deck the leafy altars, these swinging censers which perfume the breeze, these chalices of icy white and flaming crimson — surely they are consecrated to the Spirit of these realms alone? Surely this cloistered repose should be troubled by no human voice, nor these stately pillars echo back laughter or song of man?

The columns which support the mighty canopy retreat on all sides in an endless vista; each pillar a beech tree, and each beech tree a giant. Straight as ship masts, the trunks are reared; the shining bark roughened with clinging lichen and clothed with moss down to the spreading foot, which with its stealthy hold seems to grasp the earth like the velvet-covered claw of some living monster. They have all one character, that of strength and straightness, but each has its individual distinction. Some have only one band of moss down their sides, others have drawn their velvet robes around them; others are marked by a large flat fungus, which time has hardened into wood, standing out from their stems in bold relief; other beeches have received two or three or more of these fanciful ornaments, which are sometimes piled up one above the other, fifteen or twenty high, as large as footstools and as white as ivory, looking like some wonderful contrivance carved by the band of man, though the hand of man has never been near. And high overhead there is the green roof of branches, flat-grown and leafy, shutting out the light, or letting it in only with a green shade upon it, melting the gold of the sunshine, and filtering it through its network. A roof which moves and murmurs, weaving a hundred pictures with each movement, and playing a hundred tunes in each rustle, having contrasts of shadowy light and luminous shade, which no ceiling, however cunningly painted by man's hand, could ever have.

And if the living trees are beautiful, the dead trees are more beautiful still. Not those dead trees whose trunks have been hollowed out and set fire to by some stray bear-hunter, and which stand now, charred and black, like wicked ghosts, staring grimly at the traveler; those trees are weird, but they are not beautiful. The dead trees that are beautiful are those which have fallen, perhaps under the fury of a winter storm, perhaps even cut down to meet some passing human emergency. No one is responsible for these victims, and no one protects them. There they lie and rot, and the green moss creeps over them, turning them into objects fantastically beautiful, but devouring them with damp embraces, and feeding upon them day by day. A hundred times more glorious in their damp decay than they ever were in the prime of their strength, the colossal carcasses, stretched to their full length on the earth, are crusted with the enamel of lichens, and decked with moist shades of yellow-green. They seem to have borrowed the semblance of every costly thing; the glow of bronze, the sheen of satin, the fire of ruby and emerald, the refinement of fretted gold. They are inexhaustible in their variety, insatiable in their extravagance.

Two hours after sunrise the exploring party had reached the heart of this new country. They were not following any path, for there was none to follow, but wound in and out the huge pillars, surmounting the fallen trunks, or sometimes breaking through a tangle of green. The forest was not silent while they passed, though their steps could make no sound on the overgrown earth. Baron Tolnay's laugh echoed often under the leafy arches; and sometimes Gretchen asked a question, and some-times Kurt whistled the snatch of a tune. Baron Tolnay seemed in high spirits. Strangely enough, from the moment that he had set foot in the forest his historical thirst had relaxed. There was not a single reference either to Romans or Dacians in the talk which he addressed to Gretchen. It was a very brilliant talk, however — keen, ready, and just sufficiently flavored with sarcasm to make it palatable; and in spite of the want of historical element in conversation, Gretchen had found the long way very short. "You are quite sure that we are on the right road?" she had asked once or twice, when she feared that the conversationalist was gaining too much ascendancy over the guide.

"Of course, we are on the right way," said Baron Tolnay, and then for some minutes they walked on in silence, Pasha following close at his master's heels, Kurt with his hands in his pockets sauntering along as if he were merely taking a constitutional stroll, and looking at the beech trees with a sort of good-humored patronage; Gretchen rather puzzled how to explain the ever-growing exuberance of Baron Tolnay's spirits. There was a constant and unexplained laughter in his eyes; he looked almost like a man who is hugging to his heart some secret cause of delight, which touches him as so exquisite that he can scarcely keep himself from its betrayal.

"Baron Tolnay," said Gretchen, presently.

"Yes, Fraulein Mohr."

"Are you looking at the beech trees for those three crosses?"

"Of course, I am."

"I have never seen you turn your head once."

"I am turning it continually."

"What is there to laugh about?" she asked, a little piqued. "You talk as if it were a joke."

"Then you really think your father made the marks he spoke of?"

"Think! I know he did. Did he not tell you so himself?"

"To be sure."

This was incomprehensible and provoking. Could Baron Tolnay never be serious? Was that spark of mockery which lurked in his ready smile, and shone in the depth of his expressive black eyes, never to be quenched?

...they walked on in silence, Pasha following close at his master's heels;...

"If you will not look at the trees, I will," said Gretchen stepping up to the stem beside her.

But Baron Tolnay, with the most unruffled good-humor, declared his readiness not only to examine, but to bark or strip or cut down any tree, or every tree, if it gave Fraulein Mohr the slightest satisfaction. And after this no specially fine beech tree was passed unscrutinized; only that Baron Tolnay always selected for scrutiny the same tree that Gretchen had chosen, which, as she proved to him on logical grounds, was a waste of time. They found wonderful mosses and brilliant lichens enough to rejoice the heart of a botanist but the three crosses they were looking for they did not find. The only trace of human presence to be discovered was the roughly cut figure of a quadruped with crooked horns, apparently a crossbreed between the evil spirit and a goat.

"Some goatherd with a turn for art," said István, looking over Gretchen's shoulder; "you meet them sometimes in the wood here."

"This is freshly cut," said Kurt, lounging up. "Our artistic friend cannot be very far off."

There was the faintest indication of a track just discernible as it wound off to the right, while to the left a spot of blinding daylight broke in through an opening in the trees, and beyond there shone an open space of grass, as brilliant in the sunshine as the flash of a cut emerald.

"Which way ought we to go — to the right or to the left?" asked Gretchen.

"Whichever you like best; it is not of much consequence."

"But one way must lead to *Gaura Dracului*, and one must not. It stands to reason that they cannot both be right."

"I am no match for your logic, Fraulein Mohr," said István, with apparent gravity. "I should recommend the meadow, then."

To the meadow, therefore, they went, stepping out of the dim light into a blaze of sunshine, and treading, as they walked, upon thick soft grass. When they were well out on the open space, Baron Tolnay turned and offered a further piece of advice. "Now that we are on the meadow, I should recommend our taking a rest."

"It would be better to rest when we have reached *Gaura Dracului*," said Gretchen, doubtfully; but, looking round her, she could not resist the repose and beauty of the spot. The space was oval in shape, belted all round with the deep green forest. On all sides the beech trees had pressed, like a circle of invaders checked by a word of command, and standing now in close ranks, staring down with patient calm upon the spot which they guard.

"And now," said István, when they had made their halt, "now that we are sitting, is there any reason why we should not eat our sandwiches?"

"Great reason," was the prompt reply. "I intend to eat my sandwiches by the side of *Gaura Dracului*."

Gretchen had sunk on the grass; Baron Tolnay, a few paces off, leaning on his elbow, was idly plucking at the flower-stalks; Kurt, apparently in want of further exercise, was throwing sticks for Pasha to fetch.

"Do you think your resolve is quite wise?" asked István, looking up from the grass blades. "I fancy you will get rather hungry before you reach *Gaura Dracului*."

Gretchen drew out her watch. "We were to reach the spot at one; it is half-past twelve now; I can wait half an hour for my sandwiches."

Baron Tolnay appeared to be deeply absorbed in the botanical construction of a tiny flower in the grass. He made no reply.

"Is it not a pity that we did not bring ropes and torches with us?" said Gretchen, after a pause.

"What for?"

"Why, to sound the depth, of course."

"We must reach it before we sound it." "That will be in half an hour."

Again Baron Tolnay made no answer; his face was hidden, as he bent over the flower. Gretchen watched him with displeasure.

"Which way do we go when we leave the meadow, Baron Tolnay?"

Tolnay tore off the head of the tiny flower, and began pulling off the petals; when he had pulled off the last petal and thrown away the stalk, he answered slowly, still without looking up, "I have not got the slightest idea."

With a face of rigid consternation, Gretchen sat and stared at him, while he quietly searched about in the grass for another flower to dissect.

"Baron Tolnay," she managed at last to utter, "you promised to take me to the spot."

"I would take you there if I knew where it was."

"But you said that you did know; you said that you remembered it."

"Fraulein Mohr," said István, abandoning the search for the flower, and sitting up to confront her with his unabashed black eyes, "surely you understand all this, and do not require me to explain?"

"I understand nothing. You said that you would take me to *Gaura Dracului.*"

"And I say now, I would take you still, only I do not believe such a place exists."

Again, Gretchen stared, speechless for a minute. "Say that again, please — I did not quite hear."

"I do not believe that such a place or such a hole exists," repeated Baron Tolnay, deliberately.

"But papa has seen it."

Baron Tolnay raised his well-shaped shoulders ever so slightly. There was incredulity and a pity expressed in that movement which just stopped short of impertinence. Only a man as carefully polished in the furnace of the world as was this young Hungarian could venture to raise his shoulders at such a moment without appearing ill-mannered.

"I have no doubt your father believes that he has seen it; but he is an invalid — his health is broken for the moment — and invalids have strange fancies."

"But he was not an invalid when he wrote that letter; he was not broken down then."

"A man's fancy can run very wild in twenty-one years," said István.

"Do you mean to say that you know nothing about the place?"

"Upon my honor, I have never heard a word of it, far less seen it."

"Then why have you brought me up here?" Her voice shook with anger.

"Why have I brought you up here?" repeated István without changing his attitude. His hat was on the grass beside him, and his head, with its close black waves of hair, rested on his hand. Gretchen, as she asked her question, met the glance of joyful exultation which broke out of those fiery eyes — they looked very fiery for a moment. The light danced in them, but the mockery still lurked in the black shade within.

"Surely we can employ our time, now that we are up here, better than by looking for a stupid black hole."

"Stupid black hole!" There was such scornful displeasure in Gretchen's voice that István quickly corrected himself. "An interesting black hole, I should have said, Fraulein Mohr; but there are so many things that are more interesting than black holes." Baron Tolnay, as he said this, looked very confident as to the superior attraction of black eyes contra black holes.

Gretchen's face was set into an expression of judicial severity, but István did not tremble before it.

"Do you mean to say, Baron Tolnay, that you have deceived us? That you have told an untruth?"

"I would have told a hundred untruths for the sake of a walk like this."

She was not quite sure that she believed her ears; but the dancing light in his eyes was not to be mistaken.

"But that is a lie," she stammered. "I believe it is called so."

A sort of mental giddiness had come over Gretchen; her ideas of right and wrong were reeling against each other. Here was a man owning frankly to a downright lie without the slightest appearance of shame; and yet, ever since she had learned to speak, Gretchen had been taught by her father to speak the truth; had been told that falsehood was the most heinous of evils. Was not Truth the twin sister of Justice? And was not Justice Gretchen's pet virtue?

She had no words which could express this indignant bewilderment. She sat silent; but, though her eyes were on the grass, she could feel that those of Tolnay were upon her; and again, she felt helpless to impress him as she would have wished. Though she did not look at him, she knew that his gaze was one of earnest admiration, and she was aware that with each wave of angry color that flowed to her cheek his admiration was growing.

At last she raised her head.

"What do you propose doing now, Baron Tolnay?" she bitterly inquired.

"I propose that we should eat our sandwiches."

"Sandwiches!" she echoed, impatiently. "I wonder you have still the courage to talk of sandwiches! Have you nothing else to suggest? Have you no remorse for the disappointment which poor papa will have tonight?"

"There is no reason for disappointing your poor papa," said Baron Tolnay, quietly.

She looked at him with some suspicion.

"What do you mean?"

"I mean that we have only to tell him that we found the place, and that will make it all right."

"But how can we, since we have not found it?"

"Nothing could be simpler. He will believe us, if we say it, and he will never be the wiser. That is much better than disappointing him."

Gretchen turned upon the speaker a face that was positively scared. She had never before had so many successive shocks of surprise; she had never been so puzzled

by any individual of her acquaintance. Baron Tolnay was the first man whose designation in the mental catalogue had given her cause for doubt. "A man of the world,
brilliant, fascinating, good-natured, and, I think, pleasant" — such had been the first
judgment written out yesterday. Today she felt inclined to stroke out all the adjec-
tives except "brilliant," and to substitute some such qualities as "untruthful — disagreeable — hollow." Surely the words were not too harsh for a man who was quietly
proposing to her to join him in a deception which was to blind her father. But again,
there was something about the manner of the man which made her hesitate, with the
pen in her hand, figuratively speaking. His eyes, as he made the proposition, did not
in the least shrink, as the eyes of the deceitful are supposed to do. Liars ought to look
stealthy and watchful; their eyes should be cunning and disagreeable, unable to meet
the eyes of their fellow creatures. All this stood to reason, and therefore was
Gretchen's creed; but Baron Tolnay quite upset all her theories. His voice even had
a candid tone in it, and his face wore an expression of engaging frankness as he urged
the advisability of the deception. It was not as if he were indifferent to wrong-doing,
but simply as if he were incapable of seeing anything wrong in the proceeding. The
openness, almost the innocence of his gaze, was more baffling than any glance of
stealthy cunning.

What now was to become of Truth? What of Justice and Logic? How fill up the
place in the catalogue? How describe this indescribable man?

Gretchen wondered whether the singularity of the situation was her fault or his:
was it she who was stupid and dazed, or was it he, in whose mental constitution some
one element was wanting, which made him different from other men she had known?
What could that lacking element be?

For a whole minute, she made no answer at all, but when her first surprise was
past, she spoke hurriedly. "Baron Tolnay, how could you, even for one instant, imagine that I could deceive my father in this way?"

"I cannot pretend to answer that, Fraulein Mohr; but this I know, you cannot
succeed in deceiving me."

"Deceiving you!"

"This little romance about the hole is very interesting, and really very pretty; but, after all, it was no more than a graceful excuse for this charming expedition, which I hope you enjoy as much as I do. You surely did not really believe that such a place exists — as little as I believe it, who have shot bears in the hills for the last five years and never heard the place mentioned — so you cannot have really believed that we were going to find it. Do not imagine that I am venturing to blame you, Fraulein Mohr; on the contrary, I think that it was our only course, for the sake of your father's health."

Our course! Then he imagined that she had understood and tacitly agreed to his deceit. This was not to be borne a minute longer.

Gretchen started to her feet, and stood before him with flashing eyes.

"Thank you, Baron Tolnay," she said, haughtily. "I shall not ask you for your help again; I shall find *Gaura Dracului* for myself;" and with this, and a short inclination of her head, she turned on her heel and walked off straight across the meadow towards the point opposite to the one by which they had entered. She never looked back until she had reached the first beech tree, and then, throwing a stolen glance over her shoulder, she saw Kurt following, and nearer to her was Baron Tolnay, striding along with his hat pulled over his forehead, and a very serious face. Ah! so she had at last succeeded in extinguishing that mocking light. He made no attempt to speak, though he was close behind her now, and she walked on straight ahead.

She had not gone far when Pasha rushed past her, barking furiously. There was a low, dull tinkle of a bell, a sound of snapping twigs, and presently a large black-and-white goat was disclosed, interrupted in its repast, and standing in an attitude of defense.

Gretchen did not immediately think of connecting this goat with the figure she had seen carved on the tree, but her curiosity was aroused. She pressed forward a few steps and then stood still, as all at once the strangest, the weirdest of pictures was disclosed before her eyes.

Straight across the track she was following there lay a forest tree of enormous dimensions. The stump, with the marks of rude hacking upon it, clung with its mossy roots to the earth hard by, like the base of a broken pillar. The lower branches were broken into a half-withered heap; but the branches above, standing out like a young forest of trees, were still fresh. Upon this wealth of fresh leaves, five or six goats were feeding luxuriously. One black goat, the largest of the small flock, stood reared up with its front feet on the trunk, while it nibbled down the highest leaves which it could reach. A small white kid was contenting itself with the broken twigs on the ground. Perched cross-legged on the trunk crouched a strange creature. Nothing but a coarse linen shirt, of a hue as dark and undefined as the tint of his own skin, covered this boy, leaving a broad allowance of brown chest bare. A ragged, high-pointed cap, of what had once been white sheepskin, was on his head; not more ragged than his own shaggy hair, which hung from under it in a tangled black mass, over his ears and into his eyes, like the hair of a wild beast. In his thin brown fingers, he held a pipe of wood, which had seen much forest service in its days. A second shepherd, a size larger, but in every respect resembling the first, leaned against a branch hard by, chipping at the bark, and giving forth, at the same time, a low booming sound at mechanical and regular intervals. It was his way of calling the goats together; and as he looked up stupidly, and stared with his large, wild, senseless eyes, he seemed scarcely more human than the goats themselves.

"What are they?" asked Gretchen below her breath, recoiling a step in surprise and half in fear.

"Goatherds only," said Tolnay's voice beside her. "Shame upon those barbarians; they have cut down another of the finest trees; that is the way they ruin the forests for the sake of feeding their wretched goats!"

With the comprehension of the situation, Gretchen soon regained not only her self-possession, but also renewed hope; for these strange shepherds, who lived in the hills, must surely know something of the spot for which she was searching.

And so, they did; there could not be the smallest doubt of that. The mysterious word was scarcely pronounced, when an instantaneous change came over the two faces before her. A minute ago, two pairs of sullen eyes had been vacantly watching her approach; two wide-open mouths had stupidly gaped at her. Her first greeting was unanswered, apparently unheard; but upon the word *Gaura Dracului* there followed a sudden transformation. The staring eyes suddenly dilated; the boys stood before her with chattering teeth, shaking as though they had been struck with the ague; and two brown hands, gaunt already, although so young, moved up and down again, as they signed themselves on forehead and breast with the sign of the cross, after the fashion of the Greek Church.

The change was so unexpected, and the terror on both faces was so real in its wildness of expression, that Gretchen herself felt as though a shadow of superstitious dread had fallen on her. But the dread was only a new spur to curiosity, and with a dumb show of signs she attempted to enforce her question. Surely, she could overcome the obstinacy of two half-savage boys.

In vain, all in vain! Words were vain, signs were vain, money even was vain. She held it out towards them — glittering silver coins — ought that not to dazzle two starved shepherd boys?

István threw himself into the argument now; but even his tone of rough command had no effect. The goatherds never answered a single word, but stood pressed together like a couple of frightened sheep — gaping, staring, and trembling, until the smaller, and, if such a distinction were possible, the dirtier of the two, dropped his jaw and began to whimper piteously.

It took ten minutes to convince Gretchen of her defeat. Reluctantly, she put back the silver into her purse, and, without applying to Baron Tolnay for advice, she struck into what looked like a pathway and walked straight on, the others following her. Baron Tolnay never spoke, until, at the end of half an hour, they emerged, almost without warning, on a free and unshaded spot. It was a mere ledge, and Gretchen had to check her steps rather suddenly, for immediately from below her feet the ground fell sheer away — a precipitous mountainside, dotted with tufts of fine grass, and sharpened at intervals by the acute point of a rock. Beyond there stretched a view of round-topped, wooded hills.

"Where are we?" asked Gretchen.

"On the confines of Hungary, with Romania at our feet," said Baron Tolnay; and then, as Gretchen turned round, he added lower, "Are you still angry with me, Fraulein Mohr? Will you not forgive me for this once?" He looked like a child who has certainly been naughty, but means now to be very good. His face was grave, excessively so. He was quite changed from half an hour ago; he looked very penitent and very handsome.

Gretchen gave him a searching glance, a glance which she intended to be of scathing severity, but which, falling upon so meek and penitent a face, could not fail to soften a little. He certainly was the most perplexing man of her acquaintance, expressly created, it seemed, to set all logic at naught. During this last half hour, she had quite made up her mind that he was a monster of deceit; and just as she had satisfactorily decided upon this point, here was the monster standing before her in an attitude of such convincing penitence, gazing at her with eyes of such provoking sincerity, that her carefully weighed sentence fell flat to the ground. She had been angry with him for his deceit; she was almost more angry with him for this frankness which upset all her theories, which forced her to be inconsistent, which, against her own will, was disarming her. Certainly, he had been to blame, but it was difficult to believe that anyone with that open glance could mean harm. The lie which he had told had been told for — well, yes, for *her* sake. Quick as lightning a mental comparison had shot through Gretchen's mind. Baron Tolnay had said that he would not mind telling a hundred lies for her sake, and Dr. Komers would not have told a single one; of that she felt confident, without seeing it put to the test. What was the natural inference?

But she did not wish to capitulate unconditionally. She gave him her hand, but she gave it with a sort of cool reserve.

Baron Tolnay took her hand; he did not press it; he was on his very good behavior now.

"Do you still disbelieve in *Gaura Dracului?*" asked Gretchen in a tone of lofty coldness.

"I will swear to its existence. The evidence on those two faces is not to be over-turned; popular superstition has never interested me until today."

"And today it shall not baffle me," said Gretchen. "I am going back to the goat-herds; it can only be a question of florins after all."

They came to the felled tree, where the ground was strewn with bitten leaves, and where many a branch was half-stripped, but the spot was deserted. The fallen tree told them no tales, and neither goats nor goatherds were there.

Chapter XIII

"Sir Novart"

"Bring the rod, the line, the reel,
Bring, oh bring the osier creel,
Bring me flies of fifty kinds,
Bring me clouds and showers and winds."

— Thomas Stoddart

1N spite of the seclusion of the Hercules valley, such things as postmen were not entirely unknown, and letters and newspapers occasionally did stumble upon the right address; so also, an epistle of Belita's, the answer to that last of Gretchen's, written before the journey. The signature this time was no longer Belita Pegrelli, but Belita Francopazzi; for the mystic words at the altar-foot had some weeks ago transformed her into that ideal of happiness — a rich contessa.

She wrote from Switzerland, and after a description of her wedding dress (not of her wedding), she put some questions as follows: Tell me by return of post what your watering place is like; I mean, whether the *Cursalon* is favorable for showing off dresses? Promenade ditto? Would Parisian toilets find a *public sympathique?* Is it the sort of place where one can change dresses three times a day? The truth is, I am sick of Switzerland: we meet nothing but dowdy German women who wear hats which make my blood run cold, and who, I am certain, cling secretly to the tradition of the crinoline; or else big English ladies, coated, cravated, and booted like men. There is no triumph in eclipsing such rivals. I like to feel that my foemen are worthy of my steel. Besides which, Margherita — I blush for my weakness, but I have a sort of notion that I should like to see you again; or, more properly speaking, I should like to see what acquaintances you have found in your barbarous valley. You are at a critical period of life, *Bambina*, and I do not mean to lose sight of you until you have made your fortune as brilliantly as I have made mine. (Talking of that, by-the-bye, Draskócs would, of course, be all very well, if that sleepy lawyer of yours had it in him to finish the eternal suit). Do you know, Margherita, that your last letter made me rather uneasy? You have a clear head, to be sure; but Germans are never quite to be trusted. I am afraid you must have been reading some very second-rate novels. Do not again let me hear you talk such rubbish about a man saying to a woman "that she is the only woman to him, etc." Where did you pick up these ideas? I should like to see Ludovico try to say that sort of thing to me. I promise you he would not do it again. I am happy to say that I have observed no such sign of mental aberration in him. He is a nice, sensible creature.

Gretchen, replying to this letter, said she believed there was no objection to Belita changing dresses six times a day, if it gave her any pleasure. "Come and see for yourself," she added.

"But I think I have awakened the sleepy lawyer," said Gretchen to herself. "What does Belita know about his being sleepy? She has never seen him in her life."

The letter altogether was not satisfactory to Gretchen. What did Belita mean by these uncalled for and wholly superfluous warnings against sentiment? And what could she herself have meant by retaining and repeating such a ridiculously stilted phrase as the one quoted, and which she certainly had never read in any novel whether first or second rate?

It was some weeks after their arrival in the valley that this letter had reached Gretchen's hands; and during these weeks many more traveling carriages, with jingling bells, had rattled round the corner. The place was slowly waking into its summer life; the hotels began to look inhabited at corners, and rows of closed eyes opened in turn. The shops commenced a languid trade. The five men who composed the musical band played night and morning to a slowly increasing audience. At the restaurant where the Mohrs took their meals, the inferior waiters had retired into the background to make way for superior attendants; the landlord exchanged his shabby coat for an official-looking black garment, and the oleanders and pomegranates appeared along the veranda in an alternate row, quite green and flowerless as yet, as if scarcely awake after their long sleep.

The small handful of guests had now grown into a large handful. Romanian ladies — swarthy, dark-eyed, large-featured, and stout, in some cases adorned with mustaches, in one case even bearded — sat all day long in the *Cursalon*, languidly doing nothing, and very much exhausted in consequence.

"It would take very little to make any one of these Romanian women beautiful," the precocious Kurt had remarked one day; "but they all just miss it somehow."

The increase of the guests brought with it an increase of duties to the large Romanian Dr. Kokovics — social duties rather than medical. Preparations for public amusements were started on a vast scale. There were to be musical entertainments, and entertainments with fireworks, and entertainments without fireworks. The over-taxed doctor staggered under the weight of the self-imposed burden. At every hour of the day, he was to be met, covering the ground with enormous strides; his hat pushed far back from off his heated forehead, his unwashed hands crammed with paper slips, his haggard eye restlessly perusing the lists that those slips contained. The lists were not the names of his patients; they were usually connected with public amusements, or sometimes they were the rough cast of a couplet; for to write love verses in summertime was as necessary to the doctor's nature as it is necessary for a thrush to sing in April. The only difference which the verses showed this year was the sudden appearance of gray eyes in the lines, as opposed to the dark eyes of former seasons. Blue or gray eyes were scarce in the Hercules valley, while black eyes shone there as plentifully as blackberries; and perhaps for this reason Gretchen began to find herself subjected to a species of slow persecution, not the less harassing because poetical Dr. Kokovics's muse haunted her footsteps. At all hours of the day, in every imaginable place, her attention was claimed by a class of composition which would perhaps best be de- scribed as "medicinal lyrics." Omnipresence was the chief characteristic of these couplets. There was no escape from them; they came by the post, they lay in her work-basket, they fluttered down before her eyes on the pathway, they dropped out of her napkin at dinner. Dating from the moment when the doctor had thought fit to celebrate Gretchen's arrival with the cry —

"Daughter of Germania!

Welcome to our vale!

Though its rugged beauty

Beside thine turns pale" —

the flood of poetry thus heralded poured down upon her thick and fast.

These verses, which, if unsigned, were also unmistakable, breathed in their lines a scientifically colored but not the less ardent admiration. The poet-doctor seemed to be forever hovering between the extremes of his two *rôles*; for while, as the former, he celebrated the

"Nymph-like, eylph-like grace"

of the adored object — as the latter, his professional anxiety could not fail to be aroused by the apparent delicacy of that,

"Alas, too fairy-like form!"

and if she dazzled him as a brilliant beauty, she likewise interested him as a possible patient. A continual hesitation betrayed itself as to which light she should be viewed in.

But notwithstanding all this broadcast sowing of verses, Dr. Kokovics had as yet reaped nothing but contemptuous silence. The German family had made no acquaintances, and, probably by reason of Herr Mohr's precarious health, did not seem inclined to make any. Baron Tolnay alone, whose position was exceptional and supreme, had the entree of their rooms. Nor was the baron behindhand in using his privilege, nor did he appear to waste a single thought upon the remarks which his constant visits could not fail to call forth. He had been discarded as a guide, it is true;

but it was quite evident that he was accepted as an acquaintance, and as yet the only acquaintance of the family.

But there came a day at last on which the circle of the Mohrs was unexpectedly widened; and it so happened that within the same hour Kurt and Gretchen, respectively and independently, formed each an acquaintance of their own.

Brother and sister were strolling one evening up the valley by the river's side. The weather had become too hot now for anything but the laziest, most leisurely stroll, and even this was not to be enjoyed till near sunset. The sunny day hours were hotter here than anywhere else; for the sun having once gained its height, poured down its fire into the narrow valley, and the glowing rocks threw back the reflection of their heat, until a strong man would have found it an effort to crawl from one end of the short street to the other.

Kurt and Gretchen, as they strolled along by the river, perceived that a broad-shouldered gentleman in a wide-awake hat was walking in front of them. They knew him by sight; he was the pride of the season, the flower among the flock of guests, and popularly designated as "the English lord." The English lord had never been seen to talk to anybody, except to his invalid wife on the rare occasions when she was visible. Every day he might be remarked stalking up and down the promenade for a certain number of hours in grim and unapproachable dignity, and every day he was to be observed taking his meals in solitary grandeur at a table apart from the rest, and bullying the waiters in a mixture of bad French and execrable German.

It soon became evident to the two promenaders that the English lord was behaving in an even more extraordinary and eccentric fashion than usual. He walked with his eyes on the water, coming to a standstill every now and then, and frowning severely at some pool in the river. Two or three times, he descended with considerable difficulty through rolling stones and weedy undergrowth to the riverside, and proceeded to probe the shallow places with his stick; and finally, after several of these descents, he took up his position on a bridge, and leaned there with folded arms, and his eyes still fixed on the water.

It was just at this moment that Kurt, who among other precocious habits had acquired that of smoking, fumbling in his pocket, discovered that he had no matches. There being no one else in sight, he applied to the Englishman, while Gretchen wandered on by herself, expecting to be rejoined within the next dozen paces.

The Englishman, hearing himself asked for a light, took his eyes off the water, and turning to the questioner, gazed at him in surprise. He saw an individual whom he did not know whether to classify as an undersized man or an oversized boy, but who returned his look with perfect ease, and politely repeated his demand.

There are in life two contingencies in which even an Englishman considers that the ceremony of introduction may be dispensed with; one of these is the saving of life. If, for instance, you should see a fellow-creature who cannot swim tumbling into deep water, the usages of society are lenient enough to sanction your pulling him out without pausing to name yourself or to hear his name in return. In this contingency, the ceremony will follow of course, supposing the deep water not to have quite put an end to the fellow creature. But in the second contingency the ceremony is absolutely dispensed with. You can ask for a light, and you can be asked for a light, without any anxiety about your fellow creature's position and antecedents; you do not require the presence of a third fellow-creature to wave his hand, and mumble your names, and cause you to bow and scrape at each other; but having taken your light, or given your light, and having stood for one brief second with your two noses in affectionate vicinity, and not as much as the length of two cigars between your two faces as the spark is kindled in the sacred weed, you each turn upon your respective heels, and quietly drop out of each other's respective lives.

The Englishman, having recognized the second of these contingencies, complied with the request; and then, very much to his surprise, he perceived that this fellow-creature was not preparing to drop out of his life just yet.

"Have you lost anything valuable in the river, if I may ask?" began Kurt, with his cigar between his teeth.

He had become possessed at school of a respectable stock of French — not large, perhaps, but quite as much as the Englishman himself could boast of; and it was in this language that he opened conversation.

The Englishman, who had resumed his fixed gaze at the water, gave him a look of haughty astonishment.

"Thank you; I have not," was the freezing reply. But Kurt was not to be frozen in that way.

"I thought it likely, from the way you were staring at the pools." The Englishman looked at him again distrustfully. He had a true Englishman's distrust of foreigners, and this youth was evidently a foreigner. National traditions had taught him that when foreign youths address middle-aged Englishmen without introduction, it is usually for the purpose of obtaining money. This particular young man did not look much in want of money, thought the Englishman, as he ran his eye critically over his person; but it was better to be on the safe side, so the Englishman still felt distrustful.

"I fancied you might be looking for your watch or your purse, which you had dropped into the river," remarked Kurt, negligently. The allusion to the purse was suspicious; it confirmed the Englishman's worst apprehensions.

"I have not lost my purse; I have got no purse with me," he said speaking distinctly, so as to be heard through the loud rush of the water, and keeping his eye severely fixed on the young man; "and I have only got an old watch on, a silver one," he added, emphatically. By thus removing all inducement and crushing all hopes, the Englishman hoped to get rid of the young man's society; but the young man smoked on complacently, and did not move an inch.

"If you had dropped anything into the river," persisted Kurt "you would not be likely to get it back again at the rate the water is going on down there." ·

The bridge on which they stood was the last bridge up the valley. and looking down from it, you looked straight upon a foaming and gurgling spot of the Djernis, commonly called the waterfall. When the river was very high, the water, falling right over the two large boulder-stones which stood with a short space between them, made a fair imitation of a cataract; but on warm days like the present the boulder-stones were dry, and only a narrow stream trickled down between them.

The Englishman stood contemplating the large flat pool below the waterfall, and felt in his mind rather doubtful as to the young man beside him. He still wished to be on the safe side; but there was a flavor of audacity in the young man's manner which, against his own will, was arousing his admiration. Kurt, on his side, was quietly examining his companion, and wondering whether he was quite mad, or only suffering from some slight mental affection. He would not have been in the least surprised to hear him disclose himself as a raving lunatic in his next words; Kurt would have taken it quite for granted. His reflection seemed to have some ground when suddenly the Englishman, without turning his head, clutched his companion's arm and pointed towards the pool.

"Did you see? Three pounds weight at least; three and a quarter, I dare say." His whole countenance was transfigured in a way that suggested the rapture of a celestial ecstasy.

"Really?" said Kurt; "three pounds of what?"

"But a salmon-trout, I tell you — a salmon-trout, three pounds weight in that pool, jumped just that moment; didn't you see it?"

Kurt had only heard a slight splash and seen a tiny ripple, but he had now got the clue to the Englishman's apparent insanity, and his mind was at rest.

"Is not that another?" he inquired, as a second splash and a second ripple disturbed the surface of the pool.

"Yes; not such a fine one, though."

The Englishman had by this time quite abandoned the safe side — the weight of that salmon-trout had broken the ice. Kurt inquired whether the Englishman had caught much fish yet, and the Englishman replied that he had not had a throw.

"In the first place, there is no water in the river; in the second place, my tackle requires overhauling; and besides, I am not sure that I have the right flies with me for these pools."

"So you fish with flies, do you?" asked the innocent Kurt.

His new acquaintance turned and gave him a glance of wounded dignity. "Do I look as if I fished with WORM?" He pronounced the name of the ignominious reptile with an unspeakably contemptuous elongation of the word.

"Well, perhaps not," said Kurt, to whom fly-fishing and worm-fishing meant much the same thing; different forms of the same class of insanity — that was all. "So, as you can't fish for want of the water, or the flies, or whatever it is, you spend your days in walking up and down — is that it?"

"Yes, in walking up and down," repeated the Englishman, in a sort of grimly complacent tone; "there is nothing else to do in this confounded valley — nothing to do and nothing to eat. Not that I am particular on this last point; but when a man on his arrival comes to the supper-room famished, and having merely asked for a mutton-chop, a plain mutton-chop, is stared at in consequence as if he were a lunatic at large — do you not call that a hard case?"

"Perhaps so," said Kurt, out of regard for British insanity, and thinking of Chinese bird-nest soup and roast puppies as specimens of barbarous taste. "Why don't you ask for beefsteaks?"

"Didn't I ask! And do you know what happened? I said to the waiter, 'Bring me a beefsteak,' and the waiter said, interrogatively, *'Englisch!'* I said, 'Of course, English,' being too happy to have discovered anything approaching to home food. Exit the waiter with alacrity; reenter with the same alacrity after an incredibly short time, bearing on a plate a piece of meat raw and dripping with blood. When I protested indignantly, they told me it was *Englisch*. I had asked for *Englisch*, and I had got *Englisch* — why was I not satisfied? I don't believe the piece of meat had ever been within sight of the fire. And then, of course, they rush to the other extreme; they give you things uncooked which ought to be cooked, and vice versa. When I explained to the milkman with great politeness that I object to buying boiled milk, what does the milkman do but fly into a passion and cast up my nation in my teeth, by declaring, through the midst of very profane language — I concluded that it was profane by the tone — that English people always eat everything raw. If it had not been for my wife, Lady Blanche Howard's nerves, I should have taken some severe measures against that milkman."

"Lady Blanche Howard," repeated Kurt; "then you are — "

The Englishman, who had been staring moodily at a pool, started up and interrupted Kurt almost with violence. "*Not* My lord Ouare, and *not* Sir Hovart, and *not* Mr. Blanche, Esq. I entreat of you not to call me by any of these preposterous names. You may not believe it, but it is a fact that since my arrival here I have daily had my temper tried by being thus addressed; by each and all of these abominations have I been separately called. I put it to you as a man whether this is not hard?"

"Very much so," agreed Kurt, whom nothing but the merest chance had saved from a similar offence.

"I put it to you as a man whether this is not a simple case: My name is Howard, and I married an earl's daughter, being a commoner myself; consequently, my wife is Lady Blanche Howard. I have explained this over and over again, until I was hoarse; and at the end they smile thankfully and say, 'I understand, Sir Hovart,' or they simper and murmur, 'Good morning, Lady Houare.' If my father were alive, they would compromise the matter by calling me Sir Howard, junior; I know they would. They persist in turning me into a lord, and my wife into a commoner, and they harp upon the subject with every imaginable variation, only that they never alight upon the right one by any chance; enough to try the serenest temper on earth." And Mr. Howard, as he gave his pent-up feelings play, exercised part of them upon his wide-awake, which he had taken from his head and was twisting between his hands with an energy which only the texture of a best London-made hat could triumphantly resist. The crushing of the wide-awake was an evident relief to his feelings, for after a minute he put it on again, and drawing a long breath, turned a composed face upon Kurt.

"If you don't fish, what do you do?" he asked, abruptly. The transition from excitement to calmness took place without any intermediate phases.

"I mean to go up the mountains when the heat permits it."

"Ah!" Mr. Howard looked interested. "What is your object on the mountains?"

"Historical investigations, I believe. We are looking for a place which my father discovered years ago."

"Discoveries!" Mr. Howard looked more interested. "Do you go alone?"

"I go with my sister."

A sister! Mr. Howard lost his interest at once. He would have preferred the young man to be an isolated fact, unhampered by relations. This foreign youth was abnormal and exceptional, but a sister was a terrible disadvantage.

"Would you like to come with us?" suggested Kurt, good-naturedly.

"Thank you; you are very kind," said the broad-shouldered Englishman, staring down at the gnome-like figure beside him; "but — but I do not mean to make more acquaintances at present."

"Well, I thought you did not look very keen about making my acquaintance."

"H'm," said Mr. Howard. "The truth is that when you addressed me, I thought — in fact, I — I fancied — "

"Don't be shy, please," said Kurt, kindly.

"Well, I fancied that you were going to ask me for money. You were not thinking of it, were you?" With a faint revival of the former anxiety.

"No, it did not occur to me at the moment," said the imperturbable Kurt, "or I certainly should have done it."

Mr. Howard grasped the hand of his new acquaintance. "You ought to have been born an Englishman," he exclaimed, with an almost fierce energy. The coolness, the self-possession, the *insouciance* of this strange boy-man was exactly the thing that hit Mr. Howard's crooked fancy to a nicety. It was almost a regret to him when, a few minutes later, the young foreigner took his leave, saying that his sister was waiting for him on in advance.

But in this Kurt was mistaken. His sister had long since given up waiting for him, and, wandering on unprotected, had met with an adventure of her own.

Chapter XIV

The Bohemian

"Now, if ye ask me from what land I come – "

— Morris

GRETCHEN'S reflections were profound as she slowly followed the path
by the river; and it was with a look of dissatisfaction that her eyes swept
the steep hillside. She was almost tired of scanning the green wooded
slope, and of wondering where lay *Gaura Dracului*, and where stood the giant beech
which her father had marked with three crosses twenty years ago. Even had the heat
been less intense than it now was, her investigations must needs have come to a
standstill. All her inquiries had not even enabled her to find in the valley any man,
woman, or child who knew the fabulous hole, except through tradition. After the
glimpse she had had of the world above, she no longer spoke of seeking *Gaura Dracului à la bonne aventure* among its mazes. The mountains had baffled her for the
moment; Baron Tolnay had failed her — as a guide; and yet, so keen was the interest
which she felt in her father's old manuscript, that as she now wandered beside the
Djernis it was *Gaura Dracului* alone which filled her thoughts. After having succeeded in rekindling the flame of interest in her father's mind — after having been
witness of the genuine disappointment which the first failure had brought him —
she felt that now to abandon her project would be tame and spiritless. Something of
obstinacy too — something of pugnacity — may have served to fix the idea in her

head. At school, she had never tried for a prize without getting it;· and she had no more idea of being beaten by these mountains than by her school-fellows.

Meanwhile, the last glow of sunset had faded from the mountain tops., and the voice of the river grew more mysterious in the shadow. It craved Gretchen perforce to listen to the songs it was singing; and presently it seemed to her that the river was singing a song about *Gaura Dracului* — or was it her own thoughts that lent the words to the music? *Gaura Dracului*, and again *Gaura Dracului*, its bubbling voice proclaimed. It grew more distinct; it grew more human and less watery — till Gretchen, standing still to listen, could hear a man's voice singing somewhere close at hand:

> *Bats now sleep,*
> *Flowers peep,*
> *Red the dawn upon the hill.*
> *Wherefore art thou watching, lady?*
> *Wherefore art thou watching still?*
> *Beware, beware!*
> *Of Gaura Dracului beware!*
>
> *"Flies the night?*
> *Dawns the light?*
> *Without him it dawns in vain.*
> *E'er another day have broken*
> *From the wars he comes again;*
> *Then, then,*
> *He comes again!*
>
> *"Breezes sigh*
> *Far and nigh,*
> *Green the mountain, green the vale.*
> *Wherefore art thou weeping, lady?*
> *Wherefore is thy cheek so pale?*

Beware, beware!
Of Gaura Dracului beware!

"Sighs the breeze?
Bud the trees?
Shines the summer sky still blue?
Tears do blind me; for my lover
Calls me false, though I am true.
False, false,
Though I am true.

"Thunders growl,
Storm-winds howl,
Death upon the blast doth ride.
What is it thou seek'st, dark warrior —
Seek'st thus in the forest-wide?
Beware, beware!
Of Gaura Dracului beware!

"Blows the gale ?
Storms the hail?
Naught I hear but fury's cry;
For a grave I seek, a deep one,
And therein my love must lie:
Deep, deep,
My love must sleep.

"Clouds are rent,
Tree-stems bent,
Forked tongues of lightning pierce.
Wherefore must thy love die, warrior?
Wherefore is thine eye so fierce?

Fly, fly!
There Gaura Dracului doth lie!

"Tears the blast?
Speeds it fast?
Naught I feel but fury's sway;
For my love she hath betrayed me,
Whilst I tarried far away.
Far, far,
'Twas far away!

"Specters moan,
Branches groan,
Shrieks the death-crow: Thou shalt rue!
For 'tis here thy lady sleepeth,
Sleepeth with her heart so true;
Alas, alas!
*In Gaura Dracului, alas!"**

Thus ran the plaintive song, monotonous and melancholy, and the Djernis played a wild accompaniment to the melodious voice of the singer.

The singer? Yes; but where could he be? In the clouds apparently, for no human being was within eye-range. Where Gretchen now stood, the valley was extremely narrow; but the rocks at the mountain-base were broken up, and between these blocks small patches of Indian corn waved their array of broad blades, apple and cherry trees stood squeezed wherever space would permit, and despite their cramped positions had thrived so luxuriantly that a corner of thatched roof was all that betrayed the smothered farm hut.

---

*In rendering this song, more attention has been paid to literal translation than to the exigencies of English versification.

It was at the foot of one of the apple trees that Gretchen's surprise bad brought her to a standstill. Of the whole Romanian song she had understood nothing but the ever-recurring words of *Gaura Dracului*: they were enough to make her turn her eyes eagerly and curiously about her, and finally above her; for from the branches of the apple tree a shower of fresh-scented hay now came rustling down upon her.

Raising her head, she perceived that the apple tree, curiously enough, was doing duty as a haystack. With its branches groaning under the double weight of green fruit and newly cut hay, the overworked apple tree did not look unlike some strange sort of giant toadstool sprung up in the shade of the rocks.

"The singer is up there," thought Gretchen, as a renewed rustling swayed the branches above her head; and for a moment she stood hesitating as to how to address him, for to address him she was resolved.

Her hesitation was not long; calling all her linguistical powers to her aid, she raised her voice and hazarded a rather uncertain *"Bunje sara !"* (Good evening).

The rustling ceased, and a moment's silence followed; then a branch was bent aside, and a head which looked anything but a Romanian head dived out of the green leaves.

Gretchen had expected to see one of those dusky physiognomies with which the valley abounded, but to her surprise she found her glance met by a pair of singularly clear blue eyes, which gazed at her with a sort of timid inquiry from out of a pale narrow face, sun-tanned in complexion, but of a curious delicacy in all its lines. Having made a rapid inspection, Gretchen decided that this man would serve her purpose. If this gentle-looking creature possessed the necessary knowledge, there surely could be no difficulty in bending him to her will.

The blue eyes gazed at her full for some seconds, and then a sad and gentle voice answered her greeting with *"Guten Abend!"*

"German!" said Gretchen, in astonishment. "Are you a German?"

"I am a Bohemian," said the man in the tree. "I come from near Choteborschwitz."

If this gentle-looking creature possessed the necessary knowledge,
there surely could be no difficulty in bending him to her will.

"Really," said Gretchen, much relieved; for her first address had exhausted the entire stock of her Romanian. "And how do you happen to be here?"

"I was born here."

"Then how did your father come here?"

"My father also was born here,"

"Oh," said Gretchen, beginning to think that this was a rather strange sort of Bohemian; "and your grandfather, was he born here too?"

The question seemed to agitate the man in the tree considerably; and the apple tree branches caught the agitation from him and rustled noisily.

"No," he said, hurriedly, while his clear blue eyes clouded, "my grandfather was not born here, but — he died here." The man nervously plucked off a leaf and tore it in two.

"He was born at Choteborschwitz, I suppose," suggested Gretchen.

"Yes, of course, where I come from."

"Have you been there much?"

"I have never been there at all. I was born here, and have lived here all my life."

"And you call yourself a Bohemian?"

He gazed down at her wonderingly with his straight blue eyes. "Of course, I am a Bohemian; I come from near Choteborschwitz."

"Is your wife a Bohemian too?" she asked, afraid of having hurt this curious man's feelings.

Perhaps, after all, the gentle timid creature might not be as easy to deal with as she had fancied; there was a tenacity about his ideas which she had not expected to meet.

He shook his head sadly. "I have got no wife; there is no wife for me here."

"Oh, but there must be," said Gretchen, whose curiosity began to be piqued.

The Bohemian shook his head again with the same gentle, subdued melancholy. "I cannot afford the journey; my country is too far off."

"The journey! But are there no women here?"

Again, from out of the frame of green leaves and unripe apples the clear eyes were fixed on her with an expression of surprise and reproach.

"But they are Romanians!" he said, in a tone which was only a gentler and softer edition of that in which the Englishman had pronounced the obnoxious "Worm." "How could I marry a Romanian ?"

"I don't know," said Gretchen, rather puzzled, for she was not aware that to marry a Romanian is as much beneath a Bohemian's dignity as to fish with worm is for an Englishman.

"My father fetched his wife from home," went on the Bohemian. "He had more money than I have. It does not matter much," he added, simply; "perhaps it is the wish of Providence that our family should die out: this place brings us no luck."

"And you live quite alone?"

"My old mother lives with me; she has broken both her legs."

"Poor woman l"

"Oh no; she is quite happy; she lies in bed and says her beads all day. She could not be more contented if she were at home in Bohemia, instead of in this strange land."

This picture of the household in the valley was not enlivening.

"Why did your family settle here at all," asked Gretchen, "if they did not like the place?"

"He was tempted by the Government," said the Bohemian, looking not at Gretchen, but at his own apples.

"Who was tempted?"

"My grandfather. The Government wanted a man of my nation to supply the visitors here with milk and butter. They promised him this farm if he would settle here; and the prospect of fortune dazzled him, for he loved money — my grandfather — he loved it more than his soul." The Bohemian heaved a profound sigh. "But the place brought him no luck. It would have been better for him had he never seen another land but his own, and never heard or spoken another language but his own Bohemian tongue."

It was evident that for some reason this grandfather was a sore point; and afraid of having touched upon some painful family history, Gretchen left the subject for another.

"But that song you have been singing was not a Bohemian song," she said; "it was Romanian."

"So it was," conceded the man, as reluctantly as though he were apologizing for his past performance. "I have had to learn the language of this foreign land, just as I am obliged to have my milk carried by a foreign girl. But I know plenty of Bohemian songs," he added, promptly.

"I suppose so," said Gretchen, rather apprehensively, for her object was not to hear Bohemian songs just then. "But I wanted to ask whether you would translate for me the words you were singing; I only understood two of them."

"Immediately, Fraulein." His face disappeared among the leaves, the branches closed over him for a moment, in the next, he had slid down the trunk and stood before Gretchen.

Unencumbered by the apple tree leaves, the strange refinement of this peasant was even more conspicuous. He was of middle stature, slight, fair-haired, and not looking much over thirty; though the melancholy grace which pervaded his face, his manner, and his tone, made him look older in expression.

He removed his cap with a gesture of courtesy that might almost be called polished; his movements and his voice were softened and moderated as the manners of peasants rarely are.

"It is only a foolish Romanian song, Fräulein," he observed having translated to her the verses as she asked.

"Foolish? Well, yes; all songs that are mixed up with love must be more or less foolish," said Gretchen, whose fancy was taken by the song, despite the folly. "But is there any foundation for it? Is there any truth in it?"

The Bohemian shrugged his shoulders.

"I cannot say, Fräulein, whether there is any truth in it; if there is, it is not the fault of the Romanians — for when they speak the truth, it is usually by accident. They do say that long ago a Roman soldier, believing that his lady-love had betrayed him, cast her down an abyss, and went mad when he discovered her innocence."

"It does well enough for a song, at any rate," said Gretchen — "and the tune suits the words."

"Did not the Fräulein say that she understood some of the words?"

"Yes; but only two of them. I do not speak Romanian, but two of the words you sang were familiar to me."

"And which were those two words?" he respectfully inquired.

"Those which occur oftenest."

"*Gaura Dracului?*" he asked — a little anxiously, it seemed to Gretchen.

"Yes; *Gaura Dracului.*"

The Bohemian twisted his straw hat between his hands, then put it on his head nervously, and took it off again.

"These are only silly old legends," he exclaimed in haste. "Those foolish Romanian tales are not to be believed."

"But such a place as *Gaura Dracului* does exist?" asked Gretchen, keenly eying her informer.

"Why should such a place not exist?" answered the Bohemian, faintly.

"And do you know the place?"

He hesitated for a moment, and then, with his eyes fixed on a far-off patch of corn, he answered, "No, I do not."

"Yes, you do," said Gretchen, gazing still attentively at the Bohemian, as he stood two paces from her, a foreground figure, painted in pale touches and seen full against the background of dark green mountains, fast deepening to black in the gloom.

The Bohemian looked from the corn-blades to the thatched roof of his hut, from the roof to his apple trees, from the apple trees to his own feet, from these finally straight into Gretchen's face. He could not meet her eyes for a moment without speaking the truth.

"God help me," he said, "it is the first lie I have told in my life.

Yes, I know the place."

"And will you take me there?" asked Gretchen, joyfully.

"Take you there?" cried the man, starting back. "*Heilige Mutter-Gottes* of the Wunderbaum at Choteborschwitz! Not for all the gold that lies buried in that devil's hole!"

"Gold?" repeated Gretchen, forgetting her astonishment at this sudden energy in the surprise of the revelation. "Is there gold in *Gaura Dracului?*"

"Thirty-eight Turkish gold-bags, one hundred and fifty silver bags, nine hundred and ninety Russian rubles, five thousand *Bejas Jirmilik*" — enumerated the Bohemian rapidly — "three golden chalices, seventeen golden necklaces, and earrings as much as would fill three full-grown skulls; that was the list which the last of the brigands confessed in the Arad prison."

"Then it is a brigands' treasure," said Gretchen, somewhat bewildered by this dazzling ·list. "But how does the brigands' treasure come to be down the devil's hole?"

"Just because it is the devil's hole, Fräulein. The brigands knew well enough that they could find no safer hiding place for their gold than this spot haunted by evil spirits. No one knows how they reached the bottom of the terrible place, or whether they knew some secret outlet that led to and from it. The story runs that the gold lies

---

*The Turkish *gold-bag* (at 30,000 piastres) amounts to about £225; the *silver-bag* (at 500 piastres) to about £8 15s. Both the Russian ruble and the *Bejas Jirmilik* are worth 3s.

exposed, bare and open to the light of day, at a spot where the midday sun strikes it daily."

"But what good could they have of their treasure down there?" asked Gretchen, whom· the whole proceeding struck as deficient in logic.

The Bohemian gave a contemptuous laugh.

"They were Romanians, Fräulein; and give only a silver florin to a Romanian, and he will bury it at once, as a dog buries a bone. Each of these brigands had pledged himself by the most horrible oaths never to touch the gold except in presence of the others. But the band was dispersed, and the last survivor died in prison at Arad two hundred years ago. The treasure was sought for, but never found."

Gretchen stood pensive; not a word of the story had escaped her, and with each of them her interest in the mysterious hole had steadily increased.

"Will you show me the way there?" she asked again.

It had grown too dark to judge of the Bohemian's expression, but his voice betrayed renewed agitation.

"*Heilige Jungfrau von* Chotebor — "

Gretchen cut the exclamation short.

"You call yourself a Bohemian," she said, scornfully, "and you are as frightened by the foolish superstition as any Romanian could be."

An instant change came over the man. He grew all at once very quiet, and in a solemn whisper he replied,

"Frightened? Yes, Fräulein, I am frightened; but not of the devils; it is of the *Heilige Jungfrau* of Choteborschwitz that I should be frightened, were I to show you that place."

"Of Choteborschwitz?" repeated Gretchen, at a loss to see any connection between a far-off Bohemian place of pilgrimage and the abyss among the mountains.

The Bohemian had come a step nearer, and spoke still in a whisper, as though afraid that the chattering Djernis should catch up his secret and publish it to the world.

"Fräulein," he said, slowly, "I have made a vow — "

"Yes?" she asked, with strained attention.

"Never to reveal the spot of *Gaura Dracului*."

She gazed at him searchingly and in silence.

"And the reason of the vow?" she asked at last.

"That I cannot reveal. My father made me swear it to the Blessed Virgin of the Wunderbaum at Choteborschwitz. I was only seven years old at the time."

"No vow made at that age could be binding."

"Every vow is binding, Fräulein. You would not have me load my conscience with a broken oath?" and he looked at her with his beseeching blue eyes, as if entreating her not to lay this burden of guilt upon his innocent soul.

Baffled again! She could scarcely believe it. What was she to do? How to overcome these mysterious obstacles which on every side encompassed the discovery of Gaura Dracului? The person who was willing to take her there was ignorant of the spot, and the person who knew it was not willing to take her.

"And yet I must find it!" she exclaimed aloud.

"I cannot break my vow," said the Bohemian simply.

She argued eloquently in the falling dusk, and the Bohemian listened patiently, opposing to the active attack nothing but passive resistance, repeating only in his sad voice that he could not break his vow. The melancholy politeness of this gentle-spoken man was far more difficult to deal with than would have been the boorishness of a common peasant. It was hardly possible to find an answer to this despairing simplicity.

He would guide her to any other place she wished, the poor man humbly explained; he would take her up every mountain in the neighborhood — he would do anything except show her the way to *Gaura Dracului*. But nothing except *Gaura Dracului* would satisfy Gretchen. She coldly declined the proffered services, and with rising temper, she declared that she would find the place without his help.

"I hope to God that you will not, Fräulein, for that terrible spot will bring you no luck."

"*I* am not superstitious, though you may be," called back the incensed Gretchen over her shoulder, for she had already turned from him; and, without vouchsafing any answer to his timid "*Gute Nacht*, Fräulein," she walked quickly along the homeward path, leaving the Bohemian standing alone under his apple tree, and repeating mournfully to himself,

"I cannot break my vow."

Chapter XV

Devotions and Emotions

"Yes, the fashion is the fashion."

— *Much Ado about Nothing*

"**Y**ES, my dear, it is all very pretty," said the Contessa Belita Francopazzi, sauntering along the arcades on the arm of her friend — "it is all excessively pretty, but I see no toilets."

The sleeve which rested on Gretchen's arm was a chef-d'oeuvre of fashionable elegance, the color known in the Parisian world as *fumée de cigarette*, and the shape as *pétroleuse*. The dress of which that sleeve was a part, expressed in the drapery of the tunic, in every inch of the *volant à la nihiliste*, in the luster of each button, that it was a dress constructed and modeled after the highest laws of French taste. The wearer of this faultless costume was a tall, yellow-skinned, vivacious Italian. She was not handsome; and devoid of this excess of elegance, it is impossible to say whether she might not perhaps have been ugly. But she never was visible except *en toilette*; and when thus seen, it was not possible to fix your attention on the wearer, so rapidly were your thoughts taken up by the intricacies of the toilet itself. The weaker sex fell down and adored, the stronger sex stood dazzled and bewildered.

The woman was so entirely lost sight of in the dress that no one ever thought of criticizing her features, any more than people think of criticizing the features of the figurine on a French fashion-plate; and if anyone ever happened to notice the proportions of her stature, it was only to remark that she made a good lay-figure for displaying the draperies of an elaborate dress.

It was but yesterday that Belita had arrived, and already she was beginning to reproach Gretchen with her "heartless deception," as she called it. Beside her there walked a small, pale, whiskerless man, carrying her parasol, and looking up with humble admiration into his wife's face.

"But it seems to me there are a good many toilets," said Gretchen, looking about her.

"*Misericordia!* those are not toilets; they are mere dresses. I shall leave this place tomorrow."

"Nonsense! you will not. Wait till Sunday — you may see some toilets in church; and then, after that, wait till Thursday — they dance in the *Cursalon* on Thursday."

· "Do they? and they pray on Sunday! That may suit. I have a toilette de *prière*, designed expressly for a kneeling posture, and with an *abbesse* train which is very effective. And for Thursday — let me see — my Wörth with the mother-o'-pearl embroidery would be the right thing; *couleur jambe de nymphe* — not the ordinary shade, you know, but the new tint, *jambe de nymphe émue*."

The arcades at this hour held all the essence of fashionable life under its Byzantine columns. Every bench was occupied, every shop was plying a busy trade; voices ran high, and as a sort of harmonious background to this foreground of discord, the variations of a Servian *Stolo* floated out through the open door of the Cursalon.

"Who is that bowing to you?" asked Belita, as a large black hat came off to Gretchen. Dr. Kokovics was passing with a packet of lottery tickets in one hand, and a roll of tinsel paper in the other, but had found time to execute an eloquent bow and direct a languishing glance towards Gretchen. The glance did not escape Belita's attention.

"*Touché au coeur?*" she inquired. "Ah, I thought so; and now, my dear, that brings me to the question I wanted to ask. Margherita" — this more solemnly — "how stand your chances of fortune?"

"They could not stand better," was the perfectly ready answer, in which rung an unmistakable triumph. "In the first place, as I told you, Draskócs — "

"Oh, spare me Draskócs! That sleepy lawyer of yours will never — "

"The sleepy lawyer, it so happens, is down at Draskócs at this very moment; who knows what he may do there? And, Belita, in the second place — "

"Here is another hat coming off," interrupted Belita. "Who is this?"

Gretchen had no time to answer, for Baron Tolnay was already close. He stopped, as a matter of course; there was an introduction, in which the conte was forgotten by everybody, and then Baron Tolnay turned to walk once down the arcades with them.

"I wish it could be more than once," he said with a sigh, "but I have business this afternoon. Tiresome business! never so tiresome as when it robs me of such pleasure!"

The turn down the arcades did not occupy more than three minutes, but these three minutes were put to good use by Belita. In the first minute she suspected the truth, in the second she was certain of it, in the third she mentally analyzed, dissected, summed up, and approved of the case.

"My dear child," she broke out, when, after much-outspoken regret, Baron Tolnay had bowed himself off — "my dear child, is that what you meant by 'the second place?'"

"Yes," said Gretchen, in an entirely matter-of-fact tone. "Baron Tolnay is in the second place."

"Then I should certainly put him in the first; the cut of his coat is simply divine. He is the omnipotent baron who reigns in the valley, is he not? Yes? I thought so. This is a perfect prize to have gained; only — only, Margherita — "

"Only what?"

"Only you have not gained him yet. Oh, I have good eyes, my child; I can read a man at a glance, and Baron Tolnay is what I should call a slippery man. Yes, just because of those fiery eyes; they have had much practice, those eyes — frequent practice and hot practice. Don't look discouraged, Bambina; though no other woman has caught him yet, there is no reason why you should not catch this light-hearted baron. If you can, it will be a triumph!"

There was a moment's silence as the two women walked on, arm-in-arm. Gretchen's cheek was slightly flushed, but her lips remained locked, for no suitable answer occurred to her, and it would not have done to betray to Belita that which she did not like to confess to herself — namely, that her vanity was smarting sorely under the doubt thus thrown upon the conquest which she had looked on as complete. The seed, unknown to herself, was already growing fast. "If I can, it will be a triumph!" it echoed in her secret heart.

"Yes; a triumph," repeated Belita, as her friend did not speak·; "but it will require management. It will require also a little of what people call 'flirtation.' Not a bad thing in its way, though I never cared for it myself — my toilets did not give me time to cultivate the accomplishment; but I dare say, in countries where your marriages are not arranged for you, it may sometimes be useful. Such eyes as yours, however, are almost too dangerous for the game; and I perceive with anxiety that you know how to raise and lower that silken curtain with a terrible effect."

"Only as a necessary part of the process," Gretchen hastened to reply; and then went on to explain that, from her point of view, flirtation, together with dancing, social gatherings, and morning visits, ranged as a certain set of means, through which help a certain end was to be reached. It appeared further, from the tone of her apology, that what charms she possessed were regarded in the same light; and that her eyes, her complexion, and her hair were valued by her only so far as they represented a certain amount of capital to be judiciously invested.

Belita listened, and burst out laughing. "You are wasting your trouble, child. What is the use of putting on those little strong-minded airs with me? You know you only do so in order to keep up your reputation for logic. I am not in the least convinced, and again I say that flirtation may not be a bad thing — in moderation; only I fancy that it is easily overdone; and I hope, Margherita, that you do not overdo it?"

"But have I not explained myself? Why do you ask again?"

"Because, my child, I have been a little uneasy about you since that letter — you know which — that phrase about there being only one woman."

"Oh, don't tell me that again," cried Gretchen, putting her hands to her ears.

"*Misericordia!* what a temper! Well, never mind, Bambina. I meant to preach; but seeing that you are on the right road, after all, I defer my sermon. Mind, you must give me *carte blanche* for the *trousseau* — that is all I stipulate; and, of course, you must visit us in Italy. I hope we shall not quarrel. I will tell you what you must not do if we are not to quarrel."

"Flirt with your husband?" suggested Gretchen.

"No, my dear child; you may flirt with my husband as much as you like, but you must not dress better than I do. My friendship is very strong, but it is not quite strong enough for that."

"If that is all, our bond shall be immortal."

"By-the-bye, what do you think of Ludovico?" asked Belita, shrugging her left shoulder towards the conte, who had dropped behind and who appeared quite satisfied with gazing up at the back of his wife's coiffure.

"He seems very fond of you," said Gretchen.

"Margherita! I am surprised at you! I don't mean that; I mean his height. Ah, that is the one point I envy you in! You two will be a perfect match. You have no notion what difficulties I have about Ludovico's hats. I can't find them tall enough, and I can't find them to fit tight on his head. Just the one which became me best, which almost put us on the level, was blown away on the Danube. I must try the hat-shops here. Ah, there is a good hat, a wide-awake, and coming off to you too. Another acquaintance? The contessa sighed regretfully. "Ludovico can never, never wear a wide-awake; it would be perfect for setting off my bonnet, but it would cost him half a bead in stature. *Pazienza!* Everybody has a cross to bear in this world."

Mr. Howard was passing, and it was he whose wide-awake had been removed to Gretchen, for it was some time now since this Englishman had got over the disadvantage of his new friend having a sister. And more than this, he had been admitted into the secret of *Gaura Dracului*, and had developed an interest and energy which exactly suited Gretchen. Not that Mr. Howard, in his own language, cared a rush for historical investigation, nor for the idea of a black abyss without bottom; but the thought of being baffled by a set of foreign fellows was enough to set his British pugnacity in arms. He promised Adalbert, while he nearly crushed the sick man's hand between his two, that the place should be found, even though he had to knock down a few Romanians en route. In the meantime, he cultivated Kurt's society, using him as a confidant in whose ears to pour his daily stock of grievances. Today the accumulation was larger than usual, but it was not until later in the afternoon that he came across the listener he required. "Do you know what they have done to me?" said Mr. Howard, walking up to Kurt without further preamble and button-holing that young man.

Kurt confessed his ignorance.

"They have sent me Shakespeare to read," snorted Mr. Howard, "and Longfellow. Did you ever hear of such an insult? I suppose I may expect a spelling book next."

"Who is the offender?"

"That wretched little Dr. Funk; and what he means by it I cannot imagine. He looked quiet and unassuming enough; I should never have suspected him of such — such gross insolence."

"Perhaps he meant it well," suggested Kurt.

"If you had seen the note he had the audacity to send along with it, you would not think so. 'Sir, as you give yet three months to our mountains, I dare to offer you some distracting lecture,' and addressed — 'Lord Hovart, Esq.' I put it to you as a man whether that is not hard? The whole thing is a hoax, you know. If it were not for my wife Lady Blanche Howard's health, I should have nothing more to say to that doctor. And Shakespeare is not all; my temper has never before been tried to such an extent. Take my tub in the morning: what have I to undergo every day? I say, 'Give me a tub of cold water.' Can anything be simpler? Do you know what they do? They give me a little tepid water in a foot-bath. I dispatch the footbath and ask for a tub. Next day, I get a narrow barrel four feet high, smelling all over of salt herring. I can't get into that, you know, for I don't happen to have been educated as an acrobat. I explain myself clearly then — too clearly, it seems, for the result is that my room has become an exhibition for all sorts of water-holding vessels: there are low tubs and high tubs standing in unexpected places at all hours of the day; I dare not make a step without looking before me. Yesterday, I stumbled over one and flooded the passage. The waiter and the housemaids appear six times a day, with a grin and an inquiry whether I don't want more *Wasser? Wasser, Wasser, Wasser* is being dinned in my ears from morning to night. When are you going to try the hills again?"

Kurt was accustomed to these sudden transitions of ideas. "Not while this heat lasts. And when are you going to try the river?"

"When there is a little water in it."

To Kurt's uninitiated eye there seemed to be a good deal of water in the river, but Mr. Howard declared there was none.

The hills were continually in Gretchen 's thoughts; but they were unfeasible for the moment, and a more immediate object occupied her. Belita had persuaded Madame Mohr to take Gretchen to the *Cursalon* on Thursday evening, when there was to be dancing. Baron Tolnay had supported the idea, and Ascelinde had consented. "Come to me tomorrow afternoon," the contessa said to her friend, "and I will show you my *jambe de nymphe* silk." Accordingly, Gretchen went, but entering she found Belita pale, and wringing her hands with an emotion of which Gretchen had scarcely thought her capable.

"You find me disheveled and despairing," said Belita to her visitor.

"Has anything happened?"

"Eh, *sicúro!* a misfortune has happened."

"To the conte?"

"Oh, not to him; I have sent him to the telegraph office."

"To whom, then?"

"But to me, to my Wörth dress. My dear child, imagine the scene which has just taken place. I begin to unpack it — the dress I am to wear on Thursday. I knew it was in box No. 9. I open box No. 9, and there lies the body; it was like seeing the face of an old friend. I lift it out tenderly — ah, so tenderly — and put it on the bed; then I return for the skirt. I cannot believe my eyes as I look into the box, for the skirt is not there. I call my maid. 'Marietta,' I say, as calmly as I can, 'where is my *jambe de nymphe* silk skirt?' She suggests box No. 13. A minute later, she returns as pale as a sheet., and says, 'No. 13 is not there.' 'Not where?' I ask. 'Not here in our rooms; not here at all — not come to the Hercules Baths!' Margherita, can you understand my sensations? Can you feel for my sufferings?" The contessa had risen as she reached the climax, but now sat down again, wringing her hands as before; as before, despairing and disheveled — that is to say clothed in a perfectly got-up *robe de chambre*, whose details were more elaborate than the visiting dresses of ordinary mortals and with a *négligé* cap of real lace perched upon her head.

"Wear something else," said Gretchen, unfeelingly.

"My dear child, I have nothing else."

"Wear that lilac," pointing to a rich satin.

"Impossible! That dress needs a combination of circumstances. It can only be worn in the foyer of a large theatre in the height of the season, and on the evening of a *première*."

"That dirty-white, then, might do."

"That is not dirty-white, my dear child; that is the newest fashionable shade — *brebis égarée*. But it is only a standing dress — it is not meant to sit down in; and really, in this heat, I do not feel equal to standing a whole evening."

"That dark silk, then."

"That Carmélite? Why, that is a *toilette de caréme;* you taste fried fish and *maigre* soup merely by looking at it. No," said the contessa, "my Wörth dress was the dress for the occasion. Poor Ludovico! I do not blame him; he is as much in despair as I am. I have sent him to telegraph to every station on the road, but I have little hope of recovering it in time. No," with another sigh, "it is not on Thursday that my hopes are now fixed; it is on Sunday. Woe to you if you have deceived me about the toilets in church!"

Sunday came in due time — a broiling hot Sunday, when the sun, hanging in the quivering sky, glared down upon the rocks and made the cold Djernis warm. Belita's *toilette de prière* was a little oppressive in this weather, but she could be heroic in moments like this. The point to be aimed at on such a day, as she explained to Gretchen while resolutely making her way down the old street towards the Latin chapel at the end, was not so much to be cool as to look it. The Latin chapel stood at the spot where, centuries ago, the old temple of Hercules had stood in the time of the Romans. The conte, in the tallest of hats, carried his wife's prayer book after her. Gretchen was with them; for when the decisive moment came, Madame Mohr, trembling at the idea of crossing that burning space, had become imbued with a sudden desire to sit beside poor Adalbert. "I really do not feel up to the exertion," she had said with dignified melancholy; "I shall not attempt to leave the house today."

The churchgoers had reached the steps which lead up to the chapel.

"Does my tunic fall in good folds?" asked Belita of her friend, pausing halfway up the steps, and throwing an anxious glance over her draperies.

To the left of the chapel the wooded bank sloped upward, dark green against the clear blue sky; from below, on the right, the sound of rushing water came up where the Djernis tossed, moaning, over its stony bed.

"Oh, quite right," said Gretchen, looking the other way.

"You are not attending," said Belita, with displeasure; "you are looking out for Baron Tolnay, instead of telling me about my tunic."

"Oh, your tunic does not need me, you vainest of all contessas; the folds fall smoother than any moonbeams."

"Then let us come and pray," said the contessa, with a sigh of satisfaction; and they disappeared together within the shade of the chapel.

The chapel was small and crowded, the *toilette de priere* fitted very tightly, and at the end of three-quarters of an hour the contessa was glad to emerge from her bench, and to exchange the stuffy air even for the roasting sun outside.

"You have deceived me," was the first thing she said, apparently the upshot of her devotions; "there was not a toilet in church."

Gretchen made no answer; she was gazing curiously at something in the street.

"What are you looking at?" asked Belita, standing on the steps and unfurling her gray silk parasol.

"Can it be?" said Gretchen. "No, it cannot be — yes, it is — it is mamma."

"*Misericordia!* so it is! Coming down the street without a bonnet. My dear child, what does this mean? Your mother declared herself too weak to leave the house today, and here she comes in a dress which ought never to have been seen in public, and without a bonnet."

"She has got something in her hand," said Gretchen, pressing forward.

"A piece of paper," said Belita.

"A letter," suggested the conte, humbly.

"She is laughing," said Gretchen.

"No, she is crying."

"I think she is doing both," said Ludovico.

They had got near enough to the approaching figure to perceive a strange tumult of expression on Ascelinde's features. She advanced towards them with the step of a tragic heroine, her skirt trailing heavily in the dust, her uncovered head exposed to the beating sun, while, with the fixity of a stage gesture, she held out a sheet of writing towards the approaching party. Her eyes shone in a sort of intoxication, like the eyes of a queen who has been newly crowned. "What has happened, mamma?" asked Gretchen. "What is that letter?"

"Embrace me, my daughter," said the mother, superbly opening her arms. "Come, let us return thanks for the greatness of this blessing;" and she dragged Gretchen forward towards the chapel. "Ah, have they closed it already?" — for just this instant the key grated in the lock, and the sacristan tripped down the steps, light of heart, having shut up devotion for another week.

"That is a letter from Dr. Komers," said Gretchen, as she caught sight of the writing.

"Have you had good or bad news?" inquired Belita.

"Good!" said Ascelinde, in a tone of passionate grief. "Dr. Komers is a villain, a heartless, unconscientious man," she added, in the same breath.

"Mamma!" cried Gretchen, beginning to tremble, she knew not why.

"Who is Dr. Komers?" asked Belita. "Is that the sleepy lawyer?"

"He is a lawyer, at any rate," said Gretchen; "but whether sleepy or not, this letter will perhaps tell us."

"He is the family adviser," said Ascelinde; "but he is without conscience and without heart, and I — I am the happiest woman in the world;" and suddenly producing a handkerchief with an embroidered monogram and coronet, she burst into tears before their eyes.

Of the whole party, Gretchen alone retained presence of mind. Leading her mother to a retired bench, she proceeded to do the only rational thing that was to be done — namely, to extract from Madame Mohr's fingers the letter, on which several enormous teardrops had already splashed. With the eyes of the conte and contessa upon her, Gretchen read aloud the following communication:

"Hadháza, July 7th.

'DEAR MADAME, — I reached this five days ago, and send these few lines in a hurry to give you a strange piece of news. There being only one post a day from this place, I am forced to be very short in order to catch it: I can do no more than state the facts without details. I have, quite by accident and in the most extraordinary manner, come upon a will, which, though roughly drawn out, is indisputably valid, signed by your grandfather — by reason of which will Draskócs now, beyond the possibility of a doubt, belongs to your brother Alexius, though it will take a few weeks before his rights are established. I am truly sorry for any disappointment which you may feel and hope you may not be disagreeably touched. A detailed account shall be forwarded shortly. At this moment, I am called home by news of my sister's illness.

"Yours truly, VINCENZ KOMERS."

"Draskócs is won," said Gretchen, looking up with a slight flush on her face.

"Felicisco!" cried Belita, exultantly; "I would embrace you, my dear child, if it were not for my sleeves!"

"Felicisco!" repeated the small conte, like an echo.

"But it is not ours," sobbed Madame Mohr. "It would have been ours if I had not allowed myself to be persuaded out of it by Dr. Komers. He may well be sorry for the disappointment which I feel as it is his fault alone. To think that the home of my ancestors might have been ours for ten thousand florins! I shall never have such a chance again."

It was a delicate point to determine whether condolences or congratulations were the most appropriate for the occasion.

The conte looked at his wife for instructions, but Belita looked at nothing but her friend. Gretchen's face was still flushed, her eyes were shining. It was more to herself than to the others that she said, half aloud, "So after forty-three years, it is he who has ended it."

"What triumph!" burst out Ascelinde, with kindling eyes; "but there is no merit in finding a will when once it is there."

"Only that nobody else found it," said Gretchen.

"The family glory is retrieved! Dear Alexius! I shall never forgive Dr. Komers. It is the happiest day in my life. Ah, but — if Draskócs were ours!"

The struggle between smiles and tears, between triumph and dejection, was so violent that Gretchen thought it advisable quickly to regain the privacy of their apartments. Arrived there, the first thing that Ascelinde did was, with the help of the whole family, to write out a telegram of felicitation to her brother Alexius, and then burst into violent sobs as soon as it was gone. Till evening closed, and her weary head sank down on her pillow, Madame Mohr continued to vacillate between the extremes of passionate joy and frantic grief. Glances of triumph were quenched in tears; phrases begun in lamentations rose to exultant speeches. A bitter drop fell into the glass in which she was drinking to her brother's health. Alexius was alternately designated as the most exalted of mortals and the unworthy inheritor of so much magnificence. The memory of her guardian Jósika was treated sometimes with veneration, sometimes with abhorrence. On one point only did the agitated Ascelinde remain firm — persistent abuse of the family lawyer. All the evils and none of the goods of her position were to be attributed to Dr. Komers. He had misguided her by his advice; he gave no details about this mysterious will; he was leaving the place instead of remaining there to guard her brother's interests — alas! that they were not her own! "And," said Ascelinde, coming to this climax regularly at the end of every hour's talking, "he does not even take the trouble to mention how many years ago my guardian died."

It was the happiest and the most miserable day in Ascelinde's life.

Chapter XVI

Pater Dionysius

" What a strange thing is man, and what a stranger is woman!"

— Byron

ANNA KOMERS was lying on the sofa, paler and thinner than her usual self. She had been very ill, and her brother Vincenz, whom in the first fright of the attack she had summoned, sat beside her. It was but an hour ago that Vincenz came; he had been telling his sister the result of his journey.

"As I was saying," he resumed, "the house was quite shut up. I could not get admittance, and no one seems to know who is living there at present. The matter looked very hopeless. I think I might have turned back in discouragement if it had not been for the thought — "

"What thought, Vincenz?" asked Anna's thin voice so much more quavering than it was three months ago.

Vincenz passed his hand across his forehead.

"Never mind; it is only that I cannot bear being beaten. I was resolved to do something decisive. As a first step, I returned to the little inn where I had left my things, and I searched among all the papers I had brought with me — there were some addresses which Madame Mohr had given me. I scarcely hoped that they would prove of any use; but having no other clew to hold by, I remembered them now. There was, among others, the name of a family with whom Madame Mohr's mother

had been intimate. I took the slip of paper to the landlord of the inn and showed it
to him. To my agreeable surprise, he seemed to understand what I wanted in a moment. Could he direct me there? I asked. He would not only direct me there, he
would show me the way there himself; and taking his cap from the nail, he led the
way into the street. Every house in the street was of the humblest and rudest description. I could hardly fancy that the family I was in search of resided in one of these.
However, my conductor never faltered; he went straight up the whole length of the
squalid street: it was evident that the family lived outside in the country. After the
last of the houses there stood a low church of wood, stained brown; beside it a square
enclosure of planks with an unlocked gate. The landlord walked in here, apparently
with the intention of taking a shortcut through. I found myself in the middle of an
irregular and hillocky burying ground, where the nettles grew on the neglected
graves. My conductor stopped and pointed to a long row of mounds, some marked
with crosses and some without. 'That is them,' he said, laconically. Five green hillocks
was all that remained of the family! I stood and stared at the hillocks for I don't know
how long; but suddenly I remembered that I was losing my time. I thought I would
ask to see the grave of Jósika Damianovics, and I turned to ask the question; but the
landlord was gone, and I was quite alone in the cemetery. I made my way from one
cross to the other, trying to read the names on them, but many were worn out with
decay. On the fifth or sixth cross that I examined, I found the name of the old priest
who had been the friend of Madame Mohr's grandfather. He had been dead for
nearly fifty years. In leaving the cemetery, I perceived, close alongside of the church,
a house, which was a little whiter and a little larger than its neighbors. It was easy to
recognize this as the residence of the priest; and there I went, with what object in my
mind I really did not know, feeling more hopelessly discouraged than I had ever felt
before in all my life. I found a young, raw-looking priest in possession; he welcomed
me much as a good-natured peasant would, and informed me in Latin — a language
which I found much spoken by all classes down there — that he was the third suc-
cessor of the old priest whose name I mentioned, and whose grave I had seen. I assure
you, Anna, that at this stage of the proceeding there came over me a sort of Rip van

Winkle feeling. It seemed to me that I had slept a hundred years, and had awaked two generations too late. Fancy what dreary work it was making inquiries about people who had died fifty years before!"

"As if those Mohrs were worth all that trouble," said Anna, plucking with restless fingers at her coverlet. "Ah, Vincenz, believe me, they are not worth it!"

"Do not say that," said Vincenz, with a frown; "let me finish my story. I plied the young priest with questions. He could not tell me who lived at Draskócs; he had not been here long, and nobody came to church from there. He informed me that his immediate predecessor had died of low fever, and the one before that of cholera. He expected to die of the fever himself someday. 'None of them lived so long,' he said, 'as the old Pater Dionysius whose grave you have seen.' I asked whether Pater Dionysius had died of the fever also. No; he had died of some other complaint. He had preached remarkably good sermons when he was at his prime, but later he had become rather weak here — and the young priest touched his forehead significantly. It appeared that for the last few years of his life Pater Dionysius had suffered from softening of the brain. After a quarter of an hour's conversation, I made my way out; there was nothing to be got here. My visit had flattered the priest beyond measure. He accompanied me out of the door, pressing both my hands cordially. At the last moment, when I had one foot in the street already, the young priest, whose good nature was certainly greater than his intellect, seemed suddenly to have been inspired by a new view of the case. He ran after me and caught me by the sleeve. 'Are you a relation of his?' he inquired, curiously. I did not know what he meant. 'A relation of the old Pater Dionysius whose grave you have seen?' I disclaimed any connection with Pater Dionysius, and the young priest dropped my sleeve in disappointment. My curiosity was aroused in turn, and I questioned him closely. He told me that when Pater Dionysius died, there had been neither relations nor friends forthcoming to claim his few worldly effects. They had therefore been put into a wooden box, and sent to the nearest town to be deposited at the *Bezirksgericht*, where they lay ready to be claimed; but nobody had ever claimed them. I asked, with some faint movement of interest, what those worldly effects consisted in. 'Only a few rings and a few books,

I have heard,' said my host. 'If you are a relation,' he said, taking hold of my sleeve again, 'I should scarcely advise you to go and claim them now. They say that after forty years un- claimed effects are sold for the benefit of the poor. Those rings and books may be sold now; and even if they are not, you will have to pay a sum as inheritance tax; it will probably be greater than the value of the things. I should not advise you to go.' He meant it very well by me, honest man; but I went all the same. I spent two hours in searching for a conveyance, and after I found it, I spent eleven hours on the road."

"Ruin to your health," murmured Anna's pale lips.

"My health can afford it," laughed her brother. "I hardly felt the want of food, I assure you, though I subsisted on raw bacon during the drive."

Anna, thinking of the dainty dishes which she loved to serve up hot to Vincenz, could find no words here, but wrung her hands in silent anguish, as a vision of raw bacon rose before her eyes.

"I employed those eleven hours," said Vincenz, "principally in reflecting upon my folly. It did seem rather a wild goose chase to start off on the track of the meager property of an old priest, long dead. The very fact of its lying unclaimed proved that it must be worthless. But in my profession, we are taught to leave no stone unturned. I was resolved to do my best; and she should know I had done my best" — he broke off, for he met his sister's eyes fixed hard upon him. Anna did not speak; but that glance was so piercing, so penetrating, that Vincenz colored as no word could have made him color.

"It is no use," he resumed quickly, "to give you all the details of my journey and of my search. I was sent from one place to another, and from one man to another, until my brain began to reel. There was a want of limits and order, at the *Bezirksgericht* down there, perfectly perplexing to a civilized mind. Finally, the right box was hunted up, worm-eaten and falling to pieces. In it there were two rings of little value, a large stone seal, and three or four books in moldy covers. The walls of the *Bezirksgericht* were so damp that one of the books had green marks on the binding. It was the first one I took up, and in it I found some loose papers, a bill for wax candles, dated 1820, an Episcopal letter with a red seal half crumbled away; this was wrapped up in silver paper, and had evidently been prized as a treasure. There were also some papers, apparently in the dead priest's handwriting, headings for a sermon which perhaps had never been preached, also a list of the couples to be married shortly. Calligraphy and spelling did little honor to Pater Dionysius's education; but I fancy I recognized among the betrothed couples some of the names I had seen the day before on the wooden crosses in the cemetery. Alongside of this list, there was another paper, and in another handwriting. It was not more than a few lines and a signature, written out in Latin, but it was enough to repay all my trouble. Here was a contingency upon which no one had ever reckoned. The will of old Count Damianovics, Madame Mohr's grandfather, had lain here for nearly fifty years among the unclaimed effects of Pater Dionysius; and this will in a few words left the whole of his property to his eldest son Alexius, declaring that the younger, Jósika, had received his portion and was entitled to no more."

"A nice sort of friend," said Anna, querulously, "who hides away a will in that way!"

"My dear Anna, remember that the poor old man suffered from softening of the brain. The matter can now never be entirely cleared up, but as far as I understand the case, old Count Damianovics must have confided his will to the hands of the old priest, thinking that such an unusual document would be safer under ecclesiastical protection; and no doubt down in those wild parts it ought to have been. But the pater's brain must have given way very soon after his friend's death; or else, seeing the property pass into the right hands, perhaps he did not think it worth producing. It is difficult to say whether Madame Mohr's father knew that such a will existed or not. You have no notion of the way in which things are conducted down there; or rather, are not conducted, being left entirely to themselves. However, it is no use conjecturing; there the will is now, and according to it, Madame Mohr's brother is the present proprietor of Draskócs. The claim is not established yet, but the matter is clear as daylight. It was on the same day on which I found the will that your message reached me, and I came back here straight without returning to Draskócs. The rest can be done by writing, and if Madame Mohr must see the place, she will scarcely need me for that."

"So you have ended the cause after so many years," said Anna, while her fingers crept over the coverlet towards her brother's hand.

"I am proud to have done so, though it is no merit of mine; the matter was such a chance, and yet so absurdly simple. Who would have thought of a wooden box at the *Bezirksgericht*, while we were breaking our heads over irregular documents?"

"Who would have thought of it? Of course, nobody but you; and you don't imagine that that precious Count Alexius will thank you for having driven eleven hours in a cart and lived on cold bacon?"

"Poor man!" said Vincenz, with a calm smile; "I do not expect much thanks from him. I fancy he is seldom sober enough for any such sensation as gratitude. I have had no answer from Pesth, though my letter must have reached some days ago."

"You will get no thanks from anybody, Vincenz."

"I did not do it for the sake of thanks."

Anna looked at him piercingly, while she held his hand. "You are still thinking of that girl, Vincenz."

Vincenz turned away and sighed. Yes, he was still thinking of that girl; her image was burned into his soul. He did not care to deny it; he never attempted to struggle with it. He thought of her, and of her always.

Anna drew her hand slowly away, and watched him as he sat plunged in thought. Surely there had never been so fine a man as her brother Vincenz. No one was as happy as Anna Komers in her blind idolatry of devotion.

"I hardly expected you to answer my summons so soon," she said presently; and Vincenz started out of his thoughts. His thoughts had led him so far away that he had a long way to come back. "Of course, I came when I heard you were worse, Anna."

Anna plucked at the coverlet again: "Yes, yes," she said, with some asperity; "but I fancied that, being down there in those parts you would have found it shortest to return by the Hercules Baths."

"Oh, you thought so?" said Vincenz. He had thought so himself. While he was down there, he had taken much trouble to rack his brain for a plausible excuse which would justify him in going round by the Hercules Baths. He had rejected them all in turn as groundless and shallow. It had been almost a relief to turn his back upon the country, for the yearning had been a torture; but now that he had put half an empire between himself and the Hercules Baths, all those rejected reasons grew plausible again, and the torture was worse than before.

"You may be right, Anna; it would, after all, have been wiser if I had gone to the Hercules Baths and talked over the matter with Madame Mohr. However, there is nothing to be done now· I must give the details in writing."

Saying this, Vincenz went to the writing table and laid out a sheet of letter paper. Anna followed him with her eyes, and a very faint smile flickered round her pinched lips for a moment; but that was while his back was turned.

"Yes, it is too late," repeated Vincenz, as he slowly dipped his pen in ink. He said it as if he wished to be contradicted; but Anna did not offer to contradict him.

"Let me see; I must give the details in writing."

"Of course, you must," she said; "why don't you begin?"

"I was thinking," said Vincenz, laying down his pen for a moment, "that if I had known that this attack was going to be past its worst so soon, I would have followed your advice, Anna, and gone round by the Hercules Baths. It is so much easier to explain things verbally; and a business conversation — "

"*My* advice!" broke in his sister, shrilly. "I never advised you to do anything so insane. If you follow my advice, you will never go near that girl again — cold and heartless coquette as she is — who does not even know the meaning of the word 'love,' and who intends to sell herself to the first rich husband she can catch. Yes, she does. You need not shake your head — she told me so herself; and her courage in saying it is the only thing I like about her. Crush her out of your heart — that is my advice. Business conversation, indeed!"

Vincenz took up his pen again hastily and began writing rather at random. Feeling guilty made him feel angry; he had to constrain himself to be silent. He wrote half a page, but his heart was not in his writing: his eyes wandered away, and he was staring at the dusty ivy plant in the window; he looked at the shabby carpet; he counted the flowers on the wallpaper, which was a strange thing for a lawyer to do. He went through a minute calculation as to how long the letter would take to reach the Hercules Baths. On Thursday evening, it might be there; a person starting today could be there as soon as the letter.

"Did you say anything, Anna?" asked Vincenz, turning his head; he thought he had heard a sound coming from the sofa. But there was no answer, and he returned reluctantly to his writing. When he had written another line he got up quickly, for he had heard that sound again. It was not a word being spoken, but it was a sob; and as he went up and leaned over his sister, he saw that she was crying.

"Anna, dear, are you worse?" But she had taken both his hands and was kissing them.

"Vincenz, you must go; it is not right that I should keep you."

"Where to? I cannot leave you."

"You can, you must. Go down to the Hercules Baths. I shall never get well while I see you unhappy. Vincenz, if you love me, you must go."

To the Hercules Baths! Vincenz felt his heart leap with a sudden shock of joy. A delightful melody seemed to chime in his ears, as if bells were ringing all around; and they all rung out with musical tongue, "To the Hercules Baths! To her! to her!" How triumphant was the sound! He felt like a conqueror; he drew himself up, letting Anna's hands drop without noticing it. And this tumult of joy was all because he was going to avail himself of the right, which every free man has, of taking a railway ticket in any direction he chooses. He was not a conqueror — he was a rejected lover; but he was to see his scornful beauty again, and he was happy. Ah, but could he see her again? could he leave Anna just now? What selfishness to accept her sacrifice! Vincenz began to tremble as he saw his vision fading; it had sprung into life but a minute ago, yet so precious was it already that it left everything black behind it. Through the black confusion, he held blindly to one point — his duty to his sister. He would not be less generous than Anna was.

"No, Anna, I cannot go," he said, bending over her again. The sacrifice was made, but the struggle had been so fierce that Anna, looking up at him, wondered at the pallor of his face.

"There is no one to take care of you, Anna, if I go."

Anna thought deeply for a moment. "If you do not go," she said, mysteriously, "you will have to live here alone."

Vincenz did not understand.

"Did I not tell you that I have promised to visit Barbara Bitterfreund? You know how she has nursed me in my illness."

Yes. Vincenz remembered some talk of that sort. Barbara Bitterfreund had recently opened a choice establishment in a house outside the town, where young ladies were to be prepared for medical examination.

It gave Anna very little trouble to convince her brother that the country air was a necessity, if she was ever to recover her strength; and after a few minutes' talk, Vincenz, nothing loath, had become impressed by the belief that his staying in the town at present would be unpardonable selfishness on his part.

In five minutes more, he was looking up timetables with feverish eagerness. A few days ago, when down at Draskócs, it had appeared to him a ridiculous and illogical proceeding to make a journey of twelve hours in order to visit the Mohr family; now he was starting on a journey three times that length, with the same object in view, and yet he quite failed to be struck by any want of logic in the proceeding.

"If any message should come to me, Anna," said Vincenz, when the moment of departure was reached — " anything relating to Draskócs or the Mohrs — forward it on to me at once; here is the address" — and he scribbled it down upon the blank sheet of the letter which lay on the writing-table. It was the letter he had begun to Madame Mohr; but now it need not be finished, since he himself was going in its place.

Chapter XVII

Broken Glass

"Auch ich war einmal auf dem Tanz Salon."

— Karl Dahlgren

1T was quite dark when Dr. Komers reached the Hercules Baths on Thursday
evening. The dim outlines of a few large buildings, and a flood of light streaming from the central one, was all that Vincenz could gather of his surroundings.
Having made his way to the Mohrs' apartments, he found them dark, and apparently
deserted. A sleepy housemaid informed him at last that Herr Mohr had retired for
the night, and that the rest of the family were in the *Cursalon.*

"What are they doing there?"

"Dancing, of course."

"Dancing?"

"Yes, and the baron is with them."

Dr. Komers descended the stairs, feeling a little chilled. Into a place where they
were dancing he could not go, for he could not dance, and he was in his dusty traveling clothes. But, perhaps, reflected Vincenz, as he made his way towards the central
building — perhaps he could catch a glimpse of Gretchen through the windows;
without such a glimpse to live on, he did not think he could sleep that night. Who
was "the baron," he wondered, while he stumbled up and down steps in the dark,

and just saved himself on the verge of a stone pond in the Curgarten. Who was the baron, and why need the baron be with them?

Drawing near to the central building, the strains of music floated towards him through the open doors. All the doors stood open to the night air, and a small crowd of lookers-on was grouped at the entrance, under the covered arcades. Vincenz stood among them, and from over their heads he scanned the ballroom.

Between dancers and spectators there was a large society assembled; but the spectators were the larger portion, for it was only the very youngest of the young who could brave the exertion of dancing on a still and sultry summer night like this. Of the Romanian women present, even the youngest of the young were stout, and therefore preferred to sit fanning themselves indolently with palm-leaf or feather fans, rather than exert themselves in waltzes or even quadrilles. There was a pleasing medley of costume, even among the men. Wide Turkish trousers and broad leather belts were as frequent as dark coats; every shade of gray and brown was amply represented; while tailcoats were almost exclusively confined to the waiters, who darted black and noiseless across the scene — skimming between the whirling couples, and carrying refreshment to many a panting Romanian lady who languished upon her velvet seat.

Vincenz had twice looked round the room without seeing anything that he thought worth seeing, when all at once a tall, slight figure, draped in soft pink shades, floated towards him — past him. It was over in a moment, but she had been so near that he could have counted even the pearls on her neck. Would she come again? Yes, the figure in pink was coming round once more on the arm of the same partner; and this time, Vincenz did not look at her, but only at the partner. He was a young man, faultlessly attired in evening dress, waltzing to perfection, and smiling as he looked into Gretchen's face. Oh, the torture which that smile was to Vincenz!

"Will you please let me pass?" he said to the person in front of him.

The person complied, and Dr. Komers entered the big room. Perhaps the sight of so many varieties of coats had encouraged him to put his own travel-stained suit under the lamplight, or perhaps he had lost sight of all such social considerations.

It was towards Ascelinde, sitting in solitary state, that the lawyer made his way. Before he reached her, Gretchen had returned to her mother's side. Vincenz hastened his steps, but in the next moment slackened them, for the partner in the faultless evening dress had sat down beside her.

"Dr. Komers !" cried Gretchen, in an accent of unspeakable surprise.

"Dr. Komers!" echoed Ascelinde.

"How have you come?"

"When did you come?"

"Why have you come?" This last question from Ascelinde, and with rising agitation, for the horrible thought had occurred to her that Dr. Komers might be come to tell her that Draskócs was, after all, not won.

"Well," said Dr. Komers, who was not quite clear in his own mind as to why he had come, "I thought it better to make a run down here, and talk over business personally."

"Then you did not go home after all?"

"Not exactly; that is to say — yes — I did go home, but I somehow forgot that I should have come here first."

Madame Mohr was mystified, but at the same time pacified. In her gratification at this tribute of respect, she quite forgot all the indignant speeches which were to have crushed the faithless lawyer.

Vincenz, from the first word that he had said, had felt a pair of eyes fixed hard upon him. They were black, brilliant eyes, and he took an instant dislike to their expression. His answers to Ascelinde's remarks were absent and irrelevant, for no business conversation could be attempted in a ballroom; and besides, the whispering alongside disturbed his peace of mind.

"Who is that gentleman?" Baron Tolnay was inquiring in a tone which, because of the gentleman's vicinity, had to be considerably lowered.

"He is Dr. Komers, our family lawyer."

"Oh, your family lawyer!"

There was in Baron Tolnay's tone and eyes a return of that mockery which Gretchen had found so provoking on the day when they had sat on the green meadow. She answered, therefore, a little coldly,

"He is not only our lawyer, he is also our friend."

"Friend! friend! What a wide expression! The most elastic word in the dictionary."

"Do you think so?" said Gretchen, absently, for she was just then listening to Dr. Komers's stammered excuses to her mother. She decided that the excuses were lame.

"Whose friend do you mean?" Baron Tolnay asked. "Your friend? Your mother's friend?"

"Everybody's friend, of course."

"What horrible generalities! I should never be satisfied with being everybody's friend."

"Are you in danger of being that?"

"Fraulein Mohr, you crush me; you misconstrue my words."

"I hate roundabout speeches."

"I shall never be roundabout again; in the future, I shall speak like this: There is only one person whose particular friend I care to be. Is that distinct enough?"

"I think I like your roundabout speeches better, after all," said Gretchen.

By dint of listening with her left ear, she had ascertained that Dr. Komers had not offered a single rational explanation of his appearance here; and she was asking herself, merely out of curiosity, what then could have brought him?

"I am sure," said Baron Tolnay, while he gazed down reflectively at his beautifully pointed, beautifully polished, and altogether beautifully fashioned evening shoe — "I am sure that your family lawyer, or family *friend*, never makes roundabout speeches."

"Never; but how do you know that?"

Baron Tolnay cocked his right foot, which was crossed over the left, so as to get a view of his shoe *en profil.*

"Oh, because he does not look like it. A man who has so much — what shall I call it? — self-possession as to come into a ballroom in his traveling-coat, could never be guilty of any such weakness. He has a fine disregard for personal appearances;" and Baron Tolnay broke into a very subdued and perfectly inoffensive laugh. The tall, stooping man, with the spectacles and the loose gray coat certainly did make a conspicuous figure even in this big room. Twice already had unwary dancers been all but tripped up by his long legs, which he was now attempting, not very successfully, to dispose of under the red velvet bench.

After a minute, it struck Gretchen that Baron Tolnay had laughed quite enough; so she attempted to damp his merriment by inquiring whether he imagined that he would have appeared to greater advantage under the circumstances.

Of course, Baron Tolnay thought so, although he did not say so. He stopped laughing and looked grave, all except his eyes, and resumed, at the same time, the examination of his shoe, gazing at it from a birdseye point of view for a change.

"It is not fair to make me criminate myself; but given these circum-stances, I think I should have the sense to keep clear of a ballroom."

István privately thought that it would require a great deal to make him put himself as much to a disadvantage as this German lawyer was doing.

"But supposing you were very anxious to see somebody who was in the ballroom?"

"Ah!" Baron Tolnay stroked his black mustache and raised his eyebrows, "now you come to particulars; I always like particulars. In such a case" — and as he met her gaze full, there burned in his black eyes an ardor which was quite new to Gretchen — "in such a case, neither fire nor water would keep me back, let alone a dusty traveling coat."

Gretchen wished most heartily that she had kept to generalities; she sat twirling the bracelet on her arm and made no answer. These skirmishes with Baron Tolnay were always like playing with fire; there was something in his eyes, now and then, which a word or a touch could strike into flame. He frightened her somewhat, and he puzzled her still; he was both cool and hot, both self-possessed and impetuous, this brilliant, fascinating, perplexing man.

"But, Fraulein Mohr," said Baron Tolnay, gravely examining the sleeve of his evening coat, "to pursue the subject. You know more about your family friend than I do. You do not suppose that there is anybody here whom he is especially anxious to see. I thought he only came here to talk over business with Madame Mohr?"

Baron Tolnay looked up so innocently as he asked the question, that Gretchen, though she opened her lips for an impatient answer, felt herself disarmed. She was puzzled again: was this question to be taken as a piece of audacity, or was it as harmless as it pretended to be? She answered, with great decision, that of course Dr. Komers had no other object but business.

"Only business; yes, I thought so," said Baron Tolnay: "when people have reached that age, they usually do not care for anything but business."

"What age do you suppose he has reached?" asked Gretchen, who felt it her duty to defend Dr. Komers, as a friend of the family. She was quite accustomed to regarding him as belonging to an older generation, but she did not see that Baron Tolnay had any right to make jokes upon the subject.

"Oh, nothing very high; something about twice my age (twice twenty-four does not make much), and about three times yours."

Baron Tolnay happened to be twenty-eight; but he went by the elastic principle that a man is only as old as he looks.

"That would make me twelve years old. Thank you; I don't aspire to quite as much youth as that."

"Strange! I suppose it is his spectacles that make him so old-looking."

"How ill-natured you are!"

Gretchen wondered how she ever could have made the mistake of describing Baron Tolnay as the opposite. The word "good-natured" was mentally erased. Baron Tolnay's place in the catalogue was all corrections and erasures.

"Ill-natured! I! Have you not found out yet that I am the best- natured man in the world?"

He looked so genuinely surprised at her want of perspicacity, and so utterly without any ill-nature as he said it, that again Gretchen felt ashamed of having doubted him.

"Have you never seen a short-sighted man before?" she asked. "Plenty; I can tell you some excellent stories about some, about one in particular, who reminds me very much of Dr. Komers. I must keep them for later, though — I see, alas! that I am wanted. There is Kokovics making signals of distress. I cannot be blind any longer."

Dr. Komers moved into the seat beside Gretchen. He believed he had a great many things to tell her; but the only thing he could think of now was an inquiry after her father's health, to which she responded by an inquiry after his sister's. And then Vincenz appeared to be lost in thought, and Gretchen examined her fan in silence.

"You have had a great deal of trouble about Draskócs," she observed at last.

"Oh no, it was no trouble at all," said Vincenz, with a rush of joy at his heart. What were now eleven hours in a jolting cart, and three meals on raw bacon, compared with this crumb of thanks from her? What had he done to be thus rewarded?

"And you have really seen Draskócs ?" she said, looking at him with a sort of envy. "Please, Dr. Komers, tell me all about it."

Dr. Komers took off his spectacles and rubbed them. "I will tell you another time — tomorrow if you like."

"Yes, tomorrow," she agreed. It stood to reason that such a vast subject could not be done justice to in a ballroom. "Only tell me," she began; but at that moment she felt a quick tap on her shoulder, and looking up, became aware that Belita was standing before her in a magnificence of attire which baffled all description. Every face in the room was turned towards her, like flowers towards the rising sun. Before the eyes of the lazy Romanian women who paused in the middle of their ices with the cooling spoon at their lips, there seemed to float a far-off vision of Parisian glory, conjured up by that resplendent figure. Never before had such a triumph of millinery adorned this oriental *Cursalon* at the foot of the rock.

"Only tell me what?" repeated Belita, sending her eyes with the rapidity of lightning up and down the lawyer's figure, holding at the same time her handkerchief to her cheek as if she were in pain.

"So you have come after all," cried Gretchen, "in spite of your toothache. How foolish of you!"

"Congratulate me, my dear child, instead of abusing me; I have got my *jambe!* How could you expect me to stay at home? Let me sit down near you — there — a little more room for the train — and I will tell you about it. An hour ago, imagine my dejection, as, brooding in my dressing gown, I was just resigning myself to bed and to a stocking full of hot salt for the night, when enter Ludovico in a state of excitement which has doubled him in my estimation, and crying out, 'The box is come — the box is here!' Do not try to imagine my joy, for your fancy would fall short. *A basso il sale!* I flung the stocking to the ground. I am suffering the tortures of a martyr on the rack, but I am happy!"

Although Belita's left cheek was swollen out of all proportion, in a manner which gave her the appearance of a fashion plate out of a drawing, the expression of her countenance did not belie her words. There was something heroic in her bearing.

"How could you be so ridiculous as to come like this ?" said Gretchen, indignantly. "Why did you not send your dress instead of you; it would have done just as well."

"No, it would not, my dear child; it would not have been doing justice to the dress."

"How vain you are, Belita!"

"Oh, if it comes to that, not half as vain as you are, Bambina. I am only fond of my clothes; that is what confuses you. You know you would rather die than show yourself with a swollen face."

"Much rather," said Gretchen.

At this juncture, Dr. Komers was introduced by Ascelinde.

"Very happy to make the acquaintance," said the contessa aloud. "Coat fits ill — the shape of necktie out of fashion — boots antediluvian," she noted mentally. "Don't like his look at all. Come to talk over business, has he? — h'm! Where is Baron Tolnay, my dear?" she asked Gretchen.

Baron Tolnay was here, there, and everywhere. He was making himself universally agreeable and useful in his character of *quasi* host — getting chairs for old ladies, and ices for young ones; directing the waiters, and attending to everyone's wishes. Finally, he made a rush to the musicians' gallery, and presently Gretchen heard her favorite quadrille striking up. Baron Tolnay was down again in the room. Could Gretchen tell him where her brother Kurt was? There was a dancer who wanted to complete the quadrille. Gretchen believed he was in the supper-room, smoking with Mr. Howard. Baron Tolnay was in the supper-room in an instant. Had Kurt any objection to taking a place in a quadrille? No, Kurt had no particular objection, provided that the lady was not positively bad-looking and that her mustache was not more than an inch long. A minute later, Gretchen was led off by Baron Tolnay, and Vincenz found himself alone with Madame Mohr and the contessa. He scarcely counted the conte, who stood alongside with his crush hat in his hand, finding it happiness enough to look at his wife, and take note of the jealous glances which every woman in passing threw upon the *jambe de nymphe émue*.

"No, Ludovico *caro*, you had better not sit down," Belita had said earlier, when the small conte had attempted to rest his legs for a moment. "I am sorry for him," she had added aside to Gretchen; "but you see it is the only way to make up for his not being able to wear a hat in a ballroom."

Vincenz sat watching the maze of figures in a sort of dream; but he saw only one couple in all that crowd. He knew now who was "the baron," and already he had begun to hate the baron with a most unchristian-like vehemence. The unusual sounds and sights were working upon his fancy; he felt first a faint regret at not being able to dance, then an ever-growing wish that he could turn, and twist, and hold his partner's hand, as Baron Tolnay was doing over there. He never listened to the conversation beside him.

"It is a fundamental rule," the contessa was observing, "that a blonde should never wear pink — the result is usually fatal; but Margherita must be put down as an exception. I am bound to confess that I have never seen her look as lovely as she is looking tonight, and her dress is the prettiest among the dancers. You see toilets here that make you feel quite ill. Look at that colossal Romanian in green! Those rubies are lost upon such a creature! Not that perfect rubies are the fashion now; there has been quite a run upon flawed stones lately at Paris."

"Ah," said Ascelinde, "I remember some magnificent rubies among our family jewels at Draskócs. I wonder if Alexius would lend them to me? They would be mine now, had I only followed my own instinct and paid these 10,000 florins" — and she cast a bitterly mournful glance towards her legal adviser.

Thus, conversation flowed on; Belita talking of dress, and Ascelinde of Draskócs. But Vincenz never talked at all until the quadrille was over.

It was past eleven now; many people were gone; the group of spectators was dispersed, and some of the glass doors had been half-closed. When the next waltz struck up, there was a visible decrease in the number of the dancers.

The waltz was no better than the quadrille for Vincenz. What good was there in sitting beside Gretchen, since she never sat for more than a minute at a time?

"You have started a search, I hear," he began; and then a black shadow was hovering in front of Gretchen, and she was whirled off round the room.

"You have started a search among the moun — " thus he began again as soon as she had returned, and again with the same result.

"You have started a search among the mountains," he succeeded at last in saying.

She was opening her lips to answer, when once more a partner presented himself. It was Baron Tolnay this time; and it seemed, from the smile on his face, that he took a particular pleasure in interrupting conversation.

This sort of thing was very irritating, Vincenz felt; and he wished more and more that he had learned dancing in his youth. It did not look so very difficult to do after all, he thought, as he observed how Baron Tolnay turned now to the left, now to the right, sometimes getting over a great deal of ground with a few steps, sometimes revolving for a minute together on one spot.

Gretchen returned on Baron Tolnay's arm.

"You were going to tell me about the search," resumed Vincenz, doggedly.

"A search!" exclaimed Baron Tolnay, sitting down at Gretchen's other side. "Is there anything lost? I shall have the room ransacked at once. But" — in a lower tone — "if it is a glove or a flower, I hope you will not be so cruel as to ask for it. back again."

This was getting more and more irritating, Vincenz reflected, and the room certainly felt uncommonly hot.

"You will stop dancing now, I suppose, Fraulein Mohr?" he broke in; "you must be too tired almost to stand."

"Don't you know yet that nothing ever tires me, Dr. Komers?"

"Dr. Komers does not seem to have much patience for the follies of youth," laughed Baron Tolnay, in his light-hearted fashion. "Think of our tender years, and forgive us, Dr. Komers.

That "us" and the laughter in István's eyes jarred upon Vincenz. To think of "their" tender years was to think of his own sober age, and just at this moment he did not feel drawn to think of it. Before he had found an answer, again a black shadow fell, and again Gretchen was off round the room.

Baron Tolnay and Vincenz were close to each other now. Baron Tolnay with his head thrown back against the wall and his legs crossed, fanning himself with his fine cambric handkerchief, looked as thoroughly in his element as a trout in a river, or an eagle on a mountain-top; and Dr. Komers looked as thoroughly out of place as the eagle could have looked in the river, or the trout on the mountain. "This is a tropical heat," said Baron Tolnay, opening conversation.

"Quite," said Vincenz, coldly.

Baron Tolnay fanned himself more vigorously than before.

"Ah, you non-dancers have the best of it; I declare, I almost wish that I was out of the lists."

Vincenz was silent.

"It is hard work in such weather for us poor dancers, while you others can look on in coolness and comfort."

"I know that I do not feel cool," said Vincenz, with an unaccountable movement of temper; "in fact I was just thinking that I have never before had such a clear idea of what a red-hot furnace is like."

Baron Tolnay raised his eyebrows and stroked his mustache.

"Really?" he said, with polite concern. "Perhaps your journey has knocked you up?"

"I am not in the least knocked up, thank you."

"I beg your pardon; you seemed to imply it. No doubt you are tired."

"I am not in the least tired."

"Tired travelers seldom enjoy themselves in a ballroom," went on the baron, unheeding. He threw a glance which just passed over the dusty traveling suit, and then returned to the contemplation of the dancers. A hint that he would be better out of a ballroom was the very thing to make Vincenz stay there.

"You must find it dull work looking on," added Tolnay, flapping his handkerchief slowly up and down. "Perhaps you would find more amusement in the card-room; I shall be happy to show you the way. There are some old gentlemen playing whist there. I believe they want a fourth player."

"Thank you, I don't play whist," said Vincenz, feeling hotter and hotter every moment. "And I am not an old gentleman," he added to himself, with indignation.

"Ah, you don't play whist, and you don't dance," observed Baron Tolnay, with a glance which seemed to say — Then what do you do? "But I suppose you have danced in your day, Dr. Komers? Am I right? Everyone dances when they are *very* young and foolish."

There was not a single word in any of Baron Tolnay's remarks at which a rational man could have taken offense, nor anything which, taken separately, had any value in itself. Yet upon Vincenz each acted like a pin-prick, and all the pin-pricks together exasperated him beyond the bounds of endurance. He saw that figure in pink coming back towards her place, and his heart began to beat with violence, as an idea, born of desperation, took sudden shape in his head.

"Did you give up dancing long ago?" Baron Tolnay was inquiring with civil indifference.

Vincenz felt the blood rushing to his face and tingling in his ears; and in the same moment, to his own great surprise, he heard his own voice saying, suddenly, "I have not given up dancing at all;" and then he perceived that he had risen to his feet and was asking Gretchen to waltz with him.

With a look of surprise, she accepted him; and Vincenz, putting his arm round her waist, as he had seen other men do, began to tremble with a sort of tumultuous exultation at the thought that he had a right to do it as well as the others.

Now for a bold plunge into that whirlpool of dancers! He felt several pairs of eyes fixed upon him; but he was not afraid of anything at that moment, for a little hand rested on his shoulder. He forgot that he was in the dusty traveling coat; he forgot that he could not see six yards distinctly in front of him; he forgot everything except that he was holding her hand, and that he must vindicate his youth.

He made the plunge; they were carried away in the stream; other dancers made way for them precipitately, for Vincenz, resolved not to be timid like some chicken-hearted youths he had noticed, plunged onward, dancing more wildly than the wildest dancer in the room. It was not so very difficult after all, he thought, having got halfway across the floor. He had no notion of the strange and eccentric picture he made as he whirled along, storm-wind fashion, with his stooping figure, and long, unpracticed legs: self-consciousness was not one of his weak sides. Gretchen felt her breath swept away in the first second, and herself carried off the ground as if she had been a feather; her fingers were half-crushed, she fancied her arm must be bruised. Vincenz got a train under his feet, and staggered for a moment; but he recovered his balance, and Gretchen was aware of being borne down towards the lower end of the room. She could see the lamps outside through the glass doors, which stood half-closed. Only a few yards more, thought Vincenz, and the triumph would be complete; but the unaccustomed motion was making his head swim round, till the revolving couples became vague colored blotches. In an unlucky moment, he bethought himself of the skillful turns to the left with which Baron Tolnay had diversified his dancing; this would be the occasion for such a turn. He changed his direction so unexpectedly that he caused two other couples to stumble with violence; he changed it again, seeing nothing but a mass of lights and colors before his eyes, and feeling Gretchen cling more desperately to his shoulder. There was a check, a crash, some heads turned towards them, and at the same instant Vincenz, in a sudden rush of cool air, found himself standing under the arcades outside, with a heap of broken glass at his feet, and Gretchen leaning breathlessly against a pillar beside him.

"What have I done?" he gasped, thunderstruck.

"Only danced through a glass door," she answered, still breathless.

"I hope you don't mind it much," said Vincenz, rather ruefully. "I really am very sorry." She began to laugh, looking down at her arm.

"I hardly expected to get through alive; but I have come off cheap, you see — only a little scratch."

He felt that he could breathe again. The sudden transformation scene had been rather bewildering at the moment; but having realized the state of the case, his spirits began to rise. He felt on the whole that it was an exhilarating thing to have danced through a glass door: not for the last twenty years had he done anything so inspiriting. No one could say that he had not vindicated his youth. He was convinced that none of the old gentlemen who were playing whist in the card-room could have accomplished this feat. It made him feel ever so much younger than he had felt five minutes ago. He cheerfully proposed that they should dance back again.

"No, thank you," said Gretchen, retreating a step. "Perhaps we had better take a turn before going in again; it would be as wise to wait until the sensation has subsided a little. We might be mobbed, you know."

"Do you think anybody noticed it?" he asked, in perfect good faith.

"The music was very loud, I think," said Gretchen, evasively. She turned to walk down the arcade, and he walked beside her. The place was quite deserted now, except for a drowsy man who came slowly along with his ladder, putting out, one by one, the lamps which burned under each arch. The waltz music still played on inside, and on the spot where they had first stood, the broken glass lay scattered, and each glass splinter shone as in turn it caught the lamplight. They walked halfway up the arcades in silence, their steps echoing from end to end; then Gretchen stood still under an arch, and leaned against the stone pillar, still a little short of breath, while the lamp-light streamed down full upon her.

It was not one of the rare moonlight hours which visit the Djernis valley. Straight opposite, the mass of the mountain was black and unbroken; the sound of water breaking over marble and granite rocks made the night feel deliciously cool after the heat of the last hour. Gretchen drew a long breath, her lips were parted, and the pearls on her throat heaved gently with each breath.

Vincenz had gone through many experiences lately. Forty-eight hours ago, he had been a dry lawyer, immersed in parchment documents; now he found himself standing in the stillness of a summer night, having just danced through the glass door of a ballroom; and he was alone with the woman he loved. On one side, the floating music, on the other the rush of the water; nothing to disturb the solitude except the sleepy man with the ladder, who had been darkening the arcades by degrees, and now put out the light above their heads, leaving them in a sort of semi-darkness. The garden, which sloped down from their feet, was deserted — all but one figure, which came along slowly by a winding path, drawing nearer and nearer, unnoticed.

What wonder if, in the silence, Vincenz felt a thrill of wild hope shoot through his heart? He knew now what he had come here to do. Why should he not be listened to this time? After what he had seen in the ballroom, he felt he would be a fool to give more time to his rival; for Baron Tolnay was his rival — already he acknowledged that. Why should he not have as good a chance as that polished man of fashion, with his beautifully fitting coat and his beautifully pointed shoes? Vincenz, in his largeness of ideas, would never have stooped to believe that a woman could marry a man, or perhaps even love him, because of a beautiful coat or of pointed shoes. This was his time, he felt; no moment could be more favorable. If he now thought of the scattered glass at all, it was only as a pleasant recollection. He was impressed with a sort of conviction that his luck was on the turn; and that if his dancing had succeeded so well, everything else must be crowned with the same triumph.

He did not pause to look for words, but he took hold of her hand and pleaded his cause in a hurried and impassioned voice, more eloquently, more fervently than he had pleaded it on that Ash Wednesday evening when the rain was falling in the street.

It came upon Gretchen so suddenly, so utterly without warning, that she started back trembling, and stood shrinking against the broad stone pillar, staring back at him in speechless surprise. She could see the light of love shining out of his deep-set eyes — for, as in all critical moments, Dr. Komers had taken off his spectacles; but all he could see was her shrinking figure and her round arms, bare to the elbows, shining white as marble in the dim half-light.

When her first surprise was past, she drew her hand away impetuously; but she had not yet said a word, when they both started at the sound of broken glass on the pavement. An approaching figure had stepped upon one of the scattered fragments.

Vincenz relinquished her hand: he saw someone close, and there were more figures crowding out of the ballroom; but he whispered, "Gretchen, will you not give me your answer? Only one word, I implore!"

She shook her head, and shrank farther into the black of the arch. "Tomorrow, then," said Vincenz. "I will ask for my answer tomorrow. Here they are all coming."

Here they were all coming, indeed, and in the midst of them came a man with a telegram. He put it into Dr. Komers's hand.

"Anna is worse," was Dr. Komers's first thought, as he took it to the light, and, putting on his spectacles in haste, tore open the paper.

Gretchen felt herself drawn out of the dark arch. Belita had put an arm round her friend's waist.

"*Misericordia!* my dear child, I could not imagine what had become of you. What are you doing here?"

"I was so — so hot," stammered Gretchen, feeling still rather confused.

"H'm — you look hot;" and the contessa threw a curiously scrutinizing glance towards Dr. Komers. She liked his looks less than ever this time.

"Is it a business telegram?" inquired Ascelinde, burning with curiosity.

Dr. Komers started, and crushed the paper into his pocket.

"No, not exactly," he said, slowly, looking at Madame Mohr doubtfully in the light of the lamp. "It is a startling piece of news." Dr. Komers was going to have said — a sad piece of news; but, considering all the circumstances of the case, he really could not find it in his conscience to use the adjective "sad." The expression on his face was certainly that of a man who has received a shock of surprise.

"Madame Mohr, you are going home now, I presume? You will allow me to accompany you as far as your door. This telegram affects you more than anybody else."

The two walked on in advance.

Belita had her arm still linked within Gretchen's. "I shall see you tomorrow, Margherita — *early*. Goodnight, *Bambina*."

Gretchen walked away beside her brother; the tall contessa and the little conte disappeared their own way; the last of the ball-goers dispersed. In the *Cursalon*, grown suddenly dark, there was the creak of some chairs pushed aside, then the twang of a fiddle dropped to the ground by a departing musician. All was silent after that; there would not be a step more in the arcades until daylight tomorrow.

Chapter XVIII

Tristezza

"Es sind ja so mancherlei schlaue Betrüger."

— Voss's *Odyssey*

EARLY in the course of the following forenoon, the contessa was to be seen making her way from one monster hotel to the other. The little conte, left at home, thought that his wife must have some very weighty object in view; for during the six weeks of his matrimonial experience, he had never known her to have got farther than her dressing gown at ten in the forenoon.

Belita found the Mohrs' apartments in a strange state of tumult. Something abnormal had occurred; she saw that at a glance. The first visible symptoms were two youths in the passage, one holding a yard measure, the other with a packet of stuff under his arm. A little of the stuff peeped out of the paper, and Belita saw that it was black. In the first room she entered, there was a big-nosed Israelite standing sentinel beside a pasteboard box, which overflowed with fringe as with a torrent of water; but the fringe, like the stuff outside, was black. Belita opened the door of the sitting-room; and there, over all the seats, over the backs of chairs and trailing down to the ground, hung materials of all descriptions, heavy and light, thick and transparent, but all, like the packets outside, like the fringe in the box, black — a dead, unbroken black. Belita saw another larger, bigger-nosed Hebrew standing in the center of the apartment and discoursing eloquently, as he waved his hand from object to object.

She caught sight of Gretchen, barricaded by piles of black stuff; her eyes fell on Madame Mohr, sitting pale and red-eyed on a chair; and standing still at last in the doorway, she asked what had happened.

The talkative Hebrew checked his eloquence, and retired discreetly to a window, while the contessa was being told what had happened. The greatest part of Ascelinde's tears had been spent in the nighttime; but she had a few convulsive sobs remaining, wherewith to adorn more becomingly the melancholy news, which last night, on the homeward way, Dr. Komers had already broken to her.

Alexius was dead. His precarious health, it appeared, had not been proof against the shock of joy that the sudden accession of fortune had brought him. The thought of becoming thus, by one stroke of luck, the possessor of Draskócs, had been too much for his delicate constitution. This was the version which Madame Mohr gave to Belita, and the version to which she clung until her last day; but there was another version.

When Dr. Komers, in writing to his sister, mentioned the event, he expressed himself thus: "Drank himself to death immediately on getting my letter; passed twenty-four hours in his favorite pot-house, and was found at the end of that time a corpse, with fifteen empty bottles beside him. I had been told previously that the next attack of *delirium tremens* would be fatal."

It would be a willful waste of ink and paper if I attempted to depict the struggle now taking place in Ascelinde's breast. It had been her creed throughout life that Alexius was her idol. At the same time, it was a clear fact that the fall of this idol opened the direct road to Draskócs. The contention of feelings awakened by the ending of the case was weak compared to this new phase. If that had been a storm, this one was a hurricane.

"What are you going to do?" asked the contessa at the end of ten agitated minutes.

'Go to Draskócs at once." "What! Today?"

"Tomorrow: our mourning must be made first; we shall have to employ every tailor in the place. I cannot live another week without seeing Draskócs. It will only be a run-over to see if any new furniture will be required before we settle down there. I have not had time to put any questions to Dr. Komers about anything yet; and he has not been inside the house, it seems."

"How many of you are going?"

"Margherita, myself, and Dr. Komers — he accompanies us."

"Ah! he accompanies you," said Belita, reflectively.

The shopman began to insinuate some remark about material and fashions; and Belita, looking round her with the eye of a diver who scans the waves, took off her gloves instinctively and prepared for a plunge into the sea of black.

"These blacks are all abominable," she announced; "there is not one real black among them." Everybody felt rather bewildered as Belita proceeded to prove to the indignant Hebrew that he did not know black when he saw it. These were all "cheerful" blacks, a great deal too frivolous in appearance. Did he mean to say that he had none of the new *noir de cercueil*, or of the latest fashionable material called *le désespoir?* "My dear," she said to Gretchen, who sat staring in amazement, having always hitherto believed that black was black and white was white, "if you could have seen the lovely dress I was shown last month at Paris at Madame Ernestine's, in the 'Deep Affliction Department.' Just the thing to set off your hair and coloring. What a pity one cannot have presentiments!" The contessa heaved a passing sigh. "It was of a light stuff too, for summer wear — *tristezza*, and all trimmed with that new fringe *cascades des larmes*. I liked it even better than the *in memoriam* toilet they made such a fuss about. Oh, I tell you, it is a luxury to bewail your relatives when you have Madame Ernestine to equip you. Ha!" cried the contessa at that moment, pouncing upon something which her practiced eye had detected.

"What do you call this?" she asked in triumph, dragging some flimsy black stuff to the light.

"Barège," said the much-tried Hebrew.

"Oh, man, man! not to know a thing when you have it! This is *tristezza*, I tell you! Not *quite* the real *tristezza*, but not far from it. This is the only thing that will do for Margherita."

Gretchen resigned herself, so did Ascelinde; everybody had to surrender to the irrepressible contessa. There followed a quarter of an hour's wrangling, which was happiness to Belita, perplexity to Ascelinde, and weariness to Gretchen. What with "cheerful" blacks and "sad" blacks, and there being too little of this and too much of that, Belita contrived, in a wonderfully short time, to drive everybody to their wits' end.

"And now," she exclaimed, when at last alone with Gretchen- — "now I have got you all to myself! Come out from behind that fortress, Margherita, and tell me all about it." She cleared a chair for herself as she spoke, and sank into it.

Gretchen was leaning with her elbow on the top of a black heap. She had been very silent during the discussion, but there was a flush of excitement on her cheek.

"I know nothing more than mamma has told you," she answered. "Poor Uncle Alexius — "

"Whom you have never seen, and therefore cannot be sorry for, has died very opportunely, my dear. It is not that I mean — I am coming to that subject later; there is a more immediate point. Tell me the truth; has he proposed to you or not?"

Gretchen started, "What makes you think so?"

"Exactly what made everybody else think so; he danced with you the whole evening."

"Are you talking of Baron Tolnay?"

"Of whom are you talking?"

"Never mind."

"I will mind," returned Belita, with a charmingly frank smile.

The contessa knew perfectly well that there could be only one other man in the question besides Baron Tolnay.

Last night, as she stepped out of the *Cursalon*, she had seen Dr. Komers standing beside Gretchen under the arch, and her sharp eyes had enabled her to notice a circumstance which, in the dark, had escaped the others; Dr. Komers had been holding Gretchen's hand.

Of course, Belita being what she was, could not be clever about anything but trimmings and millinery, or the cut of a cloak, or the fall of a train-skirt; but undeniably, she possessed a certain feminine wit, sharp as — let us say — the scissors which shaped her fashionable garments, and bright as the needles which stitched them together. Her quickness of perception corresponded to the quickness of her ever-moving eyes, and enabled her to put twos and twos together with an almost electrical rapidity, and never allowed any chance detail, within the range of vision or hearing, to escape unnoticed. If the subject had a claim upon her interest, then Belita's eyes, both mental and bodily, quickened in proportion; and everything concerning Gretchen had an interest for the contessa. The existence of this interest was not easy to explain; Belita herself regarded it as a weakness. Constant companionship at school had first made her grow accustomed to Gretchen, as she expressed it; and intercourse had shown her in the German girl a docile disciple of her own doctrines. Since then, she had watched the progress of her pupil with mingled anxiety and pride, and today the anxiety was uppermost.

Stepping out of the *Cursalon* last night, Belita had rapidly reviewed the situation, and reflected that a man does not stand under deserted arcades, holding a girl's hand, for nothing. A certain uneasiness had preyed on her mind ever since, and it was this uneasiness which had caused her to brave the hot sun this morning, and it was the same reason which moved her to say, a minute ago, "Yes, I will mind."

Looking across the black pyramid, she now said, "You look feverish today, Margherita; your cheeks are burning."

"It is the heat," said Gretchen, shortly.

Very likely it was the heat, or possibly also her broken sleep, for her night had been restless. She had dreamed of palaces and parks; and coming drowsily to her senses this morning, her first thought had been, "My fortune is made!" Her sensations were those of a person who has suddenly been lifted on to a high pedestal. The new elevation made her feel giddy. She was scarcely calm enough to enjoy it yet.

"My dear child, you don't suppose that I have come out this way, with nothing on me, merely to get evasive answers? Beating about the bush is just the thing I cannot stand. I like things to be to the point. If Baron Tolnay did not propose to you last night, it is because you did not give him an opportunity; and if he never proposes at all, it is because of your wicked imprudence."

"Do you call it wicked imprudence to take a turn in the arcades?"

"I call it wicked imprudence to stand under an arch alone with Dr. Komers. It is a mystery to me how you came to be there at all."

"We fell through a glass door."

"No reason for not coming back through it again."

"But I had hurt my arm; it was scratched."

"I don't pity you in the least; it serves you right for dancing with that enormous man in the despairingly ugly coat and the antediluvian boots. The story will be in everybody's mouth today. Baron Tolnay says he will write to Pesth for unbreakable glass to put into the *Cursalon* windows."

Certainly, no one could accuse Belita of beating about the bush. Until this morning, Gretchen had looked upon the smash of the glass door as an amusing incident; but contemplating it from Belita's point of view, it became an ignominy. That allusion to the unbreakable glass was peculiarly mortifying.

"So you have no excuse to make," said Belita. "Do you know that you were playing a very dangerous game last night?"

"I was not playing any game at all," said Gretchen rather sulkily.

"*He* was not playing any game," the contessa returned with emphasis.

"How do you know?"

"By the evidence of my own eyes and the calculation of my own brains. What Dr. Komers said to you last night was a serious thing."

Gretchen made no denial.

"My dear child, you cannot deceive me. Perhaps you think that because I have the good fortune to live in a country where marriages are arranged, that I do not know what a man looks like when he is asking a girl to be his wife? If I had not been inspired to interrupt your *tête-à-tête* last night, that man would in another moment have had the unparalleled presumption to ask you to marry him."

"You did not come in time," said Gretchen, with a rather malicious delight.

Belita was taken aback. She had attempted a random shot; she was horrified to find how truly she had aimed.

"Do you mean to say that he had done it already?" Gretchen nodded.

"And, my dear child, if I may ask, how did he take his *congé?*"

"He did not take it at all, because you were inspired to interrupt us just then."

"Misericordia!" The contessa rose from her seat in great perturbation, and going to the glass, stared at the reflection of her hat, for the first time in her life without seeing it.

"Then he can be expected to begin again?"

"I suppose so."

"And the telegram came just at that moment," observed the contessa. "Yes — I see."

"What do you see?"

"It is as clear as daylight," said Belita, coming to a conclusion with her usual lightning-like rapidity. "It is very evident that Dr. Komers is a lawyer."

"I don't in the least understand you."

"Don't you? Don't you see that I have wronged Dr. Komers?"

"In what way?"

"By taking him for a sleepy lawyer, when in reality he has proved himself a remarkable wideawake member of his profession."

"I don't understand," said Gretchen again.

"Not yet? Well, to be sure, you have hardly had time to realize that your fortune is made at last."

"Of course, I have realized it; but what has that to do with Dr. Komers?"

"Everything possible. He has seen the advantages of the case, and he has tried to take his luck at the flood."

"That is not true, Belita!" cried the justice-loving Gretchen. "The telegram came afterwards. Dr. Komers knew nothing about it when he spoke to me. It is now that you wrong him.

"Now do not excite yourself; there is no reason whatever. I am only putting two and two together, and you can follow my calculations if you pay attention. Dr. Komers, arriving thus suddenly without any visible pretext, the telegram following on his heels, his audacious declaration — it is simple enough, in all faith, to see what it means. Your uncle died two days ago; it would be strange if Dr. Komers, who is a lawyer, could not obtain the information a little earlier than other people, even though he found it better, for his own reasons, to keep the information to himself."

"He could not have heard before; he had only just returned from Draskócs."

"Another proof for my case!" cried the contessa. "Draskócs was still fresh in his mind when he learned that it had become your mother's. Nobody could better estimate the value of a place like that than a man who is a lawyer. He has been able to calculate what your fortune would be, and he has tried to carry the situation with a bold *coup-de-main*. Dr. Komers is really a clever man, my dear. I am ready to stake my two best silk dresses that he has refrained from dwelling upon the subject of Draskócs before you. What description did he give you of the place? None? I thought so," as Gretchen shook her head; "exactly what I expected. Will you confess now that I am right?"

"No!" burst out Gretchen, rising in her black fortress; "you are wrong! Dr. Komers proposed to me three months ago, while Draskócs was still in the clouds!"

The contessa stood rooted to the spot, and for a full minute her tongue refused to move.

"Three months ago!" she managed at last to stammer. "Good heavens, child! why did you never tell me this?"

"Are you my spiritual director?"

"I almost think I am: you never made any secret about Baron Tolnay, nor Federbusch, nor any of the others. Perhaps — perhaps" — with a ray of light — "perhaps you were ashamed of this one?"

Gretchen stood silent. She was looking back at that Ash Wednesday interview. There had certainly been a keen sense of shame in the discovery that the expected suitor was not one of the coveted *partis*, but only the family lawyer. And yet, after three months' familiarity with the idea, her indignation of then appeared to her to have been almost greater than the occasion demanded.

Meanwhile, Belita had recovered her presence of mind, and rallied her scattered forces to a fresh attack.

"I understand," she exclaimed, for she chose to take Gretchen's silence for assent, "and I forgive you; the suitor certainly was not one to be proud of. But a clever man he must be all the same, though unpardonably audacious. And his ambition in wanting to marry you — "

"Belita," interrupted Gretchen rather hurriedly, "of course I put no worth on that sort of thing; but still — still, I do not believe that ambition had anything to do with it. I really think he cares for me."

"There!" cried Belita, with a sort of triumph, "did I not tell you that you are ten times vainer than I am? I blush for you, Margherita; a girl of your acuteness of perception to persist in believing that it is her charms that have fascinated that middle-aged man of the law, while it is as clear as daylight that his only motive is interest! Nor do I blame him either; for a man in his position to marry a girl in your position would always be a rising in life, even before your accession to fortune. And now that Draskócs is won, of course his ardor is redoubled. I will engage never to look at a French fashion plate again if you can deny that his second declaration was a much more passionate affair than the first."

Of course, it had been much more passionate, thought Gretchen, though she did not choose to admit it. Her clear head was not as clear as usual today; her ideas were entangled and her vanity alarmed. Was it indeed possible that Dr. Komers had wanted to marry her merely out of ambition? Well, and what of that? Why should she resent it? The point of view from which he regarded her would then be the same as that from which she herself regarded István Tolnay. It stood to reason that he had as much right to his ambition as she had to hers.

"And now, a last word of advice," said the contessa, as she drew on her many-buttoned gloves. "You will remember that only the other day, I expressed a fear as to whether you might not carry flirtation too far; and though, of course, Baron Tolnay could not possibly be jealous of a man who wears a coat of that make, still I think you have been imprudent. If you really find any amusement in it, there is no reason why you should not flirt with Dr. Komers — *moderately*, of course. I don't see the pleasure of that sort of thing myself; but I believe many people do. The mistake was, ever letting him come to a distinct declaration. Now that it has happened, all you can do is to use him prudently: play cat and mouse with him, if you like; a *soupçon* of jealousy may help to bring on Baron Tolnay."

"I thought you said that nobody could be jealous of a man with a coat like that?"

"Did I? I dare say. Let us not try to be logical, my dear; I cannot stand your logical deductions. What I advise — " The contessa raised her hand and listened to a step in the next room. "That is Dr. Komers, my dear; he is coming for his answer. I shall leave you to demolish him; but I must have a word with him first. He shall see that he is not the only person with sharp eyes in his head." Gretchen did not understand what Belita meant by her last hurried words; and there was no time to question, for Dr. Komers was in the room. She gave him her hand without looking at him, and then sat silent, trying to collect her thoughts; while Belita, having first rescued the *tristezza* on which the short-sighted lawyer was about to sit down, entered into a rapid conversation with him.

Gretchen's thoughts were not easy to collect. During the present interval of respite she was, so to say, arming herself for battle. She began to go through again the addition of those various twos and twos which Belita had summed up for her; and in the new light thrown upon the subject, it looked almost as if the sum total were, after all, correct. Nothing is so persuasive as an honest tone of conviction; and Belita's words had been imbued with the honest unwavering belief that her view was the only right one. And were not many of the things she had said the very echo of Gretchen's own thoughts on Ash Wednesday afternoon? Had she not herself been aghast at the lawyer's presumption? Penetrated by the sense of her new importance, Gretchen was more than ever ready to agree that the position in which she stood was incalculably higher than that of a poor, portionless, drudging lawyer. And yet she would have liked — she would have liked very much to know whether Belita was really right. The question could not fail to interest her vanity; for however little a woman may value a man's love, it always remains a disagreeable surprise to discover that it is not herself but only her position or her fortune that he covets.

"Ah, good morning, Dr. Komers," had been Belita's first words. "I hope you have recovered from the shock of your accident yesterday. You have come, no doubt, like me, to offer your congra— your condolences, I mean," corrected Belita, as her eye fell on the *tristezza*, which covered the sofa in a heap. "I dare not stay longer; I scarcely feel the right to take up more of Margherita's time. She has important duties now: this change of position is so sudden she scarcely realizes it herself, poor child. But I am a woman of the world, and you are a lawyer; we must help her to understand the importance of her new place."

Vincenz, who had been favored with very few words last night, did not know what to make of this gracious volubility.

"Goodbye, my little heiress," said Belita, pressing Gretchen's hand with warm significance. "She is turned into an heiress now, is she not, Dr. Komers? I suppose you will soon be having the pleasure of drawing up the marriage settlements — we all know how heiresses are snapped up nowadays. I have been trying to preach prudence a little; I think you had better do the same" — and she kissed her friend affectionately on the forehead.

"I am sure Dr. Komers agrees with me, my dear. There is so much interested motive in the world. Goodbye" — she was out of the room, throwing one more glance of warning over her shoulder.

Vincenz stood for a while, looking puzzled; he was ruminating uneasily on the meaning of the contessa's words.

Gretchen furtively watched his expression. Her own face had changed; the flush of excitement had died away, leaving her paler than usual.

Meanwhile, Belita, as she buttoned her gloves in the passage, was feeling well satisfied with herself. She took no pleasure whatever in being cruel; but she saw no cruelty in what she had been doing. It was with perfect honesty that she believed in Dr. Komers's interested motive; for she had the great advantage, or the great disadvantage, of not believing in the existence of love. The burden from which her mind now felt lightened was a fear that Gretchen, by indulging in a little too much foolish flirtation with Dr. Komers, might frighten off the other valuable captive. This was the whole extent and limit of her apprehensions.

Having buttoned her last button, she opened the door once more and stuck in her head.

"One word more: you have not seen Baron Tolnay today, Margherita?"

"Certainly not," said Gretchen, much annoyed.

"He will be here soon, I fancy, to congra— to condole. Goodbye."

Chapter XIX

More Tristezza

"Farewell! thou art too dear for my possessing,
And like enough thou know'st thine estimate."

— Shakespeare

1T was not until the contessa was half-way home that Dr. Komers spoke.

He was not embarrassed, but he was somewhat perplexed. Perhaps also his hopes, which last night in the silence of the deserted arcades had appeared to him to be nearer fulfillment, faded back into their former incertitude when looked at by this broad light of day. Even the black color on all sides tended to depress him; it threw in a gloomy background to the picture. And here, in the middle of the lugubrious piles and mournfully trailing folds, sat his lady-love in a listless attitude, looking pale by contrast to her dark surroundings.

In that moment of passion last night, when he had lost guard over himself, and avowed his love in words which he had never learned (for assuredly, he had not read them in his lawbooks, nor dug them out of his legal parchments), and which yet came so easily to his lips, he had felt it not impossible that that dimly seen, pink-robed figure should answer him with "Yes." But now she was pale, she was in black, the brilliancy was gone: what else could the black-robed figure say but "No?"

Last night had been one brief moment of happy dreaming; this was the reality of life again. Who knows? If the dream had lasted but a little while longer —

But those were foolish thoughts, useless speculations. Vincenz, passing his hand over his forehead, roused himself with an effort.

"Perhaps I ought not to have disturbed you so soon after the melancholy news which arrived last night," began Vincenz, "but you will understand my anxiety, and excuse me."

She made a sign as if to wave off the apology, but she remained silent, and Vincenz went on speaking. That burst of eloquence which had come to him unawares last night did not return to his aid now. He spoke soberly, constrainedly almost; the invigorating sensation of youth had quite departed.

"It is no use to tell you again what are my feelings towards you; you are aware of them already, and I do not want to weary you. Do not suppose me vain enough to imagine that I have won your love yet; but I still continue to hope now, as I hoped then, that I may win it in time. Can you encourage me to hope? Is it quite impossible that in time perhaps you may get to care for me?"

"Quite impossible," said Gretchen, very hurriedly.

"I beg you to reflect. I can wait for your decision, and I can wait for your love. I will wait if you only give me hope." He looked at her wistfully, but she did not meet his eyes. It was harder, she felt, to refuse a man the second than it had been the first time.

"It is no use your waiting, Dr. Komers."

"You are deciding too hurriedly," he said. "Is my love to go all for nothing?"

His love? Gretchen's curiosity as to the existence of that love returned in double force. She wished more than ever that she could feel quite convinced by Belita's theory, for that would at once have disposed of this troublesome feeling of pity, of which she was becoming faintly aware. But it was difficult to reconcile that theory with his tone and his look. She would have liked to gain some proof of the truth, whichever way it lay.

"Why will you ask me again, Dr. Komers, when I have given you one answer already?"

This was the exact juncture of the interview which an experienced coquette would have made use of for playing a game of cat and mouse, as Belita had suggested. Even Gretchen, little schooled as she was, understood that if she wished to prolong the torture of her suitor, she had only to veil her answers in a gentle cloud of vagueness, and to dole out hope and despair in equal portions. Perhaps her preoccupation today was the cause of her missing this opportunity, or perhaps she felt instinctively that this particular sort of mouse might not understand the fun of being played with, and that so large a mouse might, when under provocation, turn upon the cat. Whatever the reason was, Gretchen, with a shake of her head, added decisively, "I can never give you another answer than the first one. Pray do not think of it anymore."

"I have thought of nothing else," broke out Vincenz — "of nothing else for the last three months; my wishes are as hot today as they were on Ash Wednesday."

"Hotter, it seems to me," said Gretchen, bitterly.

"Ten thousand times hotter," echoed Vincenz, scarcely noticing the strangeness of the tone and words. "You surely do not think that any — any altered circumstances could have had an effect upon me?"

"I hope not, Dr. Komers," she answered, gravely, and this time the emphasis of the phrase made him wonder for a moment.

"Do you remember," he said, speaking almost timidly for such a giant as he was," you said then that you would never marry a poor man? but I thought — "

"That I might have changed my mind now, because we have grown rich." And, as she spoke, again there rushed upon her the desire to obtain, to call forth, to provoke, if necessary, the answer which her curiosity demanded.

"Rich?" Vincenz repeated the word with a peculiar accent, and then paused as if checking himself on the brink of some further speech. In a moment, he seemed to have recovered all his clearness.

"No," he answered, very quietly, "it was not of the change I was thinking, not of Draskócs. I never thought that Draskócs had influenced you — "

"Though it may have influenced others," said Gretchen, following a sudden impulse. In themselves, the words might have been mistaken; but the quiver of her scornful lip, the flash of her proud eyes, made their meaning clear, terribly clear to Vincenz, whose sensitive pride, put on the guard by Belita's chatter, pierced her thought on the instant. His gaze met hers: he understood, and Gretchen saw that he understood.

"Do you mean to say," asked the lawyer, slowly, having sat for a moment rigid under the effect of this revelation — " can you really believe that it is because of Draskócs that I have professed to love you? Because of Draskócs ?"

"It would not be so very unnatural to suppose," stammered Gretchen, "with some men;" and she got no farther than this, but sat silent.

Dr. Komers made a quick movement as if he were going to speak, but checked himself as suddenly as before, and for a full minute also sat silent.

During that minute, she began to tremble. This pause was fearful — Dr. Komers, in his rigid attitude, with his spectacles in his hand, and a dark flush spreading slowly over his face, struck her with a sudden awe. She fancied he was crouching for a spring-like a lion, which, in her folly, she had provoked.

The spring came, suddenly, at the end of that minute; and at the sound of his voice, so altered, so passionate that she scarcely recognized it as his. Gretchen shrank back, as though to entrench herself behind the black fortress.

"With *some* men, you say? Ay, I believe that there are such men, but I am not one of them. Oh, you misunderstand, you misunderstand me most cruelly! You insult my honor and you insult my love to you by hinting at such things. With *some* men! I dare say! You are free to refuse my love if you will not have it, but you are *not* free to insult it;" he brought down his clinched hand on the table beside him, so that it shook beneath his fist.

Gretchen sat quite still, but her breath came quick, and her eyes dilated. She had never seen Dr. Komers, the gentle, the courteous Dr. Komers, in this mood. She had never even suspected him of such passion. There was a fire in his eyes that seemed to scorch her, and yet she could not look away.

"I have loved you as few men love a woman," said the lawyer, still speaking in that rapid, deeply moved tone, and with the flush still darkening his pale face. "I have offered you my love twice, and you have refused it twice; you have rejected it, and you have doubted it. I shall never offer it again, remember that — never! I shall not beg for your love, like a beggar for a crust. If you will not give it to me freely, I shall live without it." He broke off with the same abruptness which marked his first angry words, and remained sitting as he was, staring in deep abstraction at the ground.

Still, Gretchen's self-possession failed her; still she sat in spellbound amazement. Was this the same man who a little while ago had pleaded so wistfully for her love?

It was no longer than half a minute that Vincenz had sat thus silent, when, starting out of his passing abstraction, he rose and half turned to the door; then stopping, he wheeled right round, and coming two steps straight towards Gretchen, he spoke in an altered voice, while the flush slowly faded from his face.

"I beg your pardon most humbly, Fräulein Mohr. I forget sometimes that I am no longer a young man. I have no right to lose my self-control in this way. Will you excuse my violence? I hope I have not frightened you. What I meant to say is, that as you have twice given me so decisive an answer, I shall never trouble you on this subject again."

He looked most sincerely ashamed of himself; in his heart, he felt as deeply humiliated as if he had used his brute strength against a woman. There was something tragi-comical in the alarm with which he gazed at the fragile girl before him, as though half expecting to see her shattered before his eyes like a figure of brittle porcelain.

Never again! He was gone — penitent for his outburst, but immovable in his decision.

When Gretchen met the lawyer after this, immediately before their departure, he looked a little pale, but otherwise unchanged, except that to the few hurried questions concerning Draskócs that Ascelinde found time to put to him, he gave short and rather ungracious answers. "You will see everything for yourself," he said, curtly, as he noted some necessary arrangements in his battered pocketbook.

Thanks to the united efforts of all the tailors in the place, the *tristezza* had been got into shape for the mourners. The *cascades des larmes*, so warmly recommended by Belita, were not to be procured, but an inferior sort of "tears" glittered along the outline of Ascelinde's tunic. As she walked down the staircase in her trailing black garments, where here and there a basting thread still lingered, Ma- dame Mohr felt that the most solemn epoch of her life was about to commence. For it was to take possession of the home of her ancestors, from which cruel injustice had excluded her since her most tender childhood, that she was setting off in this state of ghastly splendor.

The party of mourners had not driven more than a hundred yards down the valley when another set of bells jingled round the corner, and one traveling carriage, followed by a second, met them, and passed on at a sharp pace towards the Hercules Baths. In the first carriage, there were several people — an old gentleman, a young man, two boys. In the second, there were two ladies and a child.

For one minute, Gretchen found herself close to the younger of the two. She was leaning back, muffled in a colored burnoose; but her eyes were raised, and Gretchen saw a face which, in the dusk at least, looked beautiful. The vision swept past, vanishing into a cloud of dust.

The driver turned on his seat, and with an accent of pride, as if he were showing off a sight, he announced: "*Le mare Principe* (the great Prince) Resculescu!"

"And the lady in the second carriage, who is she?" inquired Gretchen. But the driver had cracked his whip, and the question was lost in the jingle of the bells.

Chapter XX

The Home of Her Ancestors

*"All creeping plants, a wall of green
Close matted, bur, and brake, and brier,
And glimpsing over these, just seen
High up the topmost palace spire."*

— Tennyson

T was a country of roses down there — a rose world. Enchanting designation! Pregnant with sweetest perfume, redolent of softest poetry. What life can be more fraught with dreamy delight, more removed from the dry prose of common existence, than that of a rose, living among other roses, in the midst of a rose country? What young disciple of the Muse would not sing to himself in an ecstatic moment that he'd" be a rosebud, born in a bower," and recognize the advantage of dying when the summer is o'er? The duties of a rose are light duties as a rule. To be fanned by the breeze in the daylight hours, and to listen to the song of the nightingale in the dark; to hang on a well-trimmed bush, the pride of a Northern garden; to be worshipped by well-paid gardeners in palaces of crystal, built up for them alone; to be stared at as the triumph of a metropolitan flower show; perhaps to climb up a cottage door and peep in at a scene of domestic felicity within; or, best of all, to crown a beauty's head, or scatter its dying petals on her breast.

Up there in the North, the roses arc the masters, but here in the South they are the slaves; and, like all slaves, whether human, animal, vegetable, or mineral, the roses

have a hard time of it here. No young poet, be he ever so young and ever so enthusiastic, would care to be boiled up with sugar and made into jam, nor yet to be
kneaded into the sickly *dulcezza* with which the Turkish ladies delight in spoiling
their teeth and ruining their digestion; nor even would he pine after the happiness of
being distilled into scent, or left to dry in the sun, until he had attained the necessary
degree of hardness and the coal-black hue which is requisite for the composition of
that perfumed mass, out of which the Southerners are fond of carving such fragrant,
but, alas! such hideous ornaments.

These slaves, with their pink faces and their hanging heads, are not cared for
because of their beauty — nobody takes the trouble to think of whether they are
beautiful or not: their master looks at them with a critical eye, but it is not to mark
their tenderness of hue or grace of shape — it is to calculate how much profit they
can be made to yield; for here, these queens of the flower world have sunk to the
prosaic position of potatoes or beetroot. The rose harvest is talked of here as elsewhere
the wheat harvest; and to hundreds of families, the success or the failure of the flowers
means riches or poverty. They are cut, they are stacked, they are carried away, just as
we cut, stack, and carry away our hay and our straw, our barley and our oats.

If now and then it happens that these pink-faced slaves lose their master, or that
their master slackens his hold upon them, then the slaves, breaking out of all bounds,
run wild and smother the earth, growing like weeds out of its fertile surface. Then,
missing the check of authority, they grow wanton, embracing and strangling each
other at will. Here and there, where some such colony has escaped from mastership,
the bushes bud and fade again without making anyone the richer — as for instance
on that lonely spot, where the roses year after year for a long time past have dropped
their petals unheeded upon each other, having no other duty to fulfill than to put
out their flowers as every June comes round, and weave a fantastic garland around
an old man's grave.

But those escaped slaves are few. These acres of roses around are all under the
yoke; and they are having their hardest time now, for it is late in the rose season, and
the cutters are at work. They are to be seen in the fields using their knives mercilessly,

and they are to be met on the road, coming along in the dust, bending under the load of flowers which heap the basket-casks on their backs, and staring sideways and open-mouthed at the unusual sight of a traveling carriage jogging slowly along. There is such a profusion of roses this year that no one cares if the heap shakes with each step, now and then dropping a rose-head in the dust, from where the children pick them up and play with them gleefully.

A rose burden is not necessarily a light burden, thinks Gretchen, as she watches the toil-worn faces of the laden peasant women; and though it may perhaps be pleasanter to prick one's fingers with rose thorns than with needles, that does not make the scratches in their hands less unsightly.

It is a hot day, but a day without sunshine. The hard glare of light, the dazzling brightness of the blue sky, which Gretchen has been used to for many days past, is gone today. There is an even grayness over the low-hanging sky, stretching away, unbroken and unshaded, until over there in the far west, where thunder broods in the lead-blue, metal-hued clouds, and grumbles out a faint but sullen warning, with long intervals of dead silence between. There is no breeze to carry about the scent of roses on the air: it hangs heavily over the fields, intense but unrefreshing, weighing on the senses and mingling with the breath of every evil-smelling thing, which disfigures the street of each squalid village the travelers have passed. It is strange to find one's self thus freed again from the imprisonment of the Djernis valley. The wide sky looks foreign to Gretchen, and the flat country has an uncongenial vacancy after those rocks and forests they have left behind them. They had passed by many rows of hovels, called villages; and they had passed one or two solitary buildings, standing in the middle of flat fields, and scarcely shaded by acacia trees, and these were called country houses. They were all long and low, and each had an appanage of small outbuildings; some of them were better and some of them worse. Some of them bore the stamp of poverty upon their doors and windows and the rude planking which fenced them in; others betrayed signs of rude opulence in their open granaries overflowing with Indian corn.

"Wait till you see Draskócs!" said Ascelinde, with suppressed triumph in her tone, each time that they passed one of these solitary white houses. Not one of them even distantly approached the picture in Ascelinde's mind: they all were pale and shadowy beside the vision which, with every moment and with every yard of the road traversed, was growing more distinct in her memory. The number of horses capable of being stabled at Draskócs had undergone a considerable increase since they started on their journey; every hour added a step to the flight which led up to the entrance door, the avenue grew more stately, the trees loftier with each minute, until it really appeared that if the journey were prolonged for another half day, the house of Ascelinde's ancestors would threaten to tower into the sky, and strike the beholders blind with the excess of its glory.

It was two in the afternoon when they drove past the dark wooden church with its weed-grown burying ground, and then up the dirty street of Hadháza, which Vincenz knew from his former visit. They stopped in front of the wretched little inn to water the panting horses: the poor beasts' ragged flanks were heaving, though they had jogged so slowly, for the air was heavy as lead and hot as a furnace blast.

"How slow they are in attending," said Ascelinde, impatiently, as a man leisurely filled a wooden pail with the dull water of the well. "Tell them that we are going to Draskócs, Dr. Komers, and that I am mistress of the place."

Dr. Komers appeared not to have heard; at least, he certainly did not give the information indicated; seeing which, Ascelinde gave the information herself, but was only met by a stupid stare.

"What is that man saying, Dr. Komers — I can't hear him?"

"He is saying that there will be a storm before evening, and that we had better stay here."

"How ridiculous! We shall sleep at Draskócs, of course; tell the coachman to drive on."

The landlord turned back to his inn, scratching his head, and Vincenz took his place on the box again beside the driver. The driver looked at the sky and shrugged his shoulders.

"Drive on," said Vincenz, shortly; and he folded his arms and sat staring straight in front of him, with a face as expressionless and as hard-set as a face of wood. He had worn this look throughout all the journey; and throughout all the journey, too, his lips had remained so obstinately locked that it was almost with an effort that he unclosed them when some unavoidable word had to be pronounced.

When the last house of Hadháza was left behind, the road, thick with white dust and seamed with deep cart-ruts, ran along between level fields and stretches of waste-land. It was the last stage of their journey, and Ascelinde, as she scanned the wide horizon, felt the solemnity of the impending moment settling down upon her soul.

"Are we near yet?" she asked at short intervals; and after a weary hour, at last came the answer — "We are not far now."

The sky during this hour had grown stealthily darker, and the clouds had gathered into a huddled mass. There was no one in the fields, and there was no one along the length of the deserted road.

But Ascelinde could not see the road, however much she might crane her neck. With trembling fingers, she smoothed her crape bonnet-strings and shook out the folds of her mournful tunic, which wept its inferior quality of tears around her ample person. She began to rehearse some speeches suitable for the occasion — a noble and dignified address wherewith to answer the welcome she expected. Some very unpronounced visions of enthusiastic tenantry were hovering through her brain. Mr. Howard had only the other day given her an account of a grand reception of the sort, when the farmers had taken out the horses and dragged their landlord to his door. The excitement was almost too great to be borne, and Ascelinde in this supreme moment, the culminating point as it were of her life, put out her hand mechanically, and pressed her daughter's fingers with convulsive force.

Some acacia trees were passed — five on one side, and six on the other; the carriage jolted heavily into a rut and heavily out of it again. Ascelinde saw the driver pointing his whip, as if at something ahead of them. That must be Draskócs — that must be *It!* Ascelinde could stand this no longer; she wrenched her hand away from her daughter, and she put it over her face.

She had scarcely done so when the carriage stood still. She looked up with a start. Dr. Komers was slowly descending from his seat, and Gretchen, leaning over the side, was staring eagerly on in front. Oh, irony of Fate! Had a horse come down, or had a wheel given way just as they were so near reaching the wished-for goal? Were they to be kept here in the middle of this cart track when they had all but arrived at Draskócs? Must they be detained here, at its very gates?

Ascelinde stood up in the carriage in an agony of impatience. There was a long, low, tumble-down house — a lower edition of the sort they had passed at intervals in the forenoon — staring at them over a wall of rotten planks.

"Dr. Komers, what has happened?" cried Ascelinde, trembling with agitation. "Why are we being stopped here? Are we going to be robbed? Or are the horses lame?"

Dr. Komers, having carefully descended to the ground, adjusted his spectacles and said, in a rather diffident tone, "Nothing has happened."

"Can't you take the stones out of the horses' feet, or whatever it is?" exhorted the countess. "Be quick, I implore you!"

"There are no stones in the horses' feet, Madame Mohr."

"Then the man is drunk, I am certain of it; you must take the reins."

By this time, Vincenz was rubbing his spectacles hard. "I assure you the man is perfectly sober," he said, hesitating.

"Then what have we stopped here for?" demanded the big woman, with a tragedy stare, as she stood to her full height in the carriage.

The driver was quietly filling his pipe, with the reins flung over his arm, while the horses stood with lowered heads and a dejected droop of the shoulders.

There was a long, low, tumble-down house —
a lower edition of the sort they had passed at intervals in the forenoon —
staring at them over a wall of rotten planks.

Gretchen sat still, leaning over the side, looking with a sort of fascination at the crumbling house which stood behind the rotten planks. The planks seemed to run all round in a square, and they covered half the height of the house, so that only the roof and a narrow strip of the wall remained visible. Through a chink between two boards, a pink rose had pushed its inquisitive head, and nodded them a hospitable welcome. To the right and to the left, to the back and to the front, the waste land stretched; the cart track ran on, its dust lying undisturbed by any passerby. There was no human being in sight, and no other house within eye-range, except where, in the far distance, a group of acacias seemed to denote a repetition of the place before which they found themselves.

"Madame Mohr," said Vincenz, standing with his hand on the carriage door, "I beg you to compose yourself. Be so kind as to look at those trees along the road; do they not recall anything to your memory?"

His grave tone arrested the excited words on her lips. She turned and stared back at the eleven acacia trees which they had passed, six on one side, five on the other.

"There were acacia trees at Draskócs," she said, looking at them blankly: "but there were a great many more of them, and much higher — a whole avenue."

"And that pond?" said Vincenz, pointing to an oblong piece of water which lay in a hollow outside the wall of planks, its stagnant surface coated thickly with green duck-weed, a splendid feast for a waddling flock, but spreading its luscious verdure in superfluous abundance before the solitary inhabitant of the pond. Where the supply so far exceeds the demand, even such delicacies as duckweed are lowered in the estimation of a duck.

"That pond," repeated Ascelinde, obeying Dr. Komers without knowing why she did it — "that pond? There was a lake at Draskócs — but the shape was rather like this pond, and there used to be swans upon it — large white swans," she added, looking at the small and very dingy duck that had paddled back to the near side again, and now stopped to gobble another mouthful of the floating green water-weed.

"And now," said Dr. Komers, scanning Madame Mohr's face with some agitation on his own — "and now, will you look at the house a little more carefully; does it remind you of nothing?"

Ascelinde, with a sort of notion that Dr. Komers was mad and must be humored, but with, nevertheless, a faint uneasiness at the bottom of her heart, turned away from the duck pond and stared at the tumble-down house.

There was a pause of nearly a minute while Ascelinde gazed at the house, while Gretchen looked curiously at the lawyer's face, while the coachman stuffed his pipe with his thumb, and while the dingy duck took two journeys backward and forward without any need of hurry. Then, Ascelinde looked at Vincenz, and he saw that the uneasiness had risen up steadily, and was now shining out of her eyes.

"I don't understand you," she faltered; "this does — does — not remind me of — of Draskócs."

"Look again," he said.

She did look again, blankly at first; but the uneasiness in her eyes turned gradually into real terror. Long, long-forgotten memories had begun to whisper, and were whispering louder every minute. That house was not strange to her; it had some place far back in her mind. She felt herself growing cold, but she was a strong woman — she would not give in to this absurdity.

"Dr. Komers, why are you keeping us here?" she asked, with an anger which was not quite real. "Why don't you tell the man to drive on to Draskócs?"

"We are at Draskócs already!"

Ascelinde turned pale, but she smiled a sickly smile. This was evidently a horrible dream, and it could only need a resolute effort to awake out of it; she had to clear her throat three times before she could speak distinctly.

"Yes, Draskócs," she said, looking at the lawyer rather wildly — how strange the familiar word sounded at this moment! "I suppose this is the lodge — or — or the gardener's house — but where is the house itself?"

"There is no other house; this is the house itself."

"This is Draskócs?" pointing with a desperate gesture across the plank wall. Oh, if only she could have clung to the belief that Dr. Komers was deceiving her! But, alas! what was this new light streaming in upon her reluctant eyes? As she put the question, she looked around once more, and from everywhere around her the ghosts of faraway memories seemed to start up and stare her in the face. Those acacia trees — they bore a horrible resemblance to the lofty avenue she remembered; that pond — it was growing every moment more distinctly like the lake of other days; that plank enclosure carried back her thoughts with most provoking persistency to the park-wall she had vaunted: even the tumble-down house had a ghostly, grinning likeness to the home of her earliest childhood. It was all a parody, a badly-drawn caricature; but the likeness which it bore to her memories was coming out now with rapid strokes.

"Yes, this is Draskócs." Dr. Komers said it with an effort; and having pronounced the fatal words, he turned without waiting to see the effect, and walked across the road, two or three steps away from the carriage.

This was the supreme moment then, the most dreadful half minute which Ascelinde had ever lived through; this was the moment to which Vincenz, in the first heat of his wounded pride, had looked forward to as the one of revenge. But now that it was come, the revenge was too absolute to be sweet. It was more than revenge, it was cruelty, to have kept this grim and heartless silence, to have let that unfortunate woman reach this very spot still wrapped in her insane illusions. Those two women in the carriage had grievously hurt his pride, and they were at his mercy; but it was a question whether at this moment Ascelinde or Vincenz suffered more acutely. His nature revolted against the unfair advantage he had taken. As he stood staring at the flat country, with his back generously turned to the carriage, while he printed off every cloud upon his memory with the agonized concentration of the moment, he felt that he would give everything he possessed, his sister Anna perhaps excepted, if, by a stroke of magic, the real Draskócs could have been transformed into something ten times more splendid than the imaginary Draskócs had ever been.

For a few seconds, Dr. Komers heard nothing behind him except the jingle of a carriage bell and the puffing of the driver's pipe. Ascelinde must have remained rooted and fixed as she had been when last she spoke. Then there was the sound of a heavy weight sinking down suddenly, and immediately there followed a tremendous burst of tears.

Such a burst of tears! Vincenz had never had even a distant notion of what a real burst of tears was until this moment: his ignorance was enlightened now. Ascelinde did not shed tears often, but the floodgates once let loose, they burst forth with the violence of a torrent. This woman never did things upon a small scale; her tears were only in proportion to her person. Her sobs made the carriage shake; her wails must have struck terror into the hearts of any horses not as completely deadened by fatigue as these dust-laden quadrupeds: even the driver forgot the next puff of his pipe, and the duck burst into a quack of alarm as it fluttered splashing across the pond. Small wonder if Ascelinde wept! With this flood of tears, she was weeping away whole avenues of lofty trees, whole terraces and turrets, entrance gates and flights of steps: her tears were as plentiful as the waters of her imaginary lake, her sobs as deep as the phantom mines of wealth whose fond memory she was forced to relinquish. She had been seven years old when she saw these things last; she was fifty now. During forty-three years the memories had lain and grown; what wonder that, brought thus face to face with the original, the big woman should be annihilated? At the first burst, Vincenz turned round terrified. He was but an ignorant man after all, and had but a very dim notion of what might be expected to follow upon this truly feminine hurricane. He did not look at Madame Mohr, however, he looked past her at her daughter. Would Gretchen break down? If Ascelinde's substantial frame were so shaken by this grief, then must not the effect on that perishable blossom be fatal? And he was then her murderer? Oh, the terror of suspense!

Gretchen did break down, only a minute later than her mother. She too, like Ascelinde, had been standing in the carriage; she too now sank down and threw herself back on the seat, and she too drew out her handkerchief and convulsively hid her face behind it.

Dr. Komers was just calling on the earth to open and swallow him up, when he checked his mental invocation at a sound that struck on his ear.

Oh, joy of relief! Those were not sobs; she was not weeping, she was laughing. With her face buried in her handkerchief, she was attempting to smother the irresistible laughter which overpowered her without mercy. It was a mere chance, after all, whether the ludicrous side or the tragical side of the situation came uppermost — it was such a nice question of balance between laughter and tears. For Ascelinde, it was an unbroken tragedy; for Gretchen, perhaps the solitary duck, survivor of so many fictitious swans, decided the balance in favor of comedy. Each view in its way was overpowering, and Gretchen, with her face behind her handkerchief, was entirely overpowered. Her dreams of yesterday were dispelled, her fortune was unmade again, her pedestal was shattered under her feet; and Gretchen looked at the broken pieces and realized that they were broken, and laughed with a mirth as wild as though they had been the fragments of some weight suddenly lifted from off her mind. Again and again, her laugh rose up, mingling with her mother's sobs. She laughed as only the very young and the very inexperienced can laugh, in such an excess of agony and enjoyment that the sound echoed far along the lonely road, and the deserted house stared at her in astonishment over its rotten enclosure; for it was many, many years since such a sound of mirth had struck against the crumbling walls of Draskócs.

While Ascelinde still wept and Gretchen still laughed, another sound rolled up in the distance and drowned even the wailing sobs. The rumbling thunder had burst into a loud warning, and Vincenz, looking round, saw that the great vault overhead had grown gloomy, threatening every moment to let loose a storm of rain. The over-burdened clouds hung ready to break without further warning.

It was necessary to find shelter, and there was no shelter but this desolate house alongside. The necessity for action gave back to Vincenz his lost presence of mind. Ascelinde, who appeared to have wept away all her strength for the moment, allowed herself passively to be helped out of the carriage.

They were standing close in front of what seemed to be a gate in the center of the plank wall. There was no handle, no keyhole, no bell-rope visible, no smoke issuing from the chimney of the house, and no step or movement to be heard inside the planking. A few loud raps from Dr. Komers's stick started a hollow sound but were followed by deep silence. The solitary duck in the pond was the only thing that seemed to speak of a human presence. It was a slender piece of evidence; but Gretchen argued that where there was a duck there must also be somebody who intended to eat that duck.

At a more vigorous blow against the wooden gate, the planks creaked and trembled, but held together for a moment longer; at the next blow they gave way, and two of them fell inward, but not far inward, for they were caught against the branches of the bushes within.

It was now possible to effect an entrance, but by no means easy, for a barrier of bushes confronted the travelers, or rather a tangle of interlaced branches, inextricably knit together and crowding up to the very walls of the house.

Chapter XXI

Josika's Grave

"Above the graves of buried men
The grass hath leave to grow."

— Owen Meredith

T HE three intruders paused in the entrance, struck with wonder at the singularity of the scene. The walls of the house were damp and tottering, and stained with streaks of mossy green; the old wooden shutters gaped in rotting feebleness across the black space of windows within; the plank enclosure was irregular and rough; but for all that, the spot was bewitchingly beautiful, rich with the wealth of fairy-like ornaments which it had pleased Nature to shower upon this lonely garden.

Never in the height of its best days, such as Ascelinde had persuaded her memory to remember it, had Draskócs looked as beautiful as to an artist's eye it would have seemed now in its downfall.

And yet, the sight brought with it an irresistible melancholy; for the rose season was past its height, and on all sides the overblown roses hung ready to fall at a touch. At every step the tangled bushes trembled, and shook down a rain of petals-pink petals, grown yellow and curling at the edges. But those showers which fell on all sides scarcely reached the ground: myriads of petals were caught in the arms of green branches so thickly intertwined that the rose leaves lay there in bleached and faded heaps. The three intruders were wading ankle-deep in the rose-leaves of years past; generations of rose-leaves, heaped up in every stage of decay — the highest freshly shed, the lowest crumbling already into the soft brown mold.

No oppressed nation breaking into rebellion had ever run such riot as the now neglected Draskócs roses, whose office it had once been to be cooked up with sugar and made into jam. The tyranny of man had ceased for them. Liberty! was the cry of the Draskócs roses now, and the pink roses and the white roses, meeting across the path, embraced each other with unbridled passion, or strangled each other with fierce delight. They look like intoxicated revelers, too, those pink roses with the dark purple flush which the hot sun has burned into them: no longer the shyly blushing buds of a month ago, they stare bold and unveiled into the face of the sky, while the white ones hang their heads, wan and pale, like beauties after a long night of bacchanalian dissipation.

And the rebellious flowers are not content with having their way down here. They have mounted onto higher ground; they have flung themselves on every available hold, they have peeped over the wooden barricade, they have barred up the windows more effectually than the falling planks, and scaling the walls of the house, they have hung up their red flags over the very grave of the tyrant. Two fir trees stand beside the door, and the left one has fallen a victim already to the strangling roses: there it stands, brown and dead, where a glimpse can be caught between the smothering mass of flowers; but the other still lives, vigorously pushing a glistening dark green arm outward, as though it would free itself from the certain death which has crept upon it in such beautiful guise, while above its head the triumphant roses float at a giddy height.

By dint of much perseverance, with the help of a penknife, and very much at the expense of his coat sleeves, Vincenz had succeeded in fraying a passage to the house, Gretchen following close on his steps, while Ascelinde, limp and mournful, brought up the rear, too deeply dejected to defend her trailing garments against the grasp of the roses which, stretching forth eager fingers on either side, greedily stripped off the *cascade des larmes* and shed them profusely on the ground. "There are still the rooms inside," she confided in a whisper to her daughter; "there are still the rooms and — and — the jewels."

They had struggled as far as the fir trees, and Vincenz tried the door, but it scarcely moved when he shook it, and not a sound came from within. The whitewash of the walls, no longer white, fell off in flakes and crumbled in yellowish powder on to the heads of rose bushes alongside.

The necessity of getting under shelter had grown more urgent than ever. The mass of lead-colored clouds had gathered together and hardened at the edges into thunderous rims. A white glare flashed out over the country, bathing each rose head in ghastly light, and sunk down and flashed out again.

They made their way round the house, having to force each step of the passage. It was all a repetition of the same thing — dead and dying roses on all sides. At the back, however, there was a change. Here, a small space had been cleared, and a plot of rudely planted vegetables varied the monotony of the scene. The vegetables were only a few carrots and a meager row of lettuce; but they supported the evidence of the duck, for they certainly had not come here by themselves. On the damp bed, there was the mark of a footprint. Vincenz stooped to examine it, and just then he heard Gretchen exclaim, "Oh, look! What is this?"

There was an old wooden shed behind the house, and she was pushing open the door. Inside there stood a half-starved cow, with its head turned over its shoulder, and its stupidly patient eyes fixed on the intruders, while it slowly whisked its tail.

The sight of the cow threatened to make Ascelinde break down once more. Was this all that remained of the stabling for the many horses which had grown so prodigiously in her memory?

"I beg you to compose yourself," said Vincenz, apprehensively. Ascelinde struggled with her emotion, gulped down her tears, and held out her hand to Dr. Komers. She confessed, in a shaking voice, that it was not his fault if Draskócs had come down to this; but — for her spirit even now was not quite crushed — could he not tell her

— she remembered now that he had said that land was more valuable than houses — could he not tell her how much land there was belonging to this?

There was exactly this garden and one field, Dr. Komers believed, and he communicated his belief briefly but delicately.

"This garden, one field, and a tumble-down house," summed up Gretchen to herself, "and a cow and a duck." This was the inheritance to be divided with Kurt; this was the fortune which she had suspected Dr. Komers of coveting. Oh, she could have laughed again, as she had laughed on the road! She is an heiress! An heiress to what? To this tottering ruin and to the weeds which grew around it. She could almost have resigned herself, for justice' sake, to beg Dr. Komers' pardon, only that he had interdicted the subject, and she could not find the courage to revive it.

A stealthy creak of wood aroused her; and scanning the brick-paved open passage which was the original of Ascelinde's "colonnade," they all became aware that on the edge of the unclosed door a skinny hand was resting, and that, through the chink thus formed, there stared out at them a strange face, weirdly human in its outlines, and motionless in its position.

Dr. Komers reached the door just in time to see it closed in his face; but one wrench of his arm was enough to tear open the feeble plank, and he found himself confronted straight by an old woman in a dirty orange-colored dress, and with a dirtier lemon-colored face.

She was the strangest old woman that Vincenz had ever seen.

Her face was long, lean, and withered; her left shoulder was several inches higher than her right one; her orange-colored dress had to go up a hill and down a hill again upon her deformed back. And yet hideous though she was, there yet remained something to say that she had once been handsome, perhaps even beautiful. Her eyes were faultlessly cut, although they were the eyes of a woman of eighty years; and the nose, now as sharp as the beak of a bird of prey, must have been a perfect aquiline nose sixty years ago. In spite of her deformity, she moved with a rapidity which was almost startling, and whatever her shoulders might be, her long arms were anything but the arms of a cripple. The old woman proved to be stone-deaf, shrill-voiced, and bad-tempered, and Vincenz seeing that questions were useless, took the law into his own hands, and proceeded to examine the house.

Ascelinde had suffered much, but there were still fresh disappointments to come: she had still to see the pillars of the entrance hall dwindle down to rough wooden props, the mosaic pavement of the passage to irregularly laid red bricks, the damasks into worthless, moth-eaten garments, the family rubies to a paltry string of garnets. At every step through the shabby rooms, whose windows the broken shutters darkened, and across whose rotten floor the mice scampered squeaking before them, some idol of Ascelinde's was overthrown, never to rise again.

Four moderate-sized rooms occupied the whole of the space down here; an insecure wooden staircase led up to some higher region, which Vincenz would, in all probability, have left unexplored, had not the yellow-faced woman, till now a passive and sullen spectator, suddenly placed herself across their passage, and adopted an attitude of defense.

Since she was so anxious to keep them from that staircase, argued Gretchen, it stood to reason that there was something to be hidden up there; and while Vincenz began to expostulate with the excited woman, Gretchen slipped past them and gained the landing above.

She looked round her. It was very dark up here, but she could make out two closed doors. She opened the first: a whirl of dust blew into her face; there were spiderwebs spun across the entrance. It was nothing more than a lumber room, with a few broken chairs, the wreck of a long-abandoned cradle, and a heap of rags on the ground. She put her hand on the next door. This was the door of her mother's old nursery, though Gretchen did not know it. It did not open quite as easily, but it yielded at last, and starting back in wonder and amazement, she called to the others below —

"Come up, quick, quick! There is something — there is somebody here!"

In the next instant, Dr. Komers was by her side, and Gretchen pointing forward, whispered beneath her breath —

"What is it? Is he alive?"

The room was a low attic, with a sloping ceiling and one deep-set skylight window. It was bare of ornament, and almost of furniture. Ascelinde, reaching the doorway, swept her eyes round and felt that everything was familiar, even the looking glass on the wall, even the crack which ran across it. It made her feel six years old again; it was the identical crack which, by clambering onto a chair, she had been able then to get across her nose; and now, without any clambering, the same crack mutilated the same feature. A deep leather armchair, its cover hanging in tatters, stood near the window. In this armchair there sat a motionless figure, the profile seen distinctly against the light of the window and the square of the leaden sky behind.

Gretchen might well ask whether what she saw were alive or not; for that figure, so shrunken and small, was scarcely human to look at, and the wide-open eyes were glassy and fixed. It was the figure of a very, very old man. His feet, dangling helplessly to the floor, seemed to have withered away in the loose worsted slippers; his hands showed every bone; and there was but a feeble fringe of white hair falling under the edge of his black skull-cap. And while they still stared at this dismal picture, a second figure stepped into the frame. The orange-colored dress of the old woman brushed past them, her lemon-colored face was bent over the old man in the chair.

Everything is a matter of comparison in this world; the woman of eighty looked positively young, thus closely brought in contrast with the man's petrified features. This that was written on his face and figure was not to be expressed by the mere words "old age;" the woman beside him was old, but he was more than old. Near the ashy tint of his face, the streak of angry red in her cheek might almost have been mistaken for freshness; the skin which in her had hardened into parchment, in him was worn away almost to transparency. Every muscle and bone appeared to have shriveled from the mere force of time: it seemed as though the fiber and material of which Nature had fashioned him had been used up long ago, and he had sat since then in this same tattered chair, forgotten both by his fellow-creatures and by the

Angel of Death, breathing on from day to day in a state of existence scarcely worth the name of life.

How many young souls bad been forced to take wing from out of their vigorous bodies during the century that this man had counted as his lifetime! Better and nobler and more precious lives had been cut off short without mercy: the roses outside had put out their buds and shed their leaves and beaten against the window pane for years, while this old man had sat here through summer and winter, through bright days and dull days, in a state of living torpor or torpid life, forgotten and uncared for.

The movement in the room seemed to have roused some spark of his lingering life; or perhaps the thunderclap, which at this moment shook the ceiling above his head, had awakened him. He turned his head slowly, and his blear eyes fell straight upon the figure of the girl in the doorway. Gretchen had come forward two steps; there was an overblown rose in her hand, and a bunch of roses stuck in the front of her dead-black dress — they had begun to fall already — and as she stood there, with the floating petals around her, it seemed as if the queen of the rebellious roses had broken in here, and was advancing ready to brave him to his face.

Perhaps the old man had seen some such figure long ago, for, after a minute, a voice, faint and far off, reached the listener's ears.

"Yes, I have a long life before me — a long life before me."

The words were like an echo of something heard before. Surely that phrase was familiar!

He went on nodding, with his eyes always on Gretchen, mumbling the words over again between his toothless jaws. He did not seem to hear the thunderclap, which just at this moment shook the ceiling above his head, and made the window rattle in its socket.

"They shall not touch you, Jósika!" cried the woman, bending over him. "I shall take care they shall not touch you."

"Did you hear that? She calls him Jósika," said Ascelinde, in a whisper of extreme agitation. "I know of only one Jósika, and that was my guardian. Dr. Komers, is this my guardian?"

But Dr. Komers could give her no information, although he was beginning to believe that this was indeed all that remained of Ascelinde's guardian, and that this shriveled figure in the chair was the man who, forty-three years ago, had bowed Eleonore Damianovics out of the house, and walked back into it, rubbing his hands as he laughed over the word "Justice." He had kept his word; he had survived the end of the lawsuit; but his long life was behind him now, instead of before him, and must be gone from him soon. And the deformed woman beside him — could this be the handsome housekeeper of other days'? She was the only creature who cared for his life or his death; and yet he seemed to have forgotten her presence, as his lackluster eyes hung on the girlish figure that confronted him. Most likely, he could not see her distinctly; she may have seemed like a vision of something unreal to his failing eyes — like the Angel of Death come at last to end this long, long, and useless life. But death could surely not come in so fair a shape, with hair like fretted gold and dewy lips softly parted. Hark! Is that not rather the Angel of Death riding on the blast outside, which comes with sudden tearing force sweeping right over the plain? Is that not his trumpet thundering across the sky, and his signal flashing straight into their eyes, in a sheet of blinding light?

"Yes — yes, I have a long life before me," muttered Jósika again — "a long life;" and then the eyes fixed on Gretchen seemed to go out like the flame of a candle burned down to the socket, and the eyelids closed.

The blast, tearing onward, reached the spot; it seized the rose bushes with furious strength, and all around the house there was a rush as of a mighty body of water. For the space of a second, the wind held its breath, and then the rush burst out with double strength, and roared round them on all sides. A cloud of dust was whirled past the window, and a dense shower of rose leaves was carried with it high up in the air.

Upon Gretchen, a fit of nervous terror bad descended. It had grown very dark in the room, and the first heavy drops of rain fell like blows upon the window pane. A fancy came over her that that whirling wind must carry with it something else, something beyond the dust and rose leaves which flew past in a cloud. Dust and flower petals seemed too paltry a prey for the strength of that mighty hurricane. In the glare of the lightning, she saw the old woman bending across the chair; there was a tear on her wrinkled cheek. Together with the lightning came the thunder, making the house tremble this time through every fiber of its moldering walls. But though they waited long, the old man in the chair did not open his eyes again.

Chapter XXII

Princess Tryphosa

"Let none object my lingering way –
I gain, like Fabius, by delay."

— Gay

HEN the travelers again reached the peaceful Hercules valley, they found it by no means as peaceful as when they had left it a week ago. Some people looked scared, others looked anxious; door bolts and shutter bars were being examined, and firearms were much in demand.

Alarming reports had been started, and were being circulated from mouth to mouth. These reports spoke of robber bands among the hills. It was asserted that dozens of savage men, bent upon bloodshed and pillage, and armed with death-dealing weapons, were haunting the overhanging crags. Terrifying stories were told, in which it was positively affirmed that mysterious individuals, mysteriously muffled up, had been heard at dead of night to chant mysterious songs around a roaring red fire. The Hercules valley, now at the height of its season, was thrown into a panic; and the rustic police set up guards at the two entrances by which the place might be surprised.

Every day some new version gained favor; and on the day of Madame Mohr and her daughter's return, the newest story was one referring to the rocky mountain-face which rose straight behind the *Cursalon*. At the height of some hundred feet, the rock was split by a narrow gorge, leading to the very edge of the sheer precipice. From that edge, a man could look down straight upon the Hercules Baths at his feet; and this was exactly what the robbers were reported to have been seen doing — laying their plans, no doubt, for a night attack.

Ascelinde, crushed in spirit as she already was, and now met by these startling tales, took to her bed immediately after her arrival, and declared her intention never to leave it again. In truth, it still remained a question whether a serious illness would not be the result of that journey.

But Gretchen was skeptical about the robbers; she declined to accept the evidence unsifted. "People always let their fancy run away with them," she contemptuously remarked to herself, as on the day after their return she was noting down the expenses of the Draskócs expedition in the same leather-bound volume in which she had made her estimate of fortune on the afternoon of Ash Wednesday.

It must not be supposed, in spite of Gretchen's burst of laughter at the gate of Draskócs, that the failure had left no dejection behind it. The dream had been cherished too long and tenderly to be thus yielded up without a pang. In this very account book there stood a calculation of the supposed income which she had assigned to the imaginary estate; and it was with a bitter sigh that she now drew an ink-line across it. There was no denying that her chances of fortune-making were narrowed; and, looking at her situation from a logical point of view, the upshot of her meditations was as follows:

A pretty girl without money has got one chance of success in life — marriage. I am a pretty girl without money, therefore it stands to reason that marriage is my one chance of success. Shall I throw it away, as so many foolish women have done, for the sake of beautiful whiskers or eloquent eyes? I do not think that any whiskers or beard that ever grew would look beautiful in a garret, and even the fire of eloquent eyes must be fed with something more substantial than sighs and poetry. "No, thank heavens!" said Gretchen, with a devout sigh — "thank heavens, I am sensible;" and it never struck her as she said it that all this excess of sense was in itself a folly, greater perhaps than many outspoken phases of the disease. "Thank heavens, I am sensible. People can say what they like, but it is ever so much easier to be happy when one has a whole dress on instead of a ragged one, and ever so much easier to be virtuous when one has eaten roast partridges and iced pudding than when one has dined off bread and cheese. Oh no, I have no liking at all for bread crusts; bread-and-cheese marriages may appear attractive to bread-and-butter misses, but the thing will not suit me. No," concluded Gretchen, with an almost unnecessary decision, as she drew line after line across the Draskócs calculation. "No, I am afraid — that is to say, I think that I have only one chance of fortune!"

As she reflected thus, her eyes chanced to fall on the page which faced the imaginary estimate. There was a list written there, a sort of inventory apparently; she had put it there herself not many weeks ago, and now her last ink stroke was arrested, as with sudden attention she scanned the opposite sheet.

She read it over and over again carefully, with thoughtfully puckered brow, and at last, she exclaimed aloud,

"Yes, I have another chance!"

And leaving her last ink stroke incomplete, Gretchen plunged headlong into a sea of arithmetical figures, in which she was still disporting herself when, an hour later, Belita entered the room.

The news of the Draskócs failure had been received by Belita last night with a certain amount of consternation but without any remorse. Gretchen's indignant reproaches had entirely failed in their effect — it was not possible to quarrel with the contessa. She cheerfully acknowledged that she had made a mistake, and cut the matter short by remarking that Dr. Komers must, after all, be a greater fool than she had taken him for.

"Are those the bills for your new black dresses?" she asked now, throwing a glance of interest at the account book. "If it is a dress estimate, I will help you."

"No," answered Gretchen, coming to the surface of the arithmetical sea; "it is a calculation about my fortune."

"But, my dear child — "

"Belita," said Gretchen, solemnly, "I have got a new idea about my fortune. Shall I tell you how I mean to make it?"

"What other idea can you possibly need to have beyond Baron Tolnay — provided you are lucky enough to get him?"

"But must there only be one way?" retorted Gretchen, impatiently. "Why should I not make my fortune in my own way?"

"But what way could, by any possibility, be better than the one you are on?"

"I will tell you, Belita, listen," said Gretchen, with a ring of triumphant superiority; and taking up her account book, she read from it aloud: "Thirty-eight Turkish gold bags, one hundred and fifty silver bags, nine hundred and ninety Russian rubles, five thousand bejas zirmilik, three golden chalices, seventeen golden necklaces, and golden earrings — enough to fill three full-grown skulls."

"Well," said Belita, a little startled, "who does all this belong to? Where is it to be seen? What does it mean?"

"It is the brigand's treasure," was the impressive answer.

"And what has the brigand's treasure to do with you?"

"Simply that I mean to find it."

Belita burst into a long and hearty laugh, while Gretchen, her dignity a little ruffled, proceeded to expound her views. The list in the account book had been written down from memory, on the evening after her meeting with the Bohemian. About so interesting a subject as a brigand's treasure, the methodical Gretchen could not omit to make a note at the time, even though she had then entertained no serious intentions with regard to it; it was only now that she recognized its true importance. She had spent an hour in abstruse calculation, had ascertained what proportion of the treasure she would have to relinquish to the Government, and what income, at a given rate of percentage, she could derive from the remainder.

Belita burst into a long and hearty laugh...

"The earrings can be melted down," she concluded; "but the three chalices I shall, of course, return to churches."

She could not understand what made Belita laugh. "Since the treasure had never been found, it stood to reason that it must be there still; and it only required an energetic and sensible person, unhampered by superstition, to discover it. She was a sensible and energetic person, unhampered by superstition, therefore it stood to reason," etc.

"My dear child," said Belita at last, when she had, with some difficulty, been brought to understand that Gretchen was not joking, "I am afraid that the air of the Hercules valley does not agree with you. These Waters of Hercules seem to go to everybody's head but mine; is it any mythological influence, I wonder? If you had been at school here, you certainly would never have carried off the *prix de logique*."

It was a mystery to the contessa how anyone, holding a baron in the hand, should prefer to him a mysterious treasure, which was not even in the bush, but rather hidden among millions of bushes, and which even might prove not to be, and never to have been there at all. "How on earth can you talk of finding the brigand's treasure, when you cannot even find that horrid black hole where you tell me it is buried?"

"But I intend to find *Gaura Dracului*."

"By what means?"

"By means of the Bohemian."

"But since the devout fool will not break his vow?"

"He need not break his vow; I have settled all my plans."

And Gretchen's plans were laid with a truly feminine cunning, though as a first step towards them, she herself would require to eat a slice of that most distasteful of all dishes, called humble pie. She had no more liking for humble pie than for bread crusts; but she hoped that that unsavory dish might this time be no more than an entree to the roast partridges and iced pudding. The Bohemian was to be sought out, and the offer, once so coldly rejected, was this time to be graciously accepted. Once having got him to guide her among the mountains, Gretchen had full confidence in her own skill and management in laying traps for the innocent man's secret, and causing his simple mind to betray itself unawares. As for the robbers, she settled the difficulty by not believing in them; and a couple of pistols would, in any case, be protection enough.

Belita listened with a dissatisfied air.

"Your interest in that unpronounceable place was always suspicious to me, Margherita. I cannot understand what gave you the idea of this most extraordinary wild goose chase."

"But it was papa's old manuscript — I wanted him to finish it. And oh, Belita" — there was a sudden break in Gretchen's voice, her lips quivered ominously.

"*Misericordia! Bambina*, is there anything else wrong?"

"Will — will papa ever be well enough to finish his manuscript? He is getting well so slowly."

She would call it "getting well" still, even though the first sight of his face this morning had struck her with a chill of apprehension. Yes, there was a change here too, even after this one week of absence. Of course, he was getting cured, of course, the tutelary god of the valley was not going to send him home as he came — the great Hercules had surely too much regard for his own reputation to allow of such a thing, but other people had got cured faster. Adalbert had been outstripped by many whose case had, at first sight, appeared more desperate.

"He had his forty-eighth bath today," said Gretchen, opening another page of her account book; "and I had calculated that after four dozen baths he would leave his chair, and after six dozen be able to walk up the highest mountain in the country."

"So, he will, my dear," burst in Belita, speaking with all the more rattling cheerfulness that she felt her friend's fears to be well-founded — "so he will, if you only follow my advice. Do you know what would be better for him than a hundred sulfur baths? Why, to see his daughter's fortune made, of course!"

"I have told you that I mean to make it in my own way, Belita. I will not be dictated to."

"Oh, my pretty fortune-hunter!" cried the contessa, "we are very fastidious in our choice, it seems; but how do you know that there is any choice remaining?"

"I don't understand," said Gretchen, staring at her friend.

"No; and you don't understand either what has kept me languishing on in this rocky fastness, and wasting the sweetness of Parisian toilets upon the more than desert air, when I might have been wearing my *homard écrasé* at Ostende, or my *éclipse de lune* bonnet at Baden-Baden. It is all for your sake, ungrateful Margherita!"

"I never asked you to stay," said Gretchen, completely mystified.

"But you might thank one for it. *Misericordia!* What trouble I have had! Keeping my eyes open from morning to night, and not even leaving myself time enough to write the most pressing letters to my *couturière*."

"And what have you seen while you kept your eyes open?" with an uneasy curiosity.

"Plenty, my dear — too much. Do you remember my telling you that Baron Tolnay was not caught yet?"

"Yes, I remember."

"Well, it is high time you were back. If this had gone on for another week, I should have been driven by the considerations of friendship to flirt with Baron Tolnay myself, in order to keep him away from that — No!" broke off the contessa, abruptly, "you shall find it out without me. Besides, my time is up, I have an appointment at home — some Wallachian embroidery, which Providence has cast in my path, and which forms a new and distinct interest in life. Do you dine at the restaurant today?"

"Yes," said Gretchen, further mystified.

"Well, keep your eyes open, that is all: there is a rival in the camp."

Belita walked to the door. "You have time to arm for battle," she observed, turning once more. "Baron Tolnay is at Pesth now, seeing after some international congress, I believe; and perhaps also buying unbreakable glass for the *Cursalon*." And with this parting shot, the contessa took her departure, leaving Gretchen much perturbed.

A rival in the camp! What woman's vanity would not be roused at the word? What ambition could sleep through such an alarm? Gretchen began to reflect that the brigand's treasure was not found yet, and that it would be imprudent, until it was found, to go without some second string to the bow of her fortune.

The dinner hour had never been so long in coming; and when it did come, there was nothing at first sight to satisfy Gretchen's curiosity.

The veranda was crowded: knives and forks and women's tongues contended noisily against each other. The Hercules fountain, straight opposite, tried to drown the clatter of the knives and forks and the wagging of the women's tongues, in its monotonous splash; while above, on his pedestal, the stone Hercules, leaning on his stone club, looked down with stony indifference on the doings at his feet. To this Hercules, who remembered Roman warriors, and who had gazed upon Roman beauties, the black-coated waiters who darted in and out of the veranda must have seemed indeed degenerate specimens of mankind.

There were only two vacant tables, and these stood next to each other. One of them was the table generally assigned to the Mohrs; the other was almost twice as large and assigned to whom, Gretchen did not know.

It was all the uninteresting and ordinary routine, except indeed that out of Gretchen's napkin there tumbled a more than usually eloquent and more than usually lengthy specimen of Esculapian poetry, headed by the desperately interrogative title: "Doctor or Patient?" and of which the verses ended with the alternate refrain —

"Be thou my Doctor!"

and

"Be thou my Patient!"

Whatever might be the opinion of other people, there was no doubt that Dr. Kokovics still continued to think himself as "born under a rhyming planet." But even this symptom. of unabated poetical persecution had come to be a part of normal life; and Gretchen's equanimity was scarcely disturbed by the poet-doctor's ardent desire

"To feel that lily pulse,

To view that rose-leafed tongue."

Nor even, though in the words of the bard —

"That golden head should throb,

Or ache those pearly teeth,"

was it likely that Dr. Kokovics's services should be called into requisition. Neither did Gretchen feel moved by the second appeal, in which the poet, with a spasmodic reversal of the *rôles*, groaned out the symptoms of his malady, and described the fever with which he thirsted after

"The medicine of thy smile!"

Just as the verse had been disposed of, there was a new arrival on the veranda. Heads were turned, and voices for one moment fell into a lower key, as the landlord in person, assisted by a swarm of waiters, began to set plates and chairs aright. Gretchen looked up just in time to see the vacant table alongside of them become alive, amid a great deal of creaking and clattering, and napkins being obsequiously waved, and French and Romanian being jumbled up together.

The hovering cloud of waiters dispersed at last, leaving Gretchen's view unobstructed.

At first sight, the newly-arrived family appeared to be bewilderingly large, but a short survey resolved it into the following elements: a dark and good-looking man of mature age, apparently the head of the family, presided at the table. His complexion was Oriental, but his manners were French. Except for a blood-red fez, his attire in no way fell short of the highest standard of European elegance. Alongside of him sat a ponderous, middle-aged woman, with a dark shade on her upper lip, and a suggestion of past, but very long past, beauty on her face. Beside her was placed a dark-eyed girl, ungainly of feature, and of a well-nigh mahogany complexion. Next came two pale-faced, sickly boys of twelve and fourteen, with a starved and timid tutor between them.

With her back turned straight towards the Mohrs' table, there sat another woman whose face Gretchen was not able to see. At about the height of her elbow, a small curly black head moved about restlessly. The boy of four or five, with the min-iature dagger stuck into his embroidered waistband, called the lady "maman;" but it was the Swiss *bonne* alongside who tied the napkin under his chin, and assisted him in the struggle with his eggshell. Gretchen could not even catch sight of the passive mother's profile; she was a very passive mother, there could be no doubt of that. Two or three times the curly head turned right round, and Gretchen found herself con-fronted by a pair of very black eyes, looking out of a small glowing face. It was the face of a singularly pretty boy, and, watching it, she felt her curiosity aroused. The son's good looks seemed to augur well for those of the mother. The lines of her figure, as far as could be judged by the sweep of the shoulder, were full, soft, and rounded. She wore a rather loose-fitting dress of deep purple silk, profusely trimmed and of a costly texture, but of a color too intense to be in strict accordance with the fashion of the day, which had some time since decreed that the sicklier a color was, the higher it was to be prized. Her hair, rolled up above her neck and disposed of in an edifice of massive coils and plaits, was quite black. In fact, Gret-chen thought that she had never known what really black hair was until this moment. It was not that purple or blue-black hair so much sung by poets, nor that silky black which shines in the light, but it was simply an uncompromising, unvarnished dead black. As I have mentioned the word varnish, I may as well add that this woman's hair really gave the impression of black paint which has not been varnished, for it caught no glossy reflection along the edge of its coils — it was all shadow and no light.

While Gretchen was pursuing her observations, Kurt was making vain efforts to secure the attention of the distracted waiters. The "barbarous grandees," as he called them, absorbed the mental as well as physical powers of the whole establishment. The hovering cloud of waiters had first dispersed, only to return armed with a battery of boiled eggs; then, after hovering a little longer, had dispersed a second time and reappeared a second time, bearing several melons aloft. The whole table shone with juicy, pale-red slices, while the black vultures pounced upon the ruins of the eggshells and cleared them away, all but one egg, which only now was being slowly cracked under the spoon of the unseen woman whose back-view Gretchen had been curiously contemplating. She took a long time to eat an egg, thought Gretchen, as she observed the deliberate way in which the shell was being attacked. They were strange people, certainly; it could not be good for a child of four years to gorge himself with melon, as the owner of the curly head was doing. Gretchen began to wonder what would follow upon the melon. A large soup-tureen solved the question. What had come before had only been a slight skirmishing, this was the earnest of dinner beginning. Under the claws of the vultures, the pyramid of melon rinds vanished together with the last lingering eggshell. One pale red slice remained; it was on the plate of the black-haired young woman. At this rate, she ate her way on steadily through the long and complicated meal, always a stage or two behind the rest of the party. When they were eating fish, she was eating soup; when they had reached the national *mamaliga* (a preparation of the maize grain, and first-cousin to the Italian *polenta*), she was preparing to dissect the fried trout on her plate.

Meanwhile, the brother and sister had ended their repast, and Kurt produced an elegant cigar case.

"I wish I had told Tolnay to bring me some stronger cigars from Pesth," remarked the precocious youth, as with the aid of the medicinal stanzas he kindled the spark in his "Virginia."

"I am very glad you did not," said Gretchen; "you smoke far too much for your age. I wonder where you have picked up those expensive habits!"

"At school," said Kurt, with a peculiar twinkle of his eye. "I have learned a great deal at school; smoking is not my only accomplishment. But never mind," he added, cheerfully, "I shall make Mr. Howard replenish my case. Since I have not asked him for money, it is at least fair that he should give me cigars."

"Kurt, do stop talking nonsense," said Gretchen, impatiently, while with her eyes she still followed the movements of their neighbors. As she spoke, her attention was arrested by something unlooked for.

Up to this moment, the black-haired woman had remained so immovable in her position, with her back and the massive coils of her hair turned so steadily towards the Mohrs' table, that Gretchen was positively taken by surprise to see her now slowly turning her head.

She had demolished her fried trout inch by inch, until there remained only one inch to be disposed of, and now she paused in the act of carrying the last morsel to her mouth, and, with the crisp brown tail held delicately between the fingers of her right hand, she deliberately turned in her chair and faced round towards the neighboring table. Her hand remained poised in its position, and the loose silk sleeve, falling back, showed a full and well-shaped arm. It was an expressive arm, but it was not a white arm — dark-skinned and with a soft shade over it as of a dusky down. The hand was of the same rich hue, and the well-cushioned fingers held the fishy tail with great firmness, although most delicately. Gretchen noticed that the fingertips were tinged with a deeper shade of yellow. It was only later that this yellow shade was explained to her· as the result of the innumerable cigarettes which the Romanian lady of degree fabricates for her own use and with her own skillful hands.

The turning of the stranger's neck was gradual: having reached the desired angle, she fixed her eyes first upon Kurt, and then the slow gaze moved on to Gretchen's face, and there for a full half-minute it remained fixed.

Gretchen had seen those eyes before. They had haunted her memory from the moment that the traveling carriages had passed each other on the road, until the picture of Draskócs had taken all other pictures from her mind. But seeing them again, they were at once familiar. They were as dark as her hair, and, like the hair, they seemed to want light a little; but they were beautiful eyes, long-shaped, well-cut, and velvety-black. The face was rather a full oval, with a low forehead and straight black eyebrows — almost too rich in the line of chin, and the luxurious sweep of the full red lips. She might be twenty-four, or perhaps twenty-five, thought

Gretchen, as she marked the deliberate ease of that heavy stare. Her gaze was not keen or penetrating, but it was very persevering, and it remained where it was fixed until it was satisfied. But what could be the satisfaction it wanted? This fixed gaze had an object. After eating through the previous half of her dinner with such unmoved stolidity, it had not been without reason that she now paused and turned round with the last morsel of fried trout hovering before her lips.

Gretchen went over quickly in thought the phrases which had just been said; but it was scarcely likely that the discussion of Kurt's extravagant habits, or of the vices he had learned at school, or a question as to the quality of his cigars, could have awakened any interest in this Romanian lady's mind.

For a full half-minute, the black eyes remained fixed upon Gretchen's face, and then, as slowly as she had turned round, the woman turned away again, and the hovering morsel of trout was raised to her lips and vanished there from sight.

"Who is that woman?" Gretchen asked of her brother.

Kurt shrugged his shoulders. "Cannot say, really. One of the barbarous grandees. Have not learned to particularize them yet."

"But she is beautiful!"

"I rather fancy she is," said Kurt, with the confidence of a connoisseur. "I always told you that it would take very little to make one of those Romanian women beautiful; this one has just hit it off, you see."

Undoubtedly, she had hit it off, reflected Gretchen; and all the way home she thought of nothing but the beauty of that face and the stare of those black eyes, until some words behind her roused her from her reflection.

"When is the baron to return?" one man was saying to another.

"On Thursday, I hear. She had a letter from him this morning."

"Who had a letter?" said the first voice. The answer was given in a lower tone, but Gretchen just caught it — "Princess Tryphosa."

Chapter XXIII

Fishing

"Bait the hook well; this fish will bite."

— Much Ado About Nothing

BOUT this time a fishing mania took possession of the Hercules valley. One eccentric Englishman had been enough to fire the enthusiasm of several dozen people, who immediately discovered that they had a passion for this watery sport. Everybody fished, and everybody had a different system of fishing, and everybody likewise spoke with withering scorn of every system but his own. The fish in this wild Djernis river were unwary and ignorant; and with so many systems brought to bear against them, it would go hard, surely, if some hundreds of those finny barbarians were not landed before the week was out.

Dr. Kokovics's System

Dr. Kokovics was all for energetic measures; he usually was for energetic measures, both in public and in private life. He quite deprecated any system which professed only to lure or coax the fish out of their element. He argued, amidst frantic gestures and with much throwing back of his head to clear his eyes from the fringe of hanging locks, that the fish should be got out of the water with as much noise and general rejoicing as could by any possibility be managed. This object was satisfactorily attained by the means of explosive bombs, which is thrown into the river, sent the fish floating, stunned, to the surface. In this way, the process was raised to the level of public entertainment. Seats could be arranged for the ladies by the side of the river; torches could be used; and a band of music, stationed behind the bushes, could fill up the intervals between the bombs with martial or operatic strains — so that in the case of no fish being caught, the public amusement need not suffer on that account. A choice selection of pieces bearing a piscatorial allusion, such as "Vieni la barca e pronta," or "Di pescatore ignobile," together with Schubert's " Forelle," were already noted down on one of the innumerable slips of paper to be rehearsed for the occasion.

The Conte Francopazzi's System

The Conte Francopazzi timidly objected to the foregoing system; his own nerves were not strong, and bombs had played too serious a part in the political feuds of his beloved country ever to be viewed by him in the light of mere frivolous amusement. He ventured to suggest that fish should be accustomed to the sight of man by gradual stages. Find a quiet, retired pool; go there for a week daily, with your pockets full of bread and cheese and broken meat; and — if you are not particular about your lining — cold vegetables. Empty the contents into the retired pool every day at the same hour. At the end of the week, the fish will be fat, tame, and unsuspicious. You have nothing to do now but to abuse their confidence and betray their trust by throwing in the daily meal, with the addition of hooks and lines, and you will soon have a basketful beside you. (This system, as being destructive to coat pockets, was at once extinguished by the contessa.)

Baron Tolnay's System

Baron Tolnay, being in a sort of way the King of the Djernis valley, objected to both the doctor's and the conte's systems. The bombs he considered unnecessarily destructive and the contessa's ideas with regard to the ruin of coat pockets were warmly seconded by him. He had no objection whatever to the presence of the fair sex, and he had a particular partiality for dusk; but why, he argued with a semi-royal *hauteur* — why labor with one's own hands, when there are hands enough to labor for one?

"I will order out a dozen of those lazy Romanians," he said, with that expressive smile of his which showed a flashing double row of teeth: "six of them shall wade up the river, and drive the fish before them with stones, and the others shall hold the nets across, and meantime we can sit on the bank and watch the spectacle in comfort; or, if we find anything more amusing to do, we need not watch the spectacle at all."

Mr. Howard's System

As for Mr. Howard, he regarded the bombs, the broken meat, and the wading Romanians, all with equal and unutterable contempt. This Englishman, cut after so uncompromising a pattern of his nation as to be more English than John Bull himself, recognized nothing but the severest rules of orthodox and stern-principled trout fishing. To approach a trout with any weapon but a rod of Farlowe's; to throw a March-brown in April, or a green-drake in June; to bait his hook with salmon-roe, like an English poacher, or with grasshoppers, like an unenlightened foreigner—would, in Mr. Howard's eyes, have been heresy, pure and simple; as bad as taking an advantage in a duel would be for a Frenchman, or cheating at cards for an Italian, or shooting a fox for John Bull himself. Any fish not caught in accordance with the above-named principles was, in Mr. Howard's eyes, not caught at all. "There are one or two pools here where one might possibly spin a minnow," he had said reflectively, but for the stickles there is nothing but a grilse-fly.

The Landlord's System

Flies! The landlord had no opinion whatever of those puny hooks, with little tufts of feather upon them, which Mr. Howard called flies. He would like to show them something that was like a fly indeed: a marvel of mechanism wound up by clockwork, and kept thus in motion for twenty minutes at a time. That was a fly, as large as a butterfly almost! A patented fly, too, but unfortunately as yet too little known — hardly more known than when he had first met this marvel of mechanism fifteen years ago. That had been in the landlord's obscure days — as obscure as the fate of the mechanical fly itself— when he still held a very modest position connected with knives and forks; long before the time when he had won the landlady's heart, and stepped into the place vacated in such a tragical manner.

These were the principal systems that came into fashion in the Hercules valley; but each of the fundamental ideas begot a fry of smaller ones. There were combinations and modifications, and a host of interpretations. The two young tallow-faced Resculescus, for instance, closely followed Mr. Howard's manner of managing his rod and casting his line, with only the difference of the bait; for while the elder one replaced the fly by unripe grapes, the younger was of opinion that green peas had a greater chance of success.

There were other systems of fishing, too; some of them independent of the movement started by Mr. Howard, some of them even unconnected with Djernis pools and Currents.

There was the kingfisher, who, darting out of the blue shadow of a cave, like a winged flash of color, dived for his evening meal, and came up, dripping and victorious, to carry his wriggling prey into the depth of his rocky haunt, and there sup upon it in peace.

Perhaps his system was the most successful, more successful even than that of the dark-eyed Oriental beauty, who rests in the secure consciousness that she has already landed her fish.

The kingfisher's cave is straight above the spot of the river which by courtesy is called "the waterfall" — and by a stretch of imagination may be taken for one. There the fish are leaping in a senseless manner, throwing themselves against the stones and dashing again and again at the narrow passage, in their efforts to reach the pool above. Not more than one in a dozen succeeds in its leap; the rest fall back stunned, to turn their heads perseveringly up stream again, unless indeed they are caught in the rebound by one of the two Romanian youths, who have turned their limp felt hats into impromptu landing nets. Judging from the color of the hats, ingrained with greenish-brown shades, it is not the first time that they have acted this part. One of these fishermen, with his linen trousers rolled up above his knees, has taken to the water, while the other lies flat on the slippery rock, turning from its destination many a fish, which, with an abrupt transition, finds itself landed in a well-worn felt hat, instead of in the peaceful pool above, and which, with a yet more disagreeable removal, will find itself presently landed in a frying- pan.

Gretchen, who had stopped on the bridge with Belita, began by watching; but, as she watched, she grew infected with the irresistible fishing mania. So presently, she had made her way down to the water's edge, and, armed with a green butterfly net, was rivaling the achievements of the two felt hats.

One of the fishermen was known to her by sight and name. Every now and then young Bujor would appear at the door of the Mohrs' apartment, offering for sale such natural products of the country as unfledged vultures and scorpions preserved in oil — the latter popularly regarded as a remedy against snake-bites. It was only the other day that he had brought to the door a bear-cub, which he declared to be a great bargain, but the expression of whose countenance was not reassuring, in spite of the assurance that the little monster was *multu dulce* (very gentle).

Bujor's face was of the old Roman cast so frequent in Romania — one of those clean-cut profiles and purely classical heads which are oftener found cut upon a gem, or stamped upon an antique medal, than met with in the laboring peasant.

Surely, thought Gretchen, Bujor's system of fishing was far preferable to that of Mr. Howard. A few minutes ago, they had passed the Englishman, rod in hand, stern and rigid by the riverside, followed by his two perpetual shadows, the Resculescu boys; and, upon the well-meant question as to whether he had caught anything, he had answered by a frown of displeasure, and the information given in a hushed voice, comprised in the one word "Nothing!" While Gretchen, after ten minutes, had landed almost as many sprawling little victims, very much to the disgust of Belita, who, standing on the bridge with her train gathered in one hand, chaperoned her young friend from a distance.

After a time, Gretchen became aware that Belita was signaling to her with her parasol, and apparently calling out something which the noise of the water made unintelligible. Following with her eyes the direction which the waving parasol indicated, she could see two figures approaching side by side along the path. The branches overhead threw a shifting network of shade upon them, so that Gretchen did not know them till they had drawn quite close. One of them was Baron Tolnay; the other was that black-haired beauty, whom Gretchen had heard called by the name of Princess Tryphosa.

Gretchen remembered that this was the day on which Baron Tolnay was expected back from Pesth. They had not met since the evening of the dance at the *Cursalon;* and thinking of all that had passed on that occasion — of those words and those looks, which had been flattering if they had been nothing else — it was not at all agreeable to her now to see him by the side of this Romanian beauty. Taking a rapid review of the situation, she reflected again that the brigands' treasure was not yet found, even though the first step towards her plan had been taken some days ago, the humble pie had been eaten, and the Bohemian's services accepted.

Until the appearance of this woman on the scene, she had believed that Fortune, as represented by Baron Tolnay, was a prize which lay within her grasp, ready to be taken up or left as she chose; and even though she had not yet reached the clear understanding as to whether she did choose or not, the thought had been pleasant, and the doubt now awakened was unpleasant.

The two figures approached very slowly: the woman's silk dress trailed heavily on the ground behind her. They reached the bridge, and turned on to it, and now they were standing, still side by side, looking down at the water.

All this Gretchen, without once raising her eyes, distinctly saw. From under her eyelashes, she kept the bridge in view, while to the spectators she appeared to be only fishing. And fishing she undoubtedly was, although she thought very little now about the wriggling white captives within her net. This calm indifference, this languid ignoring of the gaze upon her, it was all, according to her own theories, an advantageous laying out of capital from which she hoped a profitable return. With the net of her golden hair, with the line of her graceful arm, with the bait of her rosy lips, Gretchen was fishing — fishing for her fortune in the waters of the Djernis.

Almost any man but István Tolnay must have found his situation embarrassing. Beside him there stood a woman, and below by the water's edge there stood another woman; and his relation towards each of these women was considerably beyond that of a mere acquaintance or friend; each of them looked upon him as being in a sort of way her property, and each expected from him something which he could not possibly give to both. But István Tolnay did not find it embarrassing; he had not even taken the trouble to foresee this contingency, which sooner or later must have come to pass. It was not his habit to foresee events, or to make plans for even the most immediate future. He suffered from a species of mental short-sightedness that made it impossible for him to see what was coming. A boundless trust in his luck, or his quickness of thought, in chance, or in anything, was all the provision he made against a disagreeable contingency. The pleasure of the hour, the excitement of the hour, the pain, the passion of the hour, these alone had value; for the present was everything, the future nothing. Like the lilies of the field, he took no thought of the morrow; like them, he did not spin, neither did he weave. Fate had made him a rich man; but even had he been born poor, most assuredly he would not have been given to ask himself what he should eat on the morrow, nor wherewith he should clothe himself. Beggary, disgrace, or death could never have preyed on his mind in advance. They did not touch him as long as they were not there: a glass of red wine at the moment would be to him a more vital thing than the misfortune to be suffered next week; and a smile from a pretty woman today consolation enough for the ruin of tomorrow. Yes; and even though the future were to unclose, and show him the spot where stands his grave, István Tolnay would go forward to meet his fate as much István Tolnay as ever, whistling the air that pleases him best, with his boots polished to exactly the right degree, and his black mustache stiffened at exactly the most becoming angle.

He had found it pleasant to saunter along the path by the side of the dark-haired beauty; and now he was thinking that it would be still more pleasant to stand beside the fair-haired beauty down by the water's edge. It only wanted some faint shadow of an excuse to free him from his position on the bridge. Patience! his luck or his wit would come to his aid, he felt sure. That rock down there was coated with slippery weed; supposing she should lose her balance —

And it seemed as though his unspoken wish were to be fulfilled on the instant; for a sharp cry pierced the air.

"*Uitisce, uitisce! la kokona!*" (See, see! the young lady!) Bujor was crying.

There was a slip below, and a momentary scramble: the green gauze net was swept down the current.

"She is falling!" cried István; and he precipitately left the bridge.

"No, worse than that!" the contessa called after him, "her hat is in — her new black feather! Save it, Baron Tolnay!"

The hat would do quite as well, thought Baron Tolnay, as he made his way through the stones to the riverside. "Desolated to have to leave you in this way, princess!" he had said, with a glance to match the words, as he hurriedly left her side; and now he was smiling to himself confidentially under his mustache, as he thought how safe he would be down here from the ears, if not from the eyes, of that woman on the bridge.

Gretchen was standing bareheaded by the water-edge, with a shower of water-drops sparkling in her hair, as she directed her two Romanian assistants in the capture of the floating hat. From above, Belita, agitated spectator of the scene, called out unintelligible advice, and gazed at the sinking feather as if it had been a drowning child.

"Am I in time?" asked István, with a little artificial breathlessness, as he reached the scene of action. "Pasha would have fetched it in a moment: I wish he were here!"

"But since he is not, Baron Tolnay, would it not be more logical to wish that the hat had never fallen in?"

"But I wish nothing of the sort. If the hat were still on your head, I should be still on the bridge."

"Oh, were you on the bridge?" said Gretchen, with a movement of surprise, quite as artificial as István's breathlessness. "I have been standing there for ages."

"Indeed!" with her nose rather high in the air. "You must have found the bridge very entertaining?"

"Very; with such a picture to look at."

"You admire landscapes?"

"Not unless there are foreground figures in them."

"Those Romanians are very picturesque, certainly."

István laughed.

"You surely do not suppose that I was looking at that vermin? There, stand back!" as the triumphant Bujor held out the dripping hat. "Stand back, you dog, I say!"

"Baron Tolnay !"

The gray eyes looked almost stern for a moment. "Do you call this justice? How can you treat him in this way?"

István gazed at her in genuine surprise.

"But he is not accustomed to being treated in any other way, Fraulein Mohr!"

"*I* treat him in another way."

"But they are vermin, you know," said István, good-naturedly.

"Baron Tolnay — "

"You object? Very well, Fraulein Mohr, to oblige you, I will retract. I will not say that they are vermin. I will even go the length of saying they are not vermin should that give you the very smallest satisfaction. Look, you shall mark the generosity of my forgiving soul" — and he took a handful of loose silver from his pocket and tossed it negligently towards Bujor. "This is the only language they understand."

Gretchen half expected the insulted peasant to fold his arms, and with his foot to spurn the proffered coin, haughty and disdainful, as an ancient hero defying a tyrant. But, alas, for the degeneracy of these days! This man, who could have stood as a model of a Roman centurion, now humbly crouched down, and uttering an abject *"Mulezanim Domno!"* (I thank you, master!), patiently searched for the scattered coins which had been flung to him upon the stones of the riverside.

"How very generous of you to forgive him for having saved my hat!" said Gretchen, still with a ring of scorn in her voice.

"Not generous, magnanimous! It is positively noble of me not to grudge anyone the pleasure of having served you."

The tone of the conversation was becoming perilous, thought Gretchen; it was safer to let it drop. She was quick at these conversational skirmishes, but he was quicker; and there were moments when she felt an uneasy distrust of this man, with his brilliant conversation, his brilliant eyes, his brilliant smile, and his over-brilliant boots.

With her face turned towards the river, Gretchen stood and watched the hurrying waters; Tolnay stood beside her. The rescued hat lay beside them on the rock, slowly drying in the breeze.

A little while ago, the sunshine had been on the river; now it was gone, and with it was gone the color and the brightness of the overhanging rocks and sharp-cornered granite stones; the kingfisher's cave above the waterfall had deepened to a gloomy blue. But there was much to look at still, and much to listen to; this subdued coloring is grateful to an eye tired of the sunny glare, and flattering to a dreamy mood. Those dark-green pools where the water circles round and round so sleepily; those slanting stones down whose polished sides it slides in a sheet of smooth glass, to break at its base and curl away in frothy wavelets; those patches of milk-white foam clinging in stagnant repose to some drifted tree branch, yet torn unmercifully by the shock of the passing current — these are in themselves small pictures which together make a great one. And there is much to listen to, for there is no river more musical than the Djernis. Every drowned tree carcass caught fast between two rocks is excuse enough for this spoiled child of the mountains to break into loud-murmured and most melodious complaint: over every marble block and every boulder stone, it will fret and foam and work itself into a frenzy of bubbles and froth. There are singing voices in the currents and phantom choruses in the whirling pools. And the more you listen the more you will hear. From the hollow of a cave there floats a melody, sweet and plaintive as though the water-spirits in there were touching the strings of their harps; the wavelets which lap against the rock are playing a rippling accompaniment, and in the strong, swift sweep of the current hurrying past, there rolls back a deep-toned reply. Where the water rushes headlong over a broken bed you could fancy a peal of silver bells; and there where it flings itself with a crash and a cloud of flying spray down the rock, you seem to hear the thunder of a mighty organ played by invisible hands.

Silenced by the wildness of this varied orchestra, Gretchen stood and waited till her hat should be dry. Even Tolnay seemed to have realized that compliments, however gracefully turned, must lose some of their charm when shouted at the top of the voice.

Suddenly, Gretchen became aware that an unknown parasol-handle was being protruded before her eyes, while an unknown voice said, deliberately,

"Mademoiselle, votre chapeau."

This was all that reached her ears. The fingers which grasped the ivory handle were stained yellow at the tips. Gretchen turned round, and found herself confronted by Princess Tryphosa.

Tolnay turned also, and for a moment doubted the evidence of his eyes. A long, low whistle would have been most expressive of his feelings at this moment, but he was too well-bred to attempt anything of the sort. He was a little dismayed, though the sensation was only transitory. He had never contemplated the possibility of these few yards of shingle being actually traversed by a Romanian lady of high degree. It was a phenomenon perfectly unparalleled in his experience, and certainly, it was calculated to awake some inconvenient thoughts as to the strength of motive which must exist. Gretchen was scarcely less surprised, and it took a few seconds before she could understand what Princess Tryphosa's object was. She was offering her parasol.

There was no sun now, thought Gretchen, looking up; what was the use of a parasol? No, that was not the princess's intention: the parasol was for the rescue of the fugitive hat which for some minutes had been reposing peacefully on the rock beside her. The intention was excellent, though the offer came a little tardily. Gretchen expressed her gratitude.

"I see I am too late," said the princess, with ponderous good nature, after gazing at the damp hat intently for a minute. During this minute, Gretchen was putting her new acquaintance through a critical examination.

The princess wore a pale silk dress, long-trained, and with trimmings of lace. Her black hair was uncovered, and her neck and arms were loaded with coral ornaments. She was a little older-looking seen thus near, perhaps twenty-six, but she lost nothing in beauty. She was a rich southern flower, full-blown, and at the prime of its perfection. A little time more and the flower would be overblown; now it has attained that perfect development which has not yet been touched by decay. A few more years of indolent habits will have destroyed the symmetry of her splendid figure; some hundred-weight more of *dulcétia* will have stained the enamel of her dazzling teeth; a few thousand more cigarettes will have deepened the delicate amber-tint on her fingers to an unsightly brown; time may even develop the dark shadow above her lip, which as yet is only a silky down, into an unbecomingly masculine ornament; inaction, sickly sweetmeats, and tobacco together, will soon have deteriorated the general cast of her features. But all this will only be some years hence. She may not be beautiful for long, but certainly, she is beautiful now. Her eyes alone — eyes of the languid Oriental type — would be enough to make her beautiful. They are peculiarly deep, and instinctively you wonder what lies under that depth: is it an immense fund of brooding passion, or only an immense stupidity?

This was the question which Gretchen asked herself, even as she acknowledged Princess Tryphosa's beauty. She acknowledged it freely, without reserve and almost without a pang. There was too absolute a difference between the styles of their beauty to admit of jealousy on that score. The rival whom a beautiful woman most fears is always the one who is likest herself: a blonde will better stand being outshone by a

brunette than by one of her own complexion, just as a swarthy beauty will hate a fair-
skinned rival less than one who poaches on her own premises by being dark.
Gretchen's self-confidence was not shaken; Tryphosa's beauty was an incentive that
made her spirit rise at the thought of the coming warfare. She stood and looked full
at the princess, and the princess looked full at her; and between the two stood István
Tolnay, with a gleam of something inscrutable in his eyes, and with his most provoking smile upon his face.

"Princess!" he cried, in polite consternation — for it was necessary that somebody should throw himself into the breach — "why did you not call me to your
assistance? How shall I ever forgive myself for having let you approach thus unnoticed? I cannot plead to be either deaf or short-sighted. Apropos" — and he turned
to Gretchen — "that word reminds me — where have you left that excellent family
lawyer, or family friend, Fräulein Mohr?"

"At Draskócs."

"Oh, really? He does not seem to have drunk deeply of the Waters of Hercules;
our valley has no charm for him. I suppose he is not thinking of repeating his visit?"

"You suppose quite wrong, then. Dr. Komers is going to spend his holiday here;
he only stayed at Draskócs because — "

"Because of the noise of the waterfalls," said Princess Tryphosa, deliberately.
"You could not have heard me if I had called; and, besides, you were busy in fishing
up the hat."

"Ah, to be sure," said Tolnay, who had forgotten the offer of his assistance as
soon as it had been spoken.

"It was István who fished up the hat, was it not?" asked the princess, turning to
Gretchen with her slow smile and her steady gaze. Apparently, she did not consider
the subject of the hat exhausted quite yet, and it was against her habit to quit a subject
until she had mastered it thoroughly.

"No," answered Gretchen, wondering a little at the tone of proprietorship with
which that "István" was pronounced — "it was not Baron Tolnay who fished up my

hat; although I think he is half persuaded that he has been doing wonders of bravery, and has saved not only my hat but also my life."

Princess Tryphosa appeared to be troubled; the answer was to her bewildering, as Gretchen herself was altogether bewildering. She could not find an answer which satisfied her at the moment, but she decided to think out the question during the walk home.

It was this that kept her silent while the others talked and laughed beside her.

When they had walked some distance down the valley, they saw a big shadow, with two smaller shadows behind it.

"Have you caught anything, Sir Hovart?" called down Tolnay cheerfully; and, in his painfully hushed voice, Mr. Howard answered now as before,

"Nothing."

Gretchen and Belita laughed, and Tolnay laughed; and five minutes later, when they had forgotten the stiff fisherman with his empty basket and his unshakable dignity, Princess Tryphosa laughed — a deep and musical laugh.

The situation was not lost upon her, but it had taken a little time to penetrate.

Chapter XXIV

Public and Private Amusements

"Then one sat down and sighed,
Of finding Fortune I begin to doubt,
And fear we may have taken the wrong way."

— Lord Lytton

AN international congress of geologists had gathered together at Pesth in the interest of Science. As the interest of Science demands recreation for the overworked mind, and as the Hungarian Government was willing to pay the expense, the learned men made expeditions to various places — to the Hercules valley among others.

The Hercules valley was immensely flattered at being in this way chosen, and worked enthusiastically at preparations for the reception of the learned men. The arrangements for their food and their lodging and their amusement occupied the Hercules Waters for a week. Flower-arches and ribbon-streamers transfigured the lonely Djernis valley. It might have been fancied that the mountains were celebrating their coming of age, or that the wild Djernis itself was going to lead home a young bride. The stone Hercules, whose club was wreathed with roses for the occasion, must have been carried back in memory to the time of Roman triumphs.

Needless to say, in the department of amusements, Dr. Kokovics held complete sway. He reveled in garlands and paper scrolls; his fertile brain teemed with fireworks and colossal illuminations.

For at least a week before the great day, his dreams were exclusively of rockets and Chinese lanterns.

The learned men came one dusty forenoon; fifty learned men, with forty pairs of spectacles between them. Geologists principally; but they had brought their friends with them, disciples of various sciences. They smiled at the flower-arches, nodded at the streamers, and pretended they could read the inscriptions; after which they proceeded to refresh themselves with a bath. They then ate an excellent dinner laid out for them in the *Cursalon*, while the galleries above were crowded with spectators who wished to see what Science looked like at food. A great many toasts were drunk, and in different languages. There was a flowery French speech, and an excited Italian speech; a nasal speech pronounced by an American, whom Mr. Howard had repeatedly and indignantly to repudiate as a countryman; then a furious German got to his feet and hammered out a few angular sentences to the effect that idleness was the mother of mischief, and that everybody must work, work, work, if they wanted to get on in this world. After which he sat down, wiping the perspiration from his streaming forehead, and savagely helped himself to roast turkey and salad.

Red wine flowed uninterruptedly; and the fifty learned men, as well as some others, notably Dr. Kokovics, were in a very jovial humor when they emerged from the *Cursalon*. There was then a stroll along the river in the interest of Science; the Roman inscriptions were read by a few and pronounced interesting. One learned man went the length of chipping off a corner of a stone with his iron-shod stick, and observing that the fragment was marble. Then came the saunter back, and the prospect of the fireworks; and the next day the learned men would drive back the way they came, fully persuaded that the interests of Science had been greatly furthered by their visit to the Hercules valley.

One of the learned men, on his return from the riverside, made his way up to the Mohrs' apartments to pay his respects to a friend and colleague.

"Well, Steinwurm," said Adalbert, with a faint smile, " you don't see me much more advanced than I was in May."

"On the contrary, on the contrary," ejaculated the musty-fusty Herr Steinwurm, with his parchment-skin and his fossil smile, "I hardly expected to find you so well. One of our learned medical friends whom I met the other day was quite surprised to hear that you were still alive. I think it disappointed him," added Steinwurm, by way of a joke; for the floods of red wine, though they had not sufficed to wash away the cobwebs of antiquity, had yet raised the historian's spirits almost to the level of cheerfulness.

"Anything new at home?" asked Adalbert.

"Ah, my dear friend," sighed Herr Steinwurm, "science has had a bitter disappointment! You remember the vault of the Frauenkirche, and the inscription on that stone?"

"I should rather think I do," said Adalbert, dryly; "the stone has laid its inscription on me somewhat severely."

"Well, my dear friend, it is a sad fact that that fall has mutilated the inscription beyond all hope of recognition. I do not wish to reproach you for your part in the unfortunate accident, but Science, alas! has to bewail a heavy loss."

"So has her victim," said Adalbert, in a tone of irony quite new in him.

"Victim of Science! Glorious title!" mused Steinwurm aloud. "If you are anxious to earn the glory of the title," said Adalbert, with a gleam of his old humor, "stay here and explore the mountains. There are precipices in plenty, and there is, besides, a bottomless hole in the forest which we are searching for; and when it is found we shall have to let down a man on a rope to sound it. I think you would be the very man for that, my dear Steinwurm; your stature and your weight point you out as the appropriate instrument."

"Thank you," said Steinwurm, a little hurriedly. The program did not sound reassuring.

"I should hardly feel justified. I — I — you see, I am a family man."

"So am I," said Adalbert.

"Yes — but, do you know, I am not particularly sure of my legs in mountain-climbing; a little weakness in the knees ever since my childhood. Where — where is your charming daughter?" burst out the unfortunate historian, as a desperate transition on to safer ground. He was answered by Dr. Komers, who, sitting at a little distance, had taken no part in the discussion. It was two days since Vincenz, having wound up the small affairs of Draskócs, and seen Ascelinde's guardian laid to rest, had returned to the Hercules valley. "Fraulein Mohr has gone out to meet her brother," he said, in reply to Herr Steinwurm's question.

"Oh, has she?" answered Kurt's voice from the doorway; "her brother was not aware of the fact."

"Did you not meet your sister?" asked the lawyer; "she went up the hillside to look for you."

"Never met anybody," said Kurt, lighting a cigar. "I never went to the hill at all; I have been down to the river to see if there were no geologists to pick out of it. They were not walking over-straight when I saw them last.

And having taken place on a chair, and stretched his legs on another, Kurt proceeded to make himself comfortable with his cigar and the paper.

Dr. Komers, without further remark, quietly left the room.

Kurt continued to read his paper, and the two historians talked history, and Ascelinde, who had left her bed some days ago, occasionally wandered into the room and out of it again, looking like a ghost of her former self. And meanwhile, the dusk began to fall, and neither Gretchen nor Dr. Komers had yet returned.

At the moment when Kurt was lighting his cigar and luxuriously distributing his person between two chairs, Gretchen had already reached some distance from home; and under the delusion that her brother must be in advance, was slowly climbing the steep mountain path. The wood was quite deserted — every man, woman, and child being busy below with the entertainment of the learned men.

It was many a day since Gretchen had found herself so entirely alone; and somehow, she was not in a humor to relish her solitude just now. She was on bad terms with herself — she who hitherto had always lived on such a very satisfactory footing with her conscience, her mind, and her will. Now her conscience was uneasy, her mind was perplexed, and her will — well, as for her will, she no longer felt sure of it.

The whole of the past week had been a week of fatigue, if of amusement. Wherever Gretchen went, Baron Tolnay went; and where Baron Tolnay was, there also was Princess Tryphosa — unless, indeed, when Gretchen's steps had been turned to the mountains, for to the mountains Princess Tryphosa did not follow. Perhaps the dissatisfaction of Gretchen's mind arose from the fact that her first few skillfully set traps had failed to catch the simple Bohemian's secret; and that therefore *Gaura Dracului*, and with *Gaura Dracului* the brigands' treasure, and with the brigands' treasure her own fortune, still remained undiscovered. Or perhaps it was that she still felt uncertain of her victory over Tryphosa.

There were moments when she thought the victory secure, and there were others when she doubted it. The doubt had been sufficient to rouse her ambition with the stimulus of rivalry — to prick the side of her intent, which else might have grown faint: it had added excitement to the meetings of this past week; it had urged her to throw out the line again more than once, and to play the bait on which was to be hooked her fortune. But in the midst of the game, a certain uneasy dread had seized her more than once, and today it was on her again. Or was this dissatisfaction perhaps a little unconscious pity for Tryphosa, who, as Gretchen had long since discovered, loved István Tolnay? But since Gretchen did not believe in love, what right had she to feel pity? No; more likely it was a sense of justice. If István Tolnay had been a prize equally coveted by them both, it would have been all fair play to contend for him on a fair field; but to take from Tryphosa that which she was not sure of wanting herself, this was what Gretchen could not quite reconcile with her notions of justice and logic.

She might have become yet more deeply involved in this train of logical deduction, had not the overhanging branch of a mountain ash tree rudely caught her by the hair just as her thoughts had reached this point.

It was getting late, she discovered to her surprise, and the sun was sinking brilliantly and fast. What had become of Kurt? She ought to have met him long ago. Looking around her, she wondered to find herself so high up; for the last twenty minutes she had steadily, though unconsciously, been mounting, and now she stood on a rocky path, bordered with bilberry bushes, while the gloomy valley lay at her feet.

That uncourteous ash tree had been the last tree of this tract of forest. Here the mountain was well-nigh bare; low brushwood grew between the rocks, tufts of delicate grass covered the ground, and wild flowers shook unprotected in the breeze. Along the shoulder of the hill, the stony path continued.

Finding herself thus alone, a little awe crept into Gretchen's heart. The forest she had just passed through had grown so black behind her; she thought with dread of the dark way home.

While she stood thus hesitating, and just preparing to retrace her steps, a far-off sound fell upon her ear, and gave sudden shape to the vague alarm which oppressed her.

She listened attentively; there were footsteps approaching, and they came from the shadow of the gloomy forest. A dark figure could just be distinguished gliding along among the trees. As far as she could see, it was the figure of a tall strong man, certainly a figure that bore not the slightest resemblance to the brother she was looking for. Gretchen possessed a cool head in emergencies — at least so she always affirmed; she was inclined to be proud of her presence of mind, but her self-possession was not as perfect as usual today. The combination of the solitude, the dusk, and the sudden sight of that figure, sent a rush of cold terror to her heart. She hesitated for one moment longer, unwilling to yield to this fear; but when she heard a distinct cry, a sort of halloo come out of the wood, breaking the silence of the mountainside and echoing back from the rocks, she did not hesitate longer, but started off running in the opposite direction firmly convinced that that cry had been the signal of the robber-captain calling together his band. Five minutes ago, Gretchen did not believe in the existence of the robbers; but she is not the first philosopher who has discovered that theories will not always hold good in practice. She ran along the path, sending the loose stones flying away from under her feet, whence they leaped over the edge and went bounding down the steep hillside. She felt the evening wind rush past her ears in a current. At every turn of the path, she feared to come upon the bandit camp, but yet she dared not turn back; and in the protruding branch of every bush she saw a pistol pointed at her head. The treetops, nodding high above her seemed to be telling each other tales of murder and bloodshed each white ox-eye daisy, trembling on its stalk like a solitary star, stared at her with a pale and panic-stricken face as she flew past. Her steps slackened at last, and she stood still, breathless. Was she being pursued? She listened, holding her breath with difficulty. There was no sound whatever; but the deep shadows round her were closing in as if they would swallow her up among them.

The next thing to do was to collect her thoughts and consider her position from a logical point of view. To go back by the way she had come was out of the question; her courage was not equal to risk meeting that black figure she had seen in the wood. All around her, there were scattered rocks; but to the left a stony tract dipped down with a steep and sudden curve. According to all reasonable calculations, that tract must lead straight back towards the Hercules Baths.

She turned resolutely down it. It was rugged, and steeper than she had at first imagined. "Never mind," thought Gretchen — "if it is so steep, it stands to reason that it must be a shortcut." On each side, there was a wall of rock, bare, except where some bush pushed its thorny head from out of a slit high up. There was a narrow strip of evening sky above Gretchen's head, and nothing but rough stones under her feet.

The first few steps had been comparatively easy; but soon the path grew more precipitate, turning and twisting, and taking sudden jumps, in a way which paths, in general, do not affect. She had to steady herself by the rocks, for the stones slipped under her feet; each step sent a shower of small boulders chasing each other down the pathway.

Again, there was a sound, high above her this time, and she stood still to listen. It was only the voice of an eagle roused out of its first sleep, and scolding the intruder who dared to penetrate this solitude.

What beautiful spot was this she had come to? wondered Gretchen as she looked around her; so beautiful that it almost made her forget her fright. The walls of rock on each side had retreated for a little space, and here, before her eyes, lay a circular basin, rippling in living green waves. And yet, there was no drop of water here; the waves were only the leaves of wild harts tongue ferns, which filled the hollow to overflowing, curving over each other in graceful arches, and crowding up to the foot of the overhanging rock. Each glossy leaf, with a delicately crimped edge, rose and fell as softly as a swelling wave. More than one sharp stone reared its head right through the midst of the green pool.

Gretchen looked around her, and paused in spite of herself; she could hear her own heartbeats in the solemn silence. But she dared not linger; she traversed the oval space, walking through the midst of the waving harts tongue, and then the rocks narrowed again, and the track dipped down steeper than before. It must be a very short cut indeed, she thought, as she waded through tangles of green fern; it was all she could do to feel her way down under the thick overgrowth which masked the passage. There were dead tree-trunks across her way, and bramble-branches straggling over them. The gorge narrowed every moment, until her steps struck a hollow echo in the enclosed passage, and the air grew strangely chill. Now there was hardly room for her to pass between the two walls. In another moment, she half expected her passage to be barred, when all at once it widened again, and at the same moment Gretchen found herself suddenly brought up.

It would be a very short cut indeed to reach the Hercules Baths this way; for at her feet there fell a precipice, sheer and straight. At the two sides of the gorge's mouth the mass of rock jutted forward a little. One or two fiat-topped stone-pines, like gigantic umbrellas in shape, and somber to blackness in the evening light, flung themselves boldly forward, their twisted roots clinging to the naked stone, while the fading sky behind sharply set off each line of branch and trunk.

This was the rock at the foot of which lay the *Cursalon*, and this gorge was the narrow-slit Gretchen had so often looked at from below. The path she had followed was nothing but the stony bed which a winter torrent had left dry, and which the green hartstongue had usurped in place of the mountain stream. The Hercules Baths lay at her feet; the *Cursalon* and the monster hotels turned up their roofs towards her. She was close to them, and yet inseparably divided. She could count the windows of the houses opposite; she could even hear the band of music playing, and distinguish the voices of the people; but she would have to retrace the whole way she had come before she could be at home. With a shudder, the thought flashed upon her that this was the gorge which even from below people looked at in terror; it was here that the robbers had been seen watching the Hercules valley and planning destruction to its inhabitants. How impossible the story had sounded then! How possible it sounded now! Most alarmingly possible in the silence of this rocky solitude.

Gretchen swept a searching glance around her, and in the same moment she had to suppress an exclamation of fear. Here, indeed, was food for her terror; not two paces off there lay something black on the ground.

This was something which did not belong to the rocky solitude, which had not grown there — no product of nature. Gretchen stooped and examined it; it was a wide-brimmed felt hat — just the very hat which a bandit might be supposed to wear drawn over his brows.

For a moment she stood still, petrified with terror, unable to take her eyes off the ominous hat all at once; but, rousing herself, she reflected that every second was precious. She held her dress for fear of its rustling, and on tiptoe she prepared to leave the spot.

Before she had made two steps, she got a new fright. Here was something which belonged as little to the rocky solitude as to the bandits: for what could robbers have in common with this colored paper lantern dangling from a branch?

A stone rolled close beside her, and in the same instant a man stepped out from behind a rock and barred her passage. She screamed with the sudden start. Her first sensation was helpless terror; her second, momentary relief; her third was terror again, but terror of a different sort, for the man confronting her was no brigand — it was Dr. Kokovics.

Not that Dr. Kokovics at this moment, with his disheveled hair, his flushed face, and his somewhat disordered toilet, might not have passed for a very fair imitation of a brigand. Even through the dusk his jovial humor was evident; the excellent dinner of which, in company with the men of science, he had this afternoon partaken, had indisputably left its mark. What could be the meaning of his presence here? Gretchen asked herself in the first moment of surprise; but in the next already she had remembered the Chinese lantern, and there came back to her recollection the vast plans of illumination for this evening which Dr. Kokovics was known to entertain. Doubtless the floods of red wine which had accompanied the excellent dinner had served to render those plans more vast, and had engendered in the doctor's fertile brain the grand idea of lighting up the gorge above the *Cursalon.*

Gretchen had recoiled at the moment of recognition, but the doctor advanced, unchilled by his reception.

"By the club of Hercules," he cried, "this is luck! What happiness! What sweet and unexpected happiness!" he ejaculated rapidly, shaking back his hair as he came towards her. "To what good star do I owe this meeting with the beautiful Gretchen?"

"Thank you, I am going home," said Gretchen, retreating another step, and beginning to tremble, for the excitement about his words and gestures was unmistakable.

"You look frightened," said the doctor, stopping and gazing at her; "this solitude alarms your gentle mind. But fear nothing; trust yourself to me; Kokovics is your knight. This arm will — "

"I — I don't want to speak to you, Dr. Kokovics," said Gretchen, steadying her voice. "I wish you would let me pass."

She made a step forward, but the movement aroused the doctor's excitement to an alarming degree. He spread out his two arms in such a way as to suggest a gigantic black bat preparing to fly, and effectually to bar the narrow entrance of the gorge.

"Cruel Gretchen! By what crime have I deserved this treatment? Has not my devotion touched your heart? Why have you persisted in closing your eyes to the humble verses I have dared to lay at your feet? Why will you withhold from this poor lovesick heart

'The medicine of thy smile?'"

declaimed the Romanian with appropriate quotation from his latest stanza.

'Be thou my doctor!"

he hummed softly, wedding his thought to music on the spur of the moment. "Assuredly, oh fair physician, I am not your first case, but undoubtedly I am the most desperate. Our correspondence is my only solace, the one recipe which can cure my — "

"*Our* correspondence! How dare you spook of 'our' correspondence?" cried Gretchen, with icy scorn.

She had retreated step by step, until she now stood on the edge of the tiny platform, looking down straight at the houses below. Down there the people were talking, and the music was still playing. She could count the trees in the garden, she could distinguish the stone Hercules at his post. Ah, if the god of the valley would but scale the rock and wield his club in her assistance! To be so near help and yet so far, made the situation only the more tantalizing.

"Yes, our correspondence, fair Gretchen; but I will reproach you no longer. This *rencontre* makes up for everything; how gracious of you to meet me here, and thus by your glorious presence to sweeten my task! You find me working for the public amusement; but do not imagine that I neglect the public for the private on that account. How delightful such a task will be when shared by you! Together we will labor; together mount the rocks, and hand in hand we shall kindle the fairy lamps."

The color burned like a red flame in Gretchen's cheek; she was shaking from head to foot, for the Romanian's glittering eyes struck her with terror.

"Dr. Kokovics, will you let me pass this instant? Every word you say is an insult. I refuse any explanation. Have you forgotten that you have a wife and children?"

"Eight children!" cried the doctor, with a resounding sigh, and he plunged both his hands into the deep waves of his hair. "*Me Hercule!* Oh barbarous cruelty of woman! You are not going to cast them up all eight in my face, fair Gretchen?"

"If you do not stand aside immediately," said Gretchen, "I shall call for help to the people below."

"They could not scale the rock, fair lady; it would be a useless strain upon your delicate throat, which, as a doctor, I could not countenance. True, I have not the happiness of being your medical attendant; but in this felicitous moment who can forbid me to sing,

'Be thou my patient?'"

He came a step nearer to her. "Why this haste to terminate our delightful meeting? Consider the beauty of the spot! Look at the weirdly towering rocks all around us, the carpet of waving fern at our feet. We are in the heart of nature; what place more beautiful for a lovers' meeting? My muse inspires me — the verses are crowding to my head; I shall write a sonnet upon this happy moment!"

"Let me pass — let me pass!" cried Gretchen, in an agony, pushing out her two hands before her, for the doctor, flushed and smiling, was slowly coming nearer. On one side, this odious man, on the other, the precipice. Would not the precipice be the lesser evil of the two? In her terror, she almost thought so; she did not shrink as she measured the black and giddy cliff. Might she not save herself by clinging to a ledge, or to one of those strong-armed bushes below?

Her bewilderment was so great that she had not heard an approaching sound coming down the gorge. Now a distinct shout struck her ear; it was the same sound which had scared her in the wood a little time ago. It must be the robbers coming; but the robbers could not make matters worse than they were, and possibly they might make them better. With what delight she would yield up her purse and her earrings in order to be rid of this odious man!

"We are wasting our moments, beautiful Gretchen!" cried the doctor, advancing. "You cannot deny me one kiss!"

"If you come a step nearer, I shall jump down the rock," she said, deadly pale by this time.

"I could never allow that — as a doctor," said the Romanian; and as she stood with one foot on the brink, he seized both her hands and drew her forward.

With the fury of despair, she struggled; her teeth set, her eyes flaring wildly. The leap down the rock would have been easy at that moment, for close before her was the Romanian's flushed face. She shut her eyes, and shuddered in sickening dread; his fingers closed round her wrists with a drunken strength. The whole scene swam in her brain — rocks and trees and Chinese lanterns were blended into one formless mass.

"I could never allow that — by the club of Her — " The Romanian's customary invocation turned suddenly into something that sounded very like a curse. Was that the doctor's voice?

With a wrench Gretchen felt herself freed, and, looking up, she saw what looked like Dr. Kokovics turned into two Dr. Kokovicses, and the first Kokovics grappling with the second in the dust.

Terror had so blinded her that she could not at once understand what had happened; she could only stand by, staring helplessly at those fighting men. Had the god of the valley come indeed to her assistance? And were those the strokes of his weapon?

Gretchen felt herself freed, and, looking up, she saw what looked like Dr. Kokovics turned into two Dr. Kokovicses...

The walls of rock threw back the sounds which struck upon them, and they were ghastly sounds indeed; hot curses and heavy blows following upon each other furiously and fast. Never, until this moment, had man dared to desecrate with his passion this wild sanctuary of nature. Both combatants were tall and strong, but the Romanian was perhaps rather less steady on his legs than usual. It was not a minute after the first attack that one of the two men was down, on the very brink of the abyss, and his opponent above him, with one knee on his chest, and his hands upon his throat.

Gretchen uttered a half-stifled scream, for it seemed as if the conqueror, in the heat of his victory, was going to fling the vanquished man down that fearful rock.

At the sound of her voice, the kneeling man turned, and in the failing light, she recognized Vincenz Komers.

Chapter XXV

The Story of the Broken Heart

"I have unclaspt
To thee the book even of my secret soul."

— Twelfth Night

G RETCHEN had to look again to make sure that it was indeed Dr. Komers. Those were his features and his eyes, but they wore an expression which made him scarcely recognizable; the violence of physical movement and of mental emotion had driven the blood to his face and the fire to his eyes. He looked magnificently fierce, with his clinched hands and the quick dilation of his fine-cut nostrils.

"Dr. Komers!" cried Gretchen.

Even while she spoke, Dr. Komers had let go the grasp on his adversary's throat, and had risen from his knees to his feet. He still breathed heavily; his coat was torn, and both his hat and spectacles had fallen off in the struggle.

The Romanian doctor lay where he had fallen, giving not the smallest sign of life.

"Is he dead?" asked Gretchen, under her breath. Vincenz bent over him.

"Only stunned, I think;" and he undid the unfortunate Kokovics's collar and loosened his cravat. "Only stunned, and I dare say a good deal bruised."

The unfortunate Kokovics opened his eyes, and looked up drowsily into his enemy's face.

"Am I dead?" he inquired, in a feeble whisper.

"I hope not," said Vincenz. "Let us get you to your feet, and we shall see."

"What am I then," asked Kokovics, "if I am not killed?"

"Knocked down, that is all."

"Rather badly knocked down," murmured Kokovics, dreamily. "I have been knocked down before."

"I have no difficulty whatever in believing it," said Vincenz.

"But never quite so badly as this," finished Kokovics.

"Will you be so kind as to get to your feet? You can have my arm if you like."

Kokovics looked a little distrustful at the arm.

"You will oblige me by making haste," said Vincenz; and the Romanian struggled from the horizontal to the perpendicular.

He stood looking about him, a most piteous figure, with his long hair hanging over his eyes, and all his spirit crushed out of him.

Nobody spoke for a minute, while Dr. Kokovics slowly gathered his senses together. Then he let go Vincenz's arm, and stooped to pick up his wide-felt hat.

"Those hands of yours are like iron hammers," he said, sulkily, rubbing his bruised arms with an injured air. He crushed his hat onto his head, and turned to go up the gorge.

"Not quite so fast, if you please," interrupted Vincenz, speaking more in his usual tone. "You do not leave this spot until you have made an ample apology to this lady."

Perhaps it was the vivid recollection of the lawyer's iron fists which induced Dr. Kokovics to stand still when thus called upon. He pulled his hat farther down on his forehead, and mumbled a few words of incoherent apology.

"Let me tell you too," said Vincenz, in a studiously quiet voice, "that if you ever again dare to address a single word of any sort to Fräulein Mohr, I shall denounce you as a blackguard and a villain; and at the first hint of impertinence, I shall thrash you before the eyes of anybody who will take the trouble to look on. Is that quite distinct to you?"

"Quite," muttered the Romanian, quaking in his shoes.

Whatever harm the fall might have done to his constitution, it certainly had had the salutary effect of sobering him completely. All his blustering self-confidence of five minutes ago was vanished, leaving no trace behind it. They were of much the same stature, the Romanian and the German, yet the short-sighted lawyer looked by far the grander man of the two.

Dr. Kokovics seemed to have shrunk to half his size, as he turned and slunk away among the rocks, leaving his paper lamps abandoned to their fate. No red and blue lights will tonight rejoice the fifty learned men. Here the lamps will hang forgotten, until the rain has washed away the blue and red color, and the wind has torn them to fragments.

Dr. Kokovics waited until he had got one rock between him and his late enemy, and then, as a parting shot, he called back across this rampart,

"Good evening, valiant knight! No doubt you will now enjoy the favors which your confounded fists have taken away from me. The flower of beauty to the conqueror! Such are the fortunes of war!"

Vincent clinched his hand and made a step forward, but the doctor was flitting away like a black ghost in a hurry; and he turned back with a contemptuous shrug of his shoulders. Gretchen was leaning against a rock — her face very pale, and her lips twitching convulsively.

"I am afraid you have had a great fright," he said, looking at her anxiously.

"No, it is nothing," she managed to say with difficulty. She made a step forward, meaning to reassure him as to her strength, but stumbled and caught hold of the rock.

"I shall rest a minute," she said, faintly — "I don't think I could walk just yet."

"Upon this stone, then," said Vincenz, as, with fingers as deft and delicate as those of a woman, he cleared off the loose sticks which encumbered the low rock beside her.

"Thank you," said Gretchen, as she sat down; she would have liked to say more, but she was not sure of her voice.

Dr. Komers did not sit down; he stood some paces away from her, reflecting what else he could do for her comfort, for it was evident that she was both frightened and faint. He could hear her teeth chattering; and the thought that she might suddenly be taken ill terrified him beyond measure. The only woman he was intimately acquainted with, his sister Anna, had given him frequent and alarming examples of the frailty of the female constitution. His coat was the only available wrap, and taking it off, he put it over her knees and feet. "If you don't mind," he said, apologetically.

"Thank you," she said again. Then, after a pause, "How did you find me here?"

"Your brother came back without you," answered Vincenz, with a shade of embarrassment. "I thought I could overtake you and tell you of the mistake, for it was getting late. I walked as fast as I could; but apparently you must have walked faster, for I could not get up to you. When I came to the head of the gorge, I could hear the stones rolling farther down, and I guessed you were on in advance. Did you not hear me shout?"

"Oh, then it was you who shouted?" said Gretchen, beginning to be ashamed of her groundless alarm.

"I am afraid that villain has frightened you most terribly," he added, looking down at her with a concern that was more that of a father than of a lover.

Gretchen tried to smile. "I think you frightened me also a little."

"I frightened you!" he repeated, in a tone of the blankest consternation. "Is that possible?"

Looking at him at this moment, it did seem scarcely possible to Gretchen herself. He had quite resumed his ordinary manner — his voice and his look were gentle, almost timid.

The hands which had dealt such crushing blows a few moments ago, with what tender care had they arranged the seat for her, and placed the coat over her feet! And yet neither in the tone nor words was there the shadow of anything which could have alarmed the most sensitive delicacy. They were alone here in this wild solitude, and she knew that this man loved her; but she knew also, with as firm a conviction, that she was as safe as if her father had been by her side. This time it was not by any process of logical deduction that she reached this conclusion; the conviction sprang only from an unreasoning but not a mistaken instinct.

"Did I really frighten you?" asked Vincenz, anxiously.

The flush of movement was still on his face; and though he was calm again outwardly, the strong effort he made could not succeed in suppressing his inward excitement. A man does not pass fifteen years at desk drudgery, and then find himself suddenly plunged into a hand-to-hand fight without feeling his whole nature stirred up by it. The strength which had so long lain dormant and useless had found a subject on which to wreak itself, and instinct had told him how to use his advantages.

"You would have been frightened at yourself, if you could have seen your own face," said Gretchen.

"I am not at all sorry that I knocked him down," said Vincenz, simply; "but I am sorry I could not have knocked him down more quietly. I am afraid" — with growing anxiety — "that I must have used some rather strong language."

"Rather," said Gretchen, smiling. "I thought you were going to throw him over the rock at one moment."

Vincenz looked grave.

"I believe I was. If you had not screamed then, I should have had Dr. Kokovics on my conscience. I scarcely knew what I was doing. I felt rather wild just then. I see now that it must have frightened you terribly. Can you forgive me?"

"Oh! It is you who should forgive me," said Gretchen, catching her breath.

Dr. Komers made no answer, but turned and walked a few steps away. His back was towards her, and to all appearance, he seemed absorbed in the contemplation of a clump of trampled fern. The green tufts of harts tongue had suffered grievously in the struggle: the broken fronds lay crushed on the ground, all their juicy life stamped out of them in that brief but furious fight. It would be long before they raised their heads again.

There was a silence of some minutes. The last of the daylight was dying fast; the black stone pines frowned down from their high seats; there was not a sound in the lonely gorge. Overhead the evening stars were beginning slowly to shine; and, as though the valley had been a lake which sent back the image of each star in the sky, the lights below sprang up one by one.

Gretchen sat on the stone with her hands clasped before her. Her heart beat fast; but it was not with fright now — it was with a sort of nervous expectation. What was Dr. Komers going to say next? Was he going to tell her again that he loved her? Ah no! that was to be never again. She had forgotten that — never again!

"Fräulein Mohr," said Dr. Komers, coming back towards her, "it is no wonder that I frightened you today; the wonder is rather that I should not have frightened you long ago. Perhaps you have never guessed that I am a passionate man?"

"I have thought so — once before."

Though it was so dark, she blushed crimson; for she was thinking of the scene on the morrow of the *Cursalon* ball.

"I understand," he said, calmly. "Well, since you have seen me on that day and on this, I had better tell you at once that my temper has been my ruin. It is entirely through an act of passion that I have shipwrecked my sister's life and my own."

He hesitated for a moment before going on. "Perhaps, if it would not weary you too much, I should like to tell you the story of that day. I have not told it to anyone yet; but I think you could forgive me better for my occasional violence if you heard the rest. May I tell it to you?"

"Yes, yes; oh, please tell it to me!" she said, with an eagerness which surprised him.

"It must be the story of the broken heart that he is going to tell me," thought Gretchen.

Ever since the day of her last passage of arms with Anna Komers, an illogical curiosity had possessed her with regard to that broken heart. "Please begin," she felt inclined to say. She was as anxious as a child who has been promised a new fairy tale, and half expected the story to start with "Once upon a time."

"Thank you," said Vincenz, as if she had conferred a favor on him. "But it would be imprudent to stay here longer. I will tell you as we walk home. Would you mind making use of my arm to get back through the gorge?"

Gretchen felt stronger now, and rising to her feet, she took the arm which Vincenz almost diffidently offered her. As long as they were clambering up the torrent-bed, there was no possibility of conversation: each difficulty was increased tenfold by the darkness. There were gloomy shadows and sharp rustles all around; but Gretchen never started once. She wondered at the strength of her own nerves. Even if the robber-band had sprung out upon them, she felt as if she could have faced them coolly now. The proofs of strength which Dr. Komers had given could not fail to reassure the most timid of female minds. As they passed the circular basin, where in early spring the melted snow expands to a deep and whirling pool, the eagle put its head out of the nest above them, and expressed its displeasure at this further intrusion. It had been an evening of abnormal disturbance in the experience of this lonely eagle.

When they had gained the level path, Vincenz spoke again.

"It is a very short story I have to tell, and very simple — most despairingly simple it has proved for both Anna and me. I need not tell you that I am a poor man — for I have never concealed my poverty," said Vincenz, with an effort; "but I have not always been poor. My father was rich; until she was past twenty, Anna did not know what it was to have a wish unfulfilled. It was not long after her twentieth birthday that my father lost his fortune. It is no use troubling you with details, which at the time I did not thoroughly understand myself; the practical fact of finding that we were beggars was quite sufficient for all intents and purposes. My father's death followed soon upon the crash; Anna and I were left to manage for ourselves. Our case was not by any means desperate. In his better days, my father had had many firm friends: they did not prove themselves quite so firm in the time of misfortune; but one at least, a Count Perlenberg, occupying a high ministerial position, did not immediately turn his back upon us. He generously offered me a position that opened to me the possibility of a brilliant diplomatic career. The prospect so delighted me, that in my eyes it more than made up for the loss of fortune. I worked hard for two years, drawing so high a salary that Anna could live in ease, almost in luxury.

"Count Perlenberg had one son, a fair-haired, pink-cheeked young man. I thought him a coxcomb then, God forgive me! With what patience would I bear his coxcombry now, if I could see Conrad Perlenberg before my eyes! All this happened in Vienna, you must know. But for some months I was absent on an official mission. It was the first lengthy separation that had ever taken place be- tween Anna and me. When I met Anna again on my return, it struck me, for the first time, that my sister was pretty; there was a new bloom on her face, a happier smile on her lips, a brighter light in her eyes. She had never looked like this before, and I did not know how to explain this change.

"It was only now that I made the acquaintance of young Perlenberg. He did not occupy any recognized position in his father's office, and I was not even aware that he gave himself the show of authority.

"One morning soon after my return, on reaching the office at the usual hour I found lying on my desk the draft of an official report of some importance, whose composition had been entrusted to me, and which I had framed with particular care. It was being returned to me now, with corrections, written in an unknown hand, and evidently proceeding from some inexperienced person. Half of what I had written was stroked through, and there were remarks substituted, which displayed almost ludicrously the writer's ignorance. I never was very patient of correction; the sight of my draft, on which I had spent such scrupulous care, now thus ignominiously returned upon my hands, roused my anger on the instant. I might have borne it better if I had been alone, but the harmless chaffing of my companions stung me to the quick. I knew that I was right, and that my unknown corrector was wrong. I was very young and very hot-headed, and the sense of the injustice overpowered me as an unbearable insult.

"'The man who has written this is a fool!' I said aloud, and flung the paper to the floor.

"'You will not dare to call me a fool,' said a small voice; and through the open doorway, Conrad Perlenberg suddenly stepped forward, looking rather more white than pink this morning. We stood opposite to each other, and the young counts and barons around tittered a little as they bent over their desks. I had not expected to see Count Perlenberg; but my blood was up, beyond all power of restraint.

"'I cannot take back my words,' I said, 'even if you have written it.'

"Young Perlenberg uttered a laugh, which was half embarrassed and half hysterical.

"'This is suitable language,' he said, turning to his companions with an unsteady sneer — 'most suitable language for a man who, but for my father, might be in want of breakfast today.'

"I am convinced now that Perlenberg had lost his self-control as much as I had lost mine, for he was not a bad fellow by nature; but at the moment I felt only the taunt, and it maddened me. I don't remember making any answer; I know only that in the next moment the tittering at the desks had entirely ceased. I had struck out my right hand, and Count Perlenberg was lying on his back on the ground, while the rest of the *jeunesse dore* were dragging me back by the arms and shoulders. They might have left me alone; for at the very moment of the fall, I was already repenting having knocked down a man who was six inches below my own height."

Gretchen could not repress a rising laugh, as the picture of the prostrate Perlenberg rose before her mind's eye. Vincenz looked at her gravely.

"Does it amuse you? I dare say it was comedy to the spectators, but it turned out tragedy for us two. As soon as we had both recovered our senses, we were told that we must fight, and with pistols, as the offense had been so grave, and given before witnesses. No personal enmity was at fault. It had been entirely through a mistake that young Perlenberg had got hold of this document, and he had corrected it without knowing whose draft it was, while I had spoken unaware of the name of my corrector. But, for a hot word and a hasty act, the word decreed that each should have a shot at the other's life. I had never fought a duel before, and I was foolish enough to be rather pleased at the prospect. I took care that Anna should not guess why I left the house at so early an hour. Perlenberg had the first shot, being the offended; he aimed fairly well, and hit me in the left arm. I felt a stinging pain, but the excitement drowned every bodily sensation.

"After I had fired, which I did in absolute blindness, for I could not see six paces ahead, the young count stood upright for a moment, then staggered, and was caught in the arms of his second. He was not dead, but he was mortally wounded. He was privately removed to his house, and I went home, chilled and sobered; and at the door I was met by Anna, who had suspected something abnormal. I could not command my emotion; and my wounded arm, which I had half-forgotten, spoke for itself. Some hint dropped by a servant led her to think of a duel, and she knew me too well to believe such a thing unlikely. She insisted on binding up my arm, which still bled. I let her do it; but as I watched her preparing the bandages with such sorrowful anxiety, I felt a great discouragement come over me. 'I have done worse for him than that,' I said, gloomily. 'They tell me he can scarcely live.'

"Anna looked at me with scared eyes.

"'Who is he?' she asked. 'You must tell me, Vincenz.'

"'It is Conrad Perlenberg,' I said.

"I shall never forget the look which Anna gave me, and the cry which she uttered; it was the death-knell of her youth. The bandage she was holding dropped out of her hands, and she fell fainting on to the chair beside her. It was long before she came to herself, and then I learned the whole truth. She had loved Conrad Perlenberg, whose acquaintance she had made in my absence, and only a few days ago they had become secretly engaged. It was the first secret she had ever kept from me, and, by heavens, the innocent mystery cost her dear! God knows what she can have seen in that pink-and-white face which made her love him! But I have found since then that those are the sort of men who know how to catch a woman's fancy." How bitter sounded the sigh which went along with these words!

"There followed a fearful week," said Vincenz, continuing his story. "From the very day of the catastrophe, Anna fell into a dreadful illness. I was half distracted; every moment that I could spare from my sister I stole away and stood in the unfrequented street, where straw had been laid down before one gloomy house, watching the window of the room where Conrad lingered between life and death. It was winter, but I passed half the night at my post, wrapped in my cloak, and with my eyes on the light of that sick room. On the eighth day, I came there early; and, looking up as usual, I saw that both windows were flung wide open. It was a bitterly cold January day, and those open windows could mean but one thing."

His voice shook for a moment, and he broke off abruptly. They had come to a rough part of the pathway, and as Vincenz put out his hand as a support, Gretchen fancied it was not as steady as usual. She stole a glance up into his face, and saw the painful emotion which had been called up by that recollection.

"You should not have told me this," she whispered; "it pains you." He looked down at her quickly, and then dropped her hand.

"It does pain me; but what matters the pain? I should like you to know it all. People have sometimes been kind enough to call me a quiet, sensible man: there is no great merit in being sensible after that one experience I have had. From that fatal day in the office, Anna's life and mine were violently transformed. I sent in my resignation myself, but I had one more short interview with Conrad's father. For the sake of his old friend's memory, Count Perlenberg declined to prosecute me, for the fatal termination of the duel brought me within reach of the law. 'But it could not give me back my Conrad,' he said to me, sorrowfully. I might go where I liked, only I was never to come under his eyes again. So we went, Anna and I, like a pair of outcasts: we left Vienna, and quietly vanished out of the circles of the capital. Anna remained an invalid from the day of her recovery. Every trace of youth and bloom was swept away by that illness. She never had been beautiful; she had scarcely been pretty, except during that short period of happiness which I had destroyed. Conrad Perlenberg's love was the sun which had made her beauty bloom, and my violence was the frost that killed it. I asked her forgiveness on my knees, and she gave it to me at once: she had always idolized me since my babyhood, and her affection was not by one whit weakened after the catastrophe. We began life again at the beginning. I worked for Anna, and, thank God, I was able to keep her from starving. It was the least I could do, after all."

Vincenz paused again. He had told the facts plainly, without adding a comment; but the very bareness of the statement, given in that deeply tremulous voice, made it the more impressive. He said no word of the bitter desolation, the agony of self-reproach, which had been lived through, and which yet had to be lived down and thrust under in the battle for life on which he had then entered. A man cast in a sterner or a more callous mold would have more quickly shaken off that ghastly impression; for, after all, he had not overstepped the recognized code of honor which society had set up. But Vincenz was not of that iron hardness. His mind was too keenly sensitive, too intellectually refined, to be so easily quit of that haunting memory. The world's code of honor shrank into nothing beside the accusation of his own conscience. No one, not even Anna, had ever guessed at the moments of discouragement and self-disgust which had threatened to overpower him. For a nature like his to suppress that gnawing remorse, and to rise to the emergency of the moment, was an effort almost heroic. He had no leisure for lamentation and sterile regrets, no opportunities for indulging in self-accusing tears; even sackcloth and ashes were luxuries which he could ill afford. Stern moralists might condemn him to do penance; but how of the poor penitent who has no money to buy the sackcloth, and no time to collect the ashes?

Vincenz was forced to act at once, and to enter the lists in the vulgar battle for bare life. He had fought that battle bravely, and he had fought it alone; for Anna, successfully deceived as to the extent of their property, had never attempted to con-tribute her share of labor. She continued to bully and adore her brother now as be-fore, never by a single word of reproach hinting at the happiness which she had lost through his fault. She knew he worked, but she did not know how hard he worked; and never to this day did she suspect how Vincenz used to sit with locked door, writing all night at his desk, so as to get through double work; nor how often, when he declared he was going to dine with a friend, and she scolded him in her querulous fashion for his dissipation he would walk the streets alone, and come back looking rather pale; and all this only to lessen the butcher's bill, which he knew they could not pay.

Vincenz did not in any word refer to those past years; but some dim reflection of what must have been, could not fail to dawn in Gretchen's mind.

They had walked for some minutes in silence, when Vincenz, more in his ordi-nary voice, said,

"That is the whole of my story. I have not often indulged in a passion since then; a temper is a luxury which a poor man cannot afford to keep. That one fit of anger was an expensive thing," and he laughed bitterly; "it cost my sister's happiness, Con-rad Perlenberg's life, and my own career."

"I am glad you told me," said Gretchen, faltering. She could think of nothing else to say. "You must have been very unhappy."

"Others must have been more unhappy," he said, quietly. "Having spoiled three people's lives, I have no right to expect any happiness in my own. I was fool enough to expect it once, and I have been punished for it."

The last words were but a thought spoken aloud, and Gretchen drooped her head without answering.

They were in the valley by this time, and the blaze of the festive lights shone out close before them. But the story of the broken heart had left behind it a gloom not to be dispelled by lights or music, and the last few minutes of the walk were passed in unbroken silence.

Chapter XXVI

A Sultana

"Ich bin ein Cavalier wie andere Cavaliere."

— Faust

PRINCESS TRYPHOSA is spending the evening in her apartment. On a low ottoman against the wall, she reclines with half-closed eyes. The Resculescus occupy the most magnificent suite of rooms of the monster hotel, and Princess Tryphosa inhabits the most magnificent room of this apartment. To European ideas it would appear a comfortless room; but there is plenty of rich red velvet and luminous gilding on all sides; and every touch of color in the room, every light and every shadow, seems to be there expressly in order to throw out in relief the figure of that woman on the ottoman.

An ideal sultana, stepped straight out of the "Arabian Nights," she leans motionless among her yielding cushions. A rich and luxurious indolence is expressed in every curve of her reclining figure. There is a narcotic influence about her very presence; it hangs round her in the atmosphere, as impalpable yet as irresistible as a fragrance of poppy-heads. She is a silent protest against activity — a silent sermon on the beauty of laziness.

She is elaborately, almost gorgeously, dressed; colored stones shine upon her neck and arms, which the hanging sleeves leave bare; in her hair one red pomegranate-blossom droops, and on her cheek the black eyelashes throw a broad shadow.

The lamps have been lighted already, and pour all around them a flood of soft yellow. The summer evenings are beginning to creep in, though the days are still hot and sunny.

By the lamplight, Princess Tryphosa might be thought asleep; but she is not. There is a rosary of amber beads in her hand, and it glides slowly, very slowly through her fingers. Beside her lies open one of Paul de Kock's most doubtful novels. The novel is no doubt intended to enliven the pauses between the lengthy prayers, and the amber beads are as certainly meant to nullify any bad effect of the entertaining lecture. Paul de Kock entertained this Romanian princess very much, but not as he entertains other people. While she read him (and she read him very conscientiously) her face remained grave and her fancy untickled; she might have been believed utterly incapable of any sense of the ludicrous. That was entirely a mistake. Princess Tryphosa appreciated each joke but she usually appreciated it a little time after she had laid down the novel. While the amber beads were gliding through her fingers, and her lips slowly moving in devotion, it often happened that the point of a joke she had been reading half an hour before began to dawn in her mind, and made an irresistible smile rise to her moving lips. It was not at all infrequent to hear Princess Tryphosa break into a low soft laugh when the last half-hour had brought absolutely nothing calculated to raise merriment.

This evening she is not alone. There is a piano in the room, and at the piano a swarthy-faced girl, her younger sister, is touching the chords with an unskillful hand. The music is the only thing that disturbs the Oriental character of the picture. A Moorish serenade, or the slumber-song of the "Africaine," would have been in harmony with the rest; but these jingly variations upon *"la prière d'une vierge"* are an element foreign to the scene. Princess Tryphosa feels them to be tiresome; at least she is fully aware that something is very tiresome, although she does not attempt to analyze the precise cause.

The variations had gone on for some time, when the princess drew out her watch and looked at it. It was a beautifully enameled watch, but it was not going.

"What o'clock is it, Milena?" she inquired, raising her voice.

The *"prière d'une vierge"* was suspended for a moment, while Milena answered, "Half-past eight." She put her hands on the chords again while she added, "You have asked the hour twice, Tryphosa; do you want to go to bed? Are you tired?"

The variations went on for another half-page, and then Tryphosa's voice was heard answering,

"No, I don't want to go to bed. But I think I am rather tired," she said, lower.

The jingly prayer rambled on, causing Milena's two little brown hands to chase each other up and down the piano, and sometimes to jump clean over each other, like a couple of frisky brown mice at play. Some sound, like a heavy sigh, came from the ottoman by the wall. At the same time, the door opened, and the black eyelashes were slowly raised. But it was not the person expected; it was only a tiny figure running towards her.

"Mille pardons, madame," ejaculated the French nursery-maid behind, apologizing for the abnormal intrusion; *"mais il est d'une méchanceté ce soir!* He would insist on saying goodnight to you, *madame, et je n'ai pu l'attraper, le petit coquin."*

The small runaway meanwhile had clambered on to the ottoman and thrown himself upon his mother's neck; while Princess Tryphosa passively submitted to this strange fancy of her son's. Perhaps she had not immediately realized the meaning of his appearance, for just as the indignant Fanchette had got him as far as the door, the princess called him back to her side. She drew him towards her, and looked for a minute into his face, then pressed him once, almost with vehemence, to her breast; after which she sank back exhausted, dismissing Fanchette and her charge with a wave of her hand.

It was not more than once a week that such a scene of affection took place between the mother and the son; and yet Tryphosa was more devoted than most Romanian mothers. It had not been all at once that she had taken the little brown-faced baby to her heart, nor indeed that she had discovered herself to be possessed of a mother's heart. Codran had almost kicked himself free of his swaddling-clothes by the time that Tryphosa had, somewhat to her surprise, awakened to the fact that she really was a mother like other women, and that she really loved her child as other women do. Now the curly-headed Codran was, for her, second to only one person in the world. In a moment of danger, she might have had the devotion to sacrifice herself for her child, only that the chances are she would not have thought of it in time.

The little brown mice were beginning again to scamper over the keys, but had to break off their gambols as the door opened for the second time.

The Virgin's prayer came to a final close at last; and Tryphosa, looking up, saw her sister rising from her seat, curtseying sedately to the entering visitor.

The visitor was István Tolnay. He bowed with excessive respect to Milena, and then, advancing towards the ottoman, took Princess Tryphosa's outstretched hand and raised it to his lips. The amber rosary and the French novel were both put aside. Princess Tryphosa had more absorbing interests at this moment than prayers or novels.

Milena sat down demurely; her sister looked at her steadily for a few moments, as if meditating how to get rid of her.

"I am glad you stopped playing, Milena," she remarked now; "that air was so tiresome."

"Why did you not tell me before?" asked Milena. "I did not think of it before."

"But you patronize music, princess," said István, taking a place on a chair not very far distant from the ottoman.

The princess looked at him, but spoke to her sister. "Milena, will you say that the *dulcétia* is to be brought in?"

When Milena had reached the door, which Baron Tolnay held open for her, the princess added, "Georgin is to bring it."

Milena understood that she was not to return; and she understood also quite well why she was not to return, although she walked out of the room as demurely as any straight-laced English damsel could have done. What Milena was, Tryphosa had been; and what Tryphosa was, Milena would be in time, barring her beauty, which this swarthy-faced girl could never hope to rival. Before she had married, Tryphosa had scarcely known what the outside of a French novel was like; would have considered herself insulted if a man had offered to shake hands with her; had never been allowed to smoke a cigarette, or to cross a street except under the maternal eye. And now — well, now she is alone with István Tolnay. What is there passing between István and Tryphosa?

With the closing of the door, the mask was dropped. Milena's presence had of necessity made the first few phrases strictly conventional; but it was not for the sake of conventional conversation that István was here this evening.

"I wrote to you," said Tryphosa, not changing her position, only turning her head slowly till her eyes rested on him. "Did you not get my note?"

"I am here in obedience to it," said István, sitting down again, this time on a chair much nearer to the ottoman. He looked at Tryphosa with unveiled admiration in his eyes; she lay still in her half-reclining position, while with one hand she drew towards her a scented box, and began turning a cigarette between her fingers.

"I said eight o'clock."

"I was not back at eight o'clock."

The princess went on turning her cigarette calmly.

"Why do you always call me princess now? You used to call me Tryphosa last summer."

István winced for an instant, but in the next he laughed gayly.

"How could I know that you still allowed it this year? I shall only be too happy to call you Tryphosa again."

She appeared not to be listening to his excuse; the cigarette was done turning, but she held it unlighted in her fingers, while her eyes hung on his face as if she were maturing a thought in her mind.

"Where were you not back from at eight o'clock?"

"I took a long walk," said István, evasively.

"But not alone," said Tryphosa, with a rapidity which in her was surprising.

István pulled meditatively at his mustache. Of course, he had not been alone; but he had thought that it might have been pleasanter for all parties if the fact had remained unmentioned. He would have cheerfully told a dozen lies on the subject, if that could have done any good, for no squeamish sensitiveness as to veracity ever troubled István Tolnay. If he candidly acknowledged the truth now, it was only because he recognized that denial would do no good.

"Alone?" He laughed. "No; I enjoy my own society best in that of other people. I made an expedition with Mr. Howard and the Mohr family. We had quite a pleasant day," he added, frankly, not shrinking in the least before Tryphosa's steady gaze. Moral cowardice did not happen to be his special phase of weakness.

The cigarette was lit by this time, and a soft cloud of gray-white smoke hovered around Princess Tryphosa's head.

"Why should you fancy that I would not allow you to call me Tryphosa this year, if I allowed it you last year?"

István had hoped that that subject was dropped by this time. He began framing an answer when a welcome interruption came in the shape of a cut-glass plate filled with *dulcétia*, which just now was carried in by the servant. Never before had he so thoroughly appreciated this Oriental custom. This break in the conversation would enable a fresh subject to be started at a very convenient juncture.

But he might have known Princess Tryphosa better by this time. The slow but unfailing tenacity of her mind was not to be disturbed by such an interruption. Three lengthy meals in the interval would not have been enough for that purpose; at the end of twenty-four hours, she would have resumed the idea exactly at the place where she had dropped it. What effect could the appearance of the *dulcétia* have upon such a mind as hers?

When the glass plate was on the table and the door closed again, she spoke,

"I want you to tell me, István, what reason you have for supposing that anything is different from what it was last year?"

"Nothing is different," said István, leaning forward, and following only the impulse of the moment as he spoke. "If anything is different," she said, letting a puff of smoke escape from her lips, "it is you who have made it different, and not I; it is your doing, and not mine."

"Have I made it different?"

István leaned forward a little more. He did not say anything further at the moment, for he felt that the language of his eyes was the most appropriate language just then. He knew that his tongue spoke well, when he chose, but he knew that his eyes spoke better; it was always with them that he got over the most difficult turns in conversation.

"It is you, it is not I," she said, without lowering her eyelids under his gaze. "István, you are not what you were last year. You do not come to me; you go on expeditions; you do not call me Tryphosa. You loved me last year — "

"And I love you this year," said István, taking her hand, which hung close to him. It was by far the most convenient answer to make, although it did not happen to be the true one. Besides being convenient, it was also pleasant. Though he did not love her this year, he had loved her last year; and the memory of that impression was quite vivid enough to make him enjoy the sight of her beauty, as she reclined thus with her eyes on his face. There was a deep color glowing on her cheeks and burning on her lips; and this reflection of an inward passion brooding deep down within her made her surpassingly beautiful. In spite of many untoward circumstances, this moment was to be counted among the pleasant moments of his life. Though he did not love her this year, there was no objection to letting himself be loved by her.

After his last words she let her eyes sink deep into his for a moment; then slowly drawing away her hand, she calmly swallowed a spoonful of the *dulcétia*. Her next remark sounded irrelevant. It was always difficult to trace the embers of thought which might be smoldering in her mind.

"Mademoiselle Mohr is very beautiful."

István Tolnay started, and his eyes flashed fire. Tryphosa's image faded, and Gretchen's arose in its place. Quick as lightning, his thoughts carried him to other scenes than this; to many a pleasant moment in the forest walk today; to many a word and look exchanged in the shadow of the beech trees. Princess Tryphosa knew that that flush and that spark in his eye were not for her, even though he answered,

"You are more beautiful, my dark queen!"

"I think I am jealous of Mademoiselle Mohr," said Tryphosa, slowly.

She knew that she was much more beautiful than Gretchen, but she knew quite well what advantages the other had over her.

"It is no good being beautiful if I have lost your love."

"Have I not told you a hundred times that I love you?" asked István, with a shade of impatience this time. A woman's love was pleasant to him, but a woman's lamentations were wearisome.

Oh yes, he had told her that he loved her a hundred times, in hot and passionate words, last year: these words he said now sounded so weak beside the memory of those others; and Princess Tryphosa's memory was unfortunately so tenacious.

"István, after all the sacrifices I have made, you cannot have forgotten your promises. You told me last year that I must wait. I have been patient, and I have waited. I have lived only on the thought of you, on the hope of being your wife someday. I have given up everything. I have risked my fair fame. I have deprived my child of its father — and all, all for you. Are you going to tell me that I have done it all in vain?"

She uttered these words, so full of passion, slowly, pausing often, and giving full weight to each syllable. As she spoke, she sat up from her reclining posture; the lamplight struck red and green flashes from the rubies and emeralds on her neck.

"I have not repented one sacrifice of all those which I have made. You are not going to abandon me, now that I am free?"

"Stop this talk, in God's name!" cried István, starting up from his chair with a fierce flush on his forehead. "Do you want to hunt me down? Do you want to drive me to distraction? A man's patience can be tried too far, I tell you."

This woman's lamentations were becoming decidedly inconvenient. They required to be cut short at any price. She trembled under the glance which he shot towards her; and, womanlike, she began to undo what she had been doing.

For more than a minute, she sat collecting her thoughts; then she spoke,

"Forgive me, István — I have been wrong; you must be right. I was wrong to doubt you."

Did not even this confidence touch him with pity, or awaken some faint qualm of conscience? No; for there is a sort of cruelty which springs, not from the pleasure of seeing others suffer, but only from a sort of mental instability; and in this new way, István could be cruel. The cruelty which springs from the hardness of nature has more chance of being softened than that which comes from a light- ness of nature — for a hard nature need not necessarily be a shallow one; while here, there was no possibility of stirring the depths, because the depths themselves were wanting. Therefore, István was capable of fiery, though not of lastingly tender passions, and the impression of the moment, though paramount while it lasted, was swept away by the impression of the next. A woman's beauty was the only language that could make him feel an approach to pity. Passionate appeal and heart-rending prayers fell upon indifferent ears; but sighs could move him — when they were breathed by glowing lips; and tears could touch him — falling from beautiful eyes.

Tryphosa's beauty had lost almost the last vestige of power over him, for he was surfeited with it. There was too much of it, and it was given too profusely; the quality was too rich, and the flavor too intense. Once he had wished for her love ardently; but now that she had freed herself and laid it at his feet, he felt his ardor strangely cooled. The coveted good lost half its value when thus pressed upon him.

He had thought that the last vestige of that power was gone; but he would not have been István Tolnay if the sight of that beautiful pleading figure had not calmed his anger, though it could not touch his pity. Her hands were clasped and raised towards him; diamond drops glistened in her beseeching eyes, shining brighter than the fire of the jewels on her neck and arms. She was too beautiful to be resisted —

not too eloquent, or too loving, or too blindly devoted, but simply too beautiful. Whether he loved her or not, and whether he meant to marry her or not, the thing most natural and most agreeable at this moment was to stoop and kiss her; and István did it. There really was no other way of quieting her suspicions. It was not a necessity, of course — it was a luxury; but István had not the heart to deny himself this luxury. Make it all the harder for her afterwards? Bah! István never thought of afterwards; that was a word that did not exist in his vocabulary. *"Après moi, le deluge,"* he thought, quite gayly, as he allowed himself to be drawn down on the seat beside her. His arm was round her now, and his voice was pouring sweet promises into her ear. Even at this moment, he could scarcely be described as hypocritical. He was only taking what he liked second best, because he could not get what he liked best; he was only doing the thing most agreeable to be done at the moment. Was it his fault that he had found something else more agreeable a little time before, and might find it so again a little time after?

"And you will stay with me, István?" she murmured — and what a depth of tenderness shone in those velvety black eyes as she said it! Then, after a moment, "You will not go on any more of those expeditions in the mountains, where I cannot go?"

"Not if I can help it," said István, readily. "I only do it for the sake of that poor old gentleman who is so anxious about discovering that place."

Princess Tryphosa appeared to be ruminating upon this side of the question, but the result of her reflections was to make her repeat a remark which she had made once previously,

"Mademoiselle Mohr is very beautiful."

"As pretty as a fair-haired woman can ever be," said István, unflinchingly, pressing his lips again to the soft hand he held. "Could you suspect me of the bad taste of preferring her to you?" The effrontery with which he put the question was admirable of its kind.

The princess did not answer; she was too much in arrears for that. Her straight black brows were drawn together in deep thought.

"And you will go on no more expeditions, if you can help it; and you will come and see me often? for I must be your wife soon, István."

She turned and looked straight at him; and though those deep eyes moved so slowly, the flush which shot over his face did not escape her sight.

"We must wait, Tryphosa," he said, in his softest voice. "I told you that we must wait."

"And you say that you prefer me to her," she continued, slowly. "How long must we wait?"

It was István's conviction that the princess would have to wait much longer than she imagined; but he kept that conviction to himself.

"Oh, a little time longer; till autumn — till the season is over — till *Gaura Dracului* is found," he said, half laughing.

"*Gaura Dracului?*" she repeated. "I hate *Gaura Dracului;* it is my enemy. It takes you to the hills — it takes you from me — "

"Only to return to your side," murmured István, heedlessly.

"It takes you from me, while I must sit here and wait. Wait!" she sighed, wearily — "I have waited so long!"

And then István snatched recklessly at other arguments. To hear his fluent reasonings was almost to be convinced that marriage was a thing that required several years for its completion.

He left her, at last, with promises, which came so easily from his lips, echoing still in her ears.

Until the door was closed, he was the ardent lover. He had taken the red pomegranate blossom from her hair, and with an impassioned action he pressed it to his lips at parting.

Then with his light step he ran down the staircase, and went out whistling a gay tune as he passed into the night air.

It is not of this evening, it is of the morrow that he is thinking as he walks along. He must be at the hotel tomorrow to discuss the arrangements for one of those expeditions which, apparently, he cannot help joining — no doubt on account of the invalid gentleman whose views he is so anxious to further.

What cares he for the woman from whom he has just parted? Just as much as for the pomegranate flower which lies on the road, to be trodden into the dust by the heel of the next passerby.

And Tryphosa sits where he has left her. There is no flower in the dead blackness of her hair. On her lips, there still lingers the smile which his last kiss has left there. She is going over in thought each caress and each touch of his hand; it is almost as if only now she were tasting the full delight of his presence. Slowly, the smile dies away for her thoughts have reached another and a darker point. Her breast rises and sinks in a bitterly weary sigh.

Some people say that Princess Tryphosa is stupid; and yet István Tolnay's well-sounding protestations, his burning glances, have only half-convinced her. Not all his smiles have smoothed the line of care from her forehead; not even his kiss has lifted the weight of sadness from her heart.

Chapter XXVII

The Oath of Hercules

"Hither bend you, turn you hither,
Eves that blast and wings that wither,
Cross the wandering Christian's way,
Lead him, ere the glimpse of day,
Many a mile of maddening error
Through the maze of night and terror."

— Moore: *Song of the Evil Spirit of the Woods*

T HE spirits with whom rustic superstition peopled *Gaura Dracului* must have laughed their fiendish laugh often and often in these days, while a bootless search was leading the explorers' steps up hills and down dales, and over rocks and into gloomy forests, sometimes miles out of the right direction, sometimes across the very track which would have led them to the spot, once even within a few hundred paces of their goal; but never up to the brink of that bottomless chasm, which split the ground in a black and terrible gulf, and yawned in its secret spot, like an open grave — waiting and always waiting. In the early morning when the ivy hung wet with dew, and at sunset when the blood-red light touched it with slanting rays, and at golden midday, and at black midnight, that grave in the forest yawned and waited, like a monster that hungers for prey. But what prey could this monster crave?

Perhaps the fiendish spirits have laughed, as those blind people, who had eyes and who yet did not see, walked through the forest, searching for the three crosses cut in the bark. Those crosses were indeed cut in the bark — it was no sick man's fancy; and those blind people had been close to them and had failed to recognize the marks. If fiendish spirits have got fancies to be tickled, they certainly must have laughed often and gleefully at the idea of a person taking so much trouble in order to find his own grave. Knight or lady, youth or maiden, the spirits recked not which it was, as long as they got their rightful prey.

Those few who knew the spot declared that it was haunted. When the wind blew in the beech trees, howls, as of damned souls, mingled with the blast; the spirits danced round it at midnight, and white-robed ghosts were said to flit from the depth, and sink down again moaning at the first streak of dawn.

But the few who knew the spot were very few indeed; and they were no more than half-savage peasants, ignorant goatherds, or witless stick-gatherers. Adalbert Mohr, whose interest in the search had at first been almost as keen as his daughter's, had long since given up all hope of success. Day by day, and week by week, his strength was declining, his cheek was paling; and with the ebb of vital powers came also the ebb in his feeling towards that which had once been the passion of his life. Three months ago, he had thought himself as near to convalescence as to the discovery of *Gaura Dracului*. Now, he told himself that he was as far from the one as from the other.

It was in vain that his daughter attempted to rouse the interest slowly sinking. It might save him yet, she told herself at times, if *Gaura Dracului* were found. Something to tear him from this ever-growing despondency might yet arrest the harm. So, at least, argued the sanguine trustfulness of youth. But even the feverish interest which bound her own thoughts to the spot could wake no response in his. When she spoke of his old manuscript, he merely sighed; and when she dwelt on her hopes of finding the brigand's treasure, and proved to him by logical deductions that these hopes were grounded, he smiled with a sort of melancholy cynicism.

"Is it not a pity to have all the earrings melted down?" he suggested one day. "Had you not better keep a pair for your own use, unless the shape is too far out of date? And have you quite settled on the bank where your fortune is to be lodged? You will not take less than six percent, I suppose?" He laughed rather bitterly. "What an impostor you are, child, with your great clear eyes, your rosebud mouth, your sunbeam hair, and your logical deductions! If there could be such a thing as a strong-minded daisy, or a matter-of-fact bluebell, I think you might be compared to that, Gretchen."

Gretchen made no answer; perhaps because she felt conscious that her interest in *Gaura Dracului* was not quite as strong-minded, nor quite as matter-of-fact, as she would fain have had her father suppose.

Be the interest what it might, it had suffered no decrease. In face of all hope, she continued perseveringly to scour the mountains, and to devise what she called "traps," in which she expected to catch the Bohemian's secret, but which as yet had proved as many signal failures. The man's innocence was proof against all her wiles. He would shake his head with respectful obstinacy; he regretted his inability to fulfill her wishes; he would do anything else to please the Fräulein, but the mere mention of *Gaura Dracului* was enough to throw a spell of silence over him. Even the slightest reference to his vow he shunned with nervous dread, and all Gretchen's entreaties had not yet succeeded in eliciting the history of that mysterious oath. "I am sure it is something interesting," she said once, with a sigh of baffled curiosity.

"It is something terrible," answered the Bohemian, shuddering.

It was in the old street of the place, and beside the old stone fountain that Gretchen had on this occasion accosted the Bohemian. She was on her way home with Kurt, and her hands were full of autumn crocuses that she had gathered in her walk. Mr. Howard, with his fishing rod, and Baron Tolnay, with his dog, had joined the group; for the Hercules, fountain was a convenient spot of meeting; everyone had to pass that way, and no one could pass unobserved.

Through the first shade of dusk, the stone Hercules loomed black and gigantic above them; the waters splashed softly at his feet.

"Really," said Mr. Howard, "this will never do; this fellow's superstition will be infecting us presently. We are all, as it is, mentally deranged on the subject of this preposterous place. I, for one, am anticipating my dotage. What do you think I caught myself humming this morning in my bath? Why, the air of that ridiculous song about the Roman fellow who shoved a lady down the hole in the dark — a very ungentlemanlike thing to do, by-the-way."

"They certainly all behaved very foolishly," said Gretchen, leaning over the edge of the fountain, and looking at her reflection in the water — "everybody was always so illogical in those times. What a comfort it is that people have become more sensible and quiet now!"

"Sensible and quiet!" said Baron Tolnay, with a peculiar laugh. "Do you think so? Why, men are just the same in this age of reason as they were in the age of romance."

"The age of folly, you should call it. I am so glad it is past; that age would never have suited me."

"And I am sorry, for it would have suited me exactly."

"What part of it?" she said, laughing; "the costumes and the feasting, perhaps — but surely not the murder and the bloodshed?"

"Yes, even the murder and the bloodshed. I could do what they did, if I had motive enough."

"And what do you call motive enough?" she asked, absently.

Tolnay was leaning beside her now; she saw the reflection of his face alongside of her own in the water, and even in this imperfect mirror she could not fail to note the eagerness with which his eyes were seeking hers. The look on his face answered her. "Love would be my motive — love for you!"

Tolnay was not accustomed to set a guard upon his eyes, nor were his glances generally barred by timidity; but even he had never before dared to show his admiration so absolutely unveiled. Now, under cover of the presiding deity, he let fall for a moment the transparent mask of conventional restraint. Whose business, after all, was it to note the expression which he wore at the foot of the Hercules statue? or to analyze the nature of the gaze which he sent to the depth of the Hercules fountain?

Gretchen had often before this dimly guessed that her conquest of Tolnay was complete; she had never been sure of it until now. It was the first time in all her experience of him that she had seen that earnest look on his face and that unwonted depth in his eyes. Her heart beat tumultuously: was it with triumph? or was it with fear? "Shall I answer your question?" said István, softly, beside her; but she shook her head, and all at once, opening her fingers, she dropped the crocuses into the water, where they danced gayly on the surface, drawing a floating veil over the two faces below.

"Murder and bloodshed?" said Mr. Howard, breaking into the conversation, which had sunk to whispers by this time. "Who is standing up for murder and bloodshed? I maintain that that Roman fellow behaved disgracefully to Mrs. — whatever her name was."

"Why, Mr. Howard," said Gretchen, turning her back to the statue — for the waters of Hercules had shown her more this evening than she cared to see — "it was only yesterday you told me that you did not believe a word of the legend from beginning to end!"

"Of course, I don't," said Mr. Howard. "If you got to the bottom of the matter, you would probably find that some tipsy woodcutter broke his neck over a pitfall in the dark; and because the branches creak round the spot, the people say that it is haunted."

"They say more than that," ventured the Bohemian, who till now had stood by in respectful silence.

There is no escape for those who are marked; Hercules has sworn it on his club!

"More nonsense, you mean?" asked Mr. Howard, with a sort of unwilling curiosity.

"They say that the evil spirits who live in the abyss hunger after human lives. Ever since that innocent woman found her death there, the god of the valley has granted them a victim once in every hundred years. Some other woman or man must be sacrificed to *Gaura Dracului* in every century. There is no escape for those who are marked; Hercules has sworn it on his club!"

The Bohemian's voice had sunk to an almost inaudible whisper. He raised his blue eyes in shy terror to the stone figure above, as though diffident of speaking of the valley-god in his "sacred" presence.

It is an established fact that anything in the shape of a ghost story sounds more real in the dusk than in the dark. There was not one of the four listeners present who could have pleaded free from a certain thrill of fluttering perturbation.

The mountainside had grown gloomy by this time; the street was deserted; the Hercules fountain alone filled the silence with its gentle splash. Mr. Howard was the first to speak.

"Come!" he cried, giving himself a shake, as though to get rid of some intangible shadow of superstition — "come, this is really irresistible! Here is a fellow who is not superstitious, but who tells us, with a face as long as a yard measure and as white as paper, that somebody must fall down a black hole every hundred years, whether he wills it or no."

"I have only repeated what is the belief among the Romanians," said the Bohemian, somewhat loftily. "I did not say that I believed it."

"But you looked most remarkably as if you did a minute ago. You have not been an eyewitness to one of these century immolations, have you?"

"No," stammered the man, turning pale as ashes. "I — I — have not seen it."

"You have heard it then, or dreamed it," said Mr. Howard, planting himself straight before the Bohemian. "Come, let us go on to the end, since we are at it."

But the Bohemian had no idea of going on to the end. For one moment, he gazed at his questioner in helpless misery, then threw a wild glance around him, and turning suddenly, fairly took to his heels up the street, leaving the party to stare at each other's faces, and invent whatever solutions they could find to the riddle of his behavior.

These sorts of scenes were not calculated to cool curiosity; and despite the failures, Gretchen's courage remained unabated. Did not the failures themselves bring pleasures in their train? And though they never came to *Gaura Dracului*, did they not come to many spots beautiful in their wild solitude, untrodden perhaps for centuries, or perchance known only to the fleet chamois or the soaring eagle?

Nor was the excitement of danger a-wanting to make the enjoyment complete, for there were both the bears and the robbers to be afraid of. To be sure, the bears were said to be very shy in summer, and it had not yet been proved beyond doubt that the robbers existed. But each of these causes was enough to awaken some momentary flutters, and a gentle undercurrent of trepidation, not wholly unpleasant; and both the facts together moved Herr Mohr to insist that firearms should be taken for the protection of the party. The Bohemian, when called upon, produced a rusty gun, which had once been the property of his grandfather. He confessed to being rather surprised at the anxiety which they displayed for their lives; he did not see why people with clear consciences should require the protection of firearms, but he had no objection to humoring them by taking the gun. As to whether it would go off at the right moment, he expressed himself hopeful, though by no means sanguine. The question still remained unsolved, for neither robber nor bear had put himself within range of the Bohemian's gun. And yet there were not wanting evidence of at least the bear's existence. Passing one day through a narrow ravine, they had been startled by a shower of stones rattling down from the height. "That is a bear above us," said the Bohemian, serenely. A little later they had come upon the bleached skeleton of a horse, picked to the very bone. "It was eaten by a bear last winter," explained their guide, in the most matter-of-fact way.

No member of the party enjoyed the air, the liberty, the exhilaration of these mountain excursions as keenly as Dr. Komers. By contrast to his town life, his murky office, and his desk drudgery, the mountains were to him another world. He felt as though he were laying in a stock of sunshine and hill breezes, enough to last him for a lifetime. It was delightful to feel the physical strength which had so long lain dormant — to enjoy the powers which he scarcely knew. The works of the great machinery were coming into action at last.

Ascelinde could not imagine what kept Dr. Komers in the Hercules valley; and though, since the collapse of Draskócs, she never could be the same woman again, and had not spirit enough remaining to be actively unfriendly, still she thought it unfeeling of Dr. Komers to keep painful recollections alive by his presence. Since there was no more family cause, there could be no more need for a family lawyer.

Dr. Komers himself did not quite know why he was staying here so long, although he gave himself a great many reasons for doing so. What good could come from following Gretchen about, since he had sworn to himself that he would woo her no more, and since he meant to hold to what he had sworn? He was strong enough to keep his oath, but not quite strong enough to put the matter aside once for all, as irrevocably fixed. In fact, during these days poor Vincenz began to suspect that he was not an iron character.

The sight of Tolnay by Gretchen's side was a continual irritant, and it did much to darken the sunshine and poison the breeze. Since Gretchen could not belong to him, of course, she must belong to some other man. But, he told himself, that other man ought not to be István Tolnay. It should be an individual of peculiar excellence, and of a character more elevated than the character of any person he had ever yet met. If such a man were to be found, Vincenz felt confident that he could with calmness, almost with resignation, and perhaps a fatherly blessing on his lips, join their two hands together. He felt quite amicably disposed towards this vague man of the future; but, strangely enough, whenever the vague man threatened to become distinct, the amicable feeling turned into vehement dislike. He passed all Gretchen's acquaintances in review, and rejected them all in turn. The future man was only bearable as long as his outline remained undefined; and perhaps it was because István Tolnay's personality was so very clearly defined, both mentally and physically, that Vincenz disliked him so much. He not only disliked, he also mistrusted him. This in itself was an excellent reason for not leaving the Hercules valley. It was his misfortune that he had so many excellent reasons, and not one that could stand on its own legs. Each leaned a little against the other for support, and they ended by all knocking each other down.

It was on a clear August day that Vincenz again had taken his post of guardian and protector. The party had followed the course of the Djernis until they bad come to a ruined watch house, which marked the borders of Romania on this side.

The season had reached its climax, and had passed it. Though the change was scarcely noticeable, yet the short-lived summer glory of the Hercules Baths was slowly declining. Autumn, with its tints, was stealing over the world, "with his gold hand gilding the falling leaf." The mornings were keen and the evenings fresh already. The green brambles in the hedges were turning black; and along the path beside the Djernis, and on the rocks by the mountain foot, and over the ruin of the old watch-tower by the border, the wild grapes hung in bunches, slowly ripening in the sun.

Gretchen, with Tolnay by her side, had been gathering the tiny fruit and now made a step towards a luxuriant cluster that hung from the branches of a neighboring tree.

"Stop, Fräulein!" said the Bohemian, running to her side — "stop, for Heaven's sake! You dare not go a step farther than this!"

Gretchen stood still in alarm, and looked around to see what was the danger threatening, but there was nothing visible except a heap of dead branches across the path.

"And these withered leaves are to bar my passage?" she asked, touching them contemptuously with her foot.

"Though they be but leaves, they mark the frontier, Fräulein; and were we to be found a dozen steps beyond the frontier, we should be instantly arrested and taken off to the nearest town."

"But what for, in the name of all that is illogical?"

"I cannot say that I know what for, Fraulein; perhaps they do not know it themselves. They are always suspicious, those Romanians, and think it more natural that you should be doing harm than not."

"The Romanian grapes look twice as good as the Hungarian ones," said Gretchen, casting a longing glance at the purple berries which hung so temptingly just out of her reach. "Forbidden fruit is always the sweetest, you know."

"I have never heard that, Fräulein; and, begging your pardon, I do not think it can be true: we can never enjoy anything if our conscience be not clear."

"Well, I could make a very comfortable meal upon forbidden fruit, I think," said Tolnay; "much more enjoyable than any legitimately obtained pineapples or nectarines — at least to my thinking; but it is all a matter of taste."

"An acquired taste, perhaps?" put in Gretchen, looking at him over her shoulder.

"Exactly — caviar to such simple souls hampered by a tender conscience;" and the ironically compassionate glance which accompanied the words rested not only on the Bohemian, but on Komers as well.

"I don't like caviar," said Gretchen — "unwholesome, oily stuff, but I should like to take just one step into Romania, and to gather one bunch of Romanian grapes."

"Come, then, let us defy the laws of the country!" said Tolnay, with his irresistible smile, and offering his arm to help her over the momentous heap of branches — "let us taste of the forbidden fruit together."

And partly out of contempt for such illogical restrictions, partly out of that spirit of coquetry, which in her seemed always to be called forth by István Tolnay's presence, Gretchen accepted his arm, and together they passed the line of demarcation;

while, with a gloomy frowning brow, Vincenz watched them disappear round a corner.

All the evil that was in her nature seemed ever ready to be roused at Tolnay's will. To watch her with that man at her side was almost to believe her the cold and heartless coquette, the mercenary fortune hunter, which Anna declared her to be. "And that day," thought Vincenz — "that day when we spoke together in the gorge, I found it so easy to believe that she was a true woman, with a heart that could love, even if it cannot love me. Ah, what a pity is the change!"

"Ah, what a pity is the change!" Gretchen's own thoughts were saying at that very moment. "That day in the gorge he was like Hercules come down from his pedestal to save me; down here today he is tiresome and awkward. What a pity is the change!"

This thought was underlying all her most flippant speeches, all her most seductive smiles; and perhaps, too, this thought made her find out that forbidden fruits are only sweet in anticipation, and that even Romanian grapes can be sour. But nothing of this appeared on the surface, and she came back laughing and talking as lightly as before.

"Well, we have not been arrested, you see," she said, addressing the others.

"And by what shadow of right should you have been arrested?" said Mr. Howard. "There must be justice even in Romania."

The Bohemian's expression seemed to say that justice was much too good a thing to be found in such a country.

"By what right, I do not know; but that they do it, I know. It is sometimes much easier to walk over the Romanian frontier than to walk back again. Some years ago, there was a gentleman here who had passed the border without knowing it. He was seized and locked up as a political spy; and afterwards they forgot all about letting him out again, and if his relations had not found him out at the end of a month, he might be there still."

"A nice state of affairs," cried Mr. Howard, with rising wrath. "I should just like to see them try to lock up a free British subject!" And at the bare idea, Mr. Howard grew scarlet.

"They are an ignorant people," said the Bohemian, with a sort of contemptuous apology for Romania in general. "But they will not lock you up if you show them your papers."

"What sort of papers?" demanded the irate Englishman, who felt inclined to plunge into Romania, all paperless as he was, merely because he was warned against so doing.

"Well, just papers," said the Bohemian, serenely. "I do not think it matters much what they are; the more of them you have, the better. At home, in Bohemia, we need no such precautions; but in this strange land — "

"He means a passport," put in Tolnay.

"I always looked upon passports as an exploded superstition," remarked Kurt.

"So they should be," went on Mr. Howard; "but people in this country cling to superstitions, it seems. If you want to travel slowly, travel with a passport by all means. It is the best recipe I know for being detained at every turn and regarded as a suspicious individual. A passport is the most suspicious-looking article possible now-adays. Last year, I was traveling. I was told I must have a passport; naturally, I declined. What was the result? At the French frontier I was asked for it, and distinctly informed my questioner that I had none. A terrifying Frenchman, with a black beard and rolling eyes, glared at me ferociously for a minute, then roared, in a voice of thunder, *'Comment, monsieur, pas de passeport! Alors PASSEZ, monsieur!'* and I passed, very comfortably indeed."

"But it seems that our friends over there would say, *'Restez, monsieur,'*" laughed Kurt.

"I have got a passport," remarked Dr. Komers, who till now had been following his own thoughts, but who had caught the word under discussion.

"Really?" responded Tolnay, in that tone of half-mockery, which he always used in addressing the lawyer. "How do you come by the obsolete article? Do you keep it as a *souvenir* of extinct customs?"

"No, it is quite new — it was drawn out a few weeks ago ;" and Vincenz took out his pocketbook: and began to unfold it.

"Ah, what admirable prudence! None of us have had such care of our persons."

Vincenz continued to unfold his pocketbook, perfectly unperturbed by Baron Tolnay's pin-pricks. These pin-pricks were István's greatest pleasure. He delighted in displaying his youthfulness under the eyes of the elder man, who would fain be his rival. That the lawyer could ever succeed in being his rival, was an idea far too preposterous to have occurred to István's mind.

"I got the passport to satisfy my sister," said Vincenz, calmly, while he smoothed out the rustling document. "She believed that without it I was exposing myself to innumerable dangers."

Tolnay threw a glance of disparagement at the battered leather pocketbook from which the passport had been issued.

"Does not such a magnificent document deserve a more worthy resting place?"

"I prize this pocketbook above everything else in the world," said Vincenz, with sudden fire. "It is dearer to me than the most sacred relic." He spoke only on a thoughtless impulse, but Tolnay had caught the tone.

Quick as lightning, his glance shot towards Gretchen. A faint flush was on her cheek: she knew well enough that this old pocket-book was the same that she had once stitched together for Dr. Komers.

Of this, István Tolnay knew nothing. And yet, it was at this moment, while he stood beside the ruined watchtower, and looked from one face to the other, that there was sown in István's soul the first frail seed of a plant which was to bear bitter fruit.

Chapter XXVIII

A Modern Martyr

"Wenn dud en steilen Berg ersteigst
Wirst du beträchtlich ächzen."

— Heine

L ike a fire which has smoldered so low as to have almost reached extinction, and of a sudden leap into new flame, so did the half-forgotten robber panic reawaken with tenfold strength, when one evening it became known that the Bohemian's milk-girl had been assaulted.

A man had burst through the bushes, while she was alone on the pathway; had first torn the coin necklace from her throat, and flung it contemptuously to the ground, and had then wrenched her basket from her, and seizing on the fresh cheeses which it held, had disappeared again in the forest.

A robber who preferred milk cheeses to gold coins could not belong to the most dangerous specimens of his kind; but, by the time the story had made the round of the place, he had not only grown, but multiplied; and there seemed to cause enough for the patrols to walk about with fixed bayonets, challenging every shadow, and taking each other into custody, in the name of the king.

"I do not see any logical grounds for giving up our plan," said Gretchen, on the evening of the event, while the red-hot story was being discussed beside the fountain.

There had been a longer expedition than usual planned for the next day: they had intended to visit a cave among the mountains, and now the party was weighing the advisability of maintaining or relinquishing the idea.

The Bohemian, being consulted as to the authenticity of the robber, calmly raised his shoulders. The girl was a Romanian, he remarked, and therefore, of course, more inclined to falsehood than to truth. The account she gave was confused; superstitious terrors had bewildered her faculties. At the first appearance of the man, she had naturally jumped to the conclusion that this was the wicked spirit *Miasanoptie*, under whose evil bane falls every Romanian who is foolish enough to stand at the crossing of two roads while the sun is setting. "And," added the Bohemian, with scornful pity "the stupid girl maintains that it is the Tuesday which has brought her bad luck; for — would you believe it? — these people here call Tuesday a bad day. They will neither begin nor finish anything on a Tuesday."

"But have you not got something of that sort in Bohemia too?" Gretchen ventured to suggest.

Why, Friday is our unlucky day," said the Bohemian, with wondering simplicity; "it is only such ignorant people as these who could make Tuesday the bad day."

"Why, then Bohemians can be superstitious too?"

The Bohemian's blue eyes were fixed upon her with a sort of sorrowful reproach.

"That is not a superstition, Fräulein; that is a belief."

"Well; but to return to the robbers," said Gretchen, unwilling to waste time upon such a nice definition as Bohemian versus Romanian superstition. "Do you believe there is any danger? Should you be afraid to go to the hills alone?"

Again, the blue eyes gazed at her in mild surprise.

"I am afraid of no man, Fräulein, when my conscience is clear."

"And if we were to meet these robbers, what would they do to us?"

"Take away our money, Fräulein."

"And if we had no money?"

"Then perhaps cut our throats," said the Bohemian in an apologetic tone, as if excusing himself for mentioning such an unpleasant subject before ladies.

Gretchen's face fell a little.

"Then must we give up our expedition?"

"Oh no," said the Bohemian, with a reassuring smile: "there is no need to give it up, if our consciences are clear. For, after all, death must come sooner or later; and if our hour has struck, we cannot escape from it."

"Ye — es," said Gretchen, reflectively.

This was a salutary but not a particularly cheerful view of the case.

"Oh, our consciences are all as clear as crystal," said Baron Tolnay, breaking into the conversation with a laugh. "Let us go to the cave, by all means."

And so, finally, it was decided; the time for the start fixed, and the Bohemian dismissed.

All this time, Princess Tryphosa had stood a silent member of the group. She had made no comment whatever upon the plans; but presently, when Mr. Howard left the party, saying, "I am going to get my wading boots and have another cast in the river," the little group was electrified by the announcement from Tryphosa's lips:

"I am going too."

There was a general start and a few broken exclamations. Even Kurt's coolness was troubled for a moment. Baron Tolnay was the first to recover his presence of mind.

"But you have got no wading boots, princess."

The princess stared at him intensely. She had to reconcile the idea of the wading boots with the other idea which was present in her mind, and it took her some time to do it.

István attempted to assist the process of thought. "You want to go to the river, princess?"

"No; I want to go with you to the cave."

They had talked of the dry weather, of the departing visitors, of the principal cures of the season since then. Princess Tryphosa was still at the cave.

Here was a fresh electrical shock. Nobody believed it at first. More than one member of the party changed color. Then there followed a pause, and consciousness of general constraint; for there was no one present who could not easily guess what had moved the princess to this stupendous resolution.

The princess herself neither changed color nor expression. She sat through it all with unmoved stolidity. She waited with inexhaustible patience until the small waves of wonder, of incredulity, of only half-suppressed amusement had broken over her, as the waves of the sea break over a massive and immovable rock.

A desperate question was ventured, at last, by Gretchen. "Why are you going?"

After a minute of intense thought, the princess gave utterance to the blackest lie of which she had ever been guilty in her life:

"I am fond of caves."

Then Baron Tolnay made an effort.

"It is more than three hours' walk, princess."

"I know — but I am going."

"The way is tremendously rough."

"I know — but I am going."

Only another useless wave. It passed over, leaving no mark on the rock. The resolution had not been an impulse; Princess Tryphosa had no impulses. Every thought with her required to be carefully planted and slowly ripened until it was perfect. It had taken days, even weeks, before she had confessed to herself freely that István Tolnay was deserting her for the sake of the German girl.

That point once established, she recognized the necessity of doing something. After several more days of reflection, she resolved what that something was to be.

The principal cause of her uneasiness was those mountain expeditions, so fatally conducive to *tête-à-têtes*. Having failed to keep István from them, she had at last matured the tremendous idea of joining them herself.

Tolnay's first effort was his last. The princess's resolutions might take long to ripen; but, once ripened, no power on earth was capable of balking them. Tolnay knew the woman too well — too fatally well — not to be aware of this. After all, it mattered nothing. It was to be regarded merely as an inconvenience — merely as one more stone to be kicked out of his path. Her whole love was an inconvenience; and yet it was characteristic of István that, even when pressed hardest between his new passion and the troublesome consequences of his old one, the wish never once occurred to him that Tryphosa's love should die a natural death, and thus release him. It was only the inconvenient expression of that love to which he objected, not the love itself.

Her announced resolution provoked him; it scarcely disturbed him, and he knew that it should not balk him. Living, as he did, only in the excitement of his present passion, everything outside it dwindled in importance. He was madly in love, and he did not care who saw it. Princess Tryphosa herself must see it sooner or later. Let her see it sooner, then, if she be foolish enough to buy the information at the cost of so much personal discomfort.

The others fancied that when the moment of ascent came, and Tryphosa found herself in face of the reality, her resolution would fail. István Tolnay knew better.

This woman hated action and despised exercise; she was terrified of the robbers, she suffered from giddiness and loss of breath; but there was a feeling in her that was stronger than her hatred of action and her contempt of exercise, stronger than her dread of bodily discomfort., stronger than her fear of the robbers: it was her love for István Tolnay.

And so, to the wonder of the world, it came to pass that Princess Tryphosa, who was used to spend her day on a soft-cushioned couch, lying motionless for hours at a time; Princess Tryphosa, whose feet were used to nothing harder than embroidered

Turkish slippers; who had never in her life seen the inside of a forest, nor walked up anything steeper than the staircase of a *premier* — it came to pass that this marvel of luxurious indolence actually put her high-born feet to the base use of mountain climbing.

It may sound a small thing to English ears; but many a grander sacrifice, many a torture endured, many a bloody martyrdom, has been less heroic. It is necessary to have watched a Romanian woman dragging herself through the laziness of her everyday life before such heroism can be measured.

And Princess Tryphosa had the agony to see that it was all in vain. Her immolation was disregarded, her martyrdom was uncrowned; there was no aureole for her head, no palm for her hand. Far on in front, she could see István by Gretchen's side, giving to the light-footed Gretchen the assistance of which she, the heavy-stepping Tryphosa, stood so much in need. She had torn her long silk dress; she had walked through the soles of her shoes; her lace was banging in shreds; the amber rosary which she carried in her pocket had snapped its cord, while the yellow beads went bounding down the bill; she had struggled and panted and gasped, battling bravely through it all, and uttering no complaint. But at last, when standing breathless and flushed on the top of a steep path, she looked on and perceived that those figures in advance had vanished, and found that she herself was abandoned by all save the good-natured Kurt, who had cheered on her passage by an occasional display of his very best French — now, at last, her strong spirit seemed in danger of breaking.

Collapsing to a limp heap of lilac silk, she sank down at the foot of a beech tree, and slowly taking out a costly lace handkerchief she deliberately burst into tears.

What did Kurt do? Did he attempt to dry her beautiful eyes, as some men would have done? Was he terrified at the hysterical storm of feminine emotion, as some other sort of men might have been?

Neither of the two. Kurt put one hand into his pocket, twirled his stick with the other, and, looking down at the sobbing woman, said in an encouraging tone,

"Pleurez, madame; cela vous soulagera!"

The effect might have been expected. Tryphosa, though she was a slow woman, was yet a woman, and, being encouraged to weep, she dried her tears with something that almost approached to alacrity.

"Have we lost our way?" she asked.

Kurt did not think they had lost their way yet, but believed it not at all improbable that they should lose it presently, considering that the others were out of sight, and that he himself had never been in this part of the forest before. He hinted at the advisability of advancing.

"Not yet," said the princess. "I must rest a little longer, and I must think."

Thinking was much easier when sitting at the foot of a tree than when scrambling up a slippery path.

"Very well," said Kurt. ·

The princess began to think. She was reviewing her position. Her tactics had been a failure. She had hoped that her presence would be a check upon Tolnay, and she had found out that it was not. Nor would it ever be, for these three hours up the hill had shown her how wildly and how recklessly István was in love. Her first effort had failed; she must make another, but in another direction. That was what she required to think about.

"Does your sister always walk as fast as this?" she inquired. "Usually. I am always telling her to take things easily, but she does not listen to me. She likes preaching better than being preached to: and when I hit at her obstinacy, she hits at my expensive habits."

The princess had raised her eyes as she put her question, and they still remained fixed on Kurt's face. It was not as if she were looking at him: it was only as if she had forgotten to remove her eyes while she pursued her meditations. Kurt did not find that fixed gaze to be in the least degree embarrassing.

"She does not listen to you? Does she ever listen to anybody?"

"Not often, I admit; she has got such a terribly hard head, you see, and is so tremendously logical and strong-minded. I believe she fancies herself sent into the world as a sort of missionary to the great tribe of the illogical; what she would like best would be to distribute logic and justice all round; she says they are synonymous."

"Thank you; but please do not speak so fast."

The princess was silent, carefully dissecting the various elements of thought which were contained in Kurt's phrase.

Kurt was silent also; he found the princess puzzling, and he did not know what he was being thanked for.

Presently, he found the princess more puzzling still, when after a little silence she said, "Then you think that she would understand justice?"

"I think she would box my ears if I told her she did not," said Kurt, cheerfully; and then he proposed that they should go on.

"Yes; I am fond of caves," said the poor princess, in a rather woe-begone tone, as with the help of his arm she struggled to her feet and resumed the battle with the hill.

"Look! my shoes are all torn, and my foot is bleeding," she had said to Kurt, merely as though stating a fact, not asking for any compassion; for after that one burst of tears at the foot of the beech tree, she had made no more complaint. Her shoes were in tatters indeed, and the hem of her dress was in a fringe; but she dragged herself along, clinging to Kurt's arm, and bearing her sufferings in silent agony. There was something of an almost divine heroism about this heavily beautiful Romanian princess.

When they had reached the top of the next steep slope, her face was flushed to a deep purple, and her fourth silk flounce had given way; and yet upon her breathlessly parted lips there was a smile, for she had thought out the situation. The case was intricate, and her means well-nigh exhausted. Tears, supplications, and reproaches had all failed in reviving István's extinguished love. It is true that jealousy still remained; and Tryphosa had reflected upon the advisability of awakening István's jealousy — had carefully considered the idea, had weighed it, and rejected it. Such petty maneuverings did not suit the princess. There were none of those little weaknesses about her, and no taint of meanness. Her mind had been mapped out on a larger scale. She was going to use means more simple and more courageous — perhaps also more desperate. Having failed to work upon the man, she was going to try and work upon the woman.

"Where can they have all gone to?" asked the princess, staring all round her and above her and below her in open-mouthed wonder; for they were standing on a tiny platform with no apparent egress.

Below, there was a glimpse of rocky mountaintops, surging away like a sea of petrified waves, to break on the horizon. Around the spot on which they stood, the ground was covered with barberry bushes, where the ripe berries hung in bunches, like tassels of shaded red. Straight in front of them stood a wall of rock, and at the foot a low opening, half masked by scraggy brushwood.

"Halloo!" said Kurt; "this is the cave. I hear their voices in there. Nothing for it now but to follow them."

The princess leaned a little more heavily on his arm, and gasped — "Must I go into that hole?"

"You are fond of caves, you know, princess."

She was a courageous woman, though she was so unwieldy. She had gone through so much this day that really one discomfort more or less could not matter much. Her cup of bitterness might as well be quite full as half full. Princess Tryphosa was not a woman to do things by halves. She had walked over thorns and stones — she might as well walk into a damp cave.

"Yes; I am fond of caves," she said, rather faintly; and, rallying her resolution for the crowning effort, she went forward without another murmur, trailing her silk dress after her, carrying with her a perfume of distilled roses and a general air of mock Parisian elegance.

Never before had that wall of rock looked down upon anything as beautiful as her face or as incongruous as her costume. The rock stared down in blank and frigid surprise as the last tip of her colored train glided vanishing into the cave-like the tail of a glittering serpent.

Chapter XXIX

By Torchlight

"Leicht ist die Hülle die den Hass bedeck."

— Auffenberg

THOUGH the hole in the rock was so low that mountain gnomes alone could have entered it upright, yet it proved to be the portal of a space more suited to giants than to dwarfs.

As the party stood together in the cave, they looked no more than a tiny group, and the flames of their firwood torches were but little spots of light, lost in the vast blackness around. Their progress was not easy, for the ground was slippery with damp, and irregularly strewn with large round stones. Above their heads the vaulted ceiling rose away out of the circle of light; hollows and undefined niches blackened vaguely on all sides. But where the ceiling lowered, it was of a snowy glistening white, a fine fretwork of delicate points hanging downward, like icicles turned into stone. The air was chill and clammy; the voices of the speakers sounded unnatural, striking weird echoes against far-off corners, and rolling back towards them with a hollow murmur. And in every silence that fell, they could hear a note of melancholy music — the slow sad dropping of the ever-filtering water, which, with the patient toil of centuries, has worked out the intricacies of that wonderful fretwork ceiling.

"I suppose the rock is safe," remarked Vincenz, staring upward at the white stone icicles.

The Bohemian shrugged his shoulders.

"It may be safe, or it may not; if the day and hour for our death have come, there is no use trying to escape it."

"Let us hope for the best," said Kurt, cheerfully.

"And the best is surely a good death," returned the Bohemian, "only that I should be loath to breathe my last in this strange land." The Bohemian never lost an opportunity of airing his favorite complaint and even Gretchen had given up arguing with him on the point. In face of all logic, and despite the clearest demonstration he insisted on considering himself as a stranger and an exile. "Are we going out again soon?" asked Tryphosa, in a tone of desperate resignation.

Since they had done their duty by looking at the cave, she did not see why the torture should be prolonged.

"Going out again!" repeated Gretchen; "Why, we have scarcely come in."

"But we cannot go farther," said the poor princess, in an accent which might have moved a heart of marble. And yet the very tone, instead of softening her fair and cruel rival, seemed rather to steel Gretchen against pity.

All day long, the girl had been in strange humor — a mood of reckless gayety; different altogether from her usual self-possession. She seemed like a teetotaler who has indulged in wine and has become light-headed in consequence. Perhaps Tryphosa's presence had spurred her on to this open encouragement of Tolnay, in which she had never so undisguisedly indulged; perhaps István's homage, now quite ostentatious, had intoxicated her for the moment, giving that red-rose flush to her cheek and that deep brilliancy to her eyes. She was lovely; and yet there was about her loveliness today something that repelled even while it fascinated, something that startled even while it dazzled.

"We can go a great deal farther," she decreed, while with her torch held high she looked around her. "This is only the ground floor, and I want to see the upper stories; don't you see that we have got staircases all round us? We can explore every one of these niches up there; and I dare say we could walk all round the cave upon that ledge, although perhaps it is a little slippery."

"And we can illuminate the place with our torches," completed István, who, while Gretchen spoke, had already commenced to spring up the perilous rocks at the side. "It is quite safe, Fraulein Mohr," he said, turning.

"It is quite safe, princess," repeated Gretchen. "Are you coming up also?"

There was a flash of cruel coldness, of an almost wicked triumph, in the gaze which met Tryphosa's. The princess stood dumb before it, while her hand instinctively felt for the wrecks of the amber rosary, just as she would have sought to protect herself from the presence of some evil spirit.

She stood in a sort of trance, feeling as if every tone of that clear voice was cutting into her heart like a silver blade, knowing that every movement of that graceful figure was a step that crushed her happiness.

She saw, as if in a dream, that Gretchen was mounting the rocks and that Tolnay held out his hand to help her; she saw but these two figures alone, and she heard not a word of what the others around were speaking.

There had been a general protest at Gretchen's first step up the rocks. Mr. Howard had argued, even Kurt had objected; only Dr. Komers had stood by silent.

"Do not go up there, Fräulein; it is not safe," entreated the Bohemian.

"It is quite safe," answered Gretchen, serenely, from the slippery platform on which she stood; "and besides, you know, if my day and hour have come — "

They had reached the ledge where a niche in the rock formed a sort of sanctuary, a white stone chapel, which shone like ice in the torchlight. The stone was broken here into the finest lacework and twisted into Gothic columns.

"I have found some silver," said Gretchen, as she put up her hand, and broke off one of the glistening icicles which hung in a thick and dazzling fringe above her.

Her arm was round the pillar, and as she bent forward, her loosened plaits slipped from their hold and hung down her back. To the spectators below, she looked like some vision that was scarcely earthly; to Tryphosa's eyes she was a tempting siren, who was luring her lover into that crystal bower to hide him forever away from her sight.

As for István, he could not look away; the surroundings excited his ever-ready fancy. This scene bore something of the fairy-like glamour of that other scene, when he had found Gretchen asleep on the bank in the sunset. From the loosened waves of her hair, there seemed to pour a flood of fire. He was bewildered and blinded — he saw nothing but her. Without thinking of what he did, he put out his hand and touched the curling end of her hair.

"And I have found some gold," he said, very low, "the most beautiful that the world holds."

"Gretchen!"

Who was calling her? Whose voice was that? So familiar and yet so changed! So calm, and, in its very calmness, so startling!

"Gretchen!" said Vincenz again, and still in that studiously quiet tone, "I entreat of you to come down."

"Nobody need come up who is afraid," said Tolnay, with a laugh which was all but insolent.

Vincenz did not answer him; he did not even look at him; his eyes were fixed on Gretchen.

"I beg you to come down," he said again; "your father has made me responsible for your safety."

Still, she did not speak, standing as immovable as the stone pillar beside her, with her hand in Tolnay's, but with her eyes on those of Vincenz. She appeared to be hesitating, though she said not a word. "My dear Dr. Komers," called back István, "do you really think that nobody but yourself can take care of Fraulein Mohr? Might you not at least leave her a little choice in the matter?"

"Gretchen, come down! I insist on it!" It was his voice again, but this time raised, sharp, and peremptory.

*"Gretchen!" said Vincenz again, and still in that studiously quiet tone,
"I entreat of you to come down."*

He stood at the foot of the rock and looked upward; and Gretchen, still hesitating, looked down at him. By his attitude and by his eyes, by the pallor of his face and the suppressed passion of his tone, she knew that in a second more he would be standing beside her on the ledge and that her obedience would be taken by force, if it were not now given with her will.

"Stay here!" whispered Tolnay, beside her.

"Come down!" said Vincenz, once more.

She made no answer to either, but mechanically she dropped Tolnay's hand; and with her eyes still fixed on Vincenz, she made a step downward, then stood still, then made another step; moving all the time with the blind groping gestures of a somnambulist, conscious that her will was gone from her — that she would have liked to resist, but could not, feeling as though his eyes made it impossible for her to disobey.

After the first two steps, she staggered, and her nerve seemed all at once to give way. Climbing the rock with her back to the danger had been a very different thing from this sickening descent. She stood clinging to a ledge, not daring to move another step, not daring to look either up or down.

Before the dizziness was passed, she heard Dr. Komers's voice close beside her.

"Give me your hand," he said, in a tone of cold command, and she gave it to him.

"Lean on my shoulder."

"She obeyed, wondering at her own docility, and seeing not a step of the perilous descent before her.

Without a word, Vincenz lifted her off her feet, and in the next minute, she was standing at the bottom, released from his arm, but still trembling, and grown suddenly pale and breathless.

István had watched the scene from above, glaring down at the two figures, but offering no assistance. He descended the rock leisurely now, and came up to Dr. Komers.

"You need not have disturbed yourself," he began, in a tone of artificial politeness. "I also have got brains in my head; I also have got eyes and arms, and Fräulein Mohr's safety is as much my care as yours."

"It scarcely appeared so," said Vincenz, icily. István's eyes flashed fire.

"Do you dare to doubt?" he broke out in a higher and more offensive tone; but the lawyer stopped him —

"If you wish to quarrel with me, you must find a better place and opportunity: it cannot be here."

"Perhaps you prefer not to quarrel," muttered the Hungarian, with a glance of deadly hatred.

He had been flushed a minute ago, but he was paler now than Vincenz himself. It was a terrible revelation that had opened before his eyes. For the first time, he had felt that this man was to be feared; and István Tolnay could not fear a man without hating him. It was an alarming revelation, a rude shock to his passion, a mortal wound to his vanity.

"Certainly, I prefer not to quarrel" — and Vincenz turned his pale proud face to his rival; then, with recovered calmness, he moved away towards the others.

The Bohemian was kindling fresh torches to light their passage out; and the half-burned pieces of firwood had been stuck about into convenient cracks of the rock. High up, on the ledge where Gretchen had stood with Tolnay, there was a torch burning its last, for she had left it in the niche. It crackled and flared, dyeing the white stone all around with changeful tints, and shooting arrows of brilliant light into dimly seen, ghostly gray hollows.

While the party still stood in a group, watching the impromptu illumination, Princess Tryphosa was observed to turn pale; very gradually, of course — no change in her ever was sudden.

In a sort of shapeless alarm, the others glanced around them. The place was not soothing to human nerves; and everyone was conscious of feeling a little on the strain. Had the princess heard any noise? Seen any danger threatening?

Oh no; the cause of Tryphosa's change of color dated further back than that. She had only now distinctly realized the danger which had just been passed.

She looked up at the niche above, and shuddered. It was a very substantial shudder that passed through her frame.

"Great heavens!" she gasped, "what a danger! One false step and he would have been down there a dead man! Oh, István!" — and she clutched at his arm — "let us go, let us go away. I — I don't think I like caves very much after all; oh, come away!"

"Yes," said István, absently, for he scarcely heard her. His eyes were on Gretchen, where she sat apart on one of the round-topped stones, silently plaiting up her disordered hair.

"Come with me, István!" — Tryphosa still clung to his arm — "help me out; do not stay — there is danger for you here."

Her voice sank to a whisper. She was attempting to draw him with her; but in the same instant, she let go his arm, for he had turned and given her a look — one of those fierce looks before which she always trembled. It scarcely needed the word of warning, muttered between his teeth, to shake her from him, silent and subdued.

No one heard what he said, and the gesture by which he had released himself had been scarcely seen; but the scene wanted no interpretation; its meaning was clear, and István's next words made it clearer.

"Why, don't you know that I am far too young and unsteady for a guide?" he said, with a short and disagreeable laugh. "I can recommend you no better protector, princess, than Dr. Komers, who evidently considers himself the only sensible man of the party."

The princess did not change expression: very likely she had not yet thoroughly realized her defeat. She mechanically took the arm which Dr. Komers offered her in silence.

The others began to follow, straggling off singly. Gretchen was still busy with her hair. She had not regained either her color or her voice. From the moment of her descent from the niche, her gayety of the morning was extinguished; pale and listless she sat, and scarcely noticed what passed around her.

Tryphosa's appeal to Tolnay had been the first sound that roused her, and guessing at the slight which was given and received, for her sake, as she knew, it was scarcely triumph that she felt, but rather fear. She trembled to see what power she held over István Tolnay.

With a nervous glance after the departing figures, she rose to her feet to follow. István was the only one who had lingered behind.

"Is the last of the illumination to be wasted?" he asked. "Do you not want to see the torches burn down?"

He was not laughing as was his wont; there was about his tone and eyes a seriousness which Gretchen had rarely seen in him.

"I — I think I must go," she faltered; "the torches will be out in a moment, and we should be lost in the dark."

"Ah, I understand" — and he bent a little nearer to her — "you have to obey orders of course. Has the family lawyer given his commands?" He was laughing again, but without any mirth.

Gretchen's lips quivered, and without any answer she sat down again upon the round-topped stone beside her. At the thought of her most unaccountable obedience to Dr. Komers, she was ready to sink with shame. She could think of no logical reason to explain her conduct; but perhaps by now lingering behind she might hope to redeem at least the shadow of her independence.

There were many more of the round-topped stones scattered about; in shape like monster cheeses, and in brilliancy like crystallized sugar. István sat down upon another of these stones; and he also kept silent.

The torch that Gretchen had left in the niche still burned brightly, but it was the brightness of approaching death. Each smoldering piece of firwood sent its floating breath upward in circling wreaths. The lights leaped up and sank down, burning deep red and palest yellow by turns, while even the crackling of the firwood was enough to wake whispering echoes in the rock.

One torch flared up, scattered a few red sparks, then died down in an instant, swallowing, as it were, a whole vista of rock into darkness.

"You have made me very happy," said István at last, watching her fingers, as they moved in and out of her hair, still plaiting it up. "Your happiness is cheap, then," she said, attempting to speak lightly, though her heart was beating fast; "and I don't know how you come by it now."

"Don't you? Merely by your staying here when I asked you."

"Really, Baron Tolnay, I cannot see how so absurd a trifle should affect you one way or the other."

"A trifle!" István gave a peculiar smile. "What is a trifle? A ribbon is a trifle; a flower is a trifle; and men have killed each other for less than that."

"Men are wiser than they used to be."

"Ha! Our old dispute; the age of reason and the age of romance. Do you remember our talk that evening by the fountain?"

"Well, yes, my memory is not short," she said, with studied indifference.

"Do you remember looking into the water?"

"Yes."

"Did you see anything there, I wonder?" said István, musing. "Was there nothing written in the Waters of Hercules?"

While he spoke, a second torch grew faint and went out. There were only three more torches burning now.

Gretchen dared give no answer to István's last words. She began to understand that she had done a very foolish thing when she sat down again upon this glittering stone. Far ahead, she could see the rest of the party; the light of their torches shone towards the narrow entrance of the cave. How she longed to be with them! She would have risen, but some instinct told her that her first movement would conjure up the crisis which she dreaded; safety lay only in quiescence; she was prisoner upon her stone.

"You have made me very happy," said István again, slowly, softly, with a sort of lingering enjoyment in the words; "and you have made someone else very unhappy."

He paused for a moment, then said between his teeth, "I hate that man."

He was very pale, and his eyes glittered: but the words had been so low that Gretchen felt herself exempt from the necessity of answering. And what answer could she have made, even had she been able to command her voice? Every word seemed loaded with gunpowder, and each one might explode.

"Another torch gone," said István, almost in a whisper. "It will be dark very soon."

"Very soon," he said, watching the sinking torchlight dreamily. It was a moment of strange, luxurious, undefined, yet intense enjoyment to István Tolnay. He wished to prolong the sensation. He was drifting towards something, some crisis which he had always felt was coming, and to which he had never yet distinctly given expression, even in his own thoughts — to which, perhaps, he had no right to give expression; but that did not trouble him. The waters which carried him along breathed such a soothing perfume, such a narcotic scent, that it clouded every disturbing thought. That which he was going to do, or going to say in the next minute, he had never distinctly contemplated — not yesterday, not this morning, not even this minute exactly. He never made plans, and he had not made plans either in this. It was merely that he felt it coming, and that the sensation was one of dreamy enjoyment. He wished that he could prolong it indefinitely.

"We ought to be going," said Gretchen; "there is only one torch remaining."

"Only one more? So much the better."

The last torch was the one in the niche, and with its perishing fire it threw a golden net over Gretchen's hair. It flashed and darkened with wild changes, flickering up and sinking, only to flicker up again.

"Look!" said István, "there are words written in the fire! Can you read them?"

He spoke slowly; but his eyes were fevered with excitement. "Look! do you not see? The same words that were written in the fountain. The fire and the water speak alike. Gretchen, will you not tell me what you saw written in the Hercules fountain?"

With the last words came a sudden change of tone. Instinctively, she shrank back.

He bent quite close to her and whispered,

"Was there not written, *I love you?*'" and seizing her hand, he dragged it to his lips. "I love you, Gretchen, more than my life! and you belong to me — you belong to me!"

He was kissing both her hands and the plait of hair she held. She felt that his own fingers trembled, and were burning hot.

At the same moment, a stone displaced by one of the torches got loosened from its hold, and went rattling and bounding downward past them.

"I am frightened!" cried Gretchen, starting from her glistening seat.

Her fright was real enough; but it was not the stone which had frightened her.

And, without giving him an answer — without casting him a glance — she wrenched her hand away, and hurried on, groping her way forward to the daylight; while behind her the last torch glowed up once more, like a fiery rose fading at the foot of the white column; then, scattering its flaming petals to the air, it shriveled to a spark, to a mere point of light — then was gone altogether, and the vast cave sank back into its habitual darkness.

Chapter XXX

A Granted Prayer

" Vous l'avez voulu, Georges Dandin, vous l'avez voulu."

— Molière

THE morrow of the visit to the cave was the eve of the Francopazzi's departure from the Hercules valley, and early in the afternoon, Gretchen set forth to pay her farewell visit.

When she knocked at the door of the apartment, she was encouraged to enter by Belita's voice saying "*Avanti,*" in a somewhat muffled tone, the reason of which was soon obvious to Gretchen.

Belita was on her knees in the center of the room, with more than a dozen pins in her mouth, and she was busied in draping the folds of a long gray tunic. This gray tunic (destined to form part of the contessa's traveling dress) was at this moment worn by the conte, who, in the character of lay figure, was standing motionless and patient before his wife. He did not make a bad lay figure by any means: he possessed the requisite slenderness of waist and the requisite serenity of temper — in the matter of height alone did he fall short of the desired mark. But Belita was a woman of resources; she had obviated the difficulty by making her lord and master take up his position on a footstool, which raised his figure to the majestic proportions desirable for insuring the successful fall of the tunic.

The conte bowed with all the grace he could muster under the circumstances, and Belita, having disposed of her pins, addressed her visitor cheerfully.

"They looped up this thing so atrociously, my dear, that I have been forced to do it all over again. I could not have traveled a mile in it as it was; utterly without chic. Take a chair, my dear child, and read something; I shall be at your disposal presently. I am glad you have come, for I wanted to talk to you. A little more to the left, please, *Ludovico caro*."

Gretchen, sitting down, applied herself to the only shape of literature visible, which was French fashion papers. Here, she was informed that diamond lizards were out of fashion, and that the new shape of the jacket promised to be a wonderful success. She was begged not to suppose that *chaussure* was remaining stationary; also, she was recommended to wear diamonds, happily mixed with opals.

She tossed the paper aside, and leaned out of the window. Down there a traveling carriage, ready-packed with luggage, stood waiting for some departing visitor. The Hercules valley was beginning to wear its autumn look — a look of desertion and solitude. Every day now made the change more sensible. There were fewer people lounging in the *Cursalon*, fewer people walking in the arcades; the meals on the ole-ander-shaded veranda grew daily less noisy and less crowded. More than one shop had put up its shutters for good, and stowed away the unsold things in the big wooden packing cases which had brought them there in spring. The sun was bright, but no longer hot; the air so chilled and clear that every sound in the valley sharpened into acute distinctness. They had seen the Hercules valley slowly waking from its winter sleep, stretching itself, as it were, yawning and rubbing its many eyes; it was strange now to watch the eyes closing one by one, as the place slowly sank back into the heavy torpor which yearly overpowered it. What a gulf between those days and these! Was there not a whole lifetime, a whole world separating now and then? Then Gretchen had felt so sure that the Hercules Waters were going to restore her father to health; and now Adalbert was as far from recovery as he had been then. Ah! must she confess it at last — farther than he had been then. Then Gretchen's path in life had lain so broad and distinct before her — now she had lost her way, and there was no signpost to put her right again; then she had been so content with her prospects of fortune, and now —

There was the sound of a stumble behind her; and looking round she saw the Conte Francopazzi descending from his elevation, being released from the tunic and dismissed from the room.

"It will do now," said Belita with a sigh of relief; "in fact, I don't think I should be saying too much if I called it a *chef-d'oeuvre* of drapery. I cannot tell you how useful it is to have a husband for looping up your tunics on!"

There was no echo to the sentiment; Gretchen, without a word, flung her arms onto the wide windowsill, and stared down at the street below.

Belita looked at her friend's back, raised her eyebrows, and shook her head.

"I hope she is not losing her senses," reflected the contessa, with a twinge of anxiety; "I really must speak to her."

But before Belita had time to speak, Gretchen herself turned suddenly from the window, and put a strange, abrupt question to her friend.

"Tell me, Belita, have I been mistaken all along? Are fortune and happiness, after all, two things and not one?"

"Fortune and happiness?" Belita staggered in her stupefaction, not so much at the words as at the tone. She fell back a step, actually forgetful of the *chef-d'oeuvre* of drapery which she still held, and stood gazing at her friend with a sort of tender fear.

But Belita's presence of mind never deserted her for long. Her first care was for her tunic, her second for her friend. Taking Gretchen by the hand, she led her to a seat, and made her sit down; and Gretchen sat down with perfect submission, only upon her face and in her widely opened eyes there was a look of hungry expectation, as though she were listening for the answer of an oracle.

"Are you quite sure you are not ill?" asked Belita, affectionately. "I always said that the air of the Hercules valley did not agree with you."

"I am quite well," said Gretchen; "but you have not answered me."

"Immediately, my dear child; what doubt can you have of my answer? Of course, fortune and happiness are two names for one thing."

"But not always?"

"Of course, always."

"How do you know it?"

"By personal experience. I am rich and I am happy; therefore, it stands to reason that when you are rich — "

"Oh no," cried Gretchen, putting her hands to her ears — " stop! It does not stand to reason at all — nothing stands to reason, I think." Belita had no right to turn her own weapons against her; and for the first time it struck Gretchen that her pet phrase sounded weak and senseless.

"*Misericordia!* What a temper! Well, you can follow up the deduction for yourself; you were always the stronger of us two in logic. You know how hard I tried for the *prix de logique* which you carried off so swimmingly."

"Why will you keep harping upon that old story?" was the impatient retort.

Somehow the memory of that triumph was not a congenial thought today; and, with a start, Gretchen checked herself on the verge of the heretical reflection that the reputation of having gained a *prix de logique* is not the easiest thing in the world to live up to.

"And now," said Belita, carefully scrutinizing her friend's face "be so kind as to tell me what other possible answer you could have expected to your most incomprehensible question?"

"I thought there might be another sort of happiness, that is all." She was speaking more to herself than to Belita.

"*Misericordia!*" murmured the contessa, wringing her hands, "she has been reading books; she has got a poetical fit upon her. I wonder how these cases should be treated?

"What other sort could possibly exist?" she continued, after a disconcerting pause. "People make such a fuss about missing their happiness, and so on; but you and I, Margherita, are wiser: we know that the way is simple. You have only got to marry a rich man, who is good-natured, and who, if possible, matches you in height — whom you don't mind seeing every day, but whom you will not miss when he is away, and who can make himself useful — "

"For looping up tunics on, for instance?" suggested Gretchen.

"For looping up tunics on, exactly," said the contessa, unperturbed.

"But *are* you and I wiser, Belita? That is what I want to know. We are either much wiser or much more foolish than the rest of the world."

Perhaps the growing consternation of Belita's face alarmed Gretchen as to what she had said. Without waiting for an answer, she snatched up the fashion paper beside her.

"Why do you keep nothing but these ridiculous papers? Novels are much more interesting."

"Novels! Just as I feared," sighed Belita to herself. Her worst apprehensions were justified.

"Did you read that novel I sent you, Belita?"

"I glanced at it, my dear; but I do not think it was worth finishing. The idea of making the heroine wear a chignon, when every educated person knows that chignons were quite out of fashion in 1870. I read as far as the chignon, but I could not get over that."

"Then you do not know the end? I sat up all night reading it."

"A very foolish thing for you to do."

"I could not get to sleep without knowing whether the heroine would give up the hero or not, after he had lost his fortune."

"And she did not?"

"No, she did not."

"More fool she. But he got back his fortune, of course? They always do at the end of the third volume."

"He did get back his fortune," Gretchen reluctantly admitted. Belita shook her head.

"I do not understand you, Margherita."

"Really? How strange!"

What would not Gretchen have given to anyone at that moment who could have helped her to understand herself?

"You are not like yourself today; you have not been like yourself for some time past. It never used to be your habit to sit up reading novels by night, nor by day either, for the matter of that."

Gretchen made no answer; she was not listening. Her eyes were fixed before her, her thoughts were busily painting two pictures and putting them in contrast to each other.

One picture was painted in brilliant colors, and the canvas was somewhat crowded with gorgeous objects. There was a carriage with a baron's crown painted on the panel; there was a glimpse of brilliant apartments, a glitter of jewels: there was everything which had figured in her dreams of ambition.

On the second picture, there was very little, only a steep winding staircase, a dusty ivy plant in the window, and, as a centerpiece, a hard-worked man coming home at night weary from his desk.

Surely there could be no hesitation in the choice. Why, it was not even a matter of choice, she thought, as she detected herself contrasting these two pictures. She had twice been asked to walk up that steep staircase, and she had refused; she was not going to be asked a third time. Somebody else would water the ivy plant in the window. Perhaps Barbara Bitterfreund. She wondered what Barbara Bitterfreund was like.

Belita's voice recalled her to realities.

"Margherita — " began the contessa, abruptly. "Well?"

"Do you remember the first day, when we walked in the arcades?"

"What of it?"

"I meant then to give you a lecture upon life in general; and afterwards we met Baron Tolnay, and I did not; well, I mean to give you that deferred lecture now. Here I am on the eve of my departure, and I certainly had hoped before starting to give you my maternal benediction on an auspicious occasion. In fact, I made the sacrifice of keeping a new dress for *jour de fiançailles*, and the trimming is now *démodé*, and consequently wasted. I cannot understand why you have not brought Baron Tolnay to the point long ago; you are playing with your chances. If you were a classical beauty you could afford to wait; but I have told you often, Bambina, that, strictly speaking, you are more picturesque than beautiful. To put it clearly, without beating about the bush — which is a thing I detest — you look too breakable for many tastes, and it is only a rich man who can afford breakable luxuries. It is a mere chance whether you happen to hit a man's fancy or not."

Gretchen, as she sat listening to the empty, vapid, good-natured chatter, was wondering how she had never till now discovered its emptiness and its absurdity.

"Are you sure that is all?" she asked, with a curl of her lip. "Have you no more advice to give me?"

"Certainly, I have, and you need it all; for you are, unfortunately, a German, my dear child, and in every German there is hidden a seed which should be crushed in early childhood. Even you cannot, it seems, quite escape from the commonplace taint of sentimentality which is the ruin of your nation. You are only a German after all."

"And you are only an *Elégante!*" broke out Gretchen, with a sudden burst of indignation. "You are nothing but a heartless *Elégante*."

She felt so angry at the moment that she would not have minded quarreling even with Belita.

But nothing was farther from Belita's mind than quarreling. She left her chair, and going up to Gretchen embraced her with effusion.

"Margherita *mia*! you have made me quite happy! An *Elégante!* Why, that is the height of my ambition; the very title which I am striving to live up to. I thank you immensely for that word."

"And this," thought Gretchen, bitterly — "this is the oracle to whom I have come for advice. This is the woman who has been my friend!"

Poor Gretchen! Her logic was at fault again; she had looked for a head and a heart where all was empty. Such people as this have not got heads, they have got *coiffures*; they have not got hearts, they have got *ceintures*, or cuirasses, or whatever form of covering the fashion prescribes; they have not even got hands and feet, but only *chaussure* and *gants de Suède*, and they themselves consist much more of bodices than of bodies.

Gretchen rose from her chair to take leave.

"What! going already, *Bambina?* Are you sure you have no more questions to ask? Remember that I am always ready with my advice; always come to me when you are in doubt — promise!"

"Yes," said Gretchen, with an odd smile, "I promise. I shall always come to you when I am in doubt — about the draping of a tunic."

"Which next time will be the tunic of your wedding dress, of course: *eh, sicuro,* child; don't shake your head! What a fright you gave me, to be sure, with your 'other sort of happiness!' Why, have you not proved to me a hundred times yourself (not that I wanted it proved) that fortune is the only sort of happiness worth having, because it can buy every other?"

"I have" — it echoed in Gretchen's heart.

"Did you not boast a hundred times that your experience was gathered for you beforehand?"

"I did — oh yes, I did," thought Gretchen.

"Oh, Margherita, that I should have to remind you of this!" — there was a hysterical quiver in Belita's voice, she had seized her friend's hand between her own — "that I should have to remind you that your fortune is still to be made!"

"My fortune, yes," said Gretchen, with a start. "I — I, of course — I am going to make my fortune, but I told you that it shall be in my own way."

"And that way leads to *Gaura Dracului*, I suppose," sneered Belita. "Are you not yet cured of that pretty little fable about the brigands' treasure? Why, oh most contradictious of all maidens, will you persist in hunting for your fortune among the hills, when by merely marrying Baron Tolnay your fortune is made, and how brilliantly?"

"But," said Gretchen, slowly, "if I find the brigands' treasurer, then my fortune is made at any rate, and I can marry whom I like.

She had scarcely said it, when she took fright at herself. For the space of a few seconds, she stood, staring back into Belita's horror-stricken eyes, then hastily lowered her long lashes and guiltily drooped her head. She took fright at the fright of her friend; for if there was so much horror written in Belita's eyes, what must there be written in her own? With a rush of crimson to her cheek, Gretchen wrenched herself free, and before Belita could stop her, she had reached the door and was gone.

She ran home, almost as if she feared pursuit. It seemed to her that she could not have stood Belita's piercing gaze for a moment longer, that she could not have borne another word of Belita's; and, no doubt, with the contessa's ingrained antipathy to beating about the bush, that next word, if spoken, would have been disagreeably plain. She felt like a person with a guilty secret; like an undiscovered criminal, like a murderer whose confidence the black forest and the midnight hour have kept, but who cannot meet the sunshine without thinking, "They will see the red stain on my hands, and they will know that I am guilty."

Gretchen ran home to look for solitude and peace, but neither solitude nor peace was to be hers today. On the very threshold, a new trial lay in wait.

The afternoon post had capriciously chosen to be punctual today; and Herr Mohr, with querulous impatience, was inquiring why his daughter was not at home to read his letters aloud. This had been Gretchen's office ever since the commencement of her father's illness. She had as yet showed herself a punctual and business-like secretary; but today it was with somewhat disordered thoughts, and an anything but undivided attention, that she applied herself to her duty.

There were four letters to be read, and everything went smooth during the reading of the first three; the fourth was addressed in a handwriting not familiar to Gretchen, but it bore the postmark of Kurt s college town. Letters with this postmark had been rather frequent lately, though they had always been addressed to Kurt himself, and never to his father.

What excellent correspondents your fellow students are!" Gretchen had once remarked; and Kurt had answered, with a laugh, "Oh, aren't they, just? And so affectionate, too!"

On that occasion, Gretchen had felt a passing flash of curiosity and a passing pang of uneasiness. The great affection of Kurt's school friends had not appeared to her to be reassuring, not like the habit of schoolfellows in general. However, she had so many other things to think of, that the subject had not weighed on her mind for long; and today, as she opened the fourth letter, she scarcely noticed the postmark it bore.

"Sir, — The continued silence with which my seven previous communications have been met compels me, however much against my will, to adopt this new course, in order to obtain — "

Thus far, Gretchen had read mechanically, but all at once she drew up.

"Well," said Herr Mohr, testily, "Is that all?" and Ascelinde, who sat at the farther end of the room, an apathetic and uninterested listener, looked up with an inquiring stare.

"I — I think it is a mistake," stammered the daughter, while with lightning haste her eye skimmed the page. "Borrowed sum" "term of repayment," "money advanced to your son," and other expressions which she was able to snatch in passing, were enough to give her the key of the mystery. That vulgar old specter called "debt" had started up, and was staring her in the face; and behind it hovered all its train of hook-nosed Jews and monstrous percentages.

"A mistake!" echoed Herr Mohr. "It strikes me that you are making nothing but mistakes today; you turned the Wednesday in the date the first letter into Ash Wednesday, and you made Steinwurm talk of caves instead of crypts. What is this new mistake about?"

"It is — it is — that is to say, I think the letter is not for you, papa; it is meant for someone else;" and she crushed the perilous letter into the depth of her pocket.

"Then why do you open someone else's letter?" asked the invalid, sharply.

"Because — well, I think the address was not distinct."

"It is you who are not distinct. I could scarcely make out a line of what you read today; you never used to mumble in this way before. I suppose" — with a touch of increased asperity — "that it is not so amusing to read aloud letters to an old man as to walk about the hills with a young one."

Gretchen could not answer, though her cheek was burning. She longed to rise and be gone to her own room, but she knew that this mood of her father's was not to be escaped.

"A tiresome office," he was ·saying, still, in that tone of melancholy cynicism which had grown upon him since his illness; "but cheer up, Gretchen, you will soon be quit of it. Instead of acting the secretary, you will be commanding one. I suppose my Lady Baroness will be too grand ever to dip a pen in ink herself, or to be troubled with deciphering the crooked calligraphy of the age?"

The tears were in Gretchen's eyes; she dared not move for fear that they should fall; she dared not speak, for fear that her voice should betray her. But, silent though she was, something in her face betrayed her all the same; for with a sudden change of tone, her father said,

"Why, Gretchen, you look as woe-begone as though the splendor of your own good-fortune frightened you. You are luckier than a princess in a fairy tale; you cried for the moon, and you have got it. What is wrong with it now? Is it too big, or too bright? Does it burn your fingers? Or would your ladyship like the sun better? It was your own wish, you know."

"My own wish — yes, my own wish," repeated Gretchen to herself. True again — all quite true. Belita was right; her father was right. Everywhere there stood her own wishes, her own arguments, her own words, her own self between her and — ah, between her and what? There, indeed, was the rub; something unutterable, undefinable — something which she dared not look at, dared not think of, and yet could not crush.

She started from her chair; there was no peace here either, and no concealment for the poor criminal. In the privacy of her own chamber, she meant to seek it; and certainly, to reach her room unmolested did not seem an unreasonable desire, nor an unfeasible undertaking. But there are days when the furies will follow a man about step by step; and the spirits of evil had hold of Gretchen today. She had not got farther than the passage when there was a rustle of drapery behind her; and turning round, she found herself confronted by her mother, who had sat by, an apparently indifferent spectator of the scene just past.

But Gretchen scarcely recognized her mother now; there was a flush on her cheek, there was light again in the eyes, which, since the day when they fell upon the walls of Draskócs, had seemed to have grown dim forever. What had brought this change? What had worked this instantaneous transformation? Gretchen was soon to know.

Ascelinde did not say much, but what she said was enough for Gretchen. Flinging her massive arms around her daughter's neck, she murmured in her ear,

"I could not believe it till now; it was too good to be true. I thought that Fate had nothing but disappointments in store for us. Oh, my daughter!" and her voice swelled to exultation, "Draskócs will be Draskócs after all, for you will rebuild the house of my ancestors!"

Majestically she swept from the spot, and went to dream of the real stone walls that were to rise, and the real white swans that were to swim round the real Draskócs of the future. Hitherto, Baron Tolnay's suit had been to her a dim and far off thing — a sort of distantly twinkling star too shapeless to penetrate the profundity of that grief, the fondling and fostering and petting of which now formed her sole interest in life. It was only today, during Adalbert's pointed remarks to his daughter that roused from her apathy, that there had flashed across her mind the grand inspiration to which she had just given utterance. She was almost as happy, while she built her Draskócs in the air, while she furnished the rooms, laid the pavement, and peopled the stables, as she had been in the far off, dream-beguiled, deceptive ante-Draskócs days.

And Gretchen stood where her mother had left her, and gazed round her in the empty passage, with the stare of an animal at bay.

A cold dread was creeping over her, a nameless panic was shaking her.

She was chained and prisoned; but the chains were of her own forging, the prison of her own building; what right had she to complain? Golden chains! A golden prison wall! But ah, how heavy, how oppressive! Turn which way she might, the passage was barred. On all sides, the same assurance, the same smiles, the same unhesitating confidence, that her lot was cast.

"And it is cast!" thought Gretchen: "I have cast it myself."

She herself had composed the recipe for her happiness; there was no ingredient a-wanting — neither the silver florins, nor the golden ducats, nor the coronet. How was it, then, that the result tasted so much more bitter than sweet — so much more like misery than happiness?

In common logic and in common justice, she had no right now to reverse her fate, and she had no idea of reversing it. A desperate quiet, a numb feeling of resignation began to steal over her. She was conscious only of a helpless shrinking from the moment of the crisis. Yesterday it had been all but completed; next time it would be completed. It was impossible to meet Baron Tolnay again as a mere acquaintance. Tomorrow they were to be on the mountains again, and tomorrow her fate would be clinched. Oh, rather tomorrow than today! Rather the next hour than this hour! Rather even the next minute than this minute!

Respite was what she asked for, and in the meantime peace. Surely now, at last, she could reach her room undisturbed, and find there the solitude for which she panted.

She was not two steps from that haven when Kurt, turning the corner, met her close. At the sight of her brother, she instantly remembered that letter in her pocket, which had lain there forgotten since the moment of the broken-off reading. Without reflection, she pulled out the crumpled paper and held it towards him.

Kurt received it calmly, and read it attentively; while, speechless with sisterly indignation, and brimful of overwhelming reproaches, Gretchen watched his face.

There was not much to see on Kurt's face; nothing but an easy good-humor and a perfect self-confidence was written there.

"So you have found it out," he remarked, pleasantly, while with serene composure he folded up the paper.

"Oh, Kurt, how could you?" cried Gretchen, in her severest tone of censure, before which Kurt was accustomed not to quail.

"Yes, I am in a devil of a mess!" he said, with a particularly bright smile. "Lucky for me that the way out of it is so short!"

"At your age!" groaned his sister, wringing her hands, too excited to pay much heed to the latter half of his phrase.

"Some of us begin early and some of us begin late," returned Kurt, with all the *aplomb* of a thrice-bankrupt *roué*. "But surely a woman of your logical powers will admit that the immorality of the proceeding is not greater at sixteen than at twenty-six?"

"I admit nothing," said Gretchen; "it all comes from your smoking cigars and drinking wine, when you should have been learning your lessons in the schoolroom."

"My habits are expensive, that much I grant;" and Kurt pulled up his shirt-collar with a shade of extra complacency. "It is a great mistake my not having been born a millionaire; but it was nature who blundered there, and not I — "

"No more nonsense, please," remarked Gretchen, with a frown of judicial severity; "and let us keep to what is, not to what might have been. Why have you kept the matter a secret?"

"Why? Because it would have disagreed with my father."

"It will disagree with him all the more when he has to pay the accumulated percentages."

"Oh, well, but perhaps he won't have to pay them," said Kurt, mysteriously.

"How can that be? Have you come to any settlement? Has Dr. Komers been advising you?"

Her brother looked at her and laughed.

"Dr. Komers! Oh no, my dear Gretchen; the family lawyer is not the man to help me. It is your other friend that I look to."

"My friend! What do you mean?"

"You see," said Kurt, leisurely puffing his cigar, "I was fool enough to count upon Draskócs, or rather, Herr Mandelbaum was fool enough to count upon it for some time; and now — "

"And now, well?"

"Now I count' upon something else."

"Please explain yourself," said Gretchen, coldly.

"I have explained myself already: I told you that I counted upon your other friend."

Gretchen stared back at him with a little flush on her cheeks. "Look here," said Kurt, knocking the ashes off his cigar, "perhaps you don't mind telling me what you and Tolnay talked about yesterday in the cave when you stayed behind?"

The transition in the first moment might appear abrupt; but an uneasy suspicion was already knocking at Gretchen's heart. "What has that got to do with it? We talked about the cave, of course."

"Oh, of course, naturally; and about the beauties of nature and the geological causes of the stone formation, and so on. Oh yes, I know; but you will not go on talking about caves for much longer, I presume."

Gretchen's face had grown scarlet.

"Kurt — I — "

"Do not wish to dwell upon the subject. I understand. What I meant to say was simply that I have the greatest confidence in Tolnay's coming forward in a handsome and gentleman-like fashion, for which I esteem him highly in advance."

"Really, Kurt, this is unbearable!" cried Gretchen, turning away. "It is bad enough for a boy of your age to make debts; you need not make jokes about it too!"

"Jokes!" echoed Kurt, good-naturedly. "You have no notion how serious I am. There is no need for you to go in for such excessive unconsciousness, when everybody knows that the affair must be settled within the week."

"What affair?"

"Since you will have me speak plainly, your marriage with Baron Tolnay."

"And supposing I do not marry Baron Tolnay?" she asked turning at the door of the room.

He looked at her for a moment, then began to laugh.

"My dear Gretchen, it is you who are joking now; and I must confess that your choice of a subject is not a very happy one. You might try and hit upon something that is either more amusing or more credible."

"Do you mean to say that I am to marry Baron Tolnay in order that your debts should be paid?"

"I think you have plenty of other reasons for marrying him, and those few beggarly thousand florins can go along with it."

It was to be borne no longer; the conspiracy was unanimous. The words and the smiles on all sides agreed; and every word was a hew stone in the wall, every smile a golden link of the chain which she had forged to bind herself. Would not the very leaves on the trees lift up their voices next to taunt her? Would not the sparrows chirp, and the insects hum, into her ear," You wanted it yourself; you have your wish now; of what do you complain?"

Her courage had carried her thus far; it would carry her no farther. She turned upon her brother a gaze which was meant to be haughty, but which first wavered into despair, and then, melted into tearfulness.

"Oh, Kurt, you too!" she cried, with sudden wildness; and before her brother's eyes the cool-headed, the self-possessed, the logical-minded Gretchen burst into a storm of absolutely illogical, but not the less burning tears.

Chapter XXXI

Dulcétia and Daggers

"And she, sweet lady, dotes,

Devoutly dotes, dotes in idolatry,

Upon this spotted and inconstant man."

— *Midsummer Night's Dream*

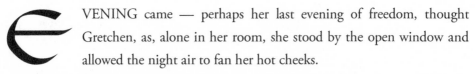VENING came — perhaps her last evening of freedom, thought Gretchen, as, alone in her room, she stood by the open window and allowed the night air to fan her hot cheeks.

It was a bright and silvery night for the world, but not for the Hercules valley.

Elsewhere, the moon is glorifying points of rock, and striking cold flashes from the water; here the rock and the water sleep untouched. But rarely the sun shines into the very heart of the valley, and more rarely still the moon, Moonlight here is a distant dream. Looking down the valley, where the space is wider and shallower, it is seen lying a transparent veil upon the hills — a still cold veil which hides nothing and beautifies everything. Here the moon must have risen very high before it can pour its light-floods down the flanks of these jealously guarding mountains. And yet the invisible moon is felt, for without the moon the night sky could not be of this transparent, quivering paleness. Never do the mountains look so black as they do when, on nights like these, each ridge on their summit, and each tiniest curve and angle of outline, is thrown out in startling contrast to the shining background. Never do the rocks frown more heavily, nor the valley wrap itself up more gloomily in its depth of darkness, than when the rest of the world is flooded and silvered with the moonlight.

Wait long enough, and presently strange effects will be seen on the hills opposite. The edge of the disk has reached the level of the hilltop, and the first white beam trembles on the mountainside. Timidly it touches some tree, and that tree, which a minute ago was only one in the millions of other trees, becomes forthwith a thing of wonderful beauty. It is the favored and chosen object of the moonlight; the moon has elected it out of the black mass around, and lavishes its favors richly. It was but a black pine a minute ago — it is now a tree worthy of fairyland; its stem is glorified, its branches are fancifully beautified, each tiny twig is dreamily idealized. The black pines around wait in sullen patience until their turn shall come. To some of them it will come, to some of them not; for it is rarely, very rarely, that the moon will pierce to the heart of this spot in the valley. It is in vain that the Djernis sings songs to the moonlight, wooing her now with laughter and now with sobs; the moonlight is not tempted by the enchanter's voice, and will not let herself be drawn down to the enchanter's embrace.

It was such an evening as this today — glory everywhere else, and blackness here. But the valley had another voice tonight besides the moaning Djernis; for Dr. Kokovics, as a last melancholy contribution to the amusement of the fast-waning public, was wandering about at the foot of the hill, making night hideous with some bulky wind-instrument of awful power. The public was decidedly amused, but scarcely as the doctor had intended. Some ungrateful people laughed, some shut their ears, others their windows.

Gretchen also shut her window at last. She must have been in a very unusual state of mind, for she did not see anything either absurd or irritating in the doctor's *Flügelhorn*.

The air which his instrument wailed forth was familiar to her. It was a Romanian song, a favorite among the peasants of the valley, a rough ditty, treating of the "Herb Forgetfulness" — the magic plant whose taste destroys memory, and which the dams of the flock search for on the mountaintops in order to blot out the memory of their butchered lambs.

Even the words were not strange to Gretchen: she knew by heart the verse in which the dying Romanian girl calls on her lover to seek forgetfulness in the mountain herb —

> *"Haste thee to the hill, my love,*
> *Since cold death doth bid us part;*
> *High up grows the magic herb*
> *That will cure thine aching heart."*

To which the lover makes reply —

> *"Tasted I each fragrant herb,*
> *Sipped I of each dewy flower;*
> *Drive thine image from my breast,*
> *Sweetheart, none could have the power."*

Having recalled this verse to her memory, Gretchen, somewhat hastily, closed the window. In the combination of the melancholy music and the far-off moonlight, she had recognized two elements that possessed the power of developing certain dangerous germs of thought, of whose existence she was conscious. The night air was chill; but it was not the fear of catching cold which caused the window to be closed so hastily. Moonlight nights are quite as conducive to mental as to bodily indispositions. She was still struggling with the bolt, when an at once a figure became visible outside. It seemed to dip up suddenly and silently out of the darkness, and was close below the window before she had noticed its approach.

Gretchen opened the pane curiously a little way and looked out.

The figure had come to a halt just below the window, and was standing with an upturned face.

"Mademoiselle, est-ce vous?" asked a woman's voice.

Gretchen recognized the Frenchwoman who was in charge of Princess Tryphosa's child.

A small three-cornered note was handed up to her — a very heavily scented little note, fragrant as some rich exotic flower. That same perfume seemed always to hang about the princess herself.

Gretchen opened the note with an uneasy conscience. It contained only a few lines, begging her earnestly and urgently to visit the princess at once. It gave no motive for the request.

"Is the princess ill?" asked Gretchen, somewhat startled.

"Madame est très fatiguée," said the maid. Madame had been all day in bed, and had only now made the great effort of putting on her dressing gown. She hoped that mademoiselle would be so kind as to come at once.

"Yes, I shall come," said Gretchen. The request was strange, unexpected, and unceremonious, but, despite her alarm, she felt no desire to avoid the meeting. Though nothing further should come of it, it would at least shorten by an hour the long sleepless night which she saw before her. Anything resembling an adventure was welcome to her overstrained nerves. She slipped noiselessly from her room, and, guided by Fanchette, very soon reached Tryphosa's apartments.

The princess was sitting when Gretchen entered; she rose very slowly and saluted the visitor.

The room was Tryphosa's bedroom, and a low lamp burned on the table. It poured a bright glare on the floor, and illuminated Tryphosa's figure distinctly to the height of her waist. Above that, the china shade dimmed the outline of things — of Tryphosa's face, among other things.

Gretchen glanced curiously round her. The room in its fundamental arrangement had not been very different from most European rooms with which she had been acquainted; it had a bed, a press, a sofa, a polished table; but an Oriental influence was visible on them all. On the bed there was flung a silken cover, so subtly blended in color that it told its Eastern tale at the first glance. Between the doors of

After the first greeting, Tryphosa put out her hand...

the half-open press there shone the folds of a Turkish shawl; on the sofa were cushions of Oriental embroidery; thick Persian carpets relieved the bareness of the polished floor. The very towels were not at all like the towels which Gretchen had ever seen before; each corner, delicate intricacy of golden and silken threads, would have been treated with tender adoration by any member of any art needlework society. It is as natural for a Romanian woman to drag about with her carpets and her embroidered pillows, as it is for an English lady to travel with her patent waterproof and fitted toilet case.

On the table there lay two soft feather fans, ruffling and fluttering noiselessly at each breath of air which touched them. Beside the feather fans, or rather half-buried under them, lay the remains of the mutilated amber rosary; next to it the last Paul de Kock novel. They lay there as if flung aside as useless — as if comfort had been sought in both and found in neither.

"Good evening, mademoiselle," said the princess, as she rose heavily from her chair. "I am grateful to you for having come so quick."

It was evident that the rapidity of Gretchen's appearance had much surprised the writer of the note. At all times, Gretchen was a puzzle to Tryphosa; her energy, her decision, the ease with which she came to a resolution, and the rapidity with which she acted upon it, were alike strange, bewildering, and tantalizing to the slow Romanian; but this case was especially salient. Considering that it had taken Tryphosa the whole forenoon to mature the idea which had first dawned in her mind yesterday, as she sat at the foot of the beech tree, and that it had taken her the whole afternoon to fabricate the note of summons which was the point and· upshot of her meditations, it was a little startling to find that it had taken Gretchen only ten minutes to answer that summons. If Gretchen's thoughts, words, and deeds had progressed at the same rate as did Tryphosa's, her appearance here ought to have taken place about this time tomorrow.

After the first greeting, Tryphosa put out her hand, and taking Gretchen's fingers in hers, drew the girl slowly forward until the lamplight was full upon her face.

Gretchen remained passive; the princess's eyes were fixed on her face steadily and scrutinizingly — *reading* her face; line by line, spelling out the meaning, very slowly but very surely.

Gretchen saw that the princess herself was very pale — that her dead black hair and eyes made her face look unnaturally white. Her eyelids were heavy, too, but the rich curve of her lips was brightly red as ever.

After that one long look into Gretchen's face, Tryphosa let go the hand she held, and with a bitter sigh, turned aside. Then she sat down, asking Gretchen with a movement to do the same.

It was all very solemn and very mysterious, thought Gretchen, beginning inwardly to wonder why she had been sent for and when the princess was going to break the long silence that followed.

The princess was watching the door, with an evident look of expectancy on her face. Gretchen found herself watching the door too, and wondering with trepidation who or what the princess was waiting for.

The door opened, and there entered a tray of *dulcétia*, borne by a servant. Could that have been what the princess was waiting for? Yes, evidently and obviously. A gradual look of satisfaction suffused Tryphosa's face. She superintended the placing of the dish, and with a whispered direction to the servant, dismissed him from the room.

When the door was closed again, it was evident that the real business of the evening was going to begin. Princess Tryphosa's nation has borrowed many Turkish habits; and no Turk will proceed to business, or pronounce a word upon any subject of importance, until the guest has partaken of refreshment.

Gretchen found herself helped to some sickly sweet stuff, which she detested at the first mouthful.

Tryphosa did not speak until after her spoon had traveled several times up and down between her lips and the little silver plate. What she said then was sufficiently startling.

"Mademoiselle, we ought to hate each other."

"I hope not," said Gretchen, hastily putting down her plate. She had not allowed herself to make any conjectures as to what Tryphosa's meaning might be in sending for her thus. She had come here with much curiosity, some anxiety, and a little uncertain, undefined hope.

Tryphosa swallowed another mouthful of the *dulcétia*, and said, "You are very beautiful — "

She said it merely as if stating a bare fact, not with flattery, and scarcely with bitterness.

"And are you not beautiful yourself?" said Gretchen, flushing; "and is that a reason why we should hate each other?"

"And he thinks so."

It was a continuation of her former phrase upon which the princess was still engaged.

The flush spread higher on Gretchen's face, but she kept silent.

"I ought to hate you," said the princess, in her deep, calm voice, "but I liked you at first, and I cannot change so soon."

The thought in Tryphosa's mind, which she intended to express, was, that having begun by liking Gretchen, it would have taken her too long to undo that liking and to mature a dislike in its place.

"If I had known what you were going to do, I should have begun by hating you."

"And what have I done?"

Oh, the fixed stare of those great dark eyes! It was hard to bear it unflinchingly. The princess very, deliberately put down her silver plate, and quite as deliberately took up a feather fan before she spoke.

"You have taken away from me the man I love; you have robbed me of the love of István Tolnay."

The word was spoken at last, the name was said; their eyes met steadily. They looked at each other, these two women, as only ri-vals can look — the one so splendidly dark, the other so gloriously fair; the one like light, the other like shade, yet both so beautiful. The black eyes were the deepest, the most intense in the heat of their slow-smoldering fire; but the gray eyes could flash as brightly, and that slight figure could draw itself up with as much proud self-reliance.

"And you sent for me to tell me that?" said Gretchen, in a voice which was hardly quite steady.

This sudden attack, so cruelly plain, so plainly pathetic, seized upon her soul with a fearful strength. It was too little European, too much Oriental; there was not enough of regard paid to the polite usages of society, and there was too much of bare, unadorned, purely human feeling. Human feeling in this undisguised state is so seldom to be seen nowadays, smothered as it is in conventional wrappings six-fold thick, that when it is seen out of its wrappings it startles us disagreeably, as something jarring, something raw — something too strong, too coarsely vigorous, for our tenderly bred nerves.

"Yes, I have sent for you to tell you that, mademoiselle."

"Then, princess, I think I shall go home," said Gretchen, rising.

"I think not," said the princess.

"And why not, pray?"

Tryphosa's eyes traveled round the room, and came back to Gretchen.

"Because the door is locked."

"I don't believe it," said Gretchen, and she went to the door and tried it. The handle moved freely, but the door remained fixed. She remembered now that whispered word of direction to the servant, and a sort of terror came over her. Was she caught in a trap? She went to the window; it was half-closed, and from the hillside opposite, where the moonlight was creeping down, chary of its precious beams, the sound of the wailing *Flügelhorn* still floated dismally on the air.

"I can call for somebody to open the door," she said, turning to Tryphosa. "I think I shall call."

"You will not."

The words were very slowly said, very calmly, and yet very decidedly.

They took hold of Gretchen as if they had been living hands. She began to understand the latent strength which existed deep down in this woman's soul — so deep down that a reflection of it rarely reached the surface.

"I shall not let you go," said Tryphosa, in the same subdued voice, "until you have told me what I want to know, and until I have told what you must know. Let us not argue. I mean to do it, and I am very desperate."

Gretchen felt that what she said was true, and that what she meant to do she would do. Against her own positive will she obeyed.

"She sat down again impatiently, and, snatching up the second feather fan from the table, began to fan her face.

"Princess," she said, with a sort of rebellious resignation, "if you have indeed any questions to ask me, please ask them quickly. Though you have me in your power at this moment, you cannot intend to keep me prisoner all night."

As she said it, her eyes fell on the spot from which she had just lifted the fan: there was a tiny dagger lying there, stuck in an enameled sheath. It was the same which the small Codran was accustomed to wear at his belt. Gretchen had drawn it once when she was playing with the boy, and she knew that the point was of sharp bright steel.

The memory of that bright point grew distinct before her at this moment. Thinking of it in connection with that calm gaze of despair in Tryphosa's eyes, the bright steel point was by no means reassuring.

"I am very desperate," Tryphosa had said, and she had said it so quietly that the words sounded all the more terrible.

Gretchen glanced at that well-shaped hand that held the feather fan just now: it could hold that little dagger as firmly, no doubt.

She had grown a shade paler, but she did not move from her place; she remained with her eyes fixed on the jeweled knife, too proud to show the alarm which might turn out to be a foolish fear, and yet not quite able to look away from that narrow-colored case where lay hidden from sight that bright point of steel. It was a consoling reflection, at any rate, to think that, even crediting the princess with so blood-thirsty an intention, the execution was not likely to be rapid. There certainly would be a margin left for defense.

Gretchen had asked the princess to put her questions quickly, and Tryphosa was honestly anxious to follow the demand; but the very word "quick" sounded like irony when applied to Tryphosa.

"Yes, I am going to tell you quickly," she said, speaking rather slower than usual. "It is very simple, my question: has István Tolnay told you that he loves you?"

"You have no right to ask me that," cried Gretchen, meeting Tryphosa's gaze. "I refuse to answer your question."

"Has István Tolnay told you that he loves you?"

Gretchen kept silent.

Tryphosa repeated the question a third time, never removing her eyes from Gretchen's face.

Again, that something undefined, which she could not explain, and from which she could not escape, took hold of her, and Gretchen answered, impatiently,

"Yes, he has."

Not the smallest change became visible in Tryphosa's face: she was quite aware of the answer, but she had put it on one side, as it were, for later consideration, being still busy with something else.

"I have a right to the question, and you shall hear what it is presently."

There was a short silence. In spite of all her fears, Gretchen felt curious. The soft flutter of the fans was the only sound in the room. Tryphosa's fan fluttered slowly, ponderously, in long, calm sweeps; Gretchen's fan moved restlessly, quivering in her hand like an imprisoned bird, up and down, in short, feverish strokes, restless and unequal.

They had been silent over a minute, when Tryphosa stopped fanning herself, and clasped her two hands against her breast with a sort of well-pondered vehemence. Her lips were trembling, and her eyebrows drawn together with a painful contraction.

"My God!" she muttered. "He has told her that he loves her. That is my death!"

She paused for a minute, then she raised her eyes again; the heavy lids, heavily fringed, rolled up slowly — a curtain which disclosed a world of beauty below.

"And you? Do you think you will marry him?"

Did she think she would marry him? Why, that was the very question which had been Gretchen's torment throughout every weary hour of this weary day; that was the question to which since morning she had vainly sought to find an answer.

"Don't ask me — oh, I don't know," she answered, hurriedly.

"You don't know? Then, I shall tell you: you *dare* not marry him!"

"And why not?"

At the defiance, her pride had risen already, armed to the teeth in its own defense. Under this new phase of danger, she forgot even her fear of that sharp steel point.

To her surprise, she was reminded of it in the next instant.

For some minutes past, Tryphosa had been intently wondering what could be the meaning of the fixed gaze which Gretchen had fastened upon the little dagger on the table. She had reached a satisfactory conclusion now.

"I know what you are afraid of, mademoiselle," she said; "you are afraid of that knife and of my despair. You think I am going to stab you."

This, again, was very plain — fearfully plain; and Gretchen recoiled, as if the words had been a blow.

The situation was so painfully intense that nothing but an attempt at lightness could relieve the strain of tension. Gretchen made that attempt.

"I don't think you would succeed," she laughed, a little harshly. "It would take you too long to do it."

"Too long? Do you think so? No, it is not that. If I want to do a thing, I do it. It may take long, but I... do it. It does not matter whether a thing is done slowly or quickly — only that it is done. It is not that," went on the princess, heavily, reasoning out the point in question — heavily, but unfailingly; "let us not be foolish. It is only that it would do no good. He would hate me for having stabbed the woman he loves; for he loves you — now. If you are afraid of that knife, throw it away."

Gretchen remained scornfully silent; she did not even look towards the knife.

The original question appeared to have become merged into this side-question. Gretchen, therefore, was not a little puzzled when the princess now repeated,

"Why not? I shall tell you why not."

She had forgotten her exact words, but Tryphosa never forgot anything she had once thoroughly understood.

"You dare not marry István Tolnay, because I have a better right to him. You have taken him away from me."

"I have not taken him away; he has taken himself away."

"Will you listen to what I say? I say I have a better right to him. He saw me before he saw you, and he loved me before he loved you. And that is not all; he promised to marry me long before he knew that you existed."

An exclamation of disbelief broke from Gretchen's lips. She had known of the last year's flirtation between Tryphosa and Tolnay; she had even this year watched its last lingering remnants; but she had never guessed at anything so grave as this, at promises made and not held. The thing was too monstrous to be grasped. Was this not only the invention of a jealous woman?

"Listen; this is not yet all. I have more rights than this. I have given up everything for him." The princess sat up on the sofa now, and the hand which held the feather fan trembled. "I have waited patiently for years for him. I have allowed my name to be talked of lightly for his sake. I have made my child fatherless. I have sacrificed" — there was a momentary pause, which seemed to promise a climax — "I have sacrificed my journey to Paris this year — and all for him."

There was a touch of absurdity, after all, in the midst of the pathos. But to a Romanian there was nothing ludicrous about it. To sacrifice a Parisian journey is to sacrifice something sacred, something inestimably precious; for to Romanian women the word "Paris" is as sweet as the word "paradise" — perhaps if the truth were known, sweeter.

"I have made my child fatherless" — those were the words that struck Gretchen's ear. She heard no others, and she stared with horror at the princess, and from the princess to the jeweled sheath on the table. "What?" she stammered, trembling; "you have — you have" — she could not finish her own extravagant thought. She recovered herself, and asked, "When did your husband die?"

A slow stare was the answer.

"My husband die? He is not dead."

"Not dead?" Gretchen got to her feet shivering. "Princess Tryphosa, are you not a widow?"

"He is not dead, he is alive. He lives in Bucharest. We are separated, but I see him often. We are very good friends."

Gretchen stood aghast, feeling as if she had been suddenly plunged into ice-cold water, which had cut her breath short for a moment. Was it her sense of hearing or her sense of understanding which was at fault? Did she hear aright? Of course, she heard aright; it was only her ignorance which was to blame. She had not mastered the A B C of the strange Romanian nation. Tryphosa's words were a shock to her own stern principles; but, in point of fact, the princess was rather behindhand in this matter. Most Romanian women of her age have two husbands alive at a time; and any lady who contents herself with conjugal affection is looked upon as eccentric, unfashionable, not to say dowdy. It is nothing at all unusual in a Bucharest salon to see a lady enter on the arm of her third husband, smilingly return the courteous bows of her two first lords, and in the course of the evening perhaps begin to throw languishing glances towards the one destined to become her fourth.

Tryphosa, seeing Gretchen's too evident distress, good-naturedly explained,

"I married very young; not because I wanted, but because they all wanted it, and really it was not worthwhile fighting about it. I could have got separated any day I liked, for in our country it is made easy for us women; but I should not have taken the trouble, only — I met István Tolnay. I saw him one year, and I loved him the next year; I shall be forced to love him all my life."

She spoke in a tone of conviction; and, no doubt, she spoke truly. Tryphosa would never find time for more than one passion in a lifetime.

It was a hard moment for Gretchen. Two feelings fought within her — disgust and pity. She was horrified at Tryphosa's confession; she was touched by her boundless love.

"What is it you want of me?" she asked, in a whisper. The princess reflected deeply. "Justice," she said, at last. "I do not understand you."

"He has sworn that he will marry me. He has not sworn it once, but twenty times. Do you not see that I am ruined if he does not hold to what he has sworn?"

"If he has sworn it he will keep it, of course. What is the use of addressing me?"

The princess only shook her head. "What I ask of you is, that you should promise not to marry him."

"I will not bind myself by any promise," said Gretchen, between pride and perplexity. "Let me go now, princess — I have listened long enough."

"You must listen to me longer," said the princess. "You cannot do me this injustice; you love justice and you love truth."

"But is this true?" thought Gretchen, in an agony of doubt.

Had Tryphosa modified the crudeness of her story, Gretchen might have been convinced; but when thus presented to her in all the hideousness of broken promises and heartless desertion, the inexperienced girl, shocked and disgusted, shrank back, taking refuge in disbelief. However much she might have sighed for liberty a few hours since, her pride revolted against having the gift forced on her by another woman. Doubts were obscuring her mind. To reject Tryphosa's demand, or to throw over István Tolnay after having thus played fast and loose with him — of the two which would be the greater sin?"

Every trifle grew fearfully weighty at this moment. Her mother's words, Kurt's debts, rose up and confronted her.

"It would be no good my promising," she said, at last, "that would not give you back his love."

"It would be some good;" and the princess frowned, as if in heavy thought. "He loves you now, but he would come back to me in time. I know it; he cannot be true to any woman for long."

"You say that, and yet you love him?"

"I do not think he is a good man — I think he is bad; and yet I love him madly."

There was a fearful suggestion of suppressed strength in that one word.

"I would sacrifice everything in the world for the sake of my child, but I would sacrifice my child for the sake of him. Do you believe now that I love him?"

There was no answer possible — none that would not have sounded weak after those slow, burning words. The revelation of passion beneath this sluggish surface was overwhelming; it stunned Gretchen for a moment.

"Will you give me the promise now?"

"Oh, I don't know — I don't know!" cried Gretchen, flinging her hands over her face. "Let me think."

"As long as you like."

How strange the deliberate words sounded after the last that had been said! The request appeared perfectly natural to Tryphosa: she was accustomed to think so much and so slowly herself, that it was not surprising to bear Gretchen say, "Let me think."

She took up her fan again. Her features were heavily passive, but the fingers which closed over the handle clutched it convulsively.

She would wait like that for an hour with perfect patience.

Gretchen felt it; she would wait like that the whole night immovably. Princess Tryphosa's patience filled her with a blank hopelessness. It was strange that, after all her agonies of today, she should not grasp at the promise as a heaven-sent means of escape; and yet it was not so very strange either, for the mystery of a woman's heart is the only labyrinth to which no clue has been invented, or ever will be found. Gretchen had much obstinacy, and she felt she would do a great deal rather than be forced into a promise; but her obstinacy beside that of the princess was like the resistance of a prickly hedge beside that of a wall of granite blocks. One of the two must break the silence, and she knew that Princess Tryphosa would not do so.

Gretchen removed her hands and made one more attempt.

"It is no use asking me to promise," she said. "If it is true that Baron Tolnay has sworn that he will marry you, then why do you not appeal straight to him?"

"Do you think that I have not appealed to him?" said Tryphosa, with a sort of bitter frankness. "I sent him word that he was to come to me today, and he has not come. I asked for five minutes' interview; he has taken no notice. I begged for one sign from him; he has given me none. That is the way he spurns me now."

The words might have sounded like abject humility, but for the sullen pride with which the admission was made.

Gretchen stood uncertain, wondering how it was to end. She felt that Tryphosa was reading her face again with that searching look. The fan had stopped moving; a new thought was dawning in Tryphosa's mind. After a little, it reached the surface. Gretchen saw the light in her eyes before she was surprised by the unexpected question.

"Tell me this; do you love István Tolnay?"

The fixed stare was hard to stand, but Gretchen would not drop her eyes. She gazed back steadily, though she felt the color ebbing from her cheek. That question at least she had a right not to answer: she stood and stared back at her questioner.

Tryphosa raised the fan to her lips, and with her teeth slowly dragged out one of the scarlet feathers of the edge. It was the only sign she gave of the suspense which was devouring her; but it told more than sighs and tears could have told. The way in which it was done made Gretchen shudder and look back from the princess to the enameled sheath on the table. Yes, that woman was quite capable of a heroic crime.

"I see," said the princess, after a long pause — "I see; of course, you love him. It could not be otherwise."

A sudden revulsion of feeling came over Gretchen; every pulse throbbed tumultuously — she seemed to lose sight and hearing.

"No, I do not love him!" she cried, passionately, thrown off her guard for the moment. "I do not love Baron Tolnay. I swear that he is nothing to me!" And then the mist seemed to clear from her eyes, and she saw Tryphosa bending forward, with the red feather still held bitten between her teeth.

There was no triumph in her eyes: wide open and dull, they were fixed full on Gretchen's face. It was impossible to read whether displeasure or satisfaction lay underneath that dull surface. Perhaps she was enraged, perhaps she felt victorious; but there was nothing in her eyes as yet. She unclosed her teeth and slowly released the scarlet feather. It fluttered softly to the ground, and lay there on the carpet at her feet, like a vivid drop of warm heart's blood shed by some cruel hand.

Chapter XXXII

István's Stirrup-Cup

"Not to be wearied, not to be deterred,
Not to be overcome."

— Southey

THE autumn morning was slowly dawning into the day, chill, and scarcely light enough to show clearly the horns, and skins, and other sportsmanlike trophies which decorated the room where István Tolnay was taking a hasty breakfast.

Outside the air was raw; the light morning mist still hovered over the valley, rolling slowly down the hillside, to leave every moment a new breadth of glistening forest and sharp-cut rock distinct in the cold air. It was one of those cautious mornings which hold out no promises, and which yet are more to be relied on than many a red-cheeked dawn that jumps out of bed in a hurry and wakes all the world with sunshiny smiles, but who finds before long that he has overtaxed his spirits, and generally ends by going into a fit of sulks or breaking into a storm of ill-tempered tears.

István Tolnay, as he took his breakfast, in which red wine appeared to be the principal feature, threw more than one glance out of the window, and decided that it was just the right sort of day for their expedition.

The room bore the stamp of wealth, of luxury even, in every detail. It spoke of the owner's tastes. Besides the trophies on the walls, there was a bearskin on the ground; there were guns and whips, and a perfectly bewildering amount of smoking appliances. Also, there was an extensive collection of photographs, exclusively female, which, from the details of their attire — sometimes the scantiness of such details — were unmistakably theatrical. They were but dimly seen in this dawning light; and the figure of István himself was still veiled in the departing shadow. He wore a costume which, by the inhabitants of the place, was considered to be sportsmanlike, and which, by Mr. Howard, had long ago been condemned as "coxcomby" and bad form. However that might be, the gray and green suit and feathered hat were most particularly becoming to the style of this young Hungarian's looks. Upon everybody else, the yellow gaiters would have looked *outré;* but István wore them in such a way that it was impossible to look at the calves of his legs with entire disapproval.

Although he was eating his breakfast with as good an appetite as usual, and although the red wine was in no danger of being neglected, István was doing something most unusual with him — he was thinking.

Two days ago, he had confessed his love to Gretchen; and her sudden withdrawal and persistent avoidance of him during the homeward walk considerably puzzled him, although it can hardly be said to have seriously alarmed him. This coyness and half-repelling reluctance were but fuel thrown on a fire, which already burned high: a little touch of difficulty gave a new charm to the wooing of this German girl. It suited his imaginative temperament — it was a change and a relief from his relations with Tryphosa; for if difficulty spurred István, too great ease made him relax. It is probable that the dreadful earnestness of the love which Tryphosa offered him had been the reason of his so rapidly cooling towards her. It oppressed him to be loved in that tragically serious manner. Of course, he liked to be loved by a woman; but, the climax once passed, he preferred to treat the matter somewhat more lightly, and, above all, somewhat more expeditiously.

For one moment in the cave, István's self-confidence had tottered. The figure of the short-sighted lawyer had seemed to obscure his path; but it had only been for one moment. His nature was elastic, and his vanity well-nigh invincible. A very little reflection had told him that the idea of that man being his rival was no more than an amusing thought, to be laughed at and dismissed. Just put his personal advantages opposite to those of Dr. Komers, and what woman could hesitate? Let alone worldly advantages, István, to do him justice, thought a great deal more of the personal than of the worldly advantages. He had been so used to riches all his life that he set no store by them. If he had set more store by them, he surely would have hesitated a little longer before abandoning the fabulously rich Romanian princess for the sake of a penniless German girl. His passion of the moment had the same effect as the light of a brightly burning lamp — it made everything very distinct all around it, as far as the rays fall, and very dark all beyond. It is only that circle of light which exists for the moment, as long as the wick has food enough to burn.

He had begun by paying attention to Gretchen, because he was struck by her beauty, because it was agreeable and amusing to pay her attention, and because he had no principles which forbade him to do an agreeable and amusing thing, even if thereby he was breaking his faith towards another woman. She had piqued him by the force of contrast. She was different in disposition, in coloring, in everything, from the women he was accustomed to meeting; different in particular, from the last woman he had loved. There could be no sharper contrast than Tryphosa and Gretchen; and if he had never known Tryphosa, István might never have loved Gretchen so hotly as he loved her now. But it was not merely with other women that she contrasted; she embodied a contrast in herself. This girl, who looked like an Ophelia and talked like a philosopher, who moved like an Undine and argued like a logician, had from the first moment caught his fancy. The harmonious discord which she presented was just of the sort to rouse István's interest. The very first words she had ever addressed to him had surprised him almost as much as though a rosebud had opened its petals to remark that two and two make four, and that therefore it stood to reason that the half of four was two.

István had begun, therefore, to pay attention to Gretchen because it was pleasant, and he had gone on because it became more pleasant.

Very likely it was only quite lately that he had reached the point of confessing to himself that his promises to Tryphosa were to count as nothing. There was no struggle to fight through, no agonies of indecision, before the wrong could triumph over the right. Nothing of the sort. Those promises were torn up by the root as easily as a plant is torn up out of the sand. It was a puzzling phenomenon, but it was true. Gretchen had once wondered what element there was missing in Istvàn's nature, the want of which made him different from other men. One element certainly had been left out in his composition, but Gretchen had not yet found it out by name. His was a face which no line of care could ever mark, which no trouble could ever alter; his fancy it was which was hot, and his heart which was cold — not so much cold as light, and capricious in its lightness.

But though he had arrived at confessing to himself that his promises were to count as nothing, he had meant that Tryphosa was not quite yet to know this truth. Not that he had taken any precautions against her knowing it — it was not in him to do so. It was an impossibility to him, physical and moral, to look ahead of the present moment. Neither had he made any effort to see Gretchen in the course of yesterday, so as to get the final answer from her lips. He preferred that the opportunity should come naturally, and he knew that it must come naturally today.

Bad weather would have crossed his plans: but the long-looked-for or long-dreaded rain was not in the sky today: it was cloudless and of a keen blue, and the mists were rolling lower every instant. The whiff of air that came in by the window brought joy and hope on its wings; it quickened his pulses and braced his nerves. Istvàn Tolnay felt very sanguine.

"One more glass of wine," he said, aloud. "Let this be my stirrup-cup; and then, Excelsior!"

He took up the bottle as he spoke: the red wine gurgled through the throat of olive-green glass. He raised the full glass to his lips, but in the same moment he turned his head, for the door handle was slowly moving. Slowly, very slowly, the door glided open.

István muttered something between his teeth, and put down the untouched glass so sharply that some drops of red wine splashed over the edge — for Princess Tryphosa was standing before him.

It was Princess Tryphosa; but it was not the glowing sultana whose beauty but a few weeks ago had still held the power of reviving for a moment the embers of a dead love; neither was it the sobbing woman who had wept at the foot of the beech tree, nor the calmly desperate woman who had sat opposite to Gretchen last night with the dagger-point between them. Her misery had reached another stage. She was dry-eyed and haggard; she was colorless and worn in face. Her hair was rough and her dress was crushed and unsightly. She had aged ten years in a few hours. Her eyes had not closed for a moment. All night she had sat, and pondered, and reflected, feeling about carefully for some way out of the straits of her despair. Gretchen had said, "Why do you not appeal to him straight?" and those words had remained fastened in her mind. Of course, she had appealed to him already; but for weeks past she had kept silent. One last and desperate appeal might yet save her. She was not a woman to leave any stone, however heavy, unturned. The curious mixture of laziness and energy, of languor and passion, which were the elements of her nature, gave her a strength of purpose which, at first sight, was not to be suspected. By morning, she had matured not only her plan but also the details. She had resolved that she should not go alone — that she should take her child with her. Her love for her child was very genuine of its kind; but it was not maternal affection which was the cause of the little Codran having been roused out of his sleep at daybreak, and dragged up out of his soft cushions. Instinct told her that that small curly head would play a useful part in the scene which she was deliberately going to provoke. Never had she been so sincerely grateful to Providence for having given her a pretty boy for her son as today, when she believed that his pretty looks might help her to touch István Tolnay's heart, or rather to fire his fancy. In a sort of dim and far off way, she felt aware that she was not beautiful today, and some impulse moved her to put her son's beauty in place of her own. Here, again, it was her knowledge of the man which guided her.

Her appearance came in such harsh contrast to his thoughts of a minute ago, that István for a moment seemed to have lost the power of speech. He stared at the white-faced woman, and the sleepy child which clung to her hand, as if he did not know them. But long before Tryphosa had succeeded in speaking, he had recovered himself.

"Princess! You're here! Is it possible?"

The princess shut the door as slowly as she had opened it, and came forward towards him.

"What imprudence! The servants might have seen you!"

The princess stood still, with her child drawn to her side, and looked back at him, still searching for words, and struggling for expression of what she felt and wanted to show. She would have preferred to give some sign more passionate and moving; but she had grown so used to the slowness that, even at a moment as critical as was this one, she was unable to move or to speak quickly. It was too unaccustomed and too strange.

"The servants *have* seen me," she said at last. "Do you think I would stop at that?"

István understood now that she was desperate; and as for the rest, he did not much care. His conduct had never been shaped to please public opinion, and if Tryphosa could brave the world, so could he. Prudence was a cloak which sat ill upon him, and Tryphosa saw how ill it sat.

"You were not usually so prudent, István, when you used to climb to my window in order to get a smile, and when you used to pick up the flowers I dropped, under my husband's eyes. Do you remember that time?"

"Excuse my surprise," said István, with convenient evasion, and still feigning stupefaction which he had already ceased to feel; "but you never leave the house so early as this."

"And when you used to carry my hair in a locket," she went on, with that despairing tenacity of hers. "There is other hair in the locket now, I suppose?"

"Nonsense, Tryphosa! There is not."

"And you used not to go to mountains at that time, or, if you went, it was with your gun and your dog alone."

"My gun and my dog have been to the mountains often enough this summer," he said, sullenly. "I am not a man to be tied to apron strings."

"You are going to the mountains again; you are going today — now. I see it by your dress, and I knew it before; that is why I came so early."

"I am going for a walk."

"You are going to the mountains, and Mademoiselle Mohr is going also."

"She may be — I don't know."

Another long stare from her eyes, before her lips said, doggedly, "She is, and you do know."

He turned with an oath upon his lips.

"Cursed be your obstinacy! Have it then, since you will; she is going, and I do know it."

"I thought so," said Tryphosa, calmly. "And what do you mean to do about me?"

"Mean? I don't mean anything. I don't know what I mean, and I can't tell you. It is stronger than I am, do you hear? It is no good speaking to me at all."

"You mean to break your promises?"

The words, plainly spoken, were ugly even to István's ears; he turned, and taking up his soft hat, began crushing it up between his hands.

The small Codran, finding his mother's conversation and movements excessively wearisome, had wandered off towards the corner, and, after affectionately pulling handfuls of hair out of the rugged bearskin, had fallen asleep upon it. His mother, going towards him, dragged him up and drew him to her side. If she had had more leisure, she would certainly have felt pity for the small victim; but at this moment, he was to her no more than a piece of decoration necessary for the scene.

"Have you never thought, Baron Tolnay, that I am not a woman to let myself be abandoned in this way?" she asked.

"Don't threaten me, Tryphosa!" and she saw a gleam in his eye — "don't threaten me: if you are desperate, so am I."

"Look at my child; I made him fatherless — for your sake."

"I never asked you to do it," he said, speaking wildly. It was a brutal thing to say, after all, that had passed between them. Even he could not have said it had he not been half out of his senses at the moment. He certainly could not have said it if she had looked at this moment as she had looked that evening when he had taken the pomegranate flower from her hair. She had been beautiful then; she was scarcely so now. The voluptuous glow of coloring about her seemed faded. She was a woman who imperiously demanded warm-tinted, luxurious surroundings. This cold morning light did not suit her; the sharp air seemed to chill her; her face looked old and hard; her very eyes were sunken. She was like any other of her countrywomen who has just missed being beautiful. Moreover, she was unwittingly pursuing the very course which with Tolnay was most fatal; she was pressing him to a distinct answer, and this pressure made him furious.

"You did ask me to do it on your knees. István, shall I kneel to you now?"

"Let me go — let me go," cried István, tearing away his arm from the grasp of her clinging hand.

"Yes, I shall let you go. I am not strong enough to hold you with my hands; but rid of me you shall never be. Oh, István! you should not have loved me — you should have loved some woman whose heart is as light as your own. István, listen to me: by all the sacrifices which I have made, by my love to my son, by the memory of your love to me, I conjure you, listen to me!"

"Enough, enough!" cried István, turning from her — for the gaze of those stupid, passionate eyes was oppressive even to him — "enough, Tryphosa; it is late, and I must go."

"You must go — to her. To tell her that you love her."

"I am accountable to none for what I may say or do."

"You have told her already that you love her."

"Think what you like."

"And I could tell you another thing."

"Could you? Ha! What is that?"

She had come a step nearer, mechanically dragging her sleepy child beside her. Now she stopped, and eyed him attentively.

"Do you think that she loves you?"

"I shall hear today;" and a smile of confidence flickered across his features.

"I can tell you."

"Ah!" He faced her, and in his eyes, there was nothing now but an expectant light. The hatred, the anger, the reckless cruelty were all held at bay for one moment by breathless suspense. He might almost have been mistaken, as he stood there, for an honest and true-hearted lover, so little power had his passions of stamping their mark on his face. And yet, at this moment, it was that his cruelty reached the point of climax. That expectant light in his eyes meant death to Tryphosa — a more bitter death than his fury of a minute ago. He viewed her only as the person who could give him information he wanted, and as such only he looked at her with interest.

The answer was long in coming, but it came at last. "I will tell you, then: she does not love you."

The words were dropped slowly, heavily, as if each word had been a leaden weight falling to the ground.

The light died out of István's eyes, only to blaze up again more hotly.

"You lie! She does love me. I know it — it must be."

He might as well have run his head against a rock. Tryphosa answered, immovably as before,

"She does not love you."

This time he turned livid pale. He knew Tryphosa too well to doubt her plain statement. He stood speechless, his hands slowly clinching by his sides, and a rush of tumultuous thought coursing fast and furious through his brain.

Tryphosa watched him; she had tried an experiment, and she was watching to see how it would work.

Suddenly upon the paleness came a painfully vivid flush of red; he sprang forward towards her and caught her by the wrist.

"Is this your revenge?" he demanded, violently. "Is this to torture me? Is it your jealousy that makes you speak? Or madness? Or is it the truth? Which is it? I must know it now — at once."

She did not shrink or waver as he touched her. There was the truth written plainly in her eyes, though she made no movement with her lips; and István saw it. He dropped her hand and turned away, taking two steps in the room and back again, with a new and sudden restlessness of manner.

"How do you know this? Quick, quick, quick!"

Quickness was out of her power, but she answered his question clearly enough.

"She told me so herself; she was with me last night. I asked her, and she told me."

"Ha, ha! Impossible!" he laughed, harshly. "She told you that — and what else?"

"She told me that," said the princess, slowly, "and she told me nothing else."

"You have something more to say — say it at once."

"She told me nothing else, but I have guessed."

"Oh, speak!" He stamped with his foot on the ground. "I think that she loves someone else."

István's teeth clinched, and he muttered a brutal curse.

"I am certain of it; she loves someone else, and he is a better man than you."

"Do not speak his name!" cried Tolnay, with sudden vehemence and a look of hatred almost diabolical in its malice. That first dawn of doubt which had risen the other day in the cave had prepared the way for this. That misgiving came to life again, and this time full-grown and near; not a mere dim, far-off possibility, which he had laughed at and scorned. The complacent self-confidence of half an hour ago made this fall from the height the ruder; the joyous hopefulness which had buoyed him up made this mortification the more intolerable. When that thought had first presented itself for consideration, he had dismissed it easily, for he had nothing but his own passing impression to go by, and vanity had argued eloquently against it: now this same thought was supported by Tryphosa's judgment; and Tryphosa's conclusions were arrived at slowly, but unfailingly.

"Do not speak his name!" he had cried, "I will not hear it; the thought is maddening. I hated that man from the first day. I will — yes, I will."

His voice was so loud that the terrified Codran set up a howl of distress; but the angry tone broke off suddenly, and István paced the room with his hands clasped behind him and his eyes fixed on the ground. He stopped by the table, and lifting the glass to his lips, drank off the wine, then put down the empty glass with such vehemence that the thin stem was shattered, and the upper half rolled broken to the ground.

Codran stopped crying, and detaching himself from his mother's hand, proceeded to make himself happy on the floor with the broken glass and the few drops of wine which still lingered about it.

István took up his hat and stick abstractedly, as if he had forgotten that he was not alone in the room.

He would not have looked at Tryphosa again, if she had not stopped him as he was passing her on his way to the door.

"Where are you going to, István?"

"To the mountains," he said, with a hard smile.

"To the mountains," she repeated. Then, after a momentary pause, "What will you do there?"

"Something; ah yes, I will certainly do something. Never fear!"

"To the mountains. And what is to become of me?"

"I don't know."

He raised his eyes from the ground for a moment. There was a curious look in them. Tryphosa thought that she knew every glance and expression of his by heart, but there was something in his face now which was new even to her. She began slowly to understand that her experiment had been a failure.

"We shall talk of that when I come back. There will be a great deal to talk about."

"You don't know — no, and you don't care."

"Perhaps not," he said, shaking her off.

Her arm remained poised, just where he had shaken it from him. Her face was white, but something was slowly kindling in her eyes. There was a spark lit beneath, and very gradually it broke to the surface: it reached it, and her black eyes flamed.

"You villain!" she panted. "You abandon me — you villain!" and she struck out her closed hand towards him.

The motion would have been a blow had it not come so slowly that Istvàn could step back in time. The scorn in her eyes was so supreme that it had the power to arrest him for a moment. She was not beautiful, perhaps, but she was well-nigh sublime in this burst of outraged pride, which, coming so late, had yet come so superbly. She had the blood of ancient Rome in her veins, and it had at last caught fire. The passion of another woman would have spent its strength long before this climax was reached; but Tryphosa's strength was all latent, dormant, difficult to be roused, but fearful when once awoke.

For the first time in his life, Istvàn quailed before a woman.

But not for long. Her hand was still outstretched, her lips were still quivering with the energy of her last words, when already that one moment of stupefaction was past, and his thoughts plunged back into the current which was dragging them on. Her very presence, so real for a moment, became again distant and indistinct.

"We shall talk when I come back — there will be much to tell," and crushing his hat onto his head, he rushed out of the room, leaving Tryphosa standing where she was.

As long as his steps could be heard, she remained fixed and listening, the light of scorn still in her eyes, the very anger seeming to have turned to stone in her face. Then, when the last step had died off, and all had been quiet for some moments, her hand slowly fell, and the rigid hardness of her face began to melt. She sank down on the seat beside her, and she wept. Those tears were for the man whom she had called "villain," whom she would have struck but a minute ago, and whom yet she loved better than all the good men in the world.

Little Codran, hearing the deep-drawn sobs, trotted to his mother's side, pulled down her hands, and held the broken glass to her lips.

"Are you tired, mamma?" he said. "Drink this little red drop — I left it for you; it is very sweet."

It was the glass from which István Tolnay had drunk, and, taking it from Codran's hand, Tryphosa dashed it to the ground. Then drawing the child onto her breast, she gave him a kiss so fierce that it seemed to scorch the freshness of his innocent cheek.

"Can I go back to bed, mamma?" asked Codran, yawning. "I am so sleepy."

Yes, he might go back to bed. The scene was played out, the curtain dropped, and the poor little piece of decoration, which had failed to decorate sufficiently, might be packed away again out of sight.

Chapter XXXIII

The Fallen Signpost

"Oh, der arme Mensch steht immer mit zugebundenen Augen vor deinem Schwerte, unhegreifliches Schicksal!"

— Jean Paul

THIS autumn season is bringing strange contrasts in its train. While below in the valley, life and activity are slowly sinking to sleep, up on the mountains a blaze of departing splendor is bursting into glory. For weeks past, Nature has been quietly at work laying in the ground — tints, and painting in one touch of bright color after the other; but it is now only that the picture is completed, and stands forth for a brief time of perfection, for soon the winter will begin to undo the summer's work.

The Hercules valley is dazzling in winter, fairy-like in spring, majestic in summer; but autumn remains its season of beauty: and this autumn is a singularly dry autumn, with no rains to rot the leaves, nothing but sunshine to wither them brilliantly. A wild fire seems to have flown over the hillside, and touched each maple-tree, till it flames like a burning brand; the low masses of bilberry bushes, clustering between the rocks, begin to warm into color, glowing hot as embers. The rocks themselves, even as sober gray rocks, do not disdain to decorate themselves, and wear patches of gaudy mosses in honor of the departing summer. What had been bright before becomes brilliant now — what had been brilliant now reaches magnificence. Green turns into rich brown, and brown changes to molten gold.

But it is in the world above that the splendor is thrown about most recklessly. Her magnificence has run riot. There is on all sides a waste of richness which almost over-surfeits the eye. Every colored lichen on the tree stems, which in summer was delicate and small, has become magnified to double its size; every tuft of moss on the rotting carcass of a fallen trunk has deepened its pile and intensified its color.

The dead trees are making preparations for their winter funeral; the monarchs of the forests are lying in state, swathed in velvet, crowned with gold, and decked out with a brilliancy of ornament well worthy of a departed king. Bright fungi are the most gorgeous among these ornaments. These mysterious and capricious children of the forest have started up in thousands immediately after the first autumn showers, and have continued to increase ever since, fed by the fatness of the soil, though no more rain has fallen. Piles of fungi, scarlet, blue, orange, and purple, have grown out of the bark of the trees, or stand in clusters covering the forest floor, each cluster like a handful of jewels that have been scattered broadcast. There are monster pearls on the branches overhead, and giant coral reared on all sides; glistening sprays, delicately cut and fancifully ramified, decorate the pathway.

It is difficult to believe that these gems are nothing but toadstools; it is still more difficult to believe that these same toadstools form an important article of diet in a Romanian peasant household. The forests thus hold an inexhaustible fund of *maigre* dishes. Moreover, there seems to be a sort of mutual understanding between Nature and the Greek Church. They have accommodated each other. Nature is kind enough to treasure up these stores for the time of fast; or perhaps the Greek Church has invented these fasts for the purpose of consuming the unlimited stores which the forests hold.

"They string them upon cords and hang them up to dry," said the Bohemian, somewhat contemptuously, as he pointed out a clump of fungi, in shape and color closely resembling a pile of ripe apricots; "or else they keep them in vinegar until they want them, and then devour them pickled. But they will not be quite as well off this year as they usually are: this is all nothing compared to the number I have sometimes seen in damp autumns — they become a positive nuisance then; you can scarcely step free of them."

Up here, in the depth of the forest, the store of *maigre* dishes ran no danger of being disturbed. Here the fungi would live their brief time of magnificence and then drop back silently into the eternal decay of nature, without having been either strung upon cords or preserved in vinegar for the fast time.

"Don't you eat toadstools in Bohemia?" inquired Kurt.

"Of course, we eat toadstools in Bohemia," said the Bohemian, with a pitying smile; "but we don't eat the blue and the red ones — we only eat the yellow ones and the white ones."

Mr. Howard here begged to explain that he utterly condemned not only blue and red, but also yellow and white toadstools; and that no power on earth could succeed in making him touch anything but an orthodox mushroom, with no suspicion of a doubt upon its character, and cooked in an orthodox English fashion.

Gretchen took no part in the discussion: she was wondering within her mind whether happiness was indeed compatible with a hut and smoked toadstools.

They had been walking for some hours now, and, contrary to her wont, she was tired. The scene with Tryphosa had excited her; her sleep had been broken and feverish: not even the autumn brilliancy around her could dispel the listless languor which weighed on her today. Ever since the moment of departure, she had instinctively kept to her brother's side, and had until now succeeded in avoiding anything but the most general and trivial conversation. She was so absorbed in her own anxieties that it was some time before she noticed the remarkable change which had come over Tolnay's manner. He was excited and flushed — talked loud at moments, and then subsided into moody silence. He seldom addressed her, and made no attempt to draw her away from the others. But whenever she happened to turn, she found his eyes fixed upon her; and once, when Dr. Komers was helping her over a tree trunk, she had been startled by a glitter in István's eyes, and· that same look of furious hatred which she had seen two days ago in the cave. Tolnay was not looking at her at the moment — he was looking at the lawyer; and instinctively Gretchen dropped the hand which Vincenz had stretched towards her and scrambled over the tree trunk unaided.

They rested at intervals, and walked on as they felt inclined. The whole day was spent in the forests thus, and it was sunset when they emerged from under the trees onto a free space of meadow.

"We have been here before," said Gretchen; "this is the meadow on which we rested the very first time I walked in the mountains."

"When I was your guide," said Tolnay beside her. "I was to have shown you *Gaura Dracului* that day; don't you remember?"

It was the same meadow, but dressed in a different garment. Brilliantly green it had been before, but here, too, autumn had been busy, and with cunning alchemy had changed the emerald into an amethyst. Crocus-heads stood closed together, so thickly sown that every step crushed half a dozen of the full-blown flowers.

"Shall I tell you what I am thinking of?" asked Tolnay, abruptly, as they walked over the crocuses.

"As you like," said Gretchen, carelessly, not choosing to betray her trepidation.

"I am wishing that I had lived in the age of romance." His tone was so peculiar that Gretchen looked up in alarm.

"Well," he said, with a harsh laugh, "what are you afraid of? We are all so quiet and sensible, you know, in this age of reason."

"Fräulein," said the Bohemian, hurrying to her side, "there is no need for our crossing this meadow; it is time to be turning homeward; look, the darkness is near."

Gretchen stopped and turned, glad of an interruption. She looked upward at the sky: the few clouds which floated there were tinged on their lower edge with the glow of rosy sunset. She looked down and saw that already the shadows were growing deep under the trees. She was half inclined to turn. If the Bohemian had not spoken again, she certainly would have turned; but a little too much anxiety is apt to spoil the very object we have at heart; and on this occasion, the Bohemian betrayed in his manner a little too much anxiety.

Had he only kept silent while Gretchen was hesitating, all would have been well, but the Fates pushed him to speak.

"Let us turn, Fräulein, and go homeward," he urged, with growing eagerness; "there is nothing to be seen over there."

Gretchen looked from the sky to his face, glanced at it, and then looked again with a faintly awakened curiosity. The anxiety in those clear eyes was very apparent. It was evident that he did not wish them to cross this meadow. The consciousness of this fact was enough to double the desire which Gretchen felt for crossing it. "Is it of robbers you are afraid?" she said; "I think we might risk them. There will be moon-light on the hills tonight to light us on the way home."

"I am not afraid of robbers, Fräulein."

"You cannot suppose that the weather will break; look at the sky — it seems as if it never could rain again."

"I am not afraid of the weather breaking, Fraulein." "Is there a spring beyond this meadow?"

There was a spring in that direction, the Bohemian reluctantly admitted, but it was some distance off — a nearer one had run dry.

"Let us go on then," said Gretchen; "I am longing for the taste of fresh water."

He was silent after this, and led the way slowly over the crocus meadow, but there was a troubled look disturbing the usual peaceful melancholy of his face, which Gretchen did not fail to notice.

They entered the shadow of the forest, Gretchen taking care to keep by her brother's side. Baron Tolnay was in advance, and Dr. Komers a little way behind them; Mr. Howard still farther to the rear.

This was the same spot they had been on once before, on the occasion of their first walk in the mountains, but they had never passed here since. It was a part of the forest little known, and even less trodden by human feet than the rest of the woods around. It did not lie in the usual beat of either hunter or woodcutter.

The aspect of the spot had so changed with the change of the season that it woke no special memory in Gretchen's mind until after a few more steps they came in sight of a huge beech tree stretched upon the ground.

She knew that tree; it was the same on which the goatherds had sat, and on the leaves of which the goats had fed.

There were no goatherds here now, and no tinkling goat bell. There was silence and desolation all around the spot. The leaves had been fresh then, and the trunk newly hewn; now the green leaves had turned brown: they strewed the ground, or hung rustling on the dead branches. Over the marks of the ax-strokes, the mosses had begun to creep, hiding the unsightly wounds with their green and yellow velvet. Then the felled giant had been still half alive — the sap had scarce had time to stand still in its course; but now it was a mere corpse — a useless heap of wood on which decay is rapidly seizing. It would be more gorgeous next autumn than it could be this autumn, for the moss and the lichens take many months to cover a dead tree — but it was well adorned even now. There was a colony of tiny fungi drawing a broad yellow streak down half its length, and single patches of color had begun to collect.

The Bohemian came to a standstill beside the tree trunk, and put down the bundle which he carried over his shoulder, and which was tied with a piece of strong rope.

"If you will sit down here, Fräulein, I will fetch you the water; it will take me a little time."

"Very well," said Gretchen; "we can wait here. Shall you be long away?"

"Fifteen minutes, perhaps — not more."

"Thank you very much," said Gretchen, sitting down on the trunk and handing him her flask. "I am sorry you have to go so far."

The Bohemian took the flask and looked at Gretchen for a moment as if he had something more to say. He turned away, however, and walked a few steps off, then returned abruptly and said; "You will wait here, Fräulein, will you not?"

"Of course, we shall wait here."

"But, I mean, you will not move from the spot? You might lose your way."

"We are not going to move from the spot," she answered, and the Bohemian again turned away and disappeared among the bushes to the left.

The trunk made a pleasant seat, cushioned as it was by nature, and Gretchen felt glad of the rest. Dr. Komers and Kurt had also sat down, for there was ample room for a dozen people more. Baron Tolnay remained standing. He held his hands behind him, and gazed fixedly at the trunk, with a look which told Gretchen that he had forgotten no detail of that day in early summer when they had first seen this fallen tree.

Presently Mr. Howard came up, holding in his hand a brilliantly colored fungus.

"I have spent five minutes in knocking this thing off a tree," he explained, as he sat down. "I am going to take it home with me in order to show my wife, Lady Blanche Howard, what the savages here feed upon. I have taken the most poisonous-looking one I could find."

"I feel almost inclined to side with the savages at this moment," said Gretchen, gazing rather longingly at the shining fungus which Mr. Howard held, and which to all appearances seemed to have been showered over with a permanent coating of dewdrops. "It looks so cool and juicy that I would risk the poison for the sake of the refreshment."

"Are you thirsty?" asked Mr. Howard.

"I am parched. The Bohemian has gone to fill my flask, but he will not be back for a quarter of an hour."

"Now this is too provoking!" cried Mr. Howard, rising. "Why did you not appeal to me? Don't you know that an Englishman is never without water? *Water, water, water,* as they din into my ears down there. I filled my flask fresh at the last spring."

Gretchen eagerly drank off the water which Mr. Howard poured into his patent cup: when the first edge was off her thirst, she began to feel sorry for the Bohemian, who had started on a useless mission.

"Call him back," said Mr. Howard; "he can't be far off," and he gave a lusty shout which seemed to shake the branches overhead. "He can walk at a tremendous pace when he chooses," said Kurt. They listened for a moment, but there was no response.

"I wish he were back," said Gretchen, wearily. "I should like to be going home."

"Well, you do look rather weather-beaten," said Kurt, contemplating his sister. "It would be a bore to have to carry you downhill. Where can that fellow be staying?"

"I shall find him," said Dr. Komers, rising to his feet.

"You will lose your way," Mr. Howard called after him; but the lawyer had already disappeared in the same direction which the Bohemian had taken some minutes before.

The evening was closing in rapidly, and the brilliant tints of the forests beginning to fade into undefined grays.

Now that she was sitting, Gretchen began to realize how tired she was. Her feverish thirst was quenched, but a sort of numb weariness was stealing over her. The day had been one long strain. She had succeeded thus far in averting an explanation with Tolnay, but the effort had told upon her. A sense of discouragement chilled her now. This very spot suggested discouragement. When she had last been here, her hopes of finding *Gaura Dracului* had been so high; but the discovery of *Gaura Dracului* had never seemed more hopeless than it did just now. After weeks of wandering about the hills, they were exactly at the same point at which they had been that day. How indignantly she had then refuted Tolnay's words, when he had laughingly declared that there was no such place as her father described! It almost seemed to her now as if Tolnay had been right. She could herself have believed *Gaura Dracului* to be a myth, were it not for that look of terror she had seen so often on the Bohemian's face. She had at last reached the point of acknowledging to herself that the Bohemian's simplicity had baffled her cunning. "Why not put a pistol to the fellow's head?" Mr. Howard had suggested, earlier in the day, having worked himself into one of the fits of passion to which the Bohemian's obstinacy periodically moved him; "he would speak fast enough then." To which Gretchen replied that, as long as the Bohemian's conscience was clear, he would not mind having a loaded cannon put to his head.

There was silence between the four people thus left alone in the forest, until István, pushing up his hat, which he had drawn over his forehead, sat down on the trunk beside Gretchen.

He took the place by her side with a sort of ostentation — an outspoken defiance, which seemed to challenge the world to dispute his right, if it dared. At this moment, Gretchen did not attempt any resistance: she felt so tired, both physically and mentally, that even if he had now seized her hand and renewed his declaration of the other day, she would have been too weary to repulse him.

But István made no such demonstration. He began digging at the lichens on the trunk beside him with the point of his stick, making, at the same time, some apparently harmless, if somewhat abrupt, remarks.

"What a much pleasanter day it was when we were here last!" he observed.

"It was warmer," said Gretchen, for want of any more original remark.

"It was warmer, and the wood was green then, and the summer was beginning instead of ending. Everything was pleasanter. Don't you think so? We were a smaller party, too."

"That is not very complimentary to Mr. Howard."

"Nor to other members of the party either," said István, striking off another tuft of gray lichen with his stick. "Complimentary? Oh no, I am not in a mood for compliments."

He said the last words rather lower, then checked himself, and bent down towards the bark of the tree stem. He seemed to have forgotten his last train of thought, and to be gazing very intently at the lichens he had just been mutilating, Gretchen followed his look, but she could see nothing that might have been supposed to call forth that fixed gaze. For a minute or so, he continued in deep silence to scrape away the moss! His whole attention was absorbed in this apparently frivolous occupation. He stooped, raised his head, stooped again, lower this time, and then, looking up, said quickly, and with a sudden laugh,

"Do you know what we are sitting on?"

"A beech tree," said Gretchen, somewhat startled.

"Not a beech tree, but the beech tree: look what I have found!"

"I did not know there was anything lost," said Kurt.

"There does not seem to be much to find," said Mr. Howard, "except these eternal toadstools."

István had now laid down his stick, and with his fingers was tearing away the moss.

"Look!" was all he said, as he pointed to the spot. Gretchen looked, and on the place which Tolnay's stick had laid bare, she saw two deep cut crosses engraved in the bark of the fallen tree.

It was long since she had given a thought to the beech tree which Adalbert had marked as signpost to *Gaura Dracului*: the recollection flashed back upon her now. In her excitement, she sprang from her seat.

"If there is a third cross, it is papa's mark," she cried. "Baron Tolnay, let me look!"

István's hand was there before hers, and while she was speaking, the third cross was disclosed.

The marks were worn with time and weather, but they were unmistakable. This beech tree bore three crosses on it, cut into the bark at what must have been the height of a man's stature, in the time when the stem had stood upright.

Just as the solution of a riddle, which we have tried in vain to guess, often provokes us by its very simplicity, so did it now appear absurd to Gretchen, and well-nigh incredible, that they should have been so near to the crosses and yet not have seen them. Why, in the midst of all their speculations, had they never contemplated the possibility of the tree which bore the marks being felled?

A minute was spent in examination and conjecture, and then followed the desire for immediate action. Gretchen had gone down on her knees to examine the marks more closely, but it was not long before she rose and looked about her, striving to recall her father's exact directions.

"When you have found that tree, you are not a hundred yards from the spot," Adalbert had said. In spite of herself, Gretchen began to tremble with the agitation of this thought.

Carefully turning in the direction which her father had indicated and calculating her paces with all possible nicety, Gretchen began her search in advance of the others.

The incertitude did not last more than five minutes.

By an ingenious combination of excessively simple circumstances, *Gaura Dracului* lay so marvelously concealed that not one person in fifty passing close to the spot would ever guess at its existence, and that fiftieth person whose ignorance was enlightened would probably reap his experience by breaking his neck in a most ghastly fashion. A dip in the ground exactly like a hundred other dips, and a tangle of bushes, scarcely more dense than in any other part of the forest, combined together to screen this black danger which lurked here in the very depth of the shadows.

Gretchen herself overshot the mark, for her eagerness upset her calculations. She was beginning again to doubt when she heard Tolnay calling to her from a little way back,

"This way, this way!"

And Mr. Howard shouted, "Yes, this way; but, in Heaven's name, be careful!"

She turned back the way she had come, stumbled over a stone, and recovered herself; broke through a narrow opening in the trees, where the low-hanging branches struck her in the face, stooped down to escape them, and, with another step, stood still.

The rich undergrowth of moss and fern at her feet opened suddenly. She was standing on the brink of a space, irregularly circular — black, vacant, and immeasurably deep.

Chapter XXXIV

Gaura Dracului

"Is this a dagger which I see before me,
The handle toward my hand?"

— Macbeth

G RETCHEN's first impulse was to exclaim in wonder, her second to recoil in fear. There was a mixture of beauty and horror about the spot which put to naught every description she had heard of the place. All around the moss and ferns wreathed in wasteful abundance. Up to the very edge of the horrible abyss did the ivy creep boldly; and not up to the edge only, but over it the green trails had ventured. There were clinging plants of all descriptions, contending with each other as to which of them should reach down the deepest to sound that gaping space below. They hung in a heavy fringe down into the darkness, scarcely stirred by the breeze, nor even touched by the sunshine; and the lowest hanging leaves of these venturesome trails were pale for want of full light, as are plants which have been grown in a cellar. Trails have hung down this way year by year, have budded in spring, and have dropped their leaves down into the gulf below them when autumn came round. Myriads of withered leaves must have fluttered down there, away from the light; but none have ever come back to tell the tale of what they had seen below.

The very beauty all around made the horror of the spot more palpable. The stately ferns waved here as peacefully as though they grew in some quiet dell; the ivy

twined as soberly as though it clothed an old church tower; and the innocent flowerets peep over the edge. But there is treason in them, one and all. They are the
beautiful mask of a hideous thing; they are the smiling ornaments which have decked
out this hidden trap. There is not one leaflet which trembles there, not one floweret
which blooms, that does not deserve to be rooted out and left to wither. Stripped of
its wreath of verdure, *Gaura Dracului* would also be stripped of half its peril. If that
black hole were cut in the naked rock, and bared on all sides to view, it would be a
frightful object, but it would no longer be the lurking danger which it now is. Nothing but fiendish cunning, you might fancy, could have contrived to turn so much
beauty to so cruel an account.

"A horrid yawning black hole," as Adalbert had said; and his words were strictly
true. And yet, not one of the four people now standing on the edge of the hole but
did not feel conscious that each had carried within them a different picture to this.
The picture in each mind would have as widely differed from the other in the painting of details, as each picture was different from the reality before them. It was not
that it was less horrible, or less black, or less beautiful than they had imagined, but
that it was horrible and beautiful in some inexplicably different way from that which
they had expected. Gretchen had known that the spot would be awful; but she had
not thought that the awfulness would make itself felt in this sensible, almost tangible
manner. Against her own will, she stepped back shuddering. The sense of immeas-
urable depth, the black vacancy, with the suggestion of a deeper, blacker vacancy
below, made her giddy. It was not difficult to understand why the peasants called the
spot haunted, and invented legends as apologies for their fear. Standing beside it now
in the gloom of twilight, Gretchen felt a shiver run over her. For centuries, this hole
had stood open: it was a necessity almost that one, or more than one, victim had
fallen into its jaws. Each of the four persons who stood now in awed silence by the
edge instinctively conjured up visions of frightful tragedies. A traveler lost in the dark
— how, when coming down the slope of that bank, could he avoid walking straight
into the arms of death? One step would be enough now to send any of them headlong
to destruction.

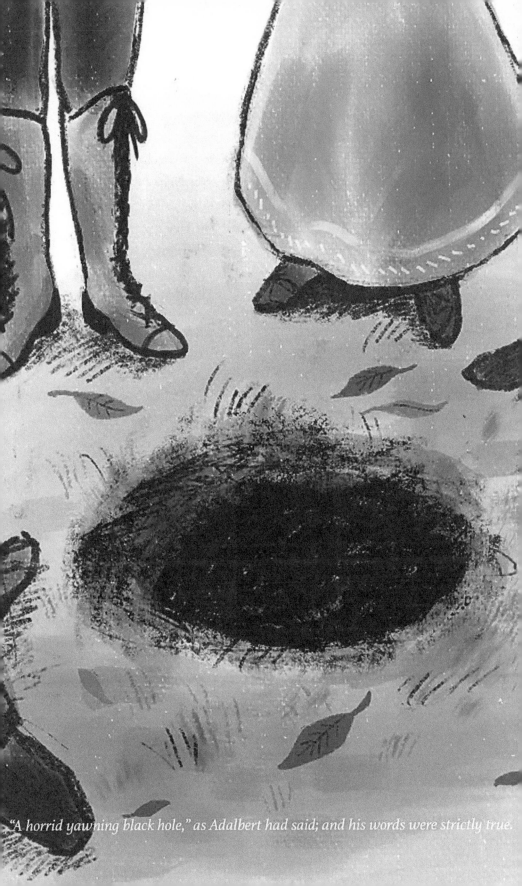

"A horrid yawning black hole," as Adalbert had said; and his words were strictly true.

Kurt was the one who appeared the least impressed. He picked up a stone and flung it down. It flashed out of sight, bounded from rock to rock, fainter and always fainter; then came an interval of silence — it must have reached the bottom: no, a far, far off sound told them that it was still falling. Not till now had they realized the awful depth. They threw another stone, and counted the time of its fall upon the second-hand of Mr. Howard's watch. There was the same flash, the same bounds, the same horribly suggestive interval of silence, and then the distant rattling sound again. During half a minute, an attentive ear could still catch the faint sound of a fall; and even then, when it died away, they were left with the impression that it had not stopped falling, but was only too far off to be heard any longer.

"They say that it leads straight to hell, don't they?" said István, suddenly. He had not spoken since Gretchen's appearance on the spot; he was now standing close to the edge, gazing down the hole with a fixed and abstracted stare. "Strange that I should never have come across it before now!"

"And we were so near it that first day," said Gretchen, drawing back another step from the edge. "I do not see how we can have missed it."

"That is because we took the turn to the left — the way the Bohemian has gone for water."

"And where does that lead?" asked Mr. Howard.

"To the frontier: we are not half an hour from Romania here."

The bushes rustled close to them, and the Bohemian appeared upon the scene, pale, disheveled, and well-nigh breathless. In his left hand, he held Gretchen's water flask; with his right, he beat his breast violently, while he stood struggling to recover his breath.

The mild face of this peacefully inclined man had never so nearly approached to passion it did at this moment.

"*Heilige Maria!*" he gasped out — "*Heilige Muttergottes* of the *Wunderbaum* at Choteborschwitz! My vow! My sacred vow! I have not broken it. *Der liebe Herrgott* knows I am innocent!"

"Of course, you are innocent," said Gretchen, laying her hand on the arm of the excited man. "We have found *Gaura Dracului,* but your vow is safe."

"No reason that I can see for such excitement," observed Kurt, composedly.

"I am thankful that we have not allowed that fellow's superstitious folly to baffle us," remarked Mr. Howard, with satisfaction.

"How did you find it?" asked the Bohemian, wiping his forehead with an unsteady hand, while, still exhausted, he leaned against a tree.

Gretchen explained to him the secret of the three crosses. "Those three crosses! I have seen them often, Fräulein, when the tree was still upright. They have puzzled me too."

He drew a long breath; and then, partially recovering his composure, offered her the water flask.

"You have waited long, Fräulein; your thirst must be terrible."

"The water!" said Gretchen, looking blankly at the flask.

"The water you sent me to fetch," the Bohemian repeated, holding the flask towards her.

"But Dr. Komers?" she said; "did you not meet him? He went after you to tell you we had already found water. Mr. Howard's flask was full."

"I did not meet the Herr Doctor. I came back to the tree trunk, and when I saw the bundle still lying there, and you gone, I guessed you would be here — I was afraid of it."

"Komers will be waiting for us at the tree," decided Kurt — "depend upon it."

"Unless he has lost his way meantime," said Tolnay, with a grim laugh.

"Which would be a nasty job about here," added Mr. Howard.

"Oh, I hope he will be careful!" cried Gretchen, drawing back another step from the abyss.

She saw a gleam of jealousy in Tolnay's eyes.

"That man is always careful," sneered István, just under his breath; "but even careful men can sometimes lose their way."

The Bohemian had by this time recovered himself to some extent, though he still leaned against the tree stem.

"Those three crosses!" he repeated, with a dissatisfied shake of the head. "If I had but known it! It always struck me that they were too well cut to be done by a goatherd. If I had but known what they meant!"

"And if you had known what they meant?"

"I should have destroyed them."

"Come!" cried Mr. Howard, "this is growing preposterous. This fellow's obstinacy beats anything in my experience. What was all that rubbish he told us about the place? What is it that the Greek fellow down there swore on his club?"

"A victim every century," said the Bohemian, and the old scared expression came back to his face.

"Why, the man looks as if he had been down the hole himself, or chucked someone else over," said Mr. Howard, eying him severely. "It can't be superstition alone that sets him shaking in his shoes this way."

"Superstition! *Heilige Jungfrau* of the *Wunderbaum* at Choteborschwitz! We are not superstitious, we Bohemians, like the people of this strange country," sighed the man, with the resignation of an exile; "and neither have I ever seen any man or woman go down into that blackness. But — but — "

"But you have heard of such a thing happening?" finished Gretchen, bending an imperious glance upon him. "Tell us the story!"

"It is the story of my vow," he faltered.

"The story of your vow can do no more harm than is already done."

It was growing too dark to see clearly the expression of the Bohemian's face; but from the pause which followed, and from the nervous motion of his hands as he twisted up the cap between them, it was evident that he was going through a sharp tussle with his conscience. Finally, the desire to justify himself against the charge of superstition triumphed, and he spoke.

"Fräulein," he began in a tremulous voice, still leaning against the tree stem beside him, "you will remember how I told you that both I and my father were born in this strange country, and that it was my grandfather who accepted the offer which the Government had made him, and left his nation to settle here. It was a rich farm which they gave him. He brought his young wife with him, and his only child was born here soon after he had settled down; and yet he should have rued the day when he came to this land. He had not been settled a year in the valley when a Wallachian, who worked on his farm, told him the story of *Gaura Dracului*, and of the treasure which the brigands had buried there, and which no one had found.

"My grandfather loved gold. The story inflamed his thirst for riches. For weeks, he dreamed of nothing else; and at last he determined, in concert with the Wallachian laborer, to whom he promised half the gain, to sound the depth of the Devil's Hole.

"The two went up in secret — not even my grandmother knew the object of the expedition; and it was only next day, when the Wallachian came back alone, halfmad with terror, and told her how the rope had broken in his hands, and his companion plunged into the abyss before his eyes — it was only then that she heard of *Gaura Dracului*."

The Bohemian broke off, and crossed himself. No one spoke for a moment. Very swift, very silent, very terrible must such a death have been.

"When I was ten years old," said the Bohemian, "my father took me up here to this place and showed it to me. He made me swear by my devotion to the *Wunderbaum* at Choteborschwitz that I would never reveal the spot to anybody. It was his mother, my grandmother — I remember her still — who had told him the story."

"But," said Gretchen, after a moment of silence, "I cannot see what logical object your father had with that vow. The more the place is known, the less danger there would be of a person stumbling in."

"That may be, Fräulein, but I was bound to hold my vow. My father meant it for the best, no doubt. I have seldom come to the spot myself, and I never cut shingles in this part of the forest. I saw something happen here long ago, when I was a child, which made me sad for many days. There were two young kids which had strayed near this place, and on that bank above they began to butt at each other in play. It was the prettiest sight you could see, and I laughed as I looked on; but I stopped laughing very soon. One of them made a false step; he had got his horns entangled with his playfellow's horns, and the two fell together down that hole. They went straight down; there was not a sound; it was all quiet in a moment."

"And I suppose that the devils had roast kid for dinner that day," observed Kurt, flippantly.

"We once carried a big stone here," went on the Bohemian, unperturbed — I and some peasants who knew of the spot. It took six of us to carry it; and when we threw it down, the breath of air which came up knocked the caps off our six heads as if with a blow."

"I should have been mightily surprised if it had not," remarked Mr. Howard; "and you took it for supernatural interference, of course."

"And another time," went on the Bohemian, calmly, "we let a man down with ropes. We had fifty yards of rope, but it was not enough. Next day, we came back with double as much rope; but when we had lost sight of the man, we heard him calling up, for he had taken fright, and after that we did not meddle with the place again."

"Bah!" said Mr. Howard, "in ten years the measurement of the depth will be reduced to a mathematical calculation."

"That is what papa says," observed Gretchen; "and he believes, too, that there is some outlet below."

"That is the secret of the mountains, Fräulein; and the mountains do not chatter. According to the story of the brigands' treasure, some such passage would need to exist. I know of one story only which seems to confirm it. My father was told by an old peasant, who died at ninety years of age, that a brother of his had a dog whom he wanted to be rid of, and so he just took him up to the wood and knocked him into the hole. He was sure never to see him again; but ten days after that, as he was leaving his house in the morning, there on the doorstep, the dog was sitting, nothing but skin and bone, and scratches all over. Nobody knows where he came from. The peasants said he was not good enough for the devils, and that therefore they let him go again."

"Too thin for roasting," suggested Kurt. "They might have made broth of him, though."

But even Kurt's irreverence failed to disturb the gravity of the others. No story of *Gaura Dracului* sounded too extravagant as long as *Gaura Dracului* lay before the listeners' eyes. In Gretchen's head, there was ringing the air of the Bohemian's melancholy song, and the monotonous refrain —

> "*Beware, beware!*
> *Of Gaura Dracului beware!*"

It seemed to her that that Roman woman, sacrificed to blind jealousy, should henceforward, from a legendary myth, become to her an authentic personage. Had she not stood beside the hapless victim's grave?

It was a place to pursue a man in his dreams, to haunt him even by broad daylight. The shiver of interest which it awoke was both exquisite and painful. While longing to be away, one yet was loath to leave it. Some such feeling it was which kept them all silent now as they stood around it. The fascination seemed to be strongest upon István. He slowly paced round the edge, with his eye fixed on the blackness below, stepping sometimes. so perilously near to the deceitful brink as to deal nervous starts to his companions, and to call forth many an invocation to the *Heilige Jungfrau* of the *Wunderbaum* at Choteborschwitz from the scared Bohemian.

"Tell me," said Gretchen to the guide, "have you ever heard of any other accident happening here, except the death of your grandfather?"

"Never any other, Fräulein: there may have been accidents here, or there may not. Those who go down there do not come back to tell us stories. You know what the peasants here say. I told you of their superstition."

"A victim every century," said Tolnay, half aloud.

"And when was it that your grandfather was killed?" asked Mr. Howard.

"In the last year of last century, *mein Herr.*"

"Ha!" cried Tolnay, raising his head. "Then the devils have not had their due this time?"

"No, Herr Baron," said the Bohemian, with a feeble attempt at a sneer — "not if we give credit to the stories of this ignorant people." But the contempt in his voice was not convincing; his simple soul could not quite escape the gloomy magic of the spot.

"Perhaps, though, their sable majesties will be content with the kids," remarked Kurt: "that immolation took place this century, you know."

"But it is a human victim they want," explained the Bohemian, with a rather inconsistent eagerness; "it is human blood which they must taste once in every hundred years: the god of the valley has sworn it on his club."

"And Hercules keeps his oaths," muttered István.

His tone was so strange that Gretchen hurriedly turned to leave the spot.

"We can do no more for today," she said; "experiments need not only daylight, but also ropes and tools. Now that the spot is found, all will be easy."

"I am not so sure of that," said Mr. Howard: "even now, enlightened as we are, we might stumble round and round the place for half an hour, or into it perhaps, before we knew where we were. That one tree is not guide enough; if you will keep your patience for half a dozen minutes longer, I shall press a few more of these giants into the sign post-service;" and he began unclasping his big English penknife, and prepared to attack the nearest beech tree.

But Gretchen had been seized with a sudden violent desire to be away from the spot. Just as a minute ago she had felt drawn to linger, so was she now consumed by a fever to be gone.

Leave it alone," she answered, impatiently; "we have already lost more time than we can afford, and besides, it is getting too dark to see what you are cutting in the bark. Mr. Howard, please come away."

"As you command," said Mr. Howard, slicing away doggedly at the beech tree. "I shall leave the others alone; but just let me mark this one fellow. I am a practical Englishman, and it revolts my common sense to leave the spot without having done something towards facilitating our next search." ·

"You are an obstinate and unpersuadable Englishman. But we are not going to stand by and watch you dig your crosses. There! If you will have the tree marked, do it this way;" and Gretchen pulled her handkerchief from her pocket, and twisted it round the lowest branch, knotting it fast with a double knot. "There! that is better than your pedantic cutting; it can be seen almost in the dark. Now, come away quick; let us lose no more time."

"I submit," said Mr. Howard, reluctantly closing his knife. "But let us sum up the matter first: From the white mark, turn to the right — mind you, *to the right;* the hole lies sharp to the left."

"Yes, yes," said Gretchen, "that will do; let us go now."

They made their way back without much difficulty. It was not so dark now, for the moon was rising early, and poured through every loophole which the branches above afforded. They had never before been on the hills at so late an hour. But even with the possibility of robbers and bears before her eyes, Gretchen felt no apprehension: she knew that both Tolnay and Mr. Howard carried revolvers in case of emergencies; and besides, was there not the gun of the Bohemian's unfortunate grandfather, which, after all, might go off at the right moment?

The prostrate beech tree was bathed in moonlight; and, sitting on the trunk, they saw the figure of Dr. Komers. He did not perceive them until they were close; then, he rose hurriedly, and came to meet them.

"At last! I could not imagine where you were."

"We could not imagine where *you* were," said Kurt.

"I missed the Bohemian, but managed to find my way back here; and seeing all the things about — plaids and so on — I concluded that my best course was to wait patiently."

"Ah, you don't know what you have missed!" said Gretchen. And then, with much question and answer, and more or less excited narrative, the lawyer's ignorance was enlightened. The Bohemian knelt on the ground, strapping up the basket which had carried their provisions.

"It is a positive pity that you have not seen it," admitted Mr. Howard. "I am bound to confess that we have nothing which beats it in its own line of horrors within the seas of Great Britain."

"Is it far from here?" asked Vincenz.

"Not three minutes' walk."

"There is no particular necessity for seeing it tonight, is there?" asked Kurt; "it is not going to close up just yet, I fancy."

Vincenz looked doubtful. As a matter of personal taste, he did not care much whether he did or did not see a black hole that was supposed to have no bottom. He took no special interest in either geological or historical researches. This black hole, however, this *Gaura Dracului*, which had played so great a part this summer, was not quite like any other black hole. He had assisted in the search for weeks past; it was an object of interest to Adalbert Mohr; above all, it was an interest to Gretchen. The position was a tantalizing one. To be the only one of the party who should come back without having seen the spot — to be so near, and to go away ignorant — it was enough to excite even a hitherto slumbering curiosity.

"Three minutes there," said Mr. Howard, with his watch in his hand, "three minutes back, and one minute to stand and shiver at the edge — seven minutes in all. We are so late already that seven minutes are neither here nor there. It will take us about that to pack up our things."

"You had better make up your mind quick, one way or the other;" remarked Kurt; "but if I were you, I should take it on trust."

"So should I," said Gretchen, as she flung her shawl around her. "It is so dark too, it would scarcely be safe. Dr. Komers, do not go?"

She had spoken low, but both Vincenz and Tolnay had heard her distinctly, and they both turned their heads towards her. For one instant, Vincenz felt his heart leap up with a sort of wild hope, but it sank down again in the next.

"I am an old fool," thought Vincenz; "it is only that she is in a hurry to get home."

"Don't go," said another voice beside him: it was Tolnay's, and there was again in it that mocking tone with which he loved to torment the lawyer. But the mockery tonight was not as light and laughing as was Tolnay's wont.

"And why should I not go?"

"Because you would see nothing; and besides — it would not be safe."

"I shall go," said Vincenz; "will anyone show me the way?"

"The Bohemian will," said Mr. Howard, as he carefully stowed away his yellow fungus in the empty provision basket.

The Bohemian looked up from the bundle he was busy with on the ground. He looked piteously towards Gretchen.

"I can't do that, Fräulein; it would be directly against my vow. I was never to reveal the spot to any living person."

"Oh, bother it!" said Mr. Howard, with magnanimity; "then I shall have to take you, I suppose."

"Yes," said Gretchen, eagerly.

"No," said Tolnay, stepping forward; "I will show you the way." There was nothing strange in the offer, and yet every person of the party looked up surprised. Tolnay's mood today had been so peculiar — so gloomy at moments and so wildly gay at others — he had showed so distinct a dislike towards Dr. Komers, that even a slight politeness of this sort struck everyone with momentary surprise.

Tolnay saw the start, saw it most clearly upon Gretchen's face, and asked somewhat defiantly,

"Well, have I said anything peculiar?"

"Nothing at all," said Mr. Howard.

"Nothing," echoed Gretchen, more faintly.

"Nothing, except that everything about him is peculiar today," remarked Kurt to himself.

In the next minute already, no one could imagine what had caused that glance of surprise. Why should not Baron Tolnay have taken it into his head to be polite for once, even to Dr. Komers?

"I am much obliged to you," said Vincenz, readily. "We had better lose no time."

"Much better," answered Tolnay; and he stood for a minute looking at Gretchen, as if he had forgotten the business in hand. Then he turned quickly and walked away, Vincenz following close behind him.

Their steps echoed on the dry crisp moss and the crackling brown of the leaves. Gretchen watched them — Tolnay in advance, Vincenz still close behind him; they would disappear among the bushes in another moment.

She got up, and, moved by some unaccountable impulse, called after them, "Don't forget the signal, the handkerchief on the tree; the tree is to the right, the hole to the left."

She was not sure she had been heard, for Vincenz kept straight on, but Tolnay turned for a moment.

"I remember," he called back.

How white his face looked in the moonlight — ghastly pale it seemed at this distance. And his eyes! Was it the moonlight alone that made them shine with that fevered brightness?

Something like dread, something like suspicion, for an instant crossed Gretchen's mind. She turned to Kurt, who was lighting a fresh cigar for the homeward journey.

"Kurt, will you not go with them? They are not out of sight yet."

Kurt laughed good-naturedly.

"My dear Gretchen, you are really very amusing. In what capacity am I to offer myself? Is not one man enough to show a hole in the ground to another man?"

"I suppose so," sighed Gretchen; and she sat down to wait, half-ashamed of the anxiety she had betrayed.

The two figures had vanished among the bushes; for a few seconds longer they could hear the crackling of the trodden leaves, and then they heard nothing more.

"We must be close to it," said Vincenz to Baron Tolnay, when they had plunged into the thicket of bushes. "Did they not call out something about a signal after us?"

István nodded without turning his head; but in the next second he came to a dead standstill, and faced straight round. He was muttering something under his breath. Vincenz did not hear what the words were; and if he had heard them, he would not have known what to make of them. What István said to himself were only the few words — "I cannot do it."

"I am not going farther," he said, louder; but his voice was so husky that Vincenz could scarcely catch even this.

They were standing in a patch of clear moonlight; and Vincenz, peering through his spectacles, thought he had never seen a man's face look as pale as István's face looked at this moment.

"Are you ill?" he asked, with sudden alarm, forgetting every thought of rivalry and petty differences in an honest fellow-feeling of sympathy. He put out his hand towards Tolnay's; but István started aside violently, as if he could not bear that touch.

"Yes — no; I don't know — perhaps I am ill, or perhaps I am mad. I am not going farther. You can find it for yourself; we are not twenty paces off."

"Do not trouble yourself," said Vincenz, with his usual courtesy. "I shall certainly find it for myself, if you will only tell me about that signal."

"It is a white handkerchief on the branch," replied Tolnay, slowly; and he broke off then, and fastened upon the lawyer's face a look so intense, so strained and fixed, that Vincenz stood wondering for a moment as to what that glance could mean.

There had been more than one moment today when Vincenz had met this man's eyes, and had puzzled over their expression. The hatred he had fancied to see in them might be explained; but there had been another element in those glances, for which he had not known how to account: that other element had looked like jealousy. What ground, in Heaven's name — what ground for jealousy could the young, the rich, the fascinating Baron Tolnay have with regard to an obscure lawyer, without fortune, shortsighted, and on the verge of forty?

Vincenz had asked himself that question earlier in the day; he did not think of it at this moment. All he saw was that Tolnay was looking strangely ill and disturbed.

"A white handkerchief on a branch," said Vincenz, recalling the other to the point in question. An István's energies seemed to have become absorbed in the intensity of that gaze.

"A white handkerchief on the branch — yes," said Tolnay.

"And when I come to it, I must turn which way?"

Tolnay looked for one moment into the face of the man before him, and he saw that he was unsuspicious and open, ready to take him at his word. He set his teeth.

"When you come to it, you must turn — " he paused — that pause was scarcely a second — "you must turn sharp to the left."

"To the left; thank you," said Vincenz, courteously.

Tolnay made no response. He stood watching the other till he passed out of sight — his own figure standing so motionless that he seemed scarcely to be drawing breath. It was not pity which he felt even at this moment — it was a furious jealousy.

When he had stood for the space of a few seconds, he turned his face in the opposite direction and broke his way through the bushes — running as if he were being pursued, as if at any price he must get away from this spot.

Vincenz walked straight on, peering about for the signal. He had not got more than twenty paces when he saw it on the tree. This signal shone so white that not even a shortsighted man could overlook it. It hung on the branch like a huge white flower, doubly pale in the moonlight. A slanting moonbeam, piercing through the branches, had touched it and made it shine out conspicuously. But though the signal on the branch was so distinct, the ground at the lawyer's feet was dark, and he did not see where he was stepping.

He stood for a moment, looking at the signal; then, exactly following Tolnay's direction, unhesitatingly, unsuspiciously, blindly, he turned, as he had been told — sharp to the left.

Chapter XXXV

A Riddle

"But long they looked, and feared, and wept.

— Bryant

T HE last of the plaids was strapped up, the provision basket had been got into traveling order; there was nothing now to do but to sit and wait till those two men came back again through the bushes. Mr. Howard and Kurt exchanged occasional remarks; the Bohemian smoked his pipe, standing a little apart; Gretchen sat silent, feeling tired, and conscious of listening rather impatiently for the sound of the returning footsteps.

"Three minutes there," said Mr. Howard, drawing out his watch, "three minutes back, and say three minutes for shuddering — nine minutes in all. They have been gone ten minutes now."

"Suppose we go on slowly, and let them follow," said Kurt.

"No," said Gretchen; "we must wait till they come."

"Oh, all right; but you looked as if you had had enough of this waiting business. I know I have."

"Four minutes for shuddering — five minutes," proclaimed Mr. Howard, holding his watch so that the moonlight fell upon it. "It is beginning to grow into an unreasonable allowance. It is wrong in them to indulge in so many shivers when they know that we are waiting."

There was a short silence, during which Mr. Howard kept his eyes on his watch, and the Bohemian puffed his pipe steadily. Then the puffs stopped, and the Bohemian stood in an attitude of attention.

"They are coming now," he said.

Mr. Howard returned his watch to his pocket, and the Bohemian hastily lighted the little lantern which was to guide them down, for in the dense parts of the forest there would be no moonlight on their path.

They all looked towards the bushes to the right. But those bushes never rustled — they slept on peacefully in the moonlight; it was from the opposite side that footsteps were approaching.

"Why, they have not been to the hole, after all," said Mr. Howard, in a tone of disgust; "they are coming from the other side."

"Fine result of all our signal-hoisting," laughed Kurt. "They will be ashamed to say it; but I bet you, nine to one, they haven't found the place."

"Just what I said," Mr. Howard wrathfully exclaimed; "we should have marked half a dozen trees at least, to make sure."

Meanwhile, from between the trees, the figure of a man was beginning to grow distinct, pacing slowly towards them.

"They are taking it easy," said Kurt, with disapproval.

"They?" repeated Mr. Howard; "I only see one. Which of them is it? Or is it neither?"

Just as he spoke, the approaching man had to cross a strip of moonlight. It was István Tolnay's face on which the moon shone.

"Halloo! What's this?" cried out Mr. Howard. "Did you not find the place?" shouted Kurt.

They shouted loud enough, but István neither hurried his pace nor made any answer to their calls. He came on somewhat laggingly, never raising his eyes from the ground before him. When he had reached them, he looked up at last, and started as if he had not expected to see them there.

"Where is Dr. Komers?" he asked.

"That is just the question we were going to put to you," laughed Mr. Howard.

"He has not come back, then?"

"No; certainly not."

"I thought not," said Tolnay; and he sat down on the trunk as if exhausted, passing his handkerchief over his damp forehead.

"But where is Dr. Komers?" repeated Gretchen.

He answered without looking at her: "I did not go with him all the way; he said he would find the place alone. I did not care to go on — I felt giddy."

Everyone was a little surprised: but the tone in which he spoke, and the pallor of his face, bore out his words. There was something subdued and exhausted about his manner. Even his eyes seemed to have no light in them. Mr. Howard could not entirely suppress a contemptuous snort. It was in his eyes a degrading spectacle to see this wretched young foreigner so entirely knocked up by a day's walk in the mountains.

"You told him about the signal?" asked Gretchen.

Still not looking at her, he answered," I told him about the signal."

"And you are sure he understood you?" ,

"I am sure he understood me."

"Then he will be back directly," said Mr. Howard, drawing out his watch with an impatient jerk.

"I hope so," said Gretchen, in a whisper.

Tolnay turned his head and looked at her as she said it, then his glance returned to the ground.

"Ten minutes for shivering he has given himself," said Mr. Howard, still watch in hand. "This is getting past a joke; it is a positive want of tact."

"Or of sense of locality," said Kurt. "Most likely he cannot find his way back."

"Of course, that is obvious," said Gretchen, somewhat irritably. "What is the use of making such self-evident remarks?"

"Shall I go and look for the Herr Doctor?'; volunteered the Bohemian, taking his pipe from his mouth.

"Look here! We have had enough of this sort of thing," objected Mr. Howard. "There have been enough cross-purposes this evening without making more. If we begin looking for each other, we shall end by each going home in a different direction. It is a golden rule, in such cases, to wait quietly at one's post."

The Bohemian submitted, but he did not look quite satisfied.

"We could call out for the Herr Doctor, at least; he may be close by without knowing it."

They shouted, first the Bohemian, then Mr. Howard, then Kurt.

The wood sank back into silence the moment they held their breath. There was not the smallest answering rustle, nor the crackling of trodden twigs, to tell them that they had been heard. Gretchen, as she sat listening, told herself that there was no cause for anxiety, and that presently she should hear the sound of parting branches, for which she was so earnestly listening.

"He may have heard, though he has not answered," said Mr. Howard. "Let us hold our tongues for a little. We might as well give him the chance of a halloo."

They did hold their tongues. They all remained as motionless as though they had been lifeless figures grown into the surroundings of the moonlit forest. But Dr. Komers apparently had missed his chance, for the answering halloo was not heard.

At last, somebody spoke. It was Tolnay. He raised his head and asked, "Why are we not going home?"

"But we are waiting for Dr. Komers," said three voices together. "To be sure;" and István's head sank down again.

It was Gretchen who spoke next —

"Where did you leave Dr. Komers exactly?"

"I left him within thirty paces of the hole."

Then silence fell again upon the waiting group. These intervals of silence were beginning to be dangerously suggestive. The intentness with which Gretchen sat listening for the sound of the bushes rustling was becoming irksome to herself. The strain grew with every second: from irksome it grew to be painful, and from painful it became torturing. Not even to herself would she acknowledge the creeping fear, which, she knew not how, had slunk into her heart, and which was slowly encircling it with an icy band. She would not even look at her brother, nor at Mr. Howard, for fear of reading in their eyes something which would strengthen the suspicion within her.

It is not possible to determine at what point exactly a fear of this sort becomes alive. Often when we are scarcely yet aware that the seed has been sown, the plant is already growing fast. By this time, they were all persuading themselves that they had not sat waiting and listening for so very long, and that there really was no reason for avoiding each other's eyes in the way they were unconsciously doing. And yet they did avoid a direct look: they stared at the bushes, at the tree trunk, at everything but each other's faces. And so sharpened do our perceptions become in moments of suspense that there was no member of the party who could not have stood a close examination as to the exact number of tree stems within sight or who could not from memory have accurately drawn the outline of that clump of bushes to the right.

That black, bottomless hole was in everybody's mind and no one had the courage to name it. The silence was unbearable; yet each felt that he would rather not be the first to break it. The first word said must be an acknowledgment of their secret fear — and it is the acknowledgment which is hardest to make.

Kurt had thrown away his cigar. The Bohemian's pipe had gone out without his noticing it. Mr. Howard it was who made the first movement. He put back his watch into his pocket, and scratched his head. Then he got up, looked around, hesitated for a moment, and said, in a studiously careless voice,

"I shall just take a cast about."

Some such signal they had waited for: they all began moving, as if with one accord.

"Why, Gretchen, you are looking as white as a ghost," said Kurt to his sister. "We shall have to carry you down the hill, after all. Hadn't you better sit here while we are beating the bushes?"

Kurt's tone was meant to be cheerful, but his supreme coolness failed him a little just now. ·

"But I mean to beat the bushes too," said Gretchen, bravely. "We are sure to find Dr. Komers at once; don't you think so, Kurt?"

"Oh, at once — naturally, of course I do," said Kurt, clearing his throat; "only I don't like to make self-evident remarks. He'll be disporting himself somewhere close at hand, depend upon it; or perhaps he has had a moon stroke, you know."

The Bohemian made a few steps to follow the party, then turned, as if struck with a thought, and picking up the lighted lantern, took it with him.

The wraps and provision basket were abandoned for a second time this evening. But they were not quite abandoned this time, for, looking back, Gretchen saw Baron Tolnay sitting where they had left him, his head still bowed and his arms folded. It seemed as if he were too exhausted to take part in the search.

This part of the wood became alive with steps and voices. Everyone felt that to make a noise was a relief after the silence and inaction from which they had just been freed. Frightened bats darted overhead, and moths flew out of the bushes around. The night birds uttered shrill cries of surprise as they winged their way towards undisturbed depths of the forest; and the day birds awoke in alarm, wondering if the night were already over.

The party separated in different directions; there was no word now said about playing at cross-purposes. They took great care in separating to inform each other that they were not going to search anywhere in particular, only to take a general look around.

Gretchen did not say much. She waited till the others were dispersed, and when she thought herself unobserved, she crept quietly in the direction of *Gaura Dracului*. She did not ask herself why she was going there; but some inward warning was drawing her in that direction. She stifled the warning with all the resolution she could muster; but, half against her will, she obeyed it. Above all, she would not have liked anyone else to guess at the horrible fear which had been born within her. She crept softly through the bushes, where the rising moon was weaving strange effects. Her quick eyes espied the signal at once — the handkerchief tied to the branch, just as she had left it. Dr. Komers could not have passed it without seeing it; and this thought for a minute revived her failing courage. Then, she stepped forward and stood at the edge of the abyss.

Its aspect was somewhat changed from what it had been half an hour ago, for the moon threw a shaft of light right into its depth. The trails of hanging plants seemed to quiver in the flood of silver; and the points of rock, the accidents of formation, were much more distinctly seen now than they had been seen then. This new distinctness added to the terror of the place; it was like scanning the bare fangs in the widely opened jaws of some monster of unearthly size.

Gretchen bent forward, intently staring into the depth; then, raising her eyes, she started, for there opposite to her were the figures of Mr. Howard and the Bohemian, both leaning forward, and peering down, as she had been doing.

Mr. Howard appeared to be no less surprised at seeing her than she felt at seeing him. Before either of them had spoken, there appeared another figure on the scene. It was Kurt.

What horrible coincidence of idea was this? thought Gretchen, with a fresh shudder. There was another half-guilty start, and then everybody began talking at once, doing their best to explain that they had come here by the merest chance, and becoming very eloquent about the great facility with which people go astray in the woods, and often wander about for hours in a circle, thus exhausting their own breath and their friends' patience. Examples were quoted and anecdotes told, mazes and labyrinths were talked of; in fact, everything which could prolong the conversation was laid hold of — for they were all as loquacious now as they had before been silent. They dreaded the first pause almost more than a little time ago they had dreaded the first word. Had not Dr. Komers missed his way once already this evening? It was quite natural that he should have missed it again. They all knew how shortsighted he was; but even in saying it, they recognized that this last argument was one that cut both ways. And then, unconsciously narrowing their circle, they argued that it would be ridiculous to suppose that a sensible man like Dr. Komers — who had, moreover, been instructed as to the meaning of the signal — could by any possibility have stumbled over the edge. An ignorant person, to hear them talk, would have supposed Dr. Komers to be possessed of as many eyes as Argus, and *Gaura Dracului* to be a roadside ditch, into which it would be scarcely unpleasant to stumble. It was quite clear that the lawyer must merely have lost his way. And again, they took to shouting and to searching the wood around, hoisting up the lantern on a long stick and waving it as a beacon light.

Their arguments were of the most convincing kind; and yet, at the end of another long half-hour, everybody was again standing round the hole, looking down with a fearful question in their eyes at the blackness below. Useless scrutiny! That hole is dumb and pitiless. It is unchanged, immovable, expressionless as before. No good in putting the dread question — Did a man pass this way? Did he fall down there — down, down out of sight? Is this the only grave he will ever have? The monster will give no answer. Truly those who go down there do not come back to tell us any stories. Perhaps the ivy leaves, rustling faintly in this breath of air, are whispering to each other about what they have seen happen in this last hour; but it is in a language which human ears cannot understand. Human beings are so helpless in a case like this. Even that noiseless bat, taking a sweep down into the abyss, and up again into the moonlight, knows more than they know. But the bat, like the ivy, tells no tales.

Tolnay gave no help in the search. He was very quiet, and apparently apathetic. He showed no disturbance when repeatedly questioned as to the exact spot on which he had parted from Dr. Komers. His mind had, for the time, sunk into a strangely indifferent state; and at this moment it had not yet occurred to him that suspicion might fasten upon him. This very indifference, perhaps, prevented the growth of suspicion.

It had occurred. nevertheless, to more minds than one. Not to the Bohemian's — he was too simple-minded for such a thought; but both upon Kurt and upon Mr. Howard such a possibility had dawned — although for the present it had not, in Kurt's case at least, got further than a mere suggestion. It did not seem to bear investigation. To begin with, there appeared to be, to the eyes of these outsiders, an utter want of motive; for neither Kurt nor Mr. Howard had ever suspected the existence of a question of serious rivalry between those two men. Neither of them had ever guessed the secret of the lawyer's love, as neither of them had ever doubted the success of Tolnay's suit. Even had they been aware of the lawyer's sentiments, the knowledge would not have helped to solve the present dilemma. It might have been worth István's while to clear a dangerous rival out of his way; but this one! The thing was inconceivable — almost as inconceivable to these outsiders as it had at first appeared to István himself. Nor had the others ever sought a more remote explanation of István's habit of ridiculing Vincenz than the young Hungarian's somewhat malicious and laughter-loving disposition. It was not likely, either, that a man who meant to do such a villainous deed would execute it in this strangely conspicuous manner. István's quietness of demeanor alone was enough to make suspicion hesitate. It did not strike his companions that this very subdued quiet was in itself unnatural. Mr. Howard, of the two, felt the more distrustful. He remembered now that he had always disliked Tolnay; and he told himself that the furious temper of young foreigners in general, and of young Hungarians in particular, was well-known and indisputable. But the motive? The motive eluded him entirely! An unexpected light was soon to fall upon the motive.

As for Gretchen, her condition was like that of a person fighting with all her failing strength against an enemy who is slowly conquering her, and into whose face she feels a strange reluctance to look. If for one moment she pauses in the fight, she knows that she will be vanquished; and after that, there will be something she shudders to think of — a sharp agony, a dreary blank — something she does not perfectly realize, which she scarcely understands, but something that she feels will stab her heart within her.

Already her courage was failing by slow degrees. Soon she would have to look that enemy in the face. She saw that the Bohemian was silently busied with the piece of rope which he had taken off the bundle. He was knotting it round the handle of the lantern. It was with a strained and palpitating curiosity that she watched him, as on his hands and knees he crept to the edge; and when, still silently, he slowly and cautiously lowered the light down into the hole, then Gretchen felt a rush of terror at her heart. That action seemed like the final acknowledgment of the dreadful thing she had feared. The visor had been torn off the face of the enemy, and she stared back helpless at him, at his gaunt features and grinning teeth. This it was she had feared, this she had shrunk from confessing, but which now she scarcely dared to doubt.

The color ebbed slowly from her face; she put out her hand to save herself from falling, for a sudden faint feeling had overpowered her. It was to Mr. Howard's arm that she found herself clinging, though she scarcely noticed who it was. She was thankful only for the steadiness and the strength which supported her in this fit of weakness. The violence of reaction had brought on a convulsive shiver, and as she clung to her support she was talking in an excited whisper.

"Oh, he is not dead! tell me that he is not dead!" she implored, trembling. "I am so frightened! I am so wretched!"

Mr. Howard looked down into the pale upturned face beside him. The eyes were imploring him for a word of hope, the lips were quivering. She was very young and very impressionable, he told himself, and no doubt German girls were more given to hysterics than English girls. It was no wonder if this scene had proved too much for the fiber of a woman's nerve.

"My dear child, I do not know; we must hope for the best," he said, tenderly almost, for so grim and middle-aged an Englishman. But his true thought penetrated all the same when he said, "He was your father's friend, was he not?"

"He was more to me than that!" she said, with a sudden burst of tears. She shook from head to foot with the vehemence of her sobs. She did not know what she had said, nor to whom she had said it. She was half wild with a new pain that had over-powered her, which was beating her spirit down to the ground without mercy and without hope.

She was very young and very impressionable, Mr. Howard repeated to himself, and Germans were undeniably given to hysterics. But neither youth, nor sensitive-ness, nor even hysterics, seemed able to account for the passionate flow of these tears. Perhaps the memory of the somewhat distant time when he had wooed and won Lady Blanche helped Mr. Howard to see the truth of this case more clearly.

Certainly, he did see the truth, and at the same moment of recognizing it, it appeared to him that a new and startling flood of light was thrown upon the events of the evening. It opened a hitherto unsuspected region of possibilities; unfortu-nately, also, it seemed to seal yet more hopelessly the fate of Vincenz Komers.

All this Mr. Howard rapidly reviewed, even while he was leading Gretchen away from the dreaded spot, and forcing her to sit down and rest. He was an English gentleman, not only as to the shape of his wide-awake and the cut of his coat, but also as to his mind and heart. He would not have allowed even her brother, could he help it, to see her weeping as she was weeping now. He felt a very keen pity for this girl, and a very earnest desire to do something towards her consolation; but as he led Gretchen away from the spot, his face betrayed far less emotion than it was wont to show at the moment of losing a particularly fine salmon-trout.

His thoughts were actively pursuing the workings of this newly discovered mo-tive. Tolnay now stood in a more suspicious light. But Mr. Howard was a practical Englishman. He would raise no accusation until he had sifted his evidence. The first thing to be done was to discover some clue that would support the suspicion thus formed. In order to do this, he must search carefully. Mr. Howard was well-acquainted with numberless instances in which such small circumstantial evidence as a wisp of straw or the impression of a boot nail had clearly established the guilt or innocence of the accused. So, while the other two were busied in lowering down to the hole the lantern whose glimmering rays scarcely attempted to pierce the black void below, Mr. Howard searched with a sort of fierce energy. He went over the ground carefully; he examined every step with minute attention, he crawled and scrutinized and calculated with dogged perseverance. And he found something. It is not necessary here to state what precise clue it was which he found. Mr. Howard himself, having found it, could not feel sure whether it pointed most towards Tolnay's guilt or his innocence. It was capable of various interpretations, and for the present he resolved to betray this clue to no one. When he emerged from the bushes, he was cautiously wrapping up some small object, and stowing it away in the depth of his coat pocket.

The lantern was standing on the moss again; they had given up their attempt. The Bohemian's gentle face was pale and grave; he had scarcely spoken since the moment of the alarm; he it was who had first given up all hope.

"If the idea were not so absurd," said Kurt to his friend, "I should be inclined to think that this business was not a mere accident. I suspect that someone might, if he chose, enlighten our ignorance."

There was no name mentioned, but Mr. Howard understood the allusion perfectly. He looked at Kurt, and seemed to hesitate for a moment.

"Look here!" he said, "I understand you quite well; but I have a reason for asking you to keep quiet for the present. Do not let that man guess that anyone suspects him. Will you promise?"

Kurt looked as much surprised as it was in his nature to be; but he sealed his assent with a nod.

Chapter XXXVI

The Day of Reckoning

"When the scourge
Inexorable, and the torturing hour
Calls us to penance."

— Milton

IT was past ten o'clock when Gretchen found herself on the homeward way. Mr. Howard had taken command of the party, decreeing that the Bohemian should guide Gretchen back, while he and Kurt pursued the search as well as they could. Nobody knew exactly where Baron Tolnay was, and nobody seemed to care very much. He had disappeared during the search; for when for the last time they returned to the tree stem, he was no longer sitting where they had left him. It was taken for granted that he had gone home in advance.

In their words, they still clung to hope, although there was very little hope alive in their hearts. They said aloud that the next day must bring a solution to the riddle of tonight; but they felt that the riddle could have no answer but one.

Gretchen obeyed Mr. Howard mechanically. She followed the glimmer of the Bohemian's lantern, round which there ever hovered a cloud of moths bumping against the hot pane, and dropping to the ground with singed wings. Her steps dragged heavily; and she was crying a little as she went along, partly from the sheer oppression. of bodily fatigue, and partly from the wretchedness against which she was too weak to fight.

That walk in the moonlight through the forest was a thing not to be forgotten. She passed by the same trees and bushes, the same groups of toadstools, which she had passed in the morning; but they stood now without color and without life — in the moonlight they all looked like the ghosts of themselves. Every spot where she remembered having exchanged a word with Vincenz Komers struck her with a shock of painful recognition. It had borne a different meaning then from what it bore now.

What a glorious day had seemed in the future the day on which *Gaura Dracului* should be discovered! And what a day of misery it had become in the present! How short-lived had been the triumph of discovery! How swift the blow which followed! It was with shuddering recoil that she turned away from the very thought of the place. But she could not escape the haunting image. It was too near and clear to be suppressed.

Her fancy was incessantly at work — hovering with feverish persistence around that spot, and painting the details of that which must have been. The step over the edge, the fall, the last wild clutch into empty air, the sickening sense of void below; and then — what was that the Bohemian had said of the fallen kids? Not another sound, everything quiet in a moment.

Everything quiet in a moment! Could any length of description have brought home the truth with a more cruel clearness?

And then, with a start and a violent effort of will, she would rouse herself and try to shake off these horrid fancies. They were but fancies after all — as yet. But her will had no power over her unnaturally strained imagination. Again and again, she pictured to herself the scene; she harrowed herself with extravagant thoughts. That he should have died this death of all others, this secret and fearful death — that it was which was the sharpest pang. In her despair now, she thought that any mode of dying which was not this mode might have been borne with resignation. She thought that the traveler who breaks his neck over a precipice in the Alps is a man not to be

pitied, but to be envied. He can lie dead in the sun- shine at least, and his body will
be carried home, and wept over by his friends, and loving hands will tend the flowers
on his grave. Even the sailor who is drowned at sea may be washed ashore someday,
and put to rest in some hallowed ground. While here, there is no coming back, no
last look, no grave even, according to the usage of the world. Oh, it was maddening,
distracting! It would have been no great wonder if, during this night walk, Gretchen's
mind had given way under the pressure of torturing thought, which she was helpless
to shake from her.

After a time, those thoughts grew so imperious, preying upon her with such
merciless persistence, that she lost the sense of her surroundings, and walked on mechanically, following the glimmer of that lantern in advance, not knowing how long
she had been walking thus, nor how much longer she would have to walk before
reaching home.

There were countless reproaches pricking her mind through the midst of the one
great grief. Each cold or unkind word which she had ever said to Vincenz Komers
came back to her memory now with unmerciful distinctness. How heavily they
weighed, and how hotly they burned!

Instinctively, she kept her eyes on the lantern, as she followed the track downward. Now she noticed that her guide was slackening his pace, and then he stopped
short altogether.

"Go on," she said, wearily, as she reached him;" I cannot rest here."

The words stood still on her lips, for, as she spoke, the man turned and held up
the lantern between them. It was not the Bohemian. Peering at her close, with the
light playing full upon his face, István Tolnay confronted her.

It was like the weird transformation of a nightmare; and, as in a nightmare, too,
Gretchen felt a cold weight of fear fall on her. There was no one else in sight; for
Tolnay had taken the lantern from the Bohemian and sent him on in advance.

As she met his eyes, Gretchen recoiled with a feeling of repulsion. He was as
loathsome to her at this moment as if he had been some poisonous reptile that had

started up in her path. She gave him one quick glance, half terror, half distrust; and then, without a second glance, and without a word, she pursued her way, walking with her head erect, and crying no longer now, for some revulsion of feeling had dried up the very tears on her cheek.

She walked hurriedly, but Tolnay kept beside her. In the very moment of recognition, when she had turned from him in disgust, he had begun to speak low and hurriedly. His words were pressed and passionate, his voice shook, and his eyes shone with a wild brightness; but Gretchen never looked towards him — she kept her gaze fixed straight ahead.

He told her that he loved her; that he must possess her or die; that no joy in this world was to him a joy without her love, and no price in the world too high to pay for it. And she walked on the while, pale and shivering, with misery in her eyes and scorn on her lips, knowing it to be useless to try and stem the current of his burning words; and knowing, too, that there was no escape for her from this — for if she attempted to run, he would stand and bar her passage. There was in his manner a violence still subdued, but ready to break out at a word or a look. For all the scornful pride in her bearing, Gretchen was yet trembling in mortal terror.

"Enough, enough!" she cried at last, as he paused. "This is not the time to talk of such things."

"This is not the time for silence," said István, "and I will be heard."

"Oh no! for pity's sake, no! What sort of man are you to speak to me of love in such a moment as this?"

"In such a moment as this!" He repeated the words with a jealous emphasis. "Is that man to stand between us always, whether alive or dead?"

"He is *not* dead," said Gretchen, fiercely. "What do you mean?"

"I mean that neither man nor ghost shall rob me of you. I mean that no wretched German scribbler, for all his caution and all his care — "

"Stop!" she cried, vehemently. "You shall not say a word against him!"

"Shall I not? But I tell you that I shall. If you put him up between you and me, I shall. You called him your friend — "

"He is my friend; I shall call him so a hundred times. There is no one whose friendship I am prouder of than his."

"And you say this to me?"

"To you or to anyone."

István laid his hand on her arm, standing still on the path and forcing her to stand still also and face him.

"You loved him," he said, in a whisper. "I have heard that; is that true?"

She felt the tightening grasp of his fingers on her arm, and she saw by the light of the lantern the frightful pallor of his face. But her terror of a minute ago vanished.

"You have heard right. I loved him — oh, with all my heart!" she cried, and burst into passionate sobs.

She felt no wonder at herself, nor at her own words, for it had not been the revelation of a moment which had made her own heart clear to her. It had been gradually growing clear during this wearisome walk through the forest. She wondered a little at not having known it before, at not having known it long ago; everything was so simple now and so hopeless. She had found the answer to all those questions which had tormented her; but alas! she had found them too late! And yet, through the very blackness of her misery, there pierced one ray of comfort: he had loved her — he had loved no other woman but her; that thought would be precious forever.

She had drooped her head, having made the confession; not in shame — she felt no shame in proclaiming her love — there was scarcely a blush on her cheek — it was only that for one moment she had allowed herself to think of what might have been. She did not see the change on Tolnay's face, but his voice tore her roughly from her dreams.

In the moment when she spoke, he had dropped her arm, and now his eyes shone dangerously.

"You loved him?" be repeated, slowly. "Then I am glad that I did what I have done."

"What have you done?" she asked, in a voice so weak and faint that it was a wonder he heard it at all.

István laughed. That laugh froze the blood in her veins.

"I showed him the way to *Gaura Dracului*."

"But you left him before you reached it."

"Yes."

"You gave him exact directions?"

"Very exact directions."

"You told him of the signal?"

"I did."

"You said a white handkerchief on the branch?"

"A white handkerchief on the branch."

"And you told him to go to the right?"

István looked at her for a moment fixedly; he drew one hard, deep breath before he answered —

"I told him to go to the left."

In the first instant, she did not perhaps realize to the full what it meant. It required a momentary look backward, a quick review of the spot in her memory, before she could understand the inevitable truth. If Vincenz Komers had turned to the left of the signal, he must have been lost. There was no possibility of escape, no margin left for hope.

It was very quick, that mental review and conclusion. She had stood for a moment fixed and motionless, all her powers of thought concentrated upon one point; then she staggered up to a tree, and remained there with her back against it. There was no color in her face, and no sound coming from her lips. If she had been a man, she would have struck him down where he stood; if she had been a Sibyl, she would have cursed him; if she had been a heroine of romance, she would have upbraided him at least with bitter words: but being only a weak girl, she did nothing and said nothing. She only stood confronting him, white and rigid, with her hands clasped convulsively across her breast, with pale lips parted and gray eyes dilated.

The very excess of the feelings which overpowered her took all expression, almost all intelligence, from her eyes; stupid and vacant, they stared back into his. There was scarcely a sign of life about her, but for the helpless twitching at the corners of her mouth. What can we do when our power of expression falls so far short of what we would express? Because she could not find words strong enough to utter, Gretchen uttered none at all.

Tolnay stood before her, grinding the heel of his boot deep into the moss, and gnawing his underlip fiercely.

Above her head, there was a flutter of great wings, and an owl flapped out into the darkness, crying Uhu-uhu, through the forest. That sound roused her; her stiffly clasped hands dropped down, and the blood began to mantle faintly in her cheek. A shivering cry broke from her lips. Back upon her fancy rushed all those fearful pictures which had haunted her before, but this time, they came as a certainty; and with them came a sense of pity, so aching, so keen, as to be almost intolerable. The wild clutch in the air — and then everything quiet! She had thought before that she was hopeless; she knew now how much she had still hoped a few minutes ago, before this word of certainty had been spoken.

When she looked up, Tolnay had come two steps nearer to her. "You wanted to know what sort of man I am — do you know it now? I have told you what I have done; ask yourself why I did it. Do you imagine that such love as this can be baffled? Do you think that a man who has not stopped at a crime will stop at any- thing less? I have proved my love well — ha, ha! What proofs has that German ever given you which could weigh against this one? Do you dare now to say that you will not belong to me, and that you will not love me?"

There was a wild triumph breaking out in his voice; it made Gretchen shrink away farther, in unutterable disgust.

"I never loved you," she said, trembling; "and now — I hate you."

"Ha! Do you say that? Then call together your friends and point to the murderer. Do you hesitate? I shall not hide myself. Tell it to the world, if you are so minded. But — " he came a step nearer, and lowered his voice — "what you will not tell them, I know, is that it is you who have made me do it."

"I?" cried Gretchen, in stupefied wonder — "I?"

"Yes, you alone. Have you not led me on, step by step, till I was mad? What have you been doing all summer but playing with me fast and loose?"

"It was not play," said Gretchen, with a sudden qualm. "I have been very foolish, but — "

"Foolish !" laughed István, roughly. "You have milder words for yourself than for me; you are only foolish, but I am criminal. Criminal I may be, but we are partners in crime at least. I claim your partnership. What have you meant with the smiles you have given me? What have you meant with your glances?"

"Nothing — nothing. Yes, I am guilty; but oh, spare me, Baron Tolnay — be merciful!"

"Have you had mercy with me all this long summer? I shall deal with you the same pity that you have dealt with me."

She was silenced. Yes, it was all true. She had played with him, she had led him on — O God! and was it this that she had led him to? Quite dumb, she stood before him; her anger even was dead within her. It was he now who was the judge, and she the sinner. There was not one word that she could say in her defense. How to tell him the truth? How to confess that his fortune and not himself had been the stake for which she had played? And at this moment, it seemed to Gretchen's roughly awakened conscience, that of the two, István was indeed the lesser criminal; and that if the blood of Vincenz Komers cried for vengeance, it was upon her head alone that the vengeance must fall.

The pang of remorseful pain which stabbed her was so sharp that she could do nothing but bow her head and suffer it in silence. She deserved it, as she deserved each bitter word from Tolnay's lips.

And Tolnay did not spare her. Now at last, his suppressed excitement broke out uncontrolled. His reproaches were fierce and cutting. He was a changed man altogether from the smooth Baron Tolnay of the salon and ballroom. The thin coat of varnish was pierced through, and close beneath it there lay the raw nature of a savage. His education and his principles were such as enabled him to shine very brilliantly in society, but they were not such as could restrain him at a moment like this. It was a very bright polish which he wore on the surface, but its quality could not stand the test of passion. There was rage and bitterness in what he said, and yet there was no word that spoke of remorse for the deed which had been done. Gretchen might well have wondered, as she had wondered often, what element it was which was missing in his nature. It was a very simple element indeed. It was only that he had no conscience. She had fancied that she saw this more than once before, but she had never believed that the want could be as total as it was here. Owing to the constitution of his mind, rather than to a personal reluctance, he would not have been capable of a premeditated crime — as little as he would have been capable of a premeditated act of any sort; but under a momentary influence, he was capable of anything, and he had been capable of this.

He paused at last in his wild reproaches, and looked for her to speak; but she had covered her face with her hands, and stood before him immovable and silent.

"And now, your answer — I am waiting for it; what have you to say?"

"Only to beg that you should leave me," she faltered, locking up.

"Gretchen!" There was a new menace in his voice; the wildness was breaking out afresh. "You dare not reject me, Gretchen!"

"I am guilty — very guilty," she said, trembling; "but Heaven knows I can give you no other answer."

He dashed the lighted lantern to the ground, so that the glass shivered and the flame went out.

"And both heaven and hell know that I have lost my soul for the love of you; and neither heaven nor hell shall cheat me of the prize!" His excitement was rising; but at this moment he checked himself, for there were sounds in the forest. Both he and Gretchen had forgotten how near they were by this time to the more frequented paths, and the voices of some woodcutters returning late from the hills struck upon them both with surprise. Gretchen uttered an exclamation of relief; Tolnay ground an oath between his teeth.

"Let it be for today; but we shall speak again — this is not the end. We have not done our reckoning yet; this night's work must be complete. Never think that I regret. Were it undone at this moment, I should begin it again; but there is no need — the work is well done. You may not be mine, but you can never be his. Is it you who are victor, or am I?"

And without waiting for any word of hers, István turned and vanished down the pathway.

Gretchen sank on her knees, half-fainting, by the tree stem. She was not far from home now; but she was so weak that she could not stand longer. She was so worn out and sick at heart that she sobbed helplessly in the dark.

Thinking of the man she loved, lying dead and alone, she prayed to God at this moment that she might die also. Must he never know of her love, nor of how her heart yearned for one word or one look of his? Every detail of his manner and look, once so familiar and so despised, became now inestimably precious: she had scarcely thought of them until this moment, when that figure was forever blotted out from her view. Ah! was it thus that her life's romance was to end? Was it thus that her love was to be slain? Had he died without one word from her?

Too late! Her chance was past. She knew it, as she crouched with her head against the tree stem. The bats and moths darted under the branches; but to her fevered fancy, they were not as ordinary bats and moths. The forest seemed peopled with flitting phantom shapes.

They circled high above her head, and shrieked through the air, "Too late! Too late!" and swooping down, they flapped their demo wings in her face and moaned — "Too late! Too late! Too late!"

Chapter XXXVII

Wisdom and Ignorance

"For reasons not to love him once I sought,
And wearied all my thought .
To vex myself and him: I now would give
My love, could be but live."

— Landor

THE next day brought no answer to the riddle.

A search was with difficulty organized; heavy payment was necessary to induce some half dozen of the more enlightened peasants of the valley to assist in sounding *Gaura Dracului*. But the enlightenment of these volunteers was after all but a question of comparison, and its measure proved to be considerably shorter than the measure of rope which was put into requisition. No man would venture beyond a certain depth; and despite hundreds of yards of rope and dozens of firwood torches, not the smallest trace was obtained. After several hours of hard labor, the men began to look at one another askance, and to murmur that a dead man's grave was not worth a live man's neck, and that it could matter little to the ill-fated German whether his bones were left to rot in the abyss, or dragged up to be pompously interred. So, throwing away their torches, and shouldering their implements, they marched downhill again, and the devils once more were left in quiet possession.

The news of the catastrophe spread quickly in the valley; the last of the departing visitors took with them this tale of horror in every shape of distorted variety. *Gaura Dracului*, of which till now no one had known the existence, was on everybody's lips today; the event was discussed at every house corner and under every doorway. The two lads who were engaged in dusting and stowing away for the winter the velvet chairs of the *Cursalon* enlivened each other's task with the latest edition of the story. In the restaurant of the old street, where the printed bill of fare had long since dwindled into a short scribbled list — quite a bill of fare *en négligé* — and where an almost unbroken quiet reigned in place of the once noisy chatter, the landlord enlarged upon the tale to the small handful of visitors. The reduced staff of waiters whispered to one another about it in their now frequent intervals of leisure. The Hercules fountain was more than ever surrounded by loiterers, whose gossiping comments mingled with the splash of the water. Even the musicians, as they made their last round this morning for a farewell concert, exchanged comments upon the deplorable event. The very children, who ran races in the deserted arcades which they had now all to themselves, spoke of the fearful thing which had happened in the mountains.

What heightened the excitement was the existence of suspense, for it was understood that there existed still a possibility of hope. It was the general run of outsiders before mentioned, those who knew least about the circumstances of the case, who most maintained this possibility. People hoped in exact proportion to their ignorance: those who knew least hoped most; the few who suspected the truth hoped less; and only the one person who knew it had said goodbye to hope. For Gretchen there existed no darkness — all was as distinct as daylight.

When she awoke that morning, after a short spell of exhausted sleep, it was with a numb feeling of some great misery, which had been deadened for the space of a few hours, and which now was waiting close at hand to seize upon her afresh.

As her mind slowly cleared, she remembered it all; her heart throbbed in dull pain, and she turned her face to the pillow. It seemed to her that at that moment her whole life stretched before her far into the future — wearisome, useless, and barren of all joy.

Many times that day did she repeat to herself the words of the Romanian song —

"My true love, ate I a hundred herbs,
Forget thee I could never more."

Ah no! Not on any mountain of the earth, not in any valley, not on any meadow however green, did there grow the herb Forgetfulness, which had power to give her oblivion.

She was ill all that day. Her head was burning, and her hands were cold as ice. Dr. Funk called it a nervous fever, and wrote a prescription of powders, which she took without resistance. Ascelinde was hysterical and tearful, pacing the room restlessly, and relieving her feelings by long outpourings to which no one listened. She was not hard-hearted, poor woman; and now that Dr. Komers had come to such a tragic end, she appeared to remember that after all he had been her family lawyer. She was rather disposed to consider it a liberty on the part of the mountains, or of *Gaura Dracului*, or of fate in general, to have dealt so summarily with a man who had conducted for so long the affairs of the Draskócs family.

What Gretchen suffered was quite a different sort of suffering from that which Ascelinde suffered, or even Adalbert. For them, there was the weight of suspense; there was a strained attention, constant listening for every sound, anxious glances from the window, nervous starts whenever the door was unexpectedly opened. Contrasted with the restlessness of the others, Gretchen's apathy looked like indifference. No sound or exclamation was enough to make her raise her head from her arm. It had not been possible to keep the truth from Adalbert. He could not look into Gretchen's face and not guess at a misfortune. With the irritation of an invalid, he had pressed them with questions, and then they told him that *Gaura Dracului* was found, but that it would have been better if the place had remained a secret to them forever. He fainted with the excitement; he was too weak to bear the shock; and from the moment that he revived from that dead faint, he sat listening in his chair for the footstep of the man who, as he querulously persisted, must still be alive, but whom Gretchen knew to be dead.

"Never fear, Gretchen," he would fretfully exclaim; "if he does not come back this morning, he will come this evening; if he does not come today, he will come back tomorrow."

Every word was a stab to Gretchen; she could answer only by a feeble smile. How she longed for this blessed ignorance! How she yearned for her former blindness! She alone to be wise, and to sit there helpless in her terrible wisdom, listening to these words of mocking encouragement! She was jealous of her parents' suspense; jealous of every start and glance which betrayed that they still could hope.

As the day wore on, the general hope grew fainter. The tidings, so hungrily looked for, did not come. The great mass of mountains lay peaceful as ever in the sunlight, and the sky above was pale and cloudless, innocent as the blue of an infant's eye.

Every hour might bring the solution of the riddle, but an hour after hour trailed by and did not bring it. Even upon Kurt's good-humored and careless face, an ever-deepening despondency had set its mark. Mr. Howard did not appear again at the hotel. He had gone away on sudden business, Kurt said, when he was questioned. Thus, the first day of suspense came to an end, and the second day began. It was an echo of the first; and the third was an echo of the second. Imperceptibly, the public excitement was losing its edge. Hope was abandoned, and the misfortune was beginning to be accepted as an accomplished fact.

Such was the general state of mind, but there was one person among the outside public who had arrived at her conclusions in a different fashion and at a different pace from the average of people. Princess Tryphosa had not forgotten a single word which István had spoken on the morning of that scene between them, and the conclusion she came to was that the lawyer's death could only be called an accident in the very widest sense of the word. She did not reach this stage in the first hour, nor even in the first day. It took her the whole first day to recover from the shock of surprise. On the second day, she said to herself, "Dr. Komers is dead;" and on the third day she said, "István has killed him."

It was on this third day, when the sun still shone with the chill brilliancy which, for so many weeks past, had been unbroken, that Gretchen formed the resolution of writing to Anna Komers. She bad scarcely thought of Anna Komers till now, nor of the blow which this would bring her. She had been too stunned herself to think of others. Now that the thought had once presented itself, it had about it a sort of bitter fascination which was not to be resisted. It was time that Anna Komers was acquainted with the truth; and Gretchen felt a jealous fear lest anyone else should break the news — for no one could do it so tenderly as she would do it. She was going to extinguish the one light of joy in a lonely woman's life; but she would extinguish it with such loving fingers that even the darkness would not be quite dark. It would be like laying a rude finger on a raw wound; but with a sort of grim satisfaction, Gretchen felt that she would have the strength to do it. She could no longer sit thus still and inactive; she must do something positive, or else this artificial fortitude would give way. Her heart would burst if she did not confide her secret to someone; and it was towards Anna Komers that she yearned — *his* sister — the meagre, querulous woman who had loved Vincenz to idolatry, and for whom Vincenz had sacrificed his whole life after having sinned so grievously against her. Anna should know now that she had triumphed. Gretchen would not spare herself. She would tell her the whole truth, and perhaps in the future she might be allowed to devote herself to the lonely old maid.

She wrote her letter sitting alone in the room which was their sitting room. It was very still, both inside the house and out. There was scarcely a living creature within sight of the windows, and there was hardly a sign of life about the short street of the place.

It was hard to write the words which told the bitter truth: the pen made many an unsteady stroke, for Gretchen's hand was shaking nervously.

She drew a long breath when that part of her task was over. Then, she hesitated for a moment, and her pale cheek flushed. Had she the courage to do the second part of her task? Would it not be better to bury the secret forever? — barren and useless secret, which could bear fruit for no one.

Her hesitation was short. It was not in her nature to do anything by halves; she would have no excuses, no modifications, no wrapping up of the truth, no patching together of the wrecks of her reasoning. Since her theories of life had failed her, she would, instead of clinging to the surviving fragments, cast their very last shred from her; since she had been too weak to live up to that reputation which the *prix de logique* had gained her, she would proclaim her mistake, instead of masking it — she would demolish her golden calf as publicly as she had erected it. So only by a courageous avowal rather than by timid concealment could the defeat bear a grim triumph of its own.

In haste, as though afraid that her resolution might waver, Gretchen went on writing.

"Do you remember the day when we quarreled, and the words that you said to me then? Perhaps you have forgotten them, but I have not. I used to boast then that I had no heart: ah, if I had not, I could not now be broken-hearted! You said to me then that I ought to be thankful for the love of such a man, that perhaps I should find out his value some day when it was too late. I want you to know that it has come true. I am more thankful for the thought that he has loved me than for any other blessing in the world. Now that he is gone, I have found out that I loved him — since when, I do not know, nor how it began. His great love, which I so little deserved, conquered me at last; but he never guessed it, since I did not guess it myself. The thought which weighs most heavily on my mind is that he should have died thinking me still the heartless creature that I tried to be. If he could have known that I never loved any man but him, and will never love any other; if he could know now that I am mourning for him — I should not have that bitter remorse in my heart. Twice he asked me to be his wife, and twice I refused. His love appeared to me then to be a trifle, or at most a burden; and now I would go on my knees, if any prayers could give me back one look of his, or one touch of his hand — one moment only to tell him of my penitence. He would not have offered me his love a third time — he vowed that he would not do it; and in time he would have found out that I am

not good enough to be his wife. But it is no use thinking of what cannot be now —
"

The color was burning high in Gretchen's face long ere she had reached this point; but she persevered — she meant to deal unmercifully with herself.

She paused for a moment, and passed her hand over her eyes; there was a mist of tears obscuring her sight, and one drop had fallen on the paper, blotting the fresh ink. Her head was aching wearily. The veins in her temples throbbed; there was a dull surging sound in her ears. The mist slowly cleared from her eyes, but that surging sound continued. It was a sound as of far-off waves washing along a coast, or the distant sigh of wind, or the murmur of many voices.

It was disagreeably persistent, and it was gradually but imperceptibly swelling. Could this be no more than a nervous fancy? The sound no longer seemed to be in her head; it was something outside her — something that was not even in the room, but which came floating through the window from down there in the valley.

Gretchen went to the window. The valley lay before her as lifeless as it had been during all this still afternoon, but not quite as silent. That sound was distinctly floating upward; it had detached itself from the aching throb of her head. It was individual and apart. It was growing less like the sweep of waves and wind, and more and more was it becoming like the murmur of many voices. And other ears than her own had heard the sounds: for here and there a window was flung open and a head was stuck out; a waiter with a napkin under his arm came out of the restaurant, and stood staring up the valley, though as yet there was nothing to be seen. Gretchen remained at the window with the pen still in her hand. She saw the empty road, without a living creature in sight; but that murmur of voices was swelling, and she kept her eyes fixed on the turn which in another moment must disclose to her the cause.

Chapter XXXVIII

The Story of a Toadstool

ONCE upon a time there was a little white toadstool, born of the damp dews, high up on the branch of a stately forest tree. It was snowy white; and when the moonbeams fell upon it, it looked like a white blossom that had grown up there by mistake. But the flowers that carpeted the forest scoffed and jeered at it, and said,

"What good are you to anyone? You are not beautiful, you are not a flower. We make the forest glorious with our painted bells, we gild the green moss, we scent the breeze, we nod from the hunter's cap, and sometimes the shepherd makes a nosegay of us for his love; but no one will gather you. No peasant even will take the trouble to eat you; for there are plenty like you at the foot of the trees. You are of no use; you are nothing but a toadstool!"

And the toadstool sighed, and repeated, humbly, "I know it; I am nothing but a toadstool!"

And summer and winter came and went for many, many years, and the toadstool still sat on the branch of the tree, and mourned over its melancholy lot. And it grew and grew, and hardened into wood, until it became as part of the tree; and as each spring came round, and the flowers awoke from their winter sleep, they looked up mockingly and began their old jests.

"What, old toadstool! are you there still?" the white anemones cried, and shook with laughter as they recognized him.

"He is grown so tough and so hard," said the spring crocuses, as they pointed up at him with their long straight fingers — "so tough and so hard that not even a hungry peasant would eat him now."

Even the violets, these spoiled children of the spring, nudged each other and tittered, as they peeped at the old weather-beaten toadstool.

"Old toadstool! Old toadstool! are you not yet tired of sitting up there? Has no one eaten you yet, old toadstool?"

And the flowers laughed till they shook again, and repeated their joke to the breeze, who liked it so well that he went murmuring through the forest, " It is only a toadstool, a useless old toadstool!" But one evening when the toadstool was weeping in the moonlight, with the dew drops sparkling all around it, the spirit of the forest passed by and said,

"Toadstool, why dost thou weep?"

And it answered, "I am weeping because I am only a toadstool; I am no use to anyone, and I have grown tough and hard. It would be more merciful if the wood-man would take his ax and strike me off the tree, to end my useless life."

The spirit answered, "Toadstool, weep no more. Listen no more to the jests of the foolish flowers: let them laugh now and jeer; they will yet bow before thee some-day. A great honor is in store for thee! I have placed thee there on the tree, and let thee grow large from year to year, so thou shouldst shine at night like a beacon and save the life of a noble man."

Hearing this, the toadstool wept no more. And when spring came round again, and the flowers crept out from under their mossy coverings, they did not laugh nor jest; the anemones hung their pale heads, the crocuses stood agape with wonder, and the violets hid their faces in the grass — for the flowers knew that though their painted bells might gild the moss and scent the breeze, though some fair shepherdess might prize them as a love token, yet they could never save a human life as the tough old toadstool had done.

Chapter XXXIX

The Political Spy

"The accident of an accident."

— Lord Thurlow

WHEN Vincenz, in blind confidence, turned, as he had been told, sharp to the left, he experienced a violent blow against his face, coming from a low-hanging branch which he had not perceived. His spectacles were struck off, as well as his hat, and it took him some minutes before he could disentangle himself from his position. Having succeeded, he looked about for his hat and spectacles. The hat was close at hand, but the spectacles were not; and the ground being in darkness, and he being half-blind without his glasses, a long and tedious search proved unavailing. He had just come to the conclusion that he must abandon the hope of finding them, when, looking up, he found himself again close to the tree with the white signal on it. The moonlight still struck upon it, and Vincenz put out his hand to feel the handkerchief.

It was no handkerchief, however, his first touch told him; he had expected to grasp thin folds, instead of which his hand came in contact with a hard and woody surface. He looked nearer, and felt it all over, unable at first to imagine what this enigmatical white object could be. It proved to be a large fungus grown out of the wood of the tree, of a shining gray texture, and whitened by the moonlight into the semblance of a dazzling pale flower. Even a man less shortsighted and less absent-

minded than Vincenz might, in this deceitful light, have taken a fungus for a handkerchief.

He had mistaken the signal then, and if the handkerchief were not on this tree,
it must be on some other tree a few paces farther on. A few paces farther on sounds
a simple matter indeed; but a few paces in which direction? was the question to be
decided. Having groped about for several minutes on the ground, Vincenz had lost
all sense of direction. He took his chance now, turning the way which seemed to him
most likely, but which happened to be one of the numerous wrong ways instead of
the only right one. He went on from tree to tree, examining each trunk, and coming
upon many more toadstools, but no handkerchief. When he had examined more
than half a dozen trees, he came to the conclusion that he had turned the wrong way,
and again changed his direction. More toadstools here, and as little sign of a handkerchief as before. The first direction must have been the right one after all, he
thought; but which way did it now lie? Who could tell him that? Not the solemn
beech trees all around, nor the squirrels that were asleep up there on the branches.
He had been walking more than ten minutes now, and he began to confess to himself
that he had lost his way. It is a confession which no one likes to make, even to himself;
and in this case, the fact was not only highly inconvenient, but might be of serious
consequences.

He quickened his pace, trusting more or less to fate; and when Vincenz chose to
put out his strength, his long-limbed frame could get over the ground at a marvelous
pace. He had relinquished his examination of the trees now, and, without any special
pang of regret, given up the hope both of the handkerchief and the hole. His only
thought was to rejoin the others. He walked on faster and faster, fancying that he
recognized the surroundings now and then, and expecting at every turn to come
upon the waiting people around the fallen tree trunk. Thus, thanks to his walking
powers, Vincenz in less than half an hour was entirely out of earshot, and getting
rapidly farther every moment from the point which he wished to reach. The trees
were all so exactly alike, and Vincenz was so helpless without his spectacles, that more
than once he was deceived into believing himself close to his object. He was sure of

it at last when all at once a faint glimmer of a light shone out far ahead. He might have been mistaken the first time, for the light was uncertain; but when it flashed out again, he saw that it was real, and with a renewal of hope and an acceleration of pace he walked straight towards it. He knew that the Bohemian carried a lantern with him, in case of their being overtaken by darkness before reaching home, as would be the case today. This certainly must be the light of the lantern, for it glowed deep orange in contrast to the white moonlight. He could see nothing of the surroundings, nor any moving figure, for the circle of light was feeble; he only saw that orange speck, and towards it he walked straight and fast.

Decidedly, it was a light kindled by human hands. It grew and grew, till it became larger even than he expected it to be — larger than a lantern. He kept his eyes upon it, not daring to look away, and it went on growing and growing, till its size could have furnished light enough for at least a dozen lanterns. It was a small smoldering fire, as Vincenz saw as he drew nearer, and therefore it was evident that this was not the place where he had left his friends. But he did not slacken his pace for all that, for by this time he was beginning to feel mildly desperate. He was weary of walking among the trees and seeing nothing but moonlight and shadow. "Where there was a fire, there must be hands that had kindled it and the same men who had hands to light a fire, might be presumed to possess tongues with which they could direct a lost traveler how to find the right way.

Then he lost sight of it, and walked on for a few minutes, seeing nothing, when all at once it started up again, close before him this time. The orange spot had become a mass of half-burned firwood still flaming here and there, and sinking lower every instant into the bed of gray ashes below. The trees around stood so close as to bar the moonlight, and the leaping of the last orange flames lighted up the underside of a few branches with vivid touches of yellow.

The sudden flood of light dazzled Vincenz; he saw nothing but the dancing flame, and some very deep shadows round it. The shadows were unusually deep — almost definite in their shape, but perfectly immovable.

He walked up close to the fire, kicked one of the outlying embers in order to assure himself of its reality, and then recovered from a violent stumble.

Strangely enough, it was over one of the immovable shadows that he had stumbled, which appeared to be more substantial than shadows usually are. At the same time, the shadow developed some other strange attributes: it started up from a horizontal into a perpendicular position, and in a very unshadow-like manner seized hold of the lawyer's arm. The shadow had a voice too, it seemed, and commenced proving the fact by muttering some unintelligible but uncomplimentary sounding expletives between its teeth.

Shadow or no shadow, Vincenz had no idea of being held in this unceremonious fashion; he shook his right arm free, but in the same instant of time felt his left arm imprisoned. The shadow on the other side of the fire had become alive also, and was unquestionably more substantial than the first. The lawyer's eyes were beginning to grow more accustomed to the light, and he now recognized on each side of him a man on whose features the firelight fell with great distinctness. He could see that the first was gaunt, unshaved, hollow-eyed, and repulsively dirty in aspect; and that the second man had all these qualities enhanced, and, as it were, enlarged by the superior size and strength of his frame.

At first, Vincenz was very much at a loss how to account for their existence and conduct; but when, after a few seconds, he was able to distinguish their appearance more closely, the truth gradually dawned upon him. He began to recall the details of the milkmaid's story, and of the picture which she had drawn of her assailant: "half a soldier and half a demon" had been the definition which she was reported to have given; and if in the individuals now before Vincenz there was nothing which, except by a stretch of the imagination could be called diabolical, there certainly was something which flavored of warfare. They both wore tattered trousers, with a narrow red line down the sides, which gave them a military stamp even in the midst of their ruin. Such trousers had been worn by the pillager of the milkmaid's cheese. It was only reasonable to suppose that he found himself in presence of the milkmaid's robber, and of a second and smaller edition of the same type. This opinion was presently confirmed by the vigor with which they ransacked his pockets — a proceeding to which he much objected, but which, in the face of two long-barreled pistols, he felt helpless to avert.

Besides the pistols, the taller of the two men possessed a musket and a steel knife, with an elaborately engraved blade, at this moment stuck in and out of his trousers just below the knee. In the ordinary course of things, the knife would have been sheathed in the top of his high boot; but in this case the arrangement was rendered unfeasible by the fact that the two men did not possess one boot between them. The handkerchief, pocketbook, and purse of the captive were thrown aside, perhaps for later consideration. Some remains of sandwich, however, were seized upon — the men tore the stale bread out of each other's hands and devoured it greedily; the flask which Vincenz had carried, and which was about half full of spirits, was joyously clutched.

The examination was over. The smaller man looked at the larger, and shook his head; the larger one returned the look, and scratched his head. They consulted together in some unknown tongue, either Servian or Romanian; then put some questions to Vincenz, which were, of course, unintelligible. Further dissatisfaction. *"Njamcz — Njamczule"* (German), they said to each other. Another short consultation, and then it was signified to Vincenz that he must take a place by the fire.

This was exactly what Vincenz desired to do; he was tired and chill, and in the midst of the lonely forest this wild fireside looked almost like a home. Despite the doubtful security of his position, it was with a sigh of heartfelt satisfaction that he let himself down on the grass. The robbers placed themselves carefully one on each side of him, and then there followed a short interval of silence. The two men looked alternately at each other and at their captive. The elder scratched his head more than once. It was very evident, now that the first excitement had subsided, that the possession of their prisoner somewhat embarrassed them. A prisoner who walks straight into his captor's hands is no doubt a valuable prize; captives are as little in the habit of doing so, as roast-pigeons are accustomed to fly into the mouths of the hungry. Such conduct was gratifying, the very *beau ideal* of a captive's behavior; but now the situation was becoming puzzling. What were they to do with him? Each man racked the small amount of brains he had in order to find a satisfactory answer to the question. During this silence, Vincenz had a fancy that he could hear somewhere in the forest, very far off, the sound of human voices shouting. He was not sure that he heard right, but yet the thought did cross his mind that those might be the voices of the party calling to him. He raised his voice upon this chance; but the shout was instantly stifled by a very dirty hand, while the unanswerable argument of a loaded pistol forced him to hold his tongue. *"Tasch! tasch!"* (hush, hush!) was hissed into his ear from either side. The distant voice soon died off in another direction, and was heard no more.

The two men resumed their position as before, again scratching their heads, and again gazing at their captive.

Vincenz saw their indecision, and waited patiently for them to decide. He made himself very comfortable by the fire in the meantime, for the glowing embers were grateful on this chill autumn night. Nothing would have been easier than for these two men to put an end to him quietly, and hide the traces forever in this dense forest. Vincenz fully recognized the force of their position and the weakness of his own, but at the same time he saw no immediate grounds for alarm.

In the first moment, the robbers had looked formidable enough, but alarm had quickly given way to pity. They looked so hungry, so ragged, so footsore and weary, that, thinking of the hundred and one stories that had been circulated in the Hercules Baths, and of the number of patrols who had walked about with fixed bayonets to protect the place from surprise, Vincenz could almost have laughed aloud. These two starved deserters from the Servian army had kept the place in terror for weeks; they were the kernel of truth, stripped of its outer shell of exaggeration. Lying on the grass beside them was the clean-picked skeleton of some small forest bird, and a number of barberry branches stripped of their very last berry. This little heap of wrecks was eloquent in its ghastly tale. Vincenz wished most heartily that he could conjure to the spot some remains of cold meat which he remembered having been thrust back into the provision basket. He could well imagine how those poor sunken eyes would kindle, had he been in the position to present a chicken bone to each man. They were a pitiful sight, poor wretches; and yet, by virtue of those long-barreled pistols, Vincenz was in their power. It was in a very amateur fashion that they now set about the examination of their booty. First, they emptied the purse, and managed to lose about half the contents in the moss while quarrelling over it; then they ransacked the pocketbook, under the delusion that it was another sort of purse: finally, they spread out the pocket-handkerchief, turned it over and over in perplexity, but could make nothing of the article. Vincenz watched the sacking of his purse with equanimity; but he winced when they attacked the pocketbook, for this was the same battered old pocket- book which, a year ago, Gretchen had stitched together for him, and for the sake of those stitches Vincenz valued it far above every other possession.

While they searched, the two men handed the articles backward and forward to each other across their prisoner, consulting at the same time as to the great question which weighed on their minds. Vincenz did not know what they were saying, but their conversation was about as follows:

"Ha, Sancu!" said the smaller bandit, who was loquacious in speech and apparently undecided in manner.

"He, Duman?" answered the larger one, who spoke laconically, and looked inflexible.

"He was hardly worth catching, was he? There is nothing of any good except the spirits in that bottle. Let's have a pull, Sancu," stretching across Vincenz a brown hand-stained with red barberry juice.

"Wait for your turn, Duman," says Sancu from behind the flask.

"Ha, Sancu!"

"He, Duman?"

"What shall we do with him?"

Upon this, Sancu scratched his head repeatedly, and having handed the flask across, proceeded dubiously to gnaw his thumbnail, as though expecting to suck wisdom therefrom.

"Ha, Sancu!"

"He, Duman?"

"Shall we let him run?" asked the smaller man, whose heart was perhaps softened by the spirits.

"Let him run and bring down the soldiers on our backs? A pistol shot would be quicker than that;" and Sancu's fingers played with the trigger for a moment.

Duman, strengthened by another pull at the flask, expressed some contemptuous opinions regarding the soldiery of the country.

"Let them come! Poor fellows, they will walk through the soles of their shoes before they get a sight of us."

"True," said Sancu; "they might lose each other, but they would not find us."

"Ha, ha! It is not everyone who knows the *muntze* (mountains) as well as his pocket; ha, Sancu ?"

"This big *Njamezule* does not, or he would not be sitting here between us now."

"It would be a pity to shoot him, I think; ha, Sancu?"

"He looks as if he could fight," said Sancu; and then the flask being drained to the last drop, both Sancu and Duman sat still, staring at their prisoner in some perplexity, and quite as curious to know what the issue would be as Vincenz himself.

A new turn was given to matters now by the introduction of tobacco on the scene. These novices had failed to discover in an inner pocket of the lawyer's coat a cigar case containing two cigars. Here was a scope for giving expression to some of the compassion which he felt towards his captors. Vincenz forgot his precarious position at sight of the absolute beatitude which spread over the two haggard faces. "Tobacco lovers who have not sniffed the scent of the divine herb for weeks past," was written on both countenances. And this was something higher than the pipe of their ordinary life. A cigar had hitherto been a sort of unattainable ideal in the eyes of these two men. But the conduct of Sancu and Duman was characteristically distinct at this supreme moment of their lives. Sancu showed his independence and decision by immediately taking up a paper which lay on the grass — one of the papers which had come to light in the examination of the booty — and pushing it into the red embers to light the cigar. Duman, on the contrary, seemed unable to make up his mind thus quickly to exhaust the spell of bliss which was contained in these three inches of brown weed. The delight was so exquisite that it required to be dwelt upon and drawn out to the utmost limits of its tension. He first gazed at the cigar, then smelled it with great enjoyment, then licked it all over, finally wrapped it up in the half-burned piece of paper which Sancu had thrown aside, and stored it away carefully inside his linen shirt. But the process did not end here. The treasure had to be taken out at intervals in order that Duman should assure himself of its reality: there were moments of indecision as to whether he would not yield to the temptation of immediate enjoyment, and then another wrapping up and another stowing away of the treasure next to his skin. Finally, a bright thought struck him. If he did not make sure of the cigar, it was certain that Sancu would take it from him by the right of might. This ended all indecision; and in another moment a second curl of smoke rose up from the lawyer's right side.

The combined effects of the spirits and the tobacco were beginning to tell upon both men. A more genial frame of mind was stealing over the bandits. They began to chant a drinking song — a monotonous drawling tune, somewhat nasal in accent, but wild and striking amid these surroundings —

> "Marko, the great Marko,
> Was a warrior strong;
> Ere he went to battle,
> Drank he deep and long.
>
> Deep drank the great Marko,
> for the wines were good,
> Steeled his arm for battle,
> Made him thirst for blood.

> *Brothers! Marko's children!*
> *This is what I think:*
> *Would ye fight like Marko,*
> *First like Marko drink!"*

It died off by degrees; it grew more drawling and more dismal. First Duman's head sank down on his arms; Vincenz thought he was asleep, but in the next moment, he looked up drowsily.

"Ha, Sancu!"

"He Duman?"

"We will not shoot him now, will we?"

Sancu was too far gone to answer with anything but a shake of the head. It was evident that the cigars had turned the scale, and that, for the present at least, the lawyer's life was in no danger.

They were both asleep, one on each side of him. Vincenz himself felt mildly drowsy. His sensations were of an agreeable sort. The position he was in was somewhat ludicrous, if also precarious.

This was a new experience of life certainly: it brought with it a pleasurable feeling of excitement; it was a refreshing change from the drudgery of desk existence. He wondered what the others would think of his disappearance, whether they would be anxious. It did not occur to him that they would conclude that he had fallen a victim to *Gaura Dracului*, especially as he had not seen *Gaura Dracului* himself, and therefore was unable to realize the danger. It was very pleasant sitting here; he was stiff and tired with his long walk, and felt a disinclination to rise, a drowsy unwillingness to move. And yet, this was the moment for escape, if ever there was one. With an effort he succeeded in rousing himself.

Sancu was snoring, Duman was breathing as softly as an innocent child in its cradle. It was best to leave them when in this Christian peacefulness of soul; after a few hours' sleep, they might change their minds about shooting him. He thought of disarming them for greater safety; but Sancu slept with his pistol in his hand, and Duman slept with his under his body, so that project had to be abandoned.

Vincenz rose to his feet softly. He had nothing to do but to walk away noiselessly; the inexperienced bandits had taken no precautions to prevent his escape. With a sort of delightful naive confidence, they had left his hands and feet untied. The lawyer stood for a moment looking down at them; they neither of them moved. He walked away a few steps and looked back; they still lay immovable. Now he quickened his pace, and paused only when he had got to a distance of fifty yards. Everything was silent. His departure had been unnoticed then, and he was free. But just now some spirit, good or evil, whispered a thought into his ear. He remembered that on the grass beside the sleeping robbers there lay that old pocketbook, which was worthless except for those few stitches in its battered cover. He had for so long held it precious as a treasure that he felt it now impossible to abandon it thus to its fate. "Was it to be fingered again by the robbers' dirty fingers, or perhaps left to lie and rot in the forest? Were the snails to crawl over it, and the spider to use it as a convenient scaffolding for its web? Was the winter snow to bury it, and the April rains to melt it into pulp? That could never be; and without giving himself time for further reflection, Vincenz had turned and was retracing his steps. It was without exception the most foolish act he had ever been guilty of in his life. For a man of his age — a man who, moreover, was generally supposed to be a cool-headed lawyer — deliberately to risk his life for the sake of a mere memory, was a rashness little short of folly.

He tried to temper his folly with prudence. When he got within a few paces of the sleeping men, he dropped on his knees, and thus on all fours approached the spot where the brigands still lay immovable. He could thus pass noiselessly over the dry, withered grass, which had crackled so obnoxiously under his footsteps. His empty purse and the scattered coins lay beside Sancu; but he scarcely saw those — he saw only the battered pocketbook on the grass. The lawyer's hand crept towards it; his fingers closed over it, and, clutching it eagerly, he turned to go the way he had come.

Perhaps his gesture had been too unguarded, for a dead twig, brittle with long dryness, snapped just then. Sancu turned his head sleepily, and for one moment Vincenz found himself staring close into a pair of startled and only half-awakened eyes. There was an oath muttered, and Sancu scrambled to his feet; while Vincenz, not waiting to see more, had risen also, and was running with all his strength and swiftness blindly into the dark forest. How he thanked Providence as he sped along for the length of limb with which it had pleased to bless him! Behind him there were angry cries and the sound of a momentary confusion; then a pause, and then the sharp crack of a pistol shot. The bullet whistled past him, several yards wide of the mark, and Vincenz ran on unhurt. He listened for more shots, but nothing followed; the cries even broke off. He stood still to recover breath. The pocketbook was tightly grasped in his hand. It was evident that he was not being pursued. That one shot, discharged in the first flurry of awakening, had been enough to salve the brigands' conscience, and they now stood staring at each other, open-mouthed indeed with wonder, but not exhibiting much distress.

"Ha, Sancu!" said Duman.

"He, Duman?" said Sancu.

"Are you sorry that the *Njamcz* is gone?"

"I am glad, Duman."

No doubt, as they turned over to sleep again on the moss, the dreams of these simple robbers will have been all the sweeter for the unlooked-for solution of their perplexity.

There was no need to run now; and Vincenz, slackening his pace, groped on in the darkness. How long he walked he did not know; he rested at intervals, and went on again, without ever coming upon a distinct path. After a time, the trees lightened, and then ceased. Vincenz found himself walking down a steep incline, clothed, as far as he could ascertain by this light, in brushwood and fine tufted grass. This was all as it should be. He had come uphill to get here, therefore he must necessarily go downhill to reach the Hercules Baths. Here also there was no path, and the grass was slippery; so, having walked some hours, and coming upon a sheltered spot, Vincenz, in sheer weariness lay down to sleep. It was no use walking on in the dark. Dawn would in all likelihood show him the Hercules Baths at his feet.

When he awoke, the first streak of dawn was in the sky. The thin, cold light of early morning was over the scene before him, but it did not show him the Hercules Baths at his feet. This was a wider landscape, with a great stretch of sky overhead. It was all a mass of undulating forest, thickly grown, and unbroken by those rocky points which gave to the Hercules valley its peculiar character of beauty. Here, too, there was much beauty, but of a tamer, less rugged sort. There was but one break in the uniformity of the autumn-tinged landscape; and that break consisted of an irregular assembly of what, at this distance, looked like dirty-white molehills, inhabited apparently by gigantic moles. What between the mistiness of the dawn, and his own ignorance, Vincenz was for a time utterly at a loss what to make of the molehills; and half in curiosity and half in hope, he set off towards them, by good luck hitting anon upon a rough cart track, which ran past the bottom of the hill, and made straight for the mysterious, yellow-white specks.

He was very cold and very hungry — furiously hungry, as he suddenly became conscious. If he thought now of the cold chicken in the provision basket, it was not for the sake of the robbers, but for his own. He was tormented by thirst, too, and there were no signs of water in sight. He walked on with the step of a hungry man, seeing no sign of life until he had drawn quite close to the molehills. Here, a bushy head stuck out of an opening told him that the inhabitants were not moles, but human beings; that the mounds, therefore, were huts, and the whole a village.

He entered the first hut — or rather descended into it, for it was no more than a square, deep hole dug in the ground, with an enclosure of plaited rushes cemented with mud, and a flat roof of the same construction. Within this enclosure, where, by reason of his stature, Vincenz could not attempt to stand upright, there were assembled a congregation consisting of one man, two women, several children (Vincenz counted five, and there seemed to be as many more indistinctly visible in corners), a cow, a sheep, and two pigs. He was stared at with very evident astonishment, and answered with shakes of the head when he tried the experiment of both German and Hungarian. The man who was evidently the master of the house was reclining on a flat wooden bench, and smoking, while two women and the elder of the children were working by the sweat of their brow.

The language in which they spoke Vincenz recognized as the same used by the peasants of the valley, and therefore Romanian. When he asked for *apa* (water), the one word of the language which circumstances had taught him, he was directed to a wooden cask that stood in a corner. Towards this, Vincenz made his way, stumbling as he passed over two pigs and several children. He dipped a small earthenware pot into the cask, and to his surprise found himself drinking a very tolerable white wine. He had not yet learned that wine is a commodity more easily obtained than water in this rich but somewhat disorganized part of Europe.

There was nothing further to be got there; and Vincenz, half-choked by the stifling atmosphere, made his way back to the fresh air.

Here a knot of curious peasants had gathered to stare at the strange phenomenon of a civilized human being. The whole village street was in a state of ferment, unable to account for the existence of this tall, bearded, and pale-faced stranger.

Vincenz was escorted by a *cortége* as he made his way onward; but he had not gone very far when his progress was unexpectedly and violently checked. A handful of ruffian-like individuals were approaching him up the street. So disreputable was their attire, and so unkempt their appearance, that had not a recent and close acquaintance with the mountain-robbers assured him of their individuality, Vincenz would have been inclined to consider that these were the bandits. Appearances are proverbially deceitful; far from being bandits, it was evident, from the respectful demeanor of the peasants, that these ragged and barefooted individuals were persons not merely "dressed in a little brief authority," but of recognized standing. As they drew nearer, Vincenz was able to see that there existed a certain uniformity about the rags they wore: each man had on his head a sheepskin cap, more or less mangy and more or less filthy; and each one also wore at least some remains of what had once been a long gray cloak.

The peasants made way as they approached; Vincenz found himself in the center of a circle. They spoke to him in Romanian, and he understood nothing; then one man stepped forward, and in Hungarian explained to him that, in case of not being able to give a satisfactory reason for his presence, he was to consider himself under arrest. Thanks to the intricacies of the Damianovics cause, Vincenz's acquaintance with the Hungarian language was sufficient for the occasion. He inquired the cause of this strange arrest.

"An unauthorized and suspicious traversing of the frontier," replied the least ragged of the ruffian-like men.

"Which frontier?" asked Vincenz, bewildered.

"The frontier of Romania."

"This, then, is Romania?"

Yes, he was told, this was the great and glorious country of Romania, which he had dared to invade unsanctioned, but which no stranger could invade unpunished. These individuals, some of whom were barefoot, and the best preserved of whom had their feet swaddled in checked woolen rags (the *Opinca* of the country), were nothing less than members of the corps of *Dorobanze* (Frontier Guardians), whose patriotic zeal had risen fifty per cent in this time of war.

"If you have papers to prove yourself harmless," said the first speaker, sternly, "produce them; if you have none, you are our prisoner: follow us!"

The ruffian-like individual's speech was received by the crowd with a murmur of applause. The peasants pressed round again to see what the stranger would do.

It was a moment of perplexity to Vincenz. He knew himself to be perfectly harmless, and in no way endangering the safety of the great and glorious Romanian State, but he wondered how he was to prove it. As was his habit at critical junctures, he put up his hand to take off his spectacles and rub them; but the movement reminded him that he had no spectacles on. However, at the same time, he remembered that though he had no spectacles, he had a passport, and that, at once, would clear the way. Had not Tolnay sneeringly observed, in reference to the passport, that Vincenz was the only member of the party who could safely pass the frontier of Romania? The thought of that paper was grateful and comforting. In his inmost soul, he blessed Anna's sisterly anxiety. When he had risked so much to recover the pocketbook, he had not thought of the papers it contained; but now, it seemed as if this piece of folly was going to bear salutary fruits after all.

He took out the battered case; he opened it. The passport was not in the first flap, it was not in the second, not in the third. In the fourth, there was a paper, but it was not the passport; it was the last letter he had received from Anna. With great distinctness, Vincenz now remembered that Sancu and Duman had lit their cigars with the fragments of a paper which exactly answered to the description of the missing passport. And he himself had presented those cigars of his own free will. Oh, irony of fate!

Involved in these painful reflections, Vincenz stood in the center of the circle, but was roused speedily out of his train of thought by his former interrogator, who calmly possessed himself of the letter which Vincenz still held, and submitted it to a close examination. It was turned over suspiciously, and handed about from man to man. Heads were shaken and shoulders shrugged. There was a great deal of murmuring and undertone whispering which resulted in the question —

"What is your name?"

"Vincenz Komers."

"What profession do you follow?"

"I am a lawyer."

A lawyer! The word was translated and repeated around the circle, amid renewed shakes of the head.

Then came a startling question — "Are you a political spy?"

"Certainly not," said Vincenz, with some surprise and a little indignation.

"He says he is not a political spy," repeated the questioner, turning triumphantly to the circle; "that is very suspicious!" And the circle echoed that it was very suspicious indeed.

"No," said Vincenz; "I have told you what I am."

The triumphant smile on the face of the questioner remained unperturbed, as this time also he translated the answer for the benefit of the circle.

"How did you come here?"

"On my legs," Vincenz felt very much inclined to answer but he said, "From the forest."

"Aha! Of course — a nest of hiding places. What were you doing there?"

"I had lost my way."

"He had lost his way!" The *Dorobanze* roared at the simplicity of the answer. As if political spies ever lost their way!

"What is your mission?" asked the chief *Dorobanze*, rolling his eyes at Vincenz, as though meditating where to take his first bite at the victim.

"My mission at present," said Vincenz, losing his temper, "is to find my way home."

"It will be a rather long way," said the chief *Dorobanze*, grimly.

It seemed to be a fundamental principle in such a case as this immediately and unhesitatingly to take for granted that the answer given was the exact reverse of the truth. Vincenz having said that he was a lawyer and not a political spy on a secret mission, seemed to lead to the natural conclusion that he was precisely what he denied, and that whatever profession he might be connected with, that profession would be anything but that of the law. The interrogator seemed to be evidently much pleased with himself and with his ingenuity — more so still when, to his great delight, and after several vain attempts, he succeeded in spelling out the name of Schleppenheim, from which Anna's letter was dated. Schleppenheim was a German town: this doubled every suspicion. Clearly the man before them was a very political spy on a very secret mission.

In a most unceremonious fashion, Vincenz was marshalled through the crowd, up the village street, and finally into a wooden cart of peculiar construction, to which were harnessed a pair of *Büffels*, shaggy and diabolical looking animals, which slowly drew the creaking construction up and down the miniature hillocks and valleys of a real Romanian cart track.

This cart did not creak merely as ordinary carts do upon an ordinarily bad road; but being framed entirely of wood, without a nail, or a morsel of metal about its whole construction, it groaned and swayed and loudly complained, until, after an hour of this experience, Vincenz, without much expenditure of imagination, could fancy himself enduring the tortures of purgatory in the midst of the aching lamentations of a host of fellow-sufferers.

He had been told that his destination was the nearest town; but as to his fate he was kept in the dark, and had ample leisure for doleful speculations on the possibilities in store for him. The man who had spelled out the date of the letter was so enchanted with his discovery that he could not part with his treasure, but sat gazing enraptured at the paper during the whole of the tedious journey. Vincenz, hungry and inexpressibly bored, began to think almost with regret of the hours he had spent in the small brigand camp, and to long for the society of Sancu and Duman in place of these morose and suspicious men. It had indeed been suggested to him, with an eloquent glance directed to his coat pocket, that in case he should feel himself in an especially liberal frame of mind, these ardent guardians of the frontier would find it possible to sacrifice a little patriotic feeling — that a few silver pieces, in fact, would have the effect of reconciling their consciences with the risk which the liberty of such a dangerous individual must necessarily bring to the great and glorious country. But alas! Vincenz knew too well that his coat pockets were empty. His memory, which a few minutes ago had so distinctly drawn for him the picture of the singed and smoldering passport, now with equal clearness showed him the little heap of scattered coins which lay strewn on the moss of the forest.

The sun was high in the sky when the groaning cart drew up at last; but the lawyer's troubles had by no means reached their end. The so-called "town" proved to be a sandy desert, with some fifty houses dropped down upon it, apparently by mistake, each without any regard to its neighbor, and standing at every possible and

Vincenz was marshalled through the crowd, up the village street, and finally into a wooden cart of peculiar construction, to which were harnessed a pair of Büffels, shaggy and diabolical looking animals

impossible angle to each other, which gave them a surprising and unpremeditated look. It was in front of the first of these unpremeditated houses that Vincenz and his escort had come to a standstill. This was a square, whitewashed construction, in front of which a man, with one boot on and with a gun on his shoulder, sauntered up and down. From his habit of standing still sometimes, without apparent cause, and going through some incomprehensible maneuver with his firearm, Vincenz concluded him to be under the impression that he was standing sentinel. There was a great deal of miscellaneous conversation and good-humored bantering between the sentinel and the men in charge of the supposed political spy. The sentinel was so delighted at some joke of one of his comrades that he felt compelled, in a friendly manner, to poke the joker in the ribs with the butt-end of his gun. Another man appeared on the scene: from the fact of his wearing two boots, Vincenz guessed him to be an officer. The cheerful and unprejudiced manner in which this man (upon duty) joined in the conversation of his subordinates was refreshing to witness, for any one accustomed to European discipline. There was, in fact, no trace of discipline or order anywhere.

There was a great deal of talking and shouting, to make up, however. Vincenz again was questioned, and again the reverse of what he said was regarded as the true statement. There being no proof for the fact of his being a political spy only made his case worse. It proved that he was well-skilled in his mission, therefore all the more dangerous. As result, Vincenz found himself confined in a small, narrow room, scrupulously whitewashed, but also scrupulously bare. There was but one window to this place of captivity, and that was crossed with iron bars. Here, finally, he was left to his own meditations, being at irregular intervals, and as it were only by accident, supplied with food in the shape of *mamaliga* — a species of porridge made of Indian corn — accompanied, incongruously enough, with a liberal supply of well-flavored wine.

As hour after hour passed, his meditations became gloomy. Up to the moment when he had entered that fatal village, there had been nothing to complain of. The adventure had been almost enjoyable until that point was reached. But now matters were changed. He had not been much alarmed at first at the prospect of arrest; it was only now that he began to recognize the disagreeables of his position. Arguments and assurances were exhausted; they had proved worse than useless. And now, as he sat in his white-washed cell, he remembered every word which the Bohemian had said on the day when he warned Gretchen against crossing the Romanian frontier in the valley: "They lock you up, and then sometimes forget all about you for weeks." Here was an inspiring prospect! Was he going to be overtaken by the same fate as that of the German gentleman whose friends had discovered him only after a month of search? It was not likely that the friends in this case would be more speedily successful, if indeed they would take so much trouble. Vincenz was not used to spend much thought upon himself; therefore, he had no true conception of the anxiety which his disappearance was causing. Least of all did he imagine that Gretchen could be made seriously uneasy by the occurrence.

This day was interminable, but the next day was worse. Nothing to do but to pace his cell, or stand staring out by the narrow grating, which could only frame one very small picture at a time.

The one-booted sentinel, the object most frequently within sight, would have been ready enough for conversation, but unfortunately the linguistic attainments of prisoner and guard did not coincide. Sometimes, a wooden cart creaked past, either very fast or very slow, according to whether it was drawn by the clumsy *Büffels* or the swift-footed small horses of the country. Peasants on the way to their fields passed also — usually the woman laden to the ears, and spinning as she went, while the man tramped behind her, leisurely puffing his pipe. It was the vintage season, and sometimes Vincenz was reminded of the fact by the monster bunches of purple and white grapes which were borne past his prison, strung upon wooden poles, and swinging heavily at each step of the bearers.

On the evening of the second day, he began to wonder how long a man could stand this sort of life without committing suicide.

According to the commencement of the proceedings, there seemed to be no rational reason why this confinement, once begun, should not continue for months, if not years. This mournful thought was in his mind when, on the morning of the third day, he stood peering through the iron bars. The dreary round of carts and laden peasant women was beginning over again. An especially creaking cart and an especially laden woman had just passed, and Vincenz was on the point of turning from his grating, when another figure appeared on the scene and immediately arrested his attention.

It was that of a peasant lad, and something in the cast of his clean-cut profile touched a chord of recognition in the lawyer's memory. Unspectacled as he was, he could not quite assure himself that he saw right; but surely that profile and that well-knit frame were familiar to him? Surely this was the peasant lad Bujor whom he had more than once seen at the door of the Mohrs' apartment, perseveringly offering for sale young bears and unfledged vultures which nobody bought?

Almost in the same moment, the question was solved; for just as Bujor passed out of the little square of vision, another, and this time unmistakable figure, presented itself. If he might have hesitated as to the Roman profile, there was no possibility of doubt as to that wide-awake and the well-cut tweed coat; and if at the sight of Bujor he had been conscious of a thrill of hope, Vincenz never doubted his rescue when in the second figure he recognized that obstinate Englishman — Mr. Howard!

Chapter XL

Gretchen's Fortune

"What more? thou knowest perchance what thing love is?"

— Morris

"Il n'y a que les morts qui ne reviennent pas."

— Barère

G RETCHEN stood at the window and listened: the murmur of voices in the valley was swelling. The crowd, heralded by some screaming children, came within sight, round the turn of the road. A struggling mass of people was pressing round some central object of interest; but of what nature this object might be, Gretchen could not distinguish, however much she craned her neck and strained her eyes. It was not even easy to determine whether this disturbance was a manifestation of joy or of grief. Our sounds of woe and of rejoicing sometimes bear a curious resemblance to each other: these piercing shrieks might do as good duty for lamentation as for glee; this frantic gesticulation was as likely to mean despair as triumph. Nothing was evident, except unlimited excitement of some sort.

The small procession came on, always nearer and always growing with each step; waiters from the restaurant, *gamins* from the roadside, and peasants on their way home, joined it as it passed. The whole place seemed to have turned out for the occasion; those who were not in the street were at the window, curtains were pushed aside and panes flung open. But there was one window which remained closed; there was one man who watched the procession indeed, but who watched it furtively and with lowering brow, scowling as he held aside the velvet folds which barred his view.

As the crowd drew nearer, Gretchen also stepped back; an uneasy suspicion had stolen over her. The horrible idea had suddenly crossed her mind that this shrieking mob was a train of mourners, and that the object of interest in their center could be nothing else but the body of Vincenz Komers, withdrawn from its deep grave in *Gaura Dracului*.

"The devils have given up their victim," she said to herself; and a cold sweat began to break on her brow. She would see his face again — see it perhaps disfigured by some cruel mutilation. No, it could not be; she never could bear that sight.

She turned away and paced the room in feverish haste, her teeth clinched, her hands tightly clasped, for she was determined to fight down this fancy.

"Ah no," she said aloud, "the devils do not give up their victims; who dies in *Gaura Dracului* is buried there. This is nonsense; I shall go and ask what the noise is about;" and she moved resolutely towards the door.

Before she reached it, it sprung open, and Mr. Howard stood before her.

"My dear," he began; but Gretchen had already started back, and pressed her hands over her eyes and ears. Her terror was too great for her; she wanted to see and hear nothing of the dreadful thing she feared.

"My dear child," said Mr. Howard in his virilous voice, which reached her in spite of herself, "are you strong enough? Are you prepared?"

"Oh no!" cried Gretchen, shuddering. "Leave me, leave me; I am not strong enough — I am not prepared for anything more!"

"But do you know what it is?" asked Mr. Howard in amazement.

"It is Dr. Komers. Tell me quickly — am I right?"

"You are right; but — "

"O God, I knew it!" She pressed her fingers more tightly across her eyes. "Oh, Mr. Howard, don't make me look at him!"

"But I shall make you look at me," said Mr. Howard, gently taking possession of her hands. "No, my dear; I see that you are not strong enough, that you are not prepared!"

Gretchen stared at him in amazement; she had expected to see a face of grave concern, instead of which she found herself gazing into a pair of eyes that shone with a triumphant light.

The grasp with which he held her hands was painful almost in its vigor, yet Gretchen did not feel it. She was giddy and confused. The murmur of voices seemed to have got into the house, and she could hear Ascelinde's voice among them, and Kurt's. There was no mistaking it now: those were sounds of joy, not of lamentation. And Mr. Howard was still holding her two hands, and there was still that light in his eyes. What did it mean? Her heart beat in uncontrollable haste. Hope was too dead within her to be called to life at a touch; she only felt a sudden incredulous, burning curi-osity to know the true cause of that disturbance outside. She would have pushed past Mr. Howard had he not held her back, and in the next moment they were all in the room.

They were all in the room. Ascelinde, Kurt, even Adalbert in his wheeled chair, and — yes, she was right, it was Dr. Komers; but it was Dr. Komers come back from the dead. His beard was somewhat unkempt, and he was pale and weary, and yet it was unmistakably Vincenz Komers. They all hung about him, all talking at once, shaking his hand, and laughing with delight. Only Gretchen made no movement towards him, and gave no sign. The sudden transition from despair, not merely to hope, but to certainty, was more like agony than joy. A drowned man called back to life may by comparison pass through some of the inexplicable phases of suffering which Gretchen was now undergoing. She had no voice, and neither tears nor laugh-ter. She could not grasp his hand as her father was doing, or hang upon his arm like Kurt.

She could only stand and stare at him in blank silence. She could not tell him what she felt, for as yet, she scarcely felt anything; she was not convinced yet whether this was real or not. In the midst of the tumult, her silence was unnoticed by most, and in the tumult also it took some time before a clear understanding of this mysterious resurrection dawned upon any person's mind.

Mr. Howard's statement was as follows: On that momentous evening of the lawyer's disappearance, after carefully searching every inch of ground, he had come upon a strange clue in the shape of a shattered pair of spectacles, which he immediately recognized as belonging to Dr. Komers. The first impression which the shattered spectacles conveyed to him, and would have conveyed to most men, was of a struggle between Komers and Tolnay. It was not at all unlikely that Tolnay, in his then state of mind, should have picked a quarrel with his rival. His British instinct warned him to keep the opinion to himself for the present; and by the time he found himself on the way homeward, and by dint of shifting the *pros* and *cons* of the situation, he ended by abandoning the idea of the struggle altogether. The position of the spot on which he had found the spectacles, led, on maturer consideration, to the belief that the lawyer had in reality never been very near the hole. A hope was now engendered in his mind; but, true to his principles, Mr. Howard maintained silence on this point too. The chances were so nicely balanced for both possibilities that he felt it would be unwise, if not unmerciful, to awaken in Gretchen's mind hopes which might prove futile.

Vincenz without his spectacles might much more likely have lost his way than Vincenz with his spectacles. Mr. Howard knew that the Romanian frontier was close at hand; he had been reminded only that evening that a wrong turn and half an hour's walk were all that was wanted to reach it, and he had not forgotten a word of what the Bohemian had said concerning the strict watch of that frontier.

It was a chance at least, and, with his natural obstinacy, Mr. Howard followed up the chance. He started, carefully avoiding to take a passport with him, but having secured Bujor as a species of guide; and for two days he had traveled along the frontier, making inquiries at every village. His determination not to be baffled by the absurdity of Romanian prejudice was strengthened by the recollection of Gretchen's despairing face, and the secret which had escaped her unawares.

By what means he had succeeded in intimidating the Romanian officials of the place into delivering up the lawyer was never distinctly known — it was enough that he had succeeded; and Mr. Howard, satisfied with the result of his expedition, had only one complaint to make, but that was a bitter one. On entering the country, the fly-book, which held all his favorite salmon-flies, had been confiscated, as containing suspicious and possibly murderous implements, by which the safety of the great and glorious Romanian nation might very likely be endangered. But even the fate of the salmon-flies lost a little of its weight at the sight of the semi-tragical, semi-comical gratitude which had shone on the face of the rescued lawyer.

It took a few minutes to make all this clear; and during all the time, Gretchen stood apart, silent and pale, feeling her benumbed power of sensation slowly waking back into life. It seemed to her a long time that the talking and laughing went on, but it was in reality only a few minutes.

She could not stand any longer; she sat down, and discovered, as she did so, that she was trembling from head to foot. The talking and laughing, the questioning and answering, the exclamations and cries, raged on for a time, then lessened and ceased. Adalbert, worn out with the excitement, was wheeled from the room; Ascelinde hastened off to order a repast for the famished captive; Kurt's emotions demanded a cigar in the open air; and Mr. Howard declared that it was an ideal fishing evening, and that he meant to land a trout before sunset.

One by one, they all dropped off; and Gretchen, raising her eyes, discovered that she and Vincenz Komers were alone in the room.

He turned towards her with his usual quiet, almost sad smile — that smile the recollection of which had tortured her for three long days.

"Will you not tell me that you are glad to see me alive?" he asked, a little wistfully; "you have not said a word to me yet."

No, she had not said a word to him, she was the only one who had not welcomed him back. Even now, she had not regained her power of speech. Her eyes were hanging upon him, scanning his features, as people look at long-lost treasures which they have thought never to see again. He was pale and weary-looking, she began to recognize now, as she met the gaze of those earnest brown eyes, which she had thought never to meet again on this side of the grave. He was waiting for her to speak, and she tried to speak. Her lips moved, but her voice seemed strangled in her throat. It was in a wretched starved little voice that she stammered at last — "Yes, I am glad."

The word struck upon her ear with a sense of almost ludicrous disproportion. Her feeling at the moment was that if she were to pass the rest of her life on her knees thanking Providence for this blessing, it would be as nothing in comparison to her gratitude. Glad! That was a word that people used when they talked of a lapdog's fortunate escape, or of a pet canary bird's recovery. How could he use it with regard to the happiness of her life?

Glad and sorry — those are the words we use: and *glad* was as little able to express what she felt now, as *sorry* would have failed to describe her feelings of the last terrible days. There was nothing in the words he used which could speak of that tremulous feeling of joy to which only now her stunned senses were beginning to awake.

Vincenz heard the little cold speech, and turned away with a sigh of disappointment. He had only hoped for some sign of friendly sympathy, nothing more.

But already Gretchen's senses were coming back to life. The sound of her own voice, and of that pitiable adjective he had used, seemed to show her all at once the astonishing depth of her happiness.

Very slowly, she raised her heavy eyelids. There close to her on the table lay that half-finished letter, which need never be finished now. *There* she had been able to express what she felt, though now she was so powerless. Despair had given her words, but joy made her dumb. Should she destroy the paper? Yes, surely. Her confession was not wanted now.

Her fingers were upon the sheet; her breath was coming fast, and every moment that rush of tremulous joy was rising higher and growing clearer in her heart.

She took the paper, but she did not tear it up; with a sudden impulse, she turned to Vincenz and placed the letter in his hand; then, walking to the open window, stood there waiting an eternity — an eternity of five minutes.

Dr. Komers, in some surprise, had taken the paper and was reading it slowly. It took him a long time to read anything without his spectacles.

Gretchen, standing with her face to the open window, was blind to the mountain range before her, and deaf to every sound in the valley. Her whole attention was concentrated upon that faint rustle of paper behind her. Even the loud voice of the rushing Djernis was for her drowned in the flutter of that paper. She did not regret what she had done, though she suffered acutely; she had been resolved not to spare herself. She did not dare to hope for that which she had forfeited; she asked for no more than his forgiveness. He should know that his great love had conquered her at last.

She heard him turn the first page, she heard him turn the second page, and then she hid her face in her hands. She knew what was written on that third page, and he was reading it now.

Then came two minutes of the most torturing suspense which Gretchen had known in her life. She heard nothing, till at last — at last she heard the sound of his voice.

"Gretchen!" he cried out, and, turning towards him, she saw his face as he stood with his arms stretched out towards her.

"Gretchen, is it to be? Is it to be after all?"

And now, at sight of the yearning love in his eyes, of the fire of happiness in his face — now Gretchen shrank back frightened at the thought of what she had done.

In her weakness and her excitement, she sunk on her knees before him,
weeping passionate tears...

She drooped her head, and stood before him trembling, while a scorching blush flowed upward and stained the whiteness of her cheek.

He came towards her with that fire still in his eyes, and all at once the long strain gave way. Her happiness was too great to be calmly borne. In her weakness and her excitement, she sunk on her knees before him, weeping passionate tears, holding his hands and kissing them in a transport of ineffable joy, of gratitude, and of love.

And, after all, it was to be. After all her dreams of greatness, and in the very teeth of the *prix de logique*, this was the pass to which the ambitious, the mercenary, the calculating Gretchen had brought herself. She had tried conscientiously to stifle the poetry of her nature; she had striven to silence her impulsive yearnings, to chill the warmth of her generous young heart; and now, she thanked Heaven that she had striven in vain.

Perhaps she had never so thoroughly deceived others as she had completely deceived herself. She certainly had not deceived Vincenz Komers. Had his lover's instinct not told him that she was other than what she painted herself, such a man could not have loved her so long. No two men are ever fascinated by the same woman for the self-same reason: the contrast between the poetical in her appearance and the prosaic in her speeches, which had so fascinated István Tolnay, would have had no power over Vincenz Komers. It was just because he looked deeper, and discerned the unreality of this display of realism, that he loved her. It was just because she was so illogical with all her logic, so foolish with all her wisdom, so ignorant with all her learning, so weak with all her strength — it was just because she was not that which she prided herself to be that Vincenz loved her.

And his reward was come at last — his loyalty crowned, his faith triumphant. Gretchen herself had defeated herself; for now, of her own free will, she had surrendered to that love which twice she had laughed to scorn.

This was the way in which Gretchen's fortune was made; this was the treasure which Gretchen found, if not in *Gaura Dracului*, yet certainly by means of *Gaura Dracului*.

Chapter XLI

The Hour and the Man

"Doch mit des Geschickes Mächten
Ist Kein ew'ger Bund zu flechten,
Und das Unglück schreitet schnell."

— Schiller

L ATE that night, a solitary bear hunter sat in the forest with his dog. He
sat before a roaring fire. A tall tree stem had been hollowed out, and
flamed upward, scattering sparks and blackening slowly at the edges. This
is a very different fire from that humble ember-pile beside which Sancu and Duman
had lain encamped; for István Tolnay is the king of the valley and of the forest, and
he can burn as many trees as it pleases him to destroy.

But there is not much expression of pleasure in the attitude of that man who sits
silent and sullen on the forest moss. From the moment when he had stood behind
his curtain, furtively watching the triumphant progress of the rival he thought to
have slain, there had been no peace for him.

It was scarcely a relief to find that he was not a murderer. In spite of his blasphe-
mous boasts to the contrary, he might not have been able to do the act over again;
but he was capable of regretting that his attempt had been a failure. He had snatched
up his long-unused gun, and under a double impulse he had plunged into the forest
thickness. He could not bear to be witness of the happiness which he knew to be in

store for his rival, and he felt that he must free himself from the desperate attempts of that other woman whom he had deceived and cast off.

She had come to his rooms again, she had again wept and upbraided him; there was no safety from her despair, except in flight.

"You told me to wait until *Gaura Dracului* was found," she had urged upon him with merciless tenacity. "I have waited, and *Gaura Dracului* is found."

As he sat there in brooding silence, with his grin cast idly beside him, he was not thinking of the game he had ostensibly come up here to hunt. He stared gloomily into the crackling fire, never lifting his chin from off his hand. Some morbid fascination had drawn him today away from his usual path, and towards this part of the forest which had been the center of interest during these last days. He had thought he would like to see the place again; but being once up here, that wish had turned to a repugnance. Though he was but a few dozen steps from the spot, he had abandoned his intention and had halted. Kindling a fire with the aid of the lad who accompanied him, he had sat down here to rest and meditate.

The forest has not changed its aspect since that night, though autumn is creeping on slowly towards winter. Soon the forest will be bleak and colorless, its moss buried in winter snow, its trees bared to the lash of the bitter November winds. Then the solitude will be more sensible even than it is now, and the bear alone will stalk across the desolate scene, master of the wide forest around. The forest has seldom been so beautiful; for, with the colors of autumn, it has preserved the fulness of summer. Throughout all the autumn, the weather has been so still and clear that scarcely a leaf has fallen; but this evening the boughs are rustling, very gently as yet, and now and then a colored leaf flutters down, blazes up for a moment, red or yellow, in the fire-light, and shrivels to ashes as it touches the burning tree.

Tolnay noticed nothing of his surroundings; he sat and stared for how long he did not know — for hours perhaps — at the crackling flame which was leaping higher and crackling more loudly in the softly rising wind. Once a red spark flew towards him and alighted on the moss at his feet. Tolnay watched it absently as it smoldered for a moment, struggled to live, almost succeeded, and then died out. The moss was very dry, he thought, as he stared back into the fire. He did not think of the spark or of the dry moss again, until presently Pasha growled beside him, and another figure showed itself within the range of firelight. The Bohemian had been at work cutting shingles in a farther part of the forest and, being on his way homeward, his attention had been attracted by the blazing tree.

His object in approaching the fire was to offer a respectful warning. "Herr Baron," he timidly began.

"Ha!" said Tolnay, with savage impatience.

"Herr Baron, I do not think such a fire is safe in such weather."

"Go to the devil," said Tolnay, sullenly; "I have not asked your opinion."

"And the wind is rising, too. Listen!"

Tolnay raised his head for a moment. There was a distant moan of branches slowly swaying, a sort of melancholy whine coming from the depth of the forest; no doubt the wind was rising. He cast a glance at the tall burning stem; the sparks were flying faster than before.

"Leave me alone," he said, irritably; "I know what I am doing."

The tone and look intimidated the Bohemian, but by no means satisfied him. He shook his head in his gentle but obstinate manner, whispered something to the lad who had been nourishing the flame with pieces of dry stick which he threw into the hollow of the burning trunk, and then withdrew from the scene, though only to a little distance. He kept well out of the circle of light where that moody hunter sat, but he felt it his duty to watch over the burning tree.

István resumed his meditations. He had forgotten the warning almost as soon as it was uttered. Once only, Pasha's uneasy moaning roused him for a minute. The dog was sitting upright, with ears erect, listening to the rising gale as though it had been the howl of a pack of hungry wolves. The Romanian lad, too, was no longer feeding the fire, but sat on his heels, staring agape and aghast into the black forest.

"Look to the fire," said István. "Why have you stopped throwing the sticks?"

"He told me not to," gasped the lad. "Is he your master, or am I?"

"But the wind, *Domnu!*" (master).

"Do as you are told, young hound!" said István, savagely. "The fire must blaze; throw the sticks, else I might be tempted to throw in your wretched carcass."

"Domne ferestje!" (so help us God!) muttered the boy, hastily flinging in a handful of dry sticks, but turning pale as he saw the fresh blaze.

Again, István sat plunged in sullen silence. He never noticed how by slow degrees that melancholy whine in the distance swelled into a howl, nor how beside him the stir of leaves grew to a rustle, and the rustle to a sharp continued rush.

It was after a long interval that the Bohemian stood beside him again and urgently renewed his warning.

When István looked up this time, he saw that the leaves were no longer fluttering singly, but were showering down in dense masses, whirled from side to side by the rising wind. They had hung on the trees ready to fall at the first breath of air, and now each new gust which swept along stripped them off by hundreds and thousands. The branches groaned and creaked, and the wind whistled fiercer every instant, rising in strength with a fearful rapidity.

"Herr Baron," urged the Bohemian, desperately, "I implore you; it will soon be too late!"

It was too late already while he spoke, though István, roused at length from his reckless apathy, had started to his feet. The trees on each side had caught the flame and were flaring up high. The flying sparks alighted on the ground, and the fire spread greedily along the dry moss.

Though the three men stamped upon the flames at their feet, and threw themselves on the ground in the hope of stifling them, it was no use; they broke out on the right just as they had been extinguished on the left. The fire flew along as though fed by a train of gunpowder. Within the space of five minutes, more than ten trees were burning; and whereas it had at first been a question of sup- pressing the fire, it had now become a problem of bare escape. The storm had risen to a hurricane; the wind no longer howled, it roared through the length and breadth of the forest. The trees comported themselves like frantic creatures. They writhed as if in agony: the lesser giants bent till they were doubled, like suppliants imploring for mercy; then springing upright, they seemed to rush at one another with threatening arms tossed on high.

They rocked and heaved and shrieked, flinging the flame to one another, and spitting out red sparks, which carried the destruction farther and ever farther. It seemed as though an army of demons had been let loose, and were playing their wild gambols with a fast and furious glee.

It would have been a glorious sight for anyone who could have dared to watch it; and for some minutes Tolnay did stand, in forgetfulness of the danger, reveling in the destruction which suited his high-strung mood so well, looking at the leaping fire as though it had been a display of fireworks lit for his enjoyment. But the flames had all but reached him, and the other men were shouting to him that he must fly.

"*Heilige Maria* of the *Wunderbaum* at Choteborschwitz!" the Bohemian called in his despair. "The forest is lost if there comes no rain!"

István turned to escape from the fire, but was pursued and surrounded by the fiery demons. To anyone with a small amount of presence of mind, the danger would not even now have been imminent; but, whether from carelessness or from excitement, István had made a mistake in his direction — he had placed himself to the windward of the burning trees. His nerves were overstrained today, and believing his retreat cut off, his coolness of mind forsook him. Instead of forcing his way to the leeward of the fire, he attempted to escape in front of it. Deafened by the noise of the hurricane, blinded by the glare of the flame, and choked by the stifling curls of smoke, he pressed onward. The air was thick with flying leaves, and hot with sparks which beat against his face.

It was scarcely possible to stand upright; he clutched onto the tree stems as he passed for support; he tried to run, not knowing where he was going, nor where were the other men. His dog, leaping on him in his distress, bewildered him yet more with

stván turned to escape from the fire, but was pursued and surrounded by the fiery demo

his terrifying howls. He had lost sight of everything except that yellow glare, and he was flying from it for his very life.

Right through the midst of the hurricane the sound of a voice calling pierced to his ears for a moment. He could hear that it was a shout of distress, but he could not know that it was a warning cry which said,

"Not that way, not that way!"

All he saw was the dazzling glare, while the cry that might have saved him was drowned in the hiss of the wind and the crash of the falling trunks.

Chapter XLII

The Missing King

"Masters, I have to tell a tale of woe,
A tale of folly and of wasted life."

— Morris.

PANIC struck upon the Hercules Baths. Late at night the cry arose —

"The woods are burning!"

Though the fire was still far, yet from below in the valley the flying sparks could be seen, the unsteady glare against the sky, and the columns of black smoke rolling hither and thither as they were driven by the furious wind.

Every person who had turned out on the road, attempting to brave the hurricane for the sake of his curiosity, stared upward at the night sky, anxiously calculating what were the chances of rain. Rain was the only hope, as those who had before witnessed such forest fires knew only too well. When the fire had reached such dimensions as this, it must rage, either until it was satisfied, or until the weather changed. The dry forests burned like matchwood, and there was no reason why they should not burn for days and weeks, if rain did not fall. The Hercules Baths themselves were in danger. Some wild attempts were made to extinguish the raging element; every man with a pair of strong arms, and a spark of adventure within him, forced his way up the hills towards the place of destruction. But they might as well have stayed at home and saved their time and their breath; they were as helpless as children in their attempts to check those leaping flames which sprung from crag to crag, and ran up and down the sides of each wooded ravine they reached in their triumphant progress.

With every hour, the excitement of the public mind grew. "Where is the baron?" was murmured at first; and then it was cried aloud, "Where is the baron?"

The panic-stricken people wanted a voice to reassure them — a recognized authority round which to rally; and they cried for the baron. The extempore firemen rushed upon their operations without method and without leader — for the baron was not there. Since the valley was in danger, why was the valley king not at his post?

Next morning broke, and again everyone looked upward at the sky. It was not blue, as the sky for so many days had been. Never had a gray sky been welcomed with such heartfelt gratitude as that one was today. There was rain in that sky, if it would only fall; but the wind hurried the drifting clouds across, and tore them to shreds in its fury. The black smoke had drawn nearer now — the very air smelled of it; but the sparks were not seen by daylight.

All day long, the clouds hurried past, and the people stood and stared from the black smoke to the gray vault above.

Late in the afternoon, a man, leading with him a dog, presented himself at the Mohrs' apartments. It was the Bohemian; he had come straight from the hills, from the place where the fire was raging, and the dog which he led with him was Pasha. All efforts to quench the fire had been abandoned, and all hopes were now placed in nothing but those gray clouds above.

The Bohemian's clothes were singed and torn, his hands were blackened with soot; he was paler than he had ever been, and his blue eyes had a look of terror in them, as if they had gazed on some dreadful sight which still pursued him in memory.

The Bohemian had a ghastly tale to tell; he shuddered and crossed himself ·as he told it, while the whining Pasha beside him uneasily scratched the floor.

"He stood like a man in a dream, staring at the flames. I shouted to him that it was time to fly; and then, at last, he turned and gazed wildly round him, and seeing the blaze on all sides, he must have lost his head, for he ran away from us instead of towards us — staggering like a drunkard. I tried to follow him; for at the moment that he turned, I remembered that straight the way he was running there lay *Gaura Dracului*. I struggled after him with all my strength, and all the time I kept shouting, 'Not that way! Not that way!' I am hoarse today with that shouting, but last night in the gale I scarcely heard my own voice. For a moment more, I caught sight of him with his arms round a tree; but the tree was burning already, and it fell with him. I heard the crash, and I saw him vanish. I knew then that I was too late, though I went on shouting in despair.

"I could not even reach the edge of the hole until this morning; for very soon it became the center of the fire. Today I was there. The tree which fell with him made a charred bridge across the place; the trunk was smoldering still, and its last sparks threw light down the black hole. His dog crouched beside the spot, and growled as I came near — the poor beast's hair is singed off half its back. Of Baron Tolnay, I saw nothing more."

The Bohemian had not yet told his terrible story when there was a sound like a gentle tap on the windowpane. It was the first raindrop, and now the second followed, and the third, and the rain was coming down fast and thick.

The Hercules Baths were saved, and the panic was past.

The fire had cost thousands of trees, and one human life.

Chapter XLIII

What People Said

*"Was der robe Aberglaube dem Teufel zur Last legt, das bürdet der halbe
Philosoph dem Schicksal auf."*

— Benzel-Sternau

T HE summer is over, and the monotonous rain pours down in torrents. The sky, which for so many weeks had been bright and distant,
like the vault of a colossal dome, has darkened now, and lowered into
the vault of a colossal dungeon; and with every hour it grows darker and sinks lower,
as though with its weight it would grind the earth to powder.

Damp veils wrap the hilltops away from sight; from morning to night the rolling
mist floats in and out of the gorge above the *Cursalon*, like the ghost of the dead
summer, returned to haunt the scenes of its glory, and to weep over the retreats that
once were its own.

Gaura Dracului lies once more solitary; but its mask is torn from it. Charred
trunks are heaped around it; the fringe of creepers has been devoured by the flames.
Retribution has fallen at last on the hypocritical flowerets that helped to hide this
danger of the forest. It will be long before *Gaura Dracului* can build up its screen
again and weave its veil anew. The aspect of the place is metamorphosed. These surviving trees that stand now so still and dripping, can they be the same that comported
themselves so frantically on the night of the fire? They stare down motionless upon

the destruction at their feet; they are shedding tears of penance over their late out-
break of fury.

A very few guests still linger at the Hercules Baths. Mr. Howard has gone back
to his native country, a little softened towards foreigners in general — which fact he
proved by nominally lending, but virtually giving to Kurt the money which is to
satisfy Herr Mandelbaum.

"I always thought that young man would prove fatal to my purse," he confided
to Lady Blanche Howard on the homeward journey. "I said so to myself on the very
first occasion when he addressed me by the riverside."

But though softened towards foreigners in general, Mr. Howard is implacable
towards Romanian officials in particular; he vows that he will get back his salmon-
flies, even though he has to go as far as the English consul at Bucharest.

Of the guests who are still here, there is one who will not leave the Hercules
Baths until he starts on the longest voyage of all. Adalbert will die at this place, which
for so many years has lived as an ideal in his mind.

Hercules and his waters, for all their power, have been too weak to undo the
harm of that Ash Wednesday catastrophe. Once Adalbert, in the prime of his youth,
standing at the foot of the beech tree in the world above, had seemed to rival the
forest king in vigor and in life; and now they might well rival each other in their ruin
— for man and tree alike are broken.

Though Adalbert has not found health in the Hercules valley, Gretchen has
found happiness there. Her father will die with his mind at rest, for he leaves his
treasure safe in the hands of an honest man.

That which was a comfort to Adalbert was a blow to Ascelinde. For a second
time, she had to unbuild her ideal Draskócs — for a second time to root up the
avenue, pull down the park wall, and turn off the waters of her lake.

One other and heavier blow she had been spared. Vincenz had thought it more
merciful not to mention to her, that in the course of winding up affairs at Draskócs,
various papers he had come across had denoted with tolerable distinctness that that

nine-pointed crown which had been the joy and pride of her life did not by any existing right belong to the name of Damianovics. It appeared that a great-grandfather's name having borne some resemblance in sound to the title in question, had become metamorphosed into count, and adorned by a crown, which was in reality fictitious. In those lower Danubian provinces on the borders of Hungary, even a title can be appropriated with tolerable impunity. As long as it belongs to no one else, a bold or ingenious aspirant is more or less welcome to have it, even if it belongs as little to himself as to the others. There was nothing to be gained by telling the truth; so Vincenz kept his discovery to himself. He could see only heartless cruelty in taking from Ascelinde the last shadow of her grandeur. What indeed would remain of the poor countess were she to be uncrowned?

Between Belita and Gretchen there is a coolness which will probably last for life. After all the counsels and pains bestowed upon what she called "the education of Gretchen's mind," her ingratitude was to be regarded as something far sharper than the serpent's tooth. "You have been an impostor," she wrote, "from beginning to end. The *prix de logique* should have been mine and not yours; but I suspected it all through, for I mistrust your nation. Farewell, Margherita! You meant well; but you are a German, and you could not escape that commonplace taint of sentimentality against which my prophetic spirit so often has warned you."

With this one outburst of bitter reproaches, the countess's letters ceased; but after a time, she softened so far as to send Gretchen a fashion-plate with the last "idea" for wedding-dresses, and since then the only form of correspondence between them as been an occasional *Journal de Modes*, addressed in Belita's hand — "To save the poor child from becoming too hopelessly dowdy," as she explained to Ludovico. "Because she has married a man who wears antediluvian boots, it is no reason why she should look like a fright herself."

Tolnay's death was much commented on, and the opinions pronounced were as numerous as various.

The Bohemian said, with a sad shake of the head, that there is no escape from fate, and that when a man's day and hour have come, he must be content to die.

There were men who said that it had not been an accident at all, but a suicide. Had it not been for the account of the Bohemian, as eyewitness, Gretchen herself might have believed this version; but though her self-confidence was shaken forever — though she had learned a bitter lesson — she was at least spared that remorse.

There were women who said that he must have been mad had be killed himself for the sake of that German girl with the golden hair and the large gray eyes; and there were others who said that, after all, her eyes were not so very large, nor her hair so very golden, and that he should have remembered that there are many other comely women in the world. "It is a pity," they said, "for he was a good- looking man!"

There was one woman who said that she would go up the mountains and fling herself after him. Princess Tryphosa meant what she said; but as the idea did not occur to her until she had returned to Bucharest, no one was alarmed by the threat.

The peasants of the valley alone took the catastrophe as the fulfilment of an inevitable doom. They bowed lower than ever as they passed the stone statue, and whispered to one another that the spirits of *Gaura Dracului* had received the sacrifice which once in every hundred years was due to them.

"It was sworn on the club of Hercules," they murmured in awe, "and therefore it was to be."

Gaura Dracului has indeed been found, but nothing has been found beyond the mere spot. The mountains have kept their secrets — perhaps they will keep them forever.

THE END

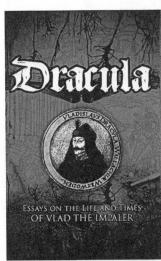

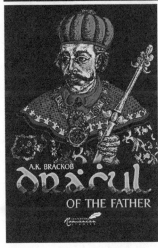
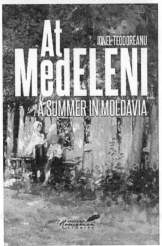